SIMON SHAW

Simon Shaw studied at Cambridge University and the Bristol Old Vic Theatre School. He worked as an actor until the publication of his first novel, *Murder Out of Tune*, in 1988, since when he has concentrated mostly on writing and journalism. *Killing Grace* is his eighth novel. He is an assistant editor of *The Week* and is a regular book reviewer for the *Mail on Sunday*.

Simon Shaw lives in London.

BY THE SAME AUTHOR

ACT OF DARKNESS
THE COMPANY OF KNAVES
MURDER OUT OF TUNE
KILLER CINDERELLA
BLOODY INSTRUCTIONS
DEAD FOR A DUCAT
THE VILLAIN OF THE EARTH

KILLING GRACE

Simon Shaw

HarperCollins*Publishers*

This novel is entirely a work of fiction. The names, characters and incidents portrayed in it are the work of the author's imagination. Any resemblance to actual persons, living or dead, events or localities is entirely coincidental.

HarperCollins*Publishers*
77–85 Fulham Palace Road, London W6 8JB

The Collins Crime website address is:
www.collins-crime.com

First published in Great Britain
in 2000 by Collins Crime

1 3 5 7 9 10 8 6 4 2

The author asserts the moral right to
be identified as the author of this work

A catalogue record for this book
is available from the British Library

ISBN 0 00 710009 4

Typeset in Meridien and Bodoni by
Palimpsest Book Production Limited,
Polmont, Stirlingshire

Printed and bound in Great Britain by
Clays Ltd, St Ives plc

1

Lewis had been sleeping with McGovern's wife for over a year before the two men actually met.

It was a Thursday evening, in the Coach and Horses. The Coach was down the road from the Simmons job, a few miles out of Petworth. It was their regular haunt when they were working in the area, and when Lewis had seen the boys in the morning they had talked about playing pool. He had driven over specially, because Bill and Charlie between them had taken a tenner off him the Friday before and he was anxious for his revenge. But when he got to the pub it was empty.

He took his Pils to the pool table anyway, and put down all the fifty-pence pieces in his pocket. It was six o'clock, the boys didn't usually work this late. He tried their mobile but it wasn't on. He decided to give them until half past. He went over to the fruit machine and lost a couple of pounds. He was restless and itching to play pool. He slotted in the first of his coins and watched the balls come tumbling down the chute. He arranged them in the triangle, selected one of the pub's collection of equally useless cues and started to chalk it.

The pub door swung open. Lewis looked up, hoping for Bill or Charlie. Instead it was Peter McGovern.

He recognized him at once, even though he only knew his face from photographs. It was such a distinctive, outsized face, the chin and nose fleshy and exaggerated, only the small pale eyes in proportion. The hair was still tight and curly, though not as red as in the wedding photograph beside the bed in which Lewis had spent most of the afternoon. The two men's eyes met across the empty room.

Lewis felt the hairs on his nape rise. McGovern must have

found out, he had followed him to make a scene. It was a good thing the boys weren't around after all. Not that Lewis was frightened of anything, far from it. McGovern's head was the only thing that was big about him. With that thin, narrow-shouldered body, he looked like a pumpkin on a stick.

McGovern, at the door, gave a slight nod, as if to acknowledge him, then walked up to the bar. Lewis heard him ask what wine they had, and settling for a glass of house red. The voice was surprising, deep with a strong Scots accent. Stronger than Lewis would have expected after so many years in England. Lewis knew a lot of biographical details about the man at the bar, like his snobbery about wine. Lewis turned to face the pool table. He practised his cueing action. The white cue ball bounced gently off the far cushion and came rolling back to him in a straight line.

'Fancy a game then?' he heard Peter McGovern say over his shoulder.

Lewis froze, not enjoying the sudden clammy feel of the cue in his hand. McGovern's tone of voice was genial, but Lewis wasn't fooled. If McGovern wanted a game he wasn't going to get it on his own terms.

Lewis straightened himself up and leant the cue carefully against the table before turning to face the other man. He folded his arms and stood back on his heels. McGovern, the pumpkin head, only came up to his chin.

'Do I know you?' Lewis asked, coolly.

McGovern hesitated. He seemed disconcerted.

'No, I . . .' He shrugged, and cleared his throat. 'I just saw you up here on your own. Thought you might fancy a game, that's all. Unless you're waiting for someone, of course.'

Lewis kept his eyes fixed on McGovern's. He didn't blink. After a few moments McGovern looked away.

'Sorry to trouble you,' the Scotsman mumbled at the floor.

I had your wife an hour ago, Lewis said with his lips only. *Had her from behind in your big bed, watching us in the mirror on the dressing table.*

'Yeah, I'll give you a game,' he said aloud. 'Heads or tails?'

He flipped one of the fifty-pence pieces on to the green baize.

'Tails.'

It was tails. McGovern smiled.

'Good start. Years since I've played though. Be a bit rusty, I expect. You'd better break.'

Lewis watched him walk around to the cue rack, murmuring more excuses under his breath. The last thing in the world he looked like was a successful dynamic businessman. No wonder Julie didn't like talking about him.

'By the way, I'm Peter McGovern.'

'Lewis Young.'

McGovern paused from chalking his cue. He sucked in his lower lip thoughtfully.

'You know, that name's familiar.'

You don't say? thought Lewis. Come on, then, out with it . . .

'Is that your van outside? The builder?'

Lewis nodded.

'That's it, then, you did some building work for me. I live near Godalming. It must have been a good year ago.'

'I do a lot round Godalming.'

'Oh, I'm sure. You know Windmill Lane, just after the Midhurst roundabout? It's an old farmhouse. Thatched. It's listed, you know. You built us a new kitchen, took us forever to get the planning permission. The old one seemed big enough to me, but my wife had other ideas, you know how it is!' He laughed. 'She was in charge, of course. I just got to write the cheque out at the end. That's how I remember your name. Lewis Young. Thought it was familiar when I saw it on the van. My accountant asked about it only the other day, going through my cheque stubs. Funny, eh?'

Very funny, thought Lewis. He couldn't make the man out. McGovern seemed twitchy and nervy, but confident at the same time. He was prattling away about his house now, and his accountant, and his accountant's obsession with golf, as if anyone could give a damn. He unwrapped the cellophane on a new packet of cigarettes as he spoke.

'You don't mind if I smoke, do you?'

Lewis shook his head. He did mind, but he didn't want to argue about it. He turned his attention to the pool table instead. He placed the cue ball and positioned himself.

'I have to smoke all I can when I'm out, you see. Julie doesn't like me to in the house.'

Lewis sliced the cue ball. It skimmed into the pack of red and yellow balls, barely dislodging them.

'Sorry, did I put you off? Shouldn't be talking while you're playing a shot. Bad habit. Julie's my wife, by the way. Talking of bad habits . . .'

He offered Lewis the cigarette packet.

'I don't.'

'Sensible. Now, let's see what you've left for me.'

He walked around the table, peering at the layout of the balls, drumming his fingers on the green baize cushion. There was an easy yellow on into the top pocket. He saw it, bent over to get himself into position and hit the cue ball with force, all in one continuous jerky movement. The yellow ball missed the pocket by six inches and smashed off the cushion into the pack, splitting it wide open.

'Oops!' said McGovern, pulling a face. He went to get his cigarette from the ashtray on the nearest table.

Lewis potted three reds in short order, then missed a tough long shot.

'You've played before,' said McGovern cheerily. 'But I think you've left me an opening.'

Lewis had, but McGovern wasn't able to take advantage of it. Lewis finished the game at his next visit to the table, without McGovern potting a ball.

'Well, that was a bit of a whitewash,' admitted McGovern as the black went in. 'Fancy another? Double or quits?'

'Double what? We weren't playing for anything.'

'That's no good, is it? You've always got to have a stake, livens up the game, concentrates the mind. Just a pound, say. You're better than me, though. How about a little handicap, for a bit of fun?'

Lewis hesitated. If this was a hustle, it was the most inept he'd ever seen.

'I'll give you two balls.'

'A man should never surrender two balls,' said McGovern with a schoolboy smirk. 'Why don't I get you another drink. A pint, is it?'

'It's a Pils, but I'm fine, thanks.'

'Sure?'

'Sure.'

McGovern went to the bar to buy himself a drink. Lewis watched him chatting to the barmaid, he all animated, she utterly bored by his patter. No wonder he got on Julie's nerves.

She had married him for his money, and had hardly even bothered to pretend otherwise. There might have been other considerations, but love had not been one of them. Julie had been only twenty-two when she met him, young enough to be impressed by the apparent worldliness of a man nearly fifteen years her senior. She was a small-town girl, from near Inverness. In those days Edinburgh, where she went to work after leaving college, had seemed like a big intimidating metropolis. McGovern had been up to stay in the hotel where she was a receptionist. He was on a working holiday, back home in Scotland for a few weeks to reconnect with his roots, as he put it, and to scout out some property for investment. He had a fat wallet, the gift of the gab, and smart city ways from his years down south. He had just moved down to Surrey after living for some time in the Midlands, set himself up in business. He said he had recently come into some money. Julie had had boyfriends before, a farmer's son back home and an insurance clerk she'd met in a takeaway queue, but never one who had known about the things McGovern knew about, about wine and food, fast cars and airplane travel, the trappings of good living. She wasn't supposed to socialize with clients, much less sleep with them, but he had been very persuasive, and she had succumbed within the week to his suggestion of room service with a personal touch. He had showered her with gifts and pestered her for a date on her night off. She had given in, and found, initially at least, that he had a softer side. He had been married, but his wife had recently left him. Just pushed off without a word, was all he said; it was obvious he didn't like talking about it. He had only just finished divorcing her on the grounds of desertion. He admitted to loneliness, and said that he was after permanence, not just a casual relationship. She had been too inexperienced to consider the possibility that he might have been lying, and, as it turned out, he wasn't. It might have been better if he had been. She had accepted his proposal partly out of boredom, but married life wasn't the solution. It didn't help that her husband had been no good in bed, but she hadn't properly understood that at the time because the farmer's boy and the insurance clerk hadn't been any good either. It was Lewis who had taught her what that was about. He knew because she told him, often, and much else besides. Over the last fifteen months or so he had learnt the whole story of her barren marriage. He wondered if the man at the bar had any idea just how much his wife despised him.

McGovern came back with his drink. He won the toss for the second time, again elected for Lewis to break. Lewis hit the pack cleanly and got a streaky yellow into a side pocket. He potted another ball.

'Oh dear, that makes us even, doesn't it?' said McGovern with a grimace. 'I'd better start playing.'

But he didn't. He didn't know how to. McGovern was the worst player Lewis had ever seen. The game ended for a second time without him potting a ball.

'It's only money,' McGovern chuckled as the black went in. He didn't seem embarrassed at his own ineptitude. He put a pound coin down on the table.

'Now we really can make it double or quits. On for another?'

'Sorry, no. I've got to go.'

McGovern looked disappointed.

'Maybe another time then?'

Lewis nodded. Everything about McGovern was annoying, his look, his voice, his conversation. But at the same time Lewis felt oddly vulnerable in his company. The shared, unspoken woman was a burden.

'Got to go,' he said again. 'Thanks for the game.'

'Don't mention it. Actually, you know, it might be a

stroke of luck my running into you like this. I was just saying the other day we needed a spot of building work doing. Spooky, eh?'

McGovern had a big grin on his face. Lewis smiled faintly.

'What do you need doing? Not the kitchen again, I hope.'

McGovern let out a short sharp laugh.

'Oh no, no. I'm not thinking of home, nothing needs doing there. No, it's a commercial job, in Guildford, where I've got my main office. There's this old storeroom at the back, it's just wasted space. I want to convert it into a private office. Not a big job, I'm afraid, but I don't want some cowboy mucking it up. It's an estate agent's, by the way. That's what I do.'

'Right. Well, give me a call sometime.'

'I will. I mean it. I'll call you very soon. Have you got a card?'

'Not on me. I'm in the phone book.'

'Of course. Mind you, I bet you anything Julie'll still have your number. She's efficient like that, a smart lassie. Maybe you remember her?'

Lewis hesitated. If this was a wind-up it had gone way beyond the funny stage. Yet McGovern appeared to be genial, sincere. Lewis looked him straight in the eye.

'No, I don't remember,' he said.

McGovern shrugged.

'Of course. You've got so many clients, and it was over a year ago. But I'm sure you'd remember if you saw her again. Pretty girl, Julie, gorgeous even. My friends are always telling me I'm a lucky feller. Just as well I'm lucky in something, eh, after my display at pool?'

McGovern laughed heartily. Lewis laughed with him. It was good to let out the tension. He started to go.

'You'll be hearing from me!' McGovern called after him.

Lewis hurried out of the pub. It was dark, and wet and cold. The fresh sharp air in his lungs, or the beer in his empty stomach, was making him feel giddy. It was the cold, he supposed as he put his key into the ignition, that was making his hand tremble.

2

His friends called Lewis a smooth operator. This is what he did.

Whenever anyone called asking for a quote he was always scrupulously polite, addressed them as sir or madam and was never pushy. He always returned calls when he said he would, and was never late for an appointment. When he turned up to give an estimate he wore a jacket and tie, and polished shoes. He was well-spoken and took care to emphasize that he was well-bred. He was so obviously not your usual common-or-garden builder that his clients were usually intrigued. If asked, he told them the name of the minor public school he had attended. He said that he could have gone to university if he'd wanted to, but as he was much more temperamentally suited to a practical rather than a professional life it would have been a waste of time. He didn't tell them that he'd been expelled from school after he'd been caught smoking cannabis at the start of his A-level term.

Generally he got a favourable response. Those of his clients who came from a similar social background trusted him, because he seemed to be one of them. They were relieved to have a builder who did what he said he'd do, when he said he'd do it, and didn't try to intimidate them. Sometimes these accountants and lawyers and doctors even hinted that they envied him. They might have social standing and well-paid jobs, but he had a kind of freedom unavailable to anyone following a more conventional career path. Those clients who came from poorer backgrounds but had worked their way up, by contrast, seemed to regard it as a feather in their caps that they should be employing a builder who sounded posher than they did. Whatever their origins, all of his clients had money. Lewis wasn't extortionate, but he knew that he had a good reputation and didn't have to strive unduly hard to be competitive. He used only good-quality materials and the men who worked for him knew what they were doing. A friend had once suggested that he advertise himself 'By appointment to the Aga-owning classes'.

Lewis was thirty-six years old. He was over six foot, broad-shouldered and in excellent physical condition. He was naturally the rugged, outdoor type, but at the same time he looked good in a suit. He still had his own hair, thick black and usually left long. He had pale-blue eyes, a classic jawline and a long aristocratic nose, like a storybook romantic hero. He would have suited long riding boots and a Regency coat. He had never had any difficulty attracting women. But he had no intention of ever giving up his single status. He didn't see the point. The sex was too good.

It would have been an exaggeration to say that women threw themselves at him, but not by much. He had always been good at chatting up women, and he didn't lack confidence, but serious relationships didn't interest him. There came a time with every girlfriend when she wanted him to settle down and become domesticated. In the long run a steady girlfriend spelt trouble. He preferred to seduce the wives of his clients.

He usually knew pretty well immediately when a woman was up for it. Like most builders he always had two or three jobs on the go at once, so it was easy to get the boys out of the way if a favourable situation arose. Then he would wait until he was sure and choose his moment. He never tried it on with a client unless she gave him the signals first, and he had never been rebuffed. He had a well-honed technique, but the trick was to be flexible. Sometimes he hardly even needed to try. Julie McGovern was a case in point.

The first time he'd seen her he hadn't been impressed. She had been gardening and was wearing dungarees, glasses and no make-up, her brown hair tied back and barely visible under a knitted woollen ski hat. She apologized for having a cold and kept her mouth covered with a handkerchief for most of their meeting. He had guessed she was about his age, a cheery outdoors type of a kind he had often encountered, a capable housewife and mother, as uncomplicated as she was bland. She had a nice voice, he noticed that, with a slight Scots burr and a warm laugh. He had given her an estimate for the kitchen, and their discussion had been brief, businesslike and devoid of flirtation. It wasn't a big job, but it did entail a bit of work, knocking down an old pantry wall to expand the kitchen, meaning a cement mixer for the screeding. She said she'd discuss the price with her husband and get back to him, but it was a good price and he guessed they'd go for it. Already he had earmarked the job for Bill and a youth experience kid who was working for him at the time.

The next time he came round he didn't recognize her. It was the second morning of the job and he was just popping in to check up on Bill. As he came up the drive he noticed that the tennis court at the side of the house was in use. Two women were playing, he presumed the one who stopped to wave at him was Julie McGovern, but he didn't pay much attention. He went into the kitchen through the back door. Julie must have followed him in.

'Hi. Is everything OK?' she asked as she came into the kitchen.

'Seems to be,' he answered after a beat, when he had got over his surprise.

Out of her dungarees and in her white tennis skirt and matching top she was unrecognizable as the same woman. Her legs, it turned out, were slim and tanned, her figure voluptuous. She was just his type; he had never gone for the anorexic model-girl look. Her hair, which she shook out of a black headband as she came in, was soft and lustrous, the face it framed, animated and flushed from exercise, pretty and sensuous. That day she was wearing lenses, not glasses, and the difference was remarkable. Her bright-blue eyes sparkled at him.

'Well, if there's anything you want, just come out and give us a shout,' she had told him. He had said that there was nothing he wanted. He wondered if she knew that he was lying.

He had a job to get back to, but that night he stopped by at the pub expressly to quiz Bill. Bill had worked with him since the beginning, he knew what Lewis was at and let him know it from time to time with wry looks and sidelong glances. There was a Mrs Bill back at a little terraced house in Guildford, a woman never referred to by her real name but by one of a dozen or so diminutives, none of them affectionate and most obscene. They had been married for thirty years and from the sound of it that pretty well amounted to sixty years of solid misery. Bill was dried up and worn down and sex had played as little a part in his life as champagne and caviar, though he hadn't a bone of resentment in his body. Lewis thought that he bathed in his own reflected glory as a ladies' man.

Julie McGovern was a nice woman, Bill told him, ever so friendly and obliging, always offering to make them coffee, and not just instant but the real thing. They'd seen her husband go off just as they were getting there both mornings, but he hadn't reappeared by going-home time. He was a funny-looking geezer, a carrot-top with shoulders so thin he was like a scarecrow. Drove a top-of-the-range Merc though, very nice. Bill had watched him go off in it, hunched over the wheel and puffing furiously on his first fag of the day. Julie – it was 'please don't call me Mrs McG' from the start – had told them he couldn't wait to get out in the morning to light up; she hated him smoking in the house. Bill, an inveterate twenty-a-day man, had taken the hint. Anyway, who'd want to be in such a hurry to get out every day, eh? Leave a woman like that behind. The youth experience kid wouldn't stop gawping at her, it was quite embarrassing. Bill had advised him to spend his wages on some looser-fitting trousers, so as not to give himself away. He laughed himself sick talking about it again in the pub, remembering how bright red the kid had gone. Lewis had had to slap him on the back to stop his coughing, and buy him another pint.

The husband had a chain of estate agents across Surrey and Sussex. Of course they had money, you only had to look at the house, his Merc and her bright-red little Toyota sports, the tennis court, the swimming pool. There didn't seem to be a lot going on in her life, though. The phone had rung a couple of times, but she hadn't been on chatting long, not your average woman at all. She spent a lot of the time reading. Although they'd moved into the area ten years ago, after they got married, they still didn't know many people. They seemed a bit stuck-up round here, was her comment. Bill had sympathized. The woman who'd been round to play tennis was a neighbour, not a friend. Julie told Bill she found him easy to talk to, he thought she was probably lonely, stuck out there in that big house, her hubby a bit of a damp squib. That was how he sounded anyway, reading between the lines. Peter – that was the hubby – worked late most nights, so she didn't get out much. When they did go somewhere it was usually some boring formal do where she was expected to smile sweetly all night at her husband's clients. When the kid had told her about some film that had just been released, and he was going to see with his mates on Friday, she said she was jealous. Peter hated the cinema, he said it was trivial. She hadn't mentioned children, but it was obvious there weren't any, the place was much too neat. A pity, Bill thought, a woman like that needed something to occupy herself.

Lewis had told her the kitchen would take a week to ten days. In the end the job lasted a month.

He'd moved Bill and the kid out the next day, sent them over to finish an extension on the other side of the county. From the little smirk Bill gave him it was obvious he'd been expecting his marching orders. Julie had looked disappointed when he had had to tell her that Bill was needed elsewhere. She seemed shy now, talking to him alone while he was working on knocking down the pantry wall. He soon put her at her ease. He knew how to put women at their ease.

She drank a lot of coffee, and he never said no when she came in to put the kettle on, although he was usually very careful about his caffeine intake. It was the autumn, and quite cool, but he always stripped down to a singlet when he worked, and when he was interested. Soon he noticed her looking at his body. He didn't let on, of course, he carried on chiselling out the bricks, turning just a little away from her so she could see his powerful arms and shoulders to advantage. He knew exactly how he looked, because he had watched himself from every angle while working out, checking for best effect in the mirrors that lined one wall at home. When he had turned round, suddenly but ever so casually, she had looked away quickly. Then he knew.

With some women it didn't work, but Lewis knew that all the stuff about men falling for women through their eyes and women falling for men through their ears was only half the picture. Lots of women liked to look too. It was just that the beer-guts and bald patches that were mostly on offer weren't too appetizing; men like him were at a premium. Lewis had always had a good body, and he took care to maintain it. Doing manual work kept him in shape, but he used the weights and the rowing machine in his bedroom every morning. He took his health seriously, was careful about what he ate and drank, and didn't have an ounce of fat on him. He was proud of his physique, but the thing with women was never to let them know you thought that. Loads of guys at the gym had good bodies, but they had egos to match. If there was one thing women hated it was vanity. They wanted you to be looking at them, not at your own reflection in every passing mirror. Of course, physique on its own was never enough. That was where the big gorillas in the gym went wrong, thinking that all they had to do was flex their pecs and the girls would come running, like one of those corny old Charles Atlas ads. Lewis understood that appearance was only an attention-grabber. After that it was down to charm. And he'd always been able to do charm.

While Julie was out shopping he had a discreet nose around in the living room. Like the rest of the house the room oozed wealth. There was a huge wide-screen TV, a video with more controls than an aeroplane, and a CD system that looked like set dressing from a futuristic movie. The carpet was inches deep, the wallpaper hand-painted and the furniture covered in exquisite red shot-silk. Beside the armchair in the window was a stack of books and magazines. The books were thick paperbacks, all written by women, each advertised in its own way as a saga of love and passion. The magazines were glossy and glamorous, with headlines on the covers such as 'Your seven-day guide to better sex', and 'How to have better orgasms'. It was a long way from the knitting patterns in the magazines his mother used to read.

The third morning he was there the neighbour came round again and she and Julie played tennis. When the neighbour had gone, Julie came into the kitchen to get some juice from the fridge. Lewis asked her how the game had gone, and they got talking. She didn't play nearly as often as she should, she said, seeing as there was a court on her doorstep. She loved the game, though she wasn't much good. Lewis told her that he'd captained the tennis team at school. He hadn't, but he'd always been good at all sports, and he was an easy liar. Julie had joked about him giving her a lesson. He had joked about being caught slacking on the job and getting the sack. It was easy to make her laugh, always a good sign. They had agreed to have a knockabout during his lunch break. She had gone off to dig out a spare racket.

The court was in excellent condition, the red-clay surface and the nets practically bran-new. They exchanged a few shots, and he could see that she was better than she'd said. He told her that he thought there might be something wrong with her grip.

He came round to her side of the net. There was nothing he could say about her grip, it was fine. Maybe she could hold the handle a little further down when she served. He told her to take up a serving position and came and stood directly behind her. He got her to go through her serve in slow motion, his right hand over hers, guiding the racket up. Gently he pressed himself against her. He told her to straighten up and laid the flat palm of his hand to her stomach, pulling her towards him. His groin brushed delicately against her buttocks. He told her it was good, murmuring his encouragement into her ear, his nose brushing her hair while he breathed her in. He asked if she'd got it, or did she need to go through it again? She said, do it again, and her voice seemed to catch in her throat. He went through it, very slowly, she obviously in no hurry for it to end. Automatically his left hand began to move up from her stomach to her breasts, but he stopped himself. He knew she wouldn't have resisted, but she might have been nervous about being in the open, even though there was no one around to see. He walked back to his side of the net, pretending to be calm, and went through the motions for another few minutes.

He had her as soon as they got back inside, over the dustsheet-covered kitchen table. There was none of the ambiguity he so often encountered, no sign of guilt at the thought of her husband, and no demand for reassurance. He was staggered by the scale of her passion, it was like a flood bursting the banks. She tore at his clothes, and dug her nails into his back, and screamed her head off as he entered her. She was so hungry for sex it felt like he was being eaten alive. When he had come she begged him to take her upstairs and do it again. He carried her up the stairs in his arms and they made love in her marriage bed. That, she told him afterwards, her eyes bright with amazement, was the first orgasm she had ever had with a man.

Julie was a textbook case, but she was also an exception. Most of his affairs were brief, partly because he enjoyed conquest at least as much as possession, but also because he was wary. With those women whose terms were much like his own there was no problem, but there were others who didn't need much encouragement to start confusing sex with love. Fortunately he was in an ideal position just to walk away from bad situations. There had been an occasion when a love-smitten woman had blurted it all out to her husband, and he had come round to Lewis's house intent on a showdown. No showdown materialized, probably because Lewis had just been working out and answered the door stripped down and looking his meanest. The only situation that had ever fazed him had been in Brighton a few years back. He didn't usually work so far afield, but he'd liked the sound of the woman's voice on the phone. When he'd got there he hadn't been disappointed, but even he had been surprised at the ease with which he'd got her into bed. Then, one afternoon just after they'd done it, she'd started running her fingers through his chest hairs and coyly murmuring something about a video camera. Would she mind if they set it up for the next time they made love? They wouldn't have to worry about anything technical, because her husband would be operating it. Lewis had made his excuses and left, feeling furious and humiliated. He hated the thought of anyone trying to take advantage of him.

He usually slept like a baby, but the night after he met Peter McGovern in the Coach he tossed and turned for hours and woke up sweating, the residue from some already-forgotten bad dream nagging in his head. He lay awake in the small hours, trying not to think of Julie's peculiar husband. Perhaps their meeting had been fate, a signal that it was time to move on. Sex with Julie was still good, but he had been getting progressively more bored with her chitchat for a while now. He was doing a quote that morning for someone called Larsen who lived near Petersfield. He didn't know what sort of a woman Mrs Larsen would be, but the prospect of finding out still excited him. He'd spoken to her on the phone but voices could be misleading. He imagined a willowy blonde, bored with her comfortable existence and her dull husband, as so many were, wanting some edge in her life before she got old. He imagined seduction, and as he lay in bed waiting for the dawn to break he went through the moves in his head.

This is what Lewis did.

3

It was Mr Larsen who opened the door. He was in his sixties and used a walking stick, though more for effect than from necessity. He explained that his wife had gone shopping, and as he was pretty much housebound he was on estimate duty. The job was to convert a small bedroom on the top floor into an *en suite* bathroom for the main bedroom. They were buying in the fittings from a local cut-price store, they just needed them installed and a connecting door put in the wall. It was something they'd been promising themselves for twenty years, Mr Larsen explained, and now that both the boys had left university and were living in London they at last had the chance. The small bedroom had been Tom's. There were pictures of Tom and his brother on the wall in the big bedroom. There was also a family group showing the boys with their parents. Mrs Larsen was about fifty-five. She looked like a plump, jolly woman, a stalwart of the WI and the local church. It turned out to be not a bad guess. While Lewis was there the phone rang and he heard Mr Larsen talking to the vicar. Mr Larsen confirmed that his wife would be hosting the next coffee-morning.

Lewis said that it all looked pretty straightforward, he'd go home and do his paperwork and let Mr Larsen have a quote within twenty-four hours. It shouldn't be more than a few days' work, either Charlie or Bill could take care of it, getting in one of their regular plumbers as and when.

It was just coming up to ten o'clock when he left the Larsen home. His work clothes were in the van, ready for him to change into later, but first he had to pay in some cheques. He never wore his work clothes into the bank, it was one of his rules. He had been using the same branch in Petersfield all his working life. Even after he'd moved out of the area he had kept his accounts there, because he knew the staff and the manager. He liked to show his face as often as possible, to keep the wheels well-oiled.

He paid in his cheques at the main desk. He had seen the girls exchange glances when he walked in and took care to respond to their flirting in kind. He said he'd like a quick word with Ralph Carter, the manager, if that was convenient. They buzzed Ralph and he came out.

The two men greeted each other with what might have passed for warmth. Lewis had done a kitchen for Ralph eighteen months earlier, and had done it very well, on schedule and at a competitive rate. He had been in need of Ralph's goodwill at the time and had even held back from attempting his pretty little red-headed wife, despite her blatant come-ons. Ralph, of course, had no idea of the extent of Lewis's magnanimity.

'Nothing come crashing down round your ears yet, I hope,' said Ralph with a big grin as he came out of his office. He always kicked off with a variation on the same remark. Lewis always managed to disguise his irritation.

'Everything still standing, touch wood,' replied Lewis, patting the counter. Ralph shrugged.

'What comes up must come down, though.'

Ralph invited Lewis into his office and offered him a coffee. Lewis accepted.

'Anything we can do for you?' asked Ralph.

'Nah. Unless you're giving away free money this week.'

Ralph laughed as if it was the funniest thing he had ever heard. He was always laughing, if he was ever in the pub Lewis knew it the second he walked in, could hear his throaty cackle over the loudest jukebox. Lewis thought of Laura Carter coming into the kitchen in her baby-doll nightie, casually crossing and recrossing her legs as she talked, giving him the full Sharon Stone treatment. That would have wiped the smirk off Ralph's jolly fat face.

'Sorry about my little difficulty last week,' said Lewis in the tone of sincere humility he reserved for such occasions.

Ralph looked at him blankly. Lewis produced the letter from the bank advising him that his current account was £400 overdrawn without authorization and passed it over.

'I'm sorry about this, Lewis,' said Ralph, looking up from the letter when he had finished reading and sounding genuinely embarrassed. 'It's automatic procedure. I'm sorry, I didn't know anything about it.'

'Oh please,' said Lewis, feigning matching embarrassment. 'I know it's nothing to do with you personally, you're much too busy to have anything to do with a trivial little matter like this.'

'No, but it's not my policy to put my longstanding trusted customers on the spot. I know all about the difficulties of cash flow and small businesses. Would you like me to see about raising your overdraft limit?'

'It might be an idea, just in case. Though everything's OK again now. I've just paid in about six grands' worth of cheques.'

'Well then, there shouldn't be any problem at all.'

The big grin was back on Ralph's face. Lewis didn't tell him that most of the six grand was earmarked for VAT and other bills at the end of the month. They chatted amiably about the possibility of building an extension on to Ralph's living room while Lewis finished his coffee. He decided, as he listened to Ralph's annoying nasal voice, that if the job went ahead he was going to have Laura Carter.

On the way out he screwed up the letter from the bank and threw it into the bin. The letter had angered him. Its tone reminded him of school, of the condescension and stupidity that went hand in glove with authority. He had self-consciously broken away from all that years ago, he hated the intrusion into his life.

He switched on his mobile as he got into his van, intending to ring Charlie and say that he was on his way. Instead he found two messages.

The first message was from Julie McGovern. One rule he was strict about with all his women was that they should never call him. The reason he gave was that he didn't want any awkward numbers appearing on an itemized phone bill, but it was also a way of ensuring that he remained in control. Julie had scrupulously followed the rule and had never called him before. The shock of hearing her voice was matched only by his surprise at her angry tone.

'For Christ's sake, Lewis, why didn't you tell me you'd met Peter? I had the shock of my life this morning when he suddenly mentioned your name, I was a nervous wreck by the time he'd finished his breakfast. I must have behaved like an idiot, I could hardly string two words together. He wanted your telephone number, by the way, said you'd agreed to do a job for him. What the hell's going on, Lewis? I said I didn't have it, that I couldn't even remember anything about you. Next time I have to lie, could you please at least give me a bit of advance warning?'

The second message was from Peter McGovern. He gave his name, said he hoped that Lewis remembered, and promised to call back later. That was all.

Lewis dialled Julie's number. She wasn't in. He gave it a few minutes and tried again, but there was still no answer. He doubted that she had gone far, he knew how little she got up to during the day. He called Charlie to say something unexpected had come up, then set off for Godalming. He stopped once on the way, at a florist's.

It took him half an hour to reach Julie's house. He saw that her car wasn't in the drive as he went past, and turned into the lane immediately after the house. He pulled up on to a grass bank rutted with tyre marks, his own. With the well-honed caution of the illicit lover he never parked in the drive, in sight of prying eyes. He tried the phone again, but there was still no answer. He decided to give her fifteen minutes, and almost immediately he saw the flash of her red car through the trees. He got out of the van and climbed over the low wooden fence that ran along the grass bank. He negotiated the flower beds and came out on to the lawn between the house and the tennis court. Julie, who was lifting shopping bags out of the boot of her car, noticed him at once. He waved as he crossed the lawn.

'I'm sorry, love,' he said with maximum contrition, offering her the dozen roses he had bought in the florist's. He saw the hardness in her eyes begin to soften.

'Oh, Lewis . . .' She glanced automatically over her shoulder, as she always did when they were out together, although the drive was invisible from any of the neighbours' houses, and no cars could be heard on the main road. 'Come on, let's go inside.'

Lewis took the shopping bags while Julie carried the roses, her nose pressed to the blooms. They were adorable, she told him. She seemed delighted. He sat in the kitchen and watched her snip and arrange the flowers in a vase. Such a simple, uncomplicated soul, he thought as he watched her, so easy to please, and get around. She would have made someone a lovely wife. A pity that someone was Peter McGovern.

'I should have rung,' he said, 'I'm sorry. I tried the mobile as soon as I got out of the pub, but I couldn't get a signal, and by the time I did I thought he must be here.'

She said she understood, and he smiled sweetly, pleased that the lie had mollified her. He explained what had happened, how her husband had walked into the pub and come over to him. He told her how at first he had been expecting a confrontation.

'From Peter?' She laughed derisively. 'You've got the wrong man there.'

He told her how weird it had been, seeing this strange man with his peculiar mannerisms, knowing so much about him but not being able to let on. His walking into the pub like that had been such a coincidence, no wonder his suspicions had been aroused. Julie agreed, and said it was odd. Peter had always said that he hated pubs, but in the last few months he had got into the habit of stopping off on his way home from the office. He was drinking more at home too, although that hadn't made him any more convivial. She had been struck by his drinking and asked if anything was the matter, but Peter, as usual these days, had brushed her off.

'Perhaps he's got work problems,' suggested Lewis.

'I don't think so,' said Julie. 'There's a housing boom, haven't you noticed? Cash isn't a problem, thank God. He

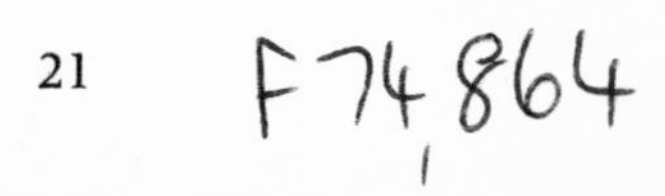

was talking last week about getting an indoor swimming pool put in.'

Julie sighed, as if the prospect of having a heated pool to flop into at will was too tedious to contemplate. Lewis did not return her wan smile. Sometimes her acquiescence in her pampered life annoyed him. She didn't like her husband, had nothing in common with him and, according to her own accounts, barely exchanged a word with him from one day to the next. They never had sex any more. It was an existence that would have driven most people spare. She seemed to come alive when she was in bed with Lewis, then slip back into a state of passiveness the moment she was on her feet again, drifting in neutral through all the featureless waypoints of her life, from the hairdresser's and the manicurist's to the tennis club and Sainsbury's, gold Amex card in hand. At least that despised creature, her husband, did something with his life. Rather to his surprise, Lewis felt a sneaking sympathy for Peter McGovern.

'It's his office in Guildford he wants me to do,' said Lewis. 'He rang this morning, I said I'd call back.'

'Be careful, Lewis.'

'How'd you mean?'

'Peter. Be careful of him. He loves getting his way with people, it's his whole life. Make an excuse, tell him you're too busy to do the job.'

'Don't worry, I won't be having anything to do with it. Bill can handle it. It'll be a doddle for him, he only lives round the corner.'

'Oh, let's not talk about boring stuff,' she said, a sudden archness in her voice.

Lewis recognized the tone. Julie wanted to play. She got up from where she had been sitting on the other side of the kitchen table and came over to him. She ran a hand through his hair as she sat down on his lap.

'Mm, you feel good,' she murmured into his ear, undoing the top button of his shirt and slipping her hand inside. She brushed her lips all the way down his cheek to his mouth, and kissed him hungrily. He began sliding his hand up under her skirt, but she stopped him with a touch.

'I think I'll go and change into something more comfortable,' she whispered, pulling away from the kiss and nuzzling his ear again. 'Would you like that?'

Lewis nodded. A year ago her knicker drawer had contained no label more exotic than Marks and Spencer, but she had since acquired a taste for playing the part of mistress, and now insisted almost as an article of faith on what she took to be the correct uniform. He didn't object. He had sometimes wondered if her husband had noticed the sudden profusion of skimpy black lace in her wardrobe, or at least the bills on her credit card, but he wasn't about to start asking questions. Their relationship had long since reached a plane of pure lust which was as close to perfection as anything in his experience, and was everything he had ever wanted in a woman. It was what had kept him coming back for more, even though their relationship was way past his usual sell-by date. She started to get up, but he seized her quickly by the wrist.

'Don't be long,' he breathed softly, dragging her lips towards his for a kiss on instalment. He kissed her hard and she responded eagerly. He knew she loved him being sexually aggressive. It was such a contrast to her feeble husband.

The ringing tone of his mobile made them both jump. He unclipped the phone from his belt and answered it impatiently.

'Ah, there you are, Lewis. You're a hard man to get hold of.'

Lewis didn't answer. Julie had settled back on to his lap and was nibbling at his other ear.

'Lewis, are you there? It's Peter McGovern.'

'Yes, I –'

Julie bit him too hard on the earlobe. He pushed her off and rose to his feet in the same movement. Julie lost her balance and fell to the floor, letting out a squeal of protest.

'Sorry, have you got company? If it's not a good time –'

'No, that's fine, Mr McGovern.'

The wounded look on Julie's face froze in place. She sat perfectly still on the floor, one leg tucked awkwardly under her, and watched him silently, as he paced into the corner of the kitchen, talking to her husband.

'Please, call me Peter. I definitely want to go ahead with that job we talked about. I was wondering if you'd be free sometime today to come and have a look at it?'

'Today?'

'Is that inconvenient?'

'Er, no, it's all right. Towards the end of the day would be better.'

They arranged to meet at McGovern's office in Guildford at six o'clock. Julie was still sitting on the floor. Lewis put down the phone and helped her up.

'That's just like him,' she said crossly. 'So damned pushy. You said you'd call back, didn't you? Everything has to be just so, the way he wants it.'

'It's no problem, Julie.'

'You don't have to live with it. He does what he wants, when he wants, he's never paid the slightest attention to me or my needs. I don't get any respect from him.'

The thought idly crossed Lewis's mind that McGovern didn't get a lot of respect from her either. He wondered, not for the first time, why the two of them were still together. He supposed he could understand it from her point of view, at least materially. Even with a hefty divorce settlement she wouldn't be able to keep up her near-luxurious standard of living, and she was probably too spoilt now to be able to revert to anything less. But why did her husband stick it? When they'd met in the pub, McGovern had sounded proud of his wife, but that had probably just been for show. Lewis only had Julie's version to go by, but there didn't seem to be a lot in it for Peter McGovern.

'Look, I think I'd better be making a move,' said Lewis suddenly. Julie seemed surprised.

'Did talking to him put you off then?'

She sounded faintly contemptuous. He took a half-hearted look at his watch, feeling suddenly cross and embarrassed.

'Of course not. I just hadn't realized how late it was. I promised Bill and Charlie I'd be in Petworth by lunchtime. I've got some paints to pick up.'

It was a feeble excuse and he presumed she knew it. But then, she must have known how utterly the erotic charge had disappeared from the room the second her husband's call came through. Going to bed now with him gnawing away at her mind was unthinkable.

'I'd like to kill him sometimes,' she said.

The queer tone of her voice surprised him. She managed to sound both venomous and matter-of-fact at the same time. She saw his perplexed look and bridled.

'I mean it, Lewis. I think about it sometimes, really I do. If I ever got a phone call from the hospital saying he'd been smashed up in a car or something, I'd whoop with delight.'

Lewis bit his lip. He had been on the point, instinctively, of saying something about the benefits of bachelorhood. He thought it instead.

'Look, I'll call you tomorrow. OK?'

She gave him a reluctant nod. He went over to give a kiss, but she turned her head away, allowing his lips barely to graze her cheek. She had adopted a sulky air that would have taken a lot more than another dozen roses to dissipate. To his annoyance he felt himself beginning to get aroused by her again. He got out of the house quickly.

There were no paints to pick up. He drove off directly to Petworth. His mind was a mess of contradictions. Erotic images of Julie swirled around inside his head. She still excited him, but lately she had been irritating him in equal measure. She would witter on so about her pointless life, and moan and moan from her secure position in the lap of luxury. As if she had anything real to complain about.

He couldn't decide whether he should find an excuse to go back that afternoon and have her, or just call the whole thing quits.

4

'So what do you think?'

Lewis gave the room another quick glance before answering the question.

'No problem. A couple of days to knock down that wall, put another door in this one. A couple more to decorate and tidy up. A week at the outside.'

'Excellent,' said Peter McGovern. 'I don't think it'll cause much disruption, do you? That's my chief concern.'

Lewis told him there wouldn't be any disruption at all. The room they were in was at the back of the building, approachable down its own little alley, so there wouldn't be builders tramping their mucky boots through the nicely carpeted front office and reception area all day. There'd be some noise, of course, but it probably wouldn't be much worse than the roar of the traffic outside. The building was bang on the main road in the middle of Guildford, a few minutes from the station. It was a lot bigger than Lewis had been expecting, and very smartly done up in front. Business was obviously booming.

'That's good,' McGovern told him, as they stood in the storeroom at the back together amidst a pile of 'For Sale' signs. 'Can you give me a rough idea of what figure we're looking at?'

'I can let you have a full estimate in the morning, but it'll be at least a grand, plus VAT and materials.'

'Really? That's not cheap.'

'If you want cheap you've come to the wrong man, Mr McGovern.'

McGovern flashed him a shrewd look, closely followed by a conciliatory smile.

'Quality costs, I know, but I won't complain if you do as good a job as you did on the kitchen. But one thing I am going to insist on: none of this Mr McGovern crap, please. Call me Pete. OK?'

'OK.'

'Good. When can you start?'

'Monday all right?'

'Perfect. You'll be here yourself, I hope.'

'Yes, of course.'

Lewis explained that he'd be getting in a plasterer for a day but that he'd be doing most of the rest himself. He didn't tell McGovern that he usually left the dull stuff to the others, but had changed his mind after seeing the very pretty dark-haired girl in the front office.

'That's good,' said McGovern. 'Come on, let's go over the road, I'll buy you a drink.'

'Well, I've got quite a bit to be getting on with –'

'Come on, a quick one'll do you no harm.'

'All right,' said Lewis reluctantly. 'As long as they don't mind me in my work clothes.'

No one in the pub seemed to notice his work clothes. It was an unusually warm evening for November, and Lewis, who didn't like the look of the smoke-filled bar, suggested that they sit outside at one of the trestle tables facing the river. McGovern lit a cigarette immediately. Lewis sat on the very edge of his seat, as far away as possible from his smoke, poised for a getaway. He reckoned he'd have to give it ten minutes before giving his excuses and leaving. McGovern had started prattling away again the moment they sat down. Trying to match him in conversation, Lewis had decided, was like trying to run against a railway engine. He fidgeted in his chair the whole time, playing with his drink and his cigarette, never looking relaxed for a second. Words tumbled out of him in a machine-like rhythm. Julie said that he either talked nonstop or was as quiet as a Trappist monk; there was nothing in the middle. His talk drove her round the bend.

'Can I get you another?' he said suddenly, cutting himself off in mid-description of his office life. Lewis hesitated. He wanted to go, but he wanted to find out more about that pretty dark-haired girl first.

'I'll get them. Same again?'

McGovern said he'd have another large one. Lewis bought himself a second bottle of Pils to keep him company, although one was his usual limit and he'd scarcely touched the first. The moment Lewis returned McGovern resumed his monologue.

'As I was saying, I only decided to make Guildford the head office last month. Godalming was where it all started, but our lease there ran out and the new place turned out to be a bit poky. I happened to be getting Guildford refurbished anyway, spent a fortune, I don't mind telling you, and it's come out a treat, hasn't it? So then I thought why not move the whole shebang over, convert that storeroom into an office? The junk you saw in there is just printed matter, we can keep it next door in that little kitchenette I showed you, though we're not short of space. I've only three people working there at the moment, you know.'

'I only saw the one young lady when I came in,' said Lewis.

'Yeah, lazy bastards, they all buggered off on the dot of half-five. That was Carol you saw, my secretary. I brought her over from Godalming. You ready for another?'

Lewis declined. He waited while McGovern went off to get a refill. Even after the first Scotch he had begun to sound light-headed. As he sipped on the third a definite slurring slipped into his speech.

'So your secretary's now working with you in Guildford, is she?' Lewis asked.

'Yes, I've got a little partition up for us both at the back of the office. It's a bit flimsy, actually, maybe you could do something about it while you're here. She'll stay there when the storeroom's complete, you see. I might move those partitions further down, give the clients a bit more privacy if they want it. I've got to take on more people, there's a bit of a feeding frenzy at the moment in the property market. Where is it you live, Lewis?'

'Why, you trying to sell me something?'

'Me? Never! No, I'm just interested. You don't strike me as the city-dweller type.'

'I'm not. I'm in the country, up Milford way. It's a barn conversion; I did it myself.'

'Making use of your skills, eh? What did you pay?'

'You get to the point, don't you? Too much, if you must know, I bought at the top of the market. But I've done a pretty good job on it, even if I do say so myself, and it's worth a damn sight more than I paid.'

'I'd like to see it sometime, out of professional interest. Nice and quiet, is it?'

'It's the middle of nowhere.'

'Well, you can't get much quieter than that. You need a good central position, it's a question of strategy. You must get around as much as I do. I was just on my way back from Arundel yesterday when I bumped into you in that pub. I'm thinking of opening a branch there. We moved down to Chichester last year, doing very well. I might be able to put a bit of business your way, you know. Clients quite often ask about builders.'

'That's very kind of you.'

'Don't mention it. Somebody does a good job for me, I won't hesitate to recommend them. There are only two sorts of people in this world, Lewis, those you can rely on and the other ninety-nine per cent of the useless wankers who make up the bulk of the human race. I've come across a lot of jealousy in my time, you know, Lewis, people who look at me in my big car going into my big house and think, yeah, I could have that if only I'd get a break. I see them thinking, what's that bastard done to deserve all that, eh? I'll tell you what that bastard's done, he's worked his bollocks off, that's all. It's as simple as that. A lot of people'll just moan about bad luck. I'll tell you something about luck, a little story, about Napoleon. You know, him of the old cocked hat, Waterloo and all that. Well, when somebody would recommend this or that general to Napoleon he used to ask them if he was lucky. Not, was he a great general or anything like that, but was he lucky? Then I read this other thing he said, his definition of luck. You see, someone had told him, Napoleon, that he was lucky, winning all his battles and that, but he shrugged it off. So what is luck? he asked. It's just the ability to exploit accidents. You get it? The ability to exploit accidents. I can show you any number of people who sit around on their arses all day complaining they don't get the breaks. But if a break does come their way do they have the balls or the nous to take advantage? I don't think so. You want to make money? Then get off your arse. It may not grow on trees but there's no mystery about where it comes from. There's money in everything. Look.'

McGovern took out a pen and a notebook from his inside pocket. He tore a piece of paper out of the book, wrote something down and passed it across the table.

'I mean it, there's money in *everything*. See.'

The paper contained one word. McGovern's scrawl was difficult to read and for a moment Lewis didn't understand, but then he recognized the form of his own name – £ewi$.

'You've got the right name for making it big time,' said McGovern, laughing. He seemed very pleased with what he'd written; very pleased with himself: 'It's down to you, it all depends how much you want it. I expect you're doing all right, mind, the prices you charge.'

'I charge the market rate.'

'I know, I know, man, I'm just joshing you. People talk more crap about money than anything else. They say, it can't buy you happiness, how many times you heard that? I tell you, if I had a quid for every time I'd heard that I'd be even more filthy rich than I am. Look at the things you can do with money. I love cars, good wines, clothes. Look at this jacket. Cashmere. These shirts are silk, ninety quid a time, I get them in Piccadilly. This is a real Rolex, by the way, in case you were wondering. Want to know how to spot a fake? It's the way the second hand moves, I'll show you sometime. All these things cost money, and, I'm telling you, they make me pretty damned happy. Good things, expensive things, please me. I've never seen the point in second best. When I was young and broke I used to wake up in the middle of the night sweating, not knowing how I was going to pay my bills. Now I've got my stash in the bank I sleep like a baby. Sure I've got a different kind of money worry now, but that's all to do with maximizing growth potential and limiting tax liability, and that's not the same thing as wondering where your next meal is coming from. You know what I mean, Lewis?'

'I know what you mean.'

'Good. I like the cut of your jib. You're a down-the-line sort of guy, no bullshit. You could be tougher on yourself, though, if you wanted to be.'

'How do you mean?'

'Stop me if you don't want me to get personal, but I have this feeling you may be a bit stuck in a rut. Sure, you've got a nice little business, good reputation and you're never going to starve, the rates you charge. But I can't see you getting up to a higher level the way things are.'

'Perhaps I like it the way things are.'

'Ah, you're sounding prickly, that's understandable, it's none of my business, I'll keep my trap shut.'

'You can say what you like. I don't mind.'

'I think you do, but that's not surprising. You're a proud man, I respect that. But you're a winner too, and I respect that more. Someone told me when I was a kid that life's a jungle. I didn't know what it meant then, but I do now and it's true. Who rules the jungle? The lions. Only thing is, there aren't many of them. I read this book once about explorers. There was a guy who was asked, what if you died in the middle of your expedition, how many of your party would be able to step into your shoes? The answer he gave was one in ten. That's about right, one in ten of us has got what it takes to be a lion. I read this other thing once, fascinating, a psychological study of men who fought in the Pacific, in the war. It wasn't like those John Wayne films. You know something, in the heat of battle there's only one man in four actually has the nerve to fire his rifle. The rest just sit there too shit-scared to do anything. Would you have been one of those with the guts to pull the trigger? The leader, or the led? I think you would, looking at you. In fact, I can see your qualities plain as day. So why are you running with the herd – the flock, I should say, the sheep? I just don't think that you're maximizing your potential.'

'You seem to have a lot of opinions about me considering we only met last night.'

'And maybe they're wrong. And maybe they're right. You've got to be prepared to make snap assessments, put yourself on the line sometimes, it's the only way to get on. The way I see it, you've got to play to your own strengths, that's the name of the game. Now last night, for example, you could have taken me to the cleaners. Pool's your game, it's not mine, but all you took off me was a quid. Why? You could have won enough off me to pay for your drinks all night.'

'What if I had? That'd make you a mug, wouldn't it?'

'I know what you're saying. I wouldn't have looked smart, but I was there to be taken, and you didn't take me. Sure, it's a trivial example, but you've got to be alert to opportunities. I was a stranger last night, and you were wary. You can't afford to be. You'd be amazed the amount of business I get talking to strangers. But it was me who called you, not the other way round. You should have been on the phone first thing to me this morning, checking out if I was for real. You've got to do that every day, it's like doing your devotions. You don't wait for God to pray to you, do you? You pray to God. I'm strict in my observances, that's the legacy of a religious upbringing, but whether it's God or Mammon it's the same rules. People overlook the fact that Jesus was a pretty good salesman. I'm not kidding, listen. Jesus had a product, and he brought it to people's attention. Don't hide your light under a bushel, that's what it says. I liked his trick of turning water into wine, too. You want another drink?'

'No, thanks, I've got to make a move.'

'I ought to as well. I'll just finish this. What do you like doing, Lewis?'

'I'm sorry?'

'What's your thing? How do you spend your time? I'm a workaholic, me, at least that's what people tell me. The same people who say you've got to have an interest. That's like a hobby, I expect. When I was a kid I was always being told to get a hobby. An aunt gave me a stamp-collecting book when I was six. I sold it to the kid next door for two bob, my first deal. I could never see the point of stuff like that. All work and no play makes Jack a dull boy. So they say. But if you're serious, and want to get on, play gets in the way. You've got to work at it, have patience, if you want to get on. You've got to take the long-term view. You know that story about Robert the Bruce and the spider, about how he watched her try and try and try again to spin her web? Probably doesn't mean as much to you as an Englishman but I'm Scots, I swallowed it down with my mother's milk. Sure you don't want another drink?'

'Sure. Thanks.'

'Fine. What do you do with your evenings?'

'Sorry?'

'What do you like doing when you're not working?'

'Oh, the usual.'

'What's that then? Watch the telly?'

'Not much.'

'You go down the pub then?'

'Sometimes.'

'You're not a drinking man?'

'No.'

'You look in pretty good shape, I have to say. You must take care of yourself.'

'I take care of myself.'

'Very sensible. A man should look after his health. You go running, weight training, that how you spend your time?'

'Some of it. It's not exactly a hobby though.'

'You got a hobby then?'

'Not exactly.'

'Married?'

'No.'

'Divorced?'

'Never married.'

'Best way. When I got shot of my first wife I thought I'd give it a rest, you know, look before you leap, which is what I should have done in the first place. You've got to give yourself the chance to correct your mistakes. Perhaps you're better off out of it. Get all you need without having to put a ring on their fingers, eh? You're a bit of a ladies' man, I reckon.'

McGovern smirked. He didn't actually lean across the table and nudge Lewis with his elbow, but he might as well have done. Lewis took his time before replying.

'I like women. Yeah. On the whole I prefer their company, because men are pretty boring in my experience, talking all the time about football, and cars, stuff like that.'

'Oh, that's a good 'un, Lewis,' said McGovern incredulously. 'You mean it's their minds you're after!'

Lewis didn't answer. He picked up his glass and finished his beer.

'You don't like talking about sex?' said McGovern. He had stopped grinning and some of the irritating bounciness had gone out of his voice.

'It's not something you talk about. It's something you do.'

'That's your credo, is it?'

'It's just my hobby, Pete. I've got to be off now.'

Lewis got up to go. McGovern knocked back the last of his drink and climbed to his feet at the same time.

'You going home now?' he asked.

'Yeah.'

'Well, that could be just dandy. Would you mind giving me a lift?'

Lewis stopped in the act of buttoning up his jacket.

'I'm sorry?'

McGovern laughed and jabbed a playful finger at his ribs.

'I'm just trying to bum a ride off you, don't look at me as if I've asked you to do something indecent. If you're going towards Milford, I'm on the way, it's only ten minutes from here.'

'What about your car?'

'I'm over the limit. I was going to take a cab, but why waste a few bob when you don't need to? I'm a Scotsman, for Christ's sake, I'm allowed to be a tight-fisted bastard.'

McGovern threw back his head and let out a loud yelp of laughter. As if to emphasize the fact that he'd drunk more than he should he lost his balance as he tried to get up and had to clutch at Lewis for support. Lewis helped steer him out on to the pavement.

'Thanks, son, you're a brick. Well, you're a builder, what else would you be?'

McGovern practically bent double at his own joke. Somewhere along the line his laughter turned into a cough. He stayed bent over, his hands resting on his knees, while the coughing racked his lungs.

'Should get that seen to,' said Lewis idly.

'Yeah, bit of flu I can't seem to shake off. Had it for weeks, sore throat, the lot. My own fault, though. Should be cutting these out.'

He had had another cigarette out ready. He put it back into the packet as Lewis led him across the road to where he'd parked.

'So you've not got your van then?' asked McGovern, with some surprise, as they stopped at Lewis's rust-coloured old Range Rover.

'One of my men has got it tonight.'

'That's not good, Lewis. The van's got your name on, it's free advertising.'

'I'll try and remember that in future.'

'Ah, I've offended you. I didn't mean to. I just don't like to see you pass up opportunities. You've got to build your firm foundations, Mr Builder!'

Lewis left him chuckling to himself and leaning against the bonnet as he went round to unlock the driver's door. He checked his mobile while he waited for McGovern to clamber in beside him. There were no messages. He put his key into the ignition.

'I wonder if Julie'll remember you,' said McGovern quietly.

Lewis turned on the ignition. He looked at his two hands, firmly on the steering wheel. He gave it a mental count of three before speaking.

'You mean your wife?'

'Yeah, that's right. I asked if she still had your number, but she said she didn't remember you. Maybe if she sees you it'll jog her memory.'

'Yeah? Maybe.'

Lewis pulled out and headed off towards Godalming. He had mapped out the route in his head, worked out where he would have to feign ignorance and ask for directions. When they got there, he had decided, he would just stop at the end of the drive and let McGovern walk the rest of the way. He had a picture in his head of Julie glancing up and noticing him through the kitchen window, supporting her half-drunk husband on his arm. He had other pictures of Julie in his head too, and had a strange uncomfortable sensation that her husband could somehow see into his transparent skull. It was nonsense, he knew, but like a rationalist who can't help glancing over his shoulder in a haunted house, there was nothing logic could do to banish the feeling. And the more he tried to put Julie from his thoughts the more stubbornly she clung to her unwelcome tenancy. All he could do was put his foot to the floor and make the journey pass as quickly as possible.

McGovern, mercifully, had lapsed into temporary silence. Lewis turned on the radio, twiddled the knob till he found mindless pop and left it up loud. McGovern seemed to like it. He slumped into his seat and nodded his head in time to the music. It was like having your own full-size nodding-dog mascot, Lewis decided.

He had been preparing a spiel about how he was late and couldn't afford to waste another second, but when they reached the top of the drive McGovern reached for the door handle without being prompted.

'Ring any bells?' he called out over his shoulder as he got down on to the pavement.

'Yeah, I remember.'

'See you Monday then.'

With a cheery wave McGovern set off jauntily up the drive. The kitchen light wasn't on, Lewis noticed to his relief. He imagined Julie sitting in the living room watching the TV or reading one of her slushy novels. He imagined her again, in the bedroom, shiny with sweat in her whorish livery and squealing with pleasure. He saw McGovern fumbling with his door keys in the evening gloom, and it killed the image, like a bromide to the brain. He put the Range Rover into gear and drove off at top speed. He was home, as usual, in twenty minutes. He could have set his watch by the time it took to make that journey.

Peter McGovern watched the taillights of the Range Rover disappear. The cold night air had sobered him up, though in truth he wasn't as drunk as he had thought, or he had pretended to be. He had enjoyed his talk with Lewis, and perhaps (he reflected as he put his key into the lock) he had allowed himself to get a little too carried away. He had got under Lewis's skin much more easily than he would have expected. Lewis had a lot of pride, he was one of those men whose antennae were constantly picking up slights, real or imagined. In his own way he was impressive, not just tough-looking but hard with it. He could do that cold don't-mess-with-me look with his eyes. Peter McGovern respected him for that; he admired men with a physical presence. It was a useful asset in so many situations, and he had always regretted its absence in his own armoury. It meant, though, that one just had to try that little bit harder, and that was no bad thing. How much more satisfying it was to achieve one's ends through recourse to wit and intelligence, not brawn.

'Hi, darling, I'm home!' he said as he closed the door behind him.

She wouldn't have heard, or if she had she would pretend she hadn't. She was in the living room, he could see a strip of light under the door and hear the TV. What would she be watching? *Brookside*, or *Coronation Street*, or *Eastenders*? *Neighbours* was earlier, he had picked up that much somewhere along the line, although there was little in the world that interested him less than his wife's viewing habits. He opened the living room door and went in.

It was *Coronation Street*. He smiled to himself at the thought that at least she had lost none of her capacity never to surprise him.

'Hello, darling, have you had a nice day? We got an offer on that house out on the Downs, the one with the stables and the dressage arena. The full nine hundred, straight out, not even a hint of a haggle. It was through an agent, I think he works for an Arab gentleman. A very satisfactory day, all in all. How was yours?'

He watched her features compress with annoyance as he spoke. She hated anyone talking while she was watching her programmes.

'I didn't hear your car,' she said in a clipped voice, reaching for the remote control.

'I was in the pub, I left it behind. I got a lift from Lewis. You know, the builder. He's going to do that job in the office I told you about. I had a drink with him. Well, a couple of drinks, to be honest. Nice guy. You should drop in sometime, say hello. What's for tea then? I'm starving!'

She turned up the volume on the remote control, not taking her eyes from the TV screen for an instant. Her screwed-up concentration amused him.

'We'll eat after this,' she murmured.

'You're watching your programme. Sorry to disturb you, I'll shut up. Is it good? Can't say I've ever understood the appeal myself. Real life's got enough to be going on with, I've always thought. I think I'll go and have a shower. Yes, I'd like to freshen up. Have I got time? Julie? Have I got time?'

'Yes,' she hissed, barely audible above the actors' voices.

'That's grand then.'

He closed the living room door behind him and went up to the bedroom, loosening his tie as he climbed the stairs. An almost beatific smile had settled on his face, the private acknowledgement of a job well done. After ten sterile years, the capacity to irritate his wife beyond endurance remained the only compensatory feature of his marriage.

5

Lewis's barn was a few miles off the A286, between Milford and Haslemere. He had bought the property just when the craze for barn conversions was at its height and he was conscious that he had paid over the odds, but it had still been worth every penny. The barn was reached via a windy lane that didn't even feature on most maps. The farm to which it had once belonged was over the other side of a thick copse. Lewis saw the farmer at most half a dozen times a year, and the brusque nods they exchanged at a distance represented the full extent of contact with the neighbours. That suited him perfectly. The only problem with his home was that it was still unfinished. In the first six months or so he had worked all the hours God sent, filling his weekends and spare evening time with his own busman's holiday, more building. He had done most of it himself, though Charlie and Bill had lent the occasional hand. But after completing the upstairs he had run out of steam. The upstairs was the heart of the project, and its completion made the barn habitable. Ever since, for the best part of five years, he had been coming home to a half-built house.

The uncompleted downstairs comprised a small kitchen/dining room and a large workshop, their respective sizes reflecting his own priorities. The kitchen, though designed as minimally as possible, was the least finished room in the house, the bare walls and floor still untiled and the pine cupboards still doorless. The small cooker, fridge/freezer, microwave and washing machine were lined up against one wall like goods in a second-hand shop. Opposite was a shelf at which he ate, perched on a barstool. The workshop next door was scarcely nearer completion, though it was much better equipped. Two large solid workbenches ran down either side, and the wall racks were bursting with tools. He had electric drills and saws, sanders and strippers, and, his pride and joy, a superb professional's lathe. There should have been a hallway connecting the downstairs rooms and giving out on to the front door, but the partitions were still stacked against the wall and some faded strips of masking tape were all that remained to hint at the larger design. In the middle of what would have been the hall was an iron spiral staircase.

The top of the barn, the former loft, was Lewis's masterpiece. It was split-level, with two main areas, and the staircase spiralling on halfway up the wall and opening out on to a third, a railed gallery where he had his bed. Beneath the gallery was his workout space, where he kept his weights and his bicycling and rowing machines, in front of the full-length wall mirrors. Near to the back was his office, a desk and the filing cabinets which contained his records. Against the other side wall was a big leather recliner facing a TV, which along with the CD was connected to half a dozen strategically placed speakers. This part of the room he called the Bunker, because no sound ever intruded from the outside world. The rest of the upper area was occupied by a pool table he had bought cheaply after refitting a pub.

Three shallow steps flush to the wall led down to the lower part of the room, where a huge black leather sofa faced a low glass table and an expanse of thick white carpet. There was nothing else, except glass and light.

The whole end wall of the upper barn had been replaced with glass. A skylight extended to half the depth of the roof as well, letting the whole room fill with sun by day. The window was south facing, and in the summer could become a sheet of brightness that dazzled the naked eye. There were blinds and shutters to act as shields, but Lewis was rarely there in the day to use them. The times he liked best were dawn and dusk, when he could watch the sun rising or dipping over the trees. He called this part of the room the Aquarium.

When Lewis arrived home after dropping off Peter McGovern

he showered and changed, then had a quick meal, grilled chicken and fresh green vegetables and salad. He took his bottle of Evian and vitamin supplements upstairs and sat in the Aquarium, sprawling on the big black sofa, the lights behind him dimmed so that he could appreciate the night sky. It was a pretty good life, he thought to himself. He worked hard but he was his own boss, and he wasn't beholden to anybody. He might not drive a top-of-the-range Mercedes or live in a house with its own swimming pool. So what? He had the man's wife whenever he wanted. He hadn't needed money to broker that deal.

Why did he keep thinking, then, about what McGovern had said? No woman's head turned when McGovern walked into a room, except maybe as the prelude to a laugh. Men like McGovern might think they'd got it made, but Lewis measured himself by different criteria. Lewis had the edge, he was confident of that. He knew things that others didn't. McGovern was rich and successful, granted, but he was Lewis's dupe. He would never know it, of course. Perhaps that was the problem. Lewis believed that he lived a life to be envied, but the best of it he had to keep to himself. Sometimes he felt like an explorer who'd walked on his own to the South Pole but hadn't been able to tell anyone about it. What was the point of being number one if no one else appreciated the fact?

He felt restless. He thought of Peter McGovern and he thought of Julie McGovern, two separate strands that had become one. Husbands had never been a real issue before; they had been background figures, meaningless. Not that he felt guilt; why should he have done? Guilt was just a hang-up, a residue of the stale moral code they'd tried to ram down his throat in the school chapel. Society might disapprove of what he got up to with other men's wives, but as far as he was concerned he was just following his natural impulses, and what could be wrong with that? It wasn't as if he'd ever coerced anyone; far from it. No, his conscience was clear. Besides, he understood instinctively the truth of what McGovern had been telling him. Success made its own rules. The masses were just passive, so many sheep. If McGovern had but realized it, thought Lewis, the man he had spent a half-hour lecturing in the pub was a living embodiment of his philosophy.

Why then did he feel so uneasy? Why, specifically, did he feel as if McGovern knew something he didn't? He wished he could have washed him out of his skin, as easily as he had washed out the day's muck and grime in the shower. One thing was sure, sitting in the semi-darkness thinking endlessly about him wasn't going to make him go away. He held his watch close up to his eyes, straining to read the hands. It was about nine, and it was a Friday night. No time to be stewing in his own juices.

He picked up his jacket and car keys and went out. There were innumerable places in the area he could have gone, but on a Friday the choice was easy. He drove to a country pub about ten minutes down the road.

The pub was the England's Rose, formerly the Rose and Crown, a garishly modern conversion of a once pretty building, kitted out with the usual complement of fake horse brasses and cheap pine fittings. The beer wasn't much good either, but on Fridays it was Singles Night, and the Rose was transformed into the easiest pick-up joint between London and the coast. As local wisdom had it, you had to be Quasimodo with halitosis if you couldn't score in the Rose on Singles Night, or 'Nite' as it was advertised on the board outside.

The only drawback was the disco, which was manned by a near-adolescent with a taste for the kind of aggressive tuneless noise you got in the London clubs. But the Rose wasn't a young club scene. The average age of the clientele was thirtysomething, and over-forties were more common than under-twenties. That was why it was so good: the men and women who frequented it were all consenting adults after the same thing. Nobody liked the music, but at least it provided the springboard for a chat-up line.

Lewis paused in the doorway to scout out the land. It was still early, uncrowded and pleasantly unsmoky. Three men were at the bar, joking with each other and the barmaid, putting on a show of loud confidence that almost certainly signified a complete lack of it. The only other man in the room was doing rather better, chatting to two miniskirted girls in the corner by the fruit machine. Lewis looked at the girls critically, thinking there should be a law against shops being allowed to sell miniskirts to women with fat legs. He turned his attention to the other half of the room.

Two pairs of girls were sitting at separate tables. That was usual, women rarely hunted alone, and this early they always outnumbered the men. For some reason men seemed to think it was macho to turn up late, but Lewis saw no reason to give the competition a clear run. A casual glance was enough to dismiss the first pair, over-made-up shopgirls. The other two were a classier-looking brunette and a blonde. The blonde had her back to him, but the brunette looked quite tasty. He started for the bar, and halfway across saw that the brunette had clocked him. She leaned forward to say something to her friend over the music and the blonde turned round. For a moment her eyes and Lewis's locked together.

Lewis was usually good at disguising interest, but the blonde took him by surprise. It wasn't just that she was pretty – she was, but no more than the brunette – it was more her own reaction. Her eyes went wide when she saw him and her lips parted in frank amazement. He knew at once that he'd scored big time, and he wasn't quite sharp enough to conceal the fact that he knew it. He turned away abruptly and signalled to the barmaid. He asked for a mineral water.

He kept his back to the two girls while he waited for his drink. If he'd glanced up he could have caught a glimpse of them in the mirror behind the bar, so he forced himself to keep his eyes down. He had to look cool. If the blonde thought he thought he'd made her without even trying she would go right off him, and he didn't want that. He played the picture of her over in his mind's eye. It was a very pretty face, round almost to the point of plumpness but with good cheekbones; big blue eyes with long lashes, full lips and clear white skin. In her late twenties, he guessed. Hard to tell, sitting down, but around five-six. Dressed in a dark-brown velvety trouser suit, impossible to get much idea of her figure, but slim-looking, chic. He wondered briefly if the two of them would be on for a threesome, but thinking about it he realized that he had forgotten what the brunette looked like already. It was the blonde he wanted.

He pocketed his change and took a sip of his water. He waited patiently for the grungy track on the turntable to end, then rose smoothly from his barstool as the DJ started his prattle and walked over to the table in the corner.

'Hi! Mind if I join you?'

'Sure,' said the brunette. He sat down between them.

'I'm Lewis.'

'Nikki,' said the brunette.

Lewis turned to the blonde. She said something but he didn't catch it over the music, which had started up again, really loudly. Lewis leant towards her, making a joke of it as he cupped his ear.

'Grace!' she yelled above the music. 'And don't say amen!'

'I wasn't going to,' replied Lewis, taking advantage of the noise to lean in a little closer, enough to catch the scent of her perfume. Over his shoulder the brunette was saying something he couldn't quite catch. Reluctantly he leant back in his seat, spreading his attention to take them both in.

'I said do you need a drink?' shouted Nikki at him.

'I'm all right, but let me,' he said, starting to rise. Nikki clamped her hand on his arm and pushed him down again.

'No, no, it's my turn,' she said. She pointed inquisitively at her friend's half-finished white wine. Grace shook her head. 'See you later,' Nikki shouted at them both, and made for the bar.

Lewis wondered what unseen signal had passed between them, and marvelled at it. No man would ever have got the message and cleared the decks so smoothly. When it came to getting laid, women were streets ahead of men.

'So,' said Grace, leaning in close so that her mouth was only inches from his ear. 'Do you come here often?'

It wasn't a line he would ever have tried, even with the broad knowing smile she used for accompaniment. Lewis shook his head.

'Not my scene really. Yourself?'

'Nah. It was Nikki's idea. Look!'

Grace nodded towards the bar and nudged Lewis's arm. He glanced round. Nikki was standing amongst the men at the bar, flirting simultaneously with all of them.

'She was never very fussy,' said Grace, laughing.

'Unlike you, I suspect,' said Lewis.

'That's very astute of you.'

Grace leant back in her chair and folded her arms, giving him a look of mock-appraisal. He wondered what she did, and decided that he would put money on her being a teacher. Something about her suggested that she was used to being in control, that she knew how to raise her voice and make her presence felt if she had to. It was also obvious that she'd been speaking the truth when she said that coming to the Rose was her friend's idea. She was the only woman in the room not in a skirt, and her white blouse was buttoned up far too high to afford a glimpse of cleavage. She just didn't have that cattle-market look at all.

'God!' she said, suddenly pressing her hands to her ears. 'Why does the music have to be so loud?'

'Good question,' said Lewis. 'I think they want to stop people talking to each other.'

'I thought that was the idea?'

'Yeah, so did I. Doesn't make much sense, does it?'

Grace glanced quickly over in Nikki's direction. Lewis couldn't see what she saw, but it clearly amused her. When she looked back at him she was wearing a big smile. She leant in so close that her lips almost brushed his ear.

'Why don't we go somewhere else then?'

He had known she was confident, but he was still surprised. Of course it wasn't difficult making a pick-up in the Rose, but even he usually had to try a little harder than this.

'OK,' he said, trying to be casual about it. She was already on her feet, scooping up a big brown leather shoulder bag from the floor. She headed for the door without waiting for him.

'Thank God!' she said, when he joined her outside. 'Any more of that and my eardrums would burst.'

'What about your friend?' asked Lewis.

'What about her?'

Grace threw back her head and laughed. She was taller than Lewis had thought, and she wasn't wearing heels. He wondered if her legs were as good as they looked in her loose-fitting trousers.

'There's quite a decent wine bar down the road,' he said. 'Why don't we go there?'

'No. Let's go back to your place.'

For a moment he was speechless. Fortunately she was looking for something in her bag and didn't notice his surprise. She produced a packet of chewing gum.

'Want some?'

Lewis shook his head.

'Nor do I really. But I have to have something to stop me smoking. It's been three months now, sheer hell every minute. Let's not stand here all night, it's bloody freezing.'

'My car's over there.'

'And mine's over here. We'll go in mine.'

Her tone was utterly matter-of-fact, and didn't admit even to the possibility of dissension. Lewis imagined her standing in front of a classroom of wild children, and quelling them with a look. She set off towards a small white Renault. He followed after a moment, when his reactions had caught up with him. She had already started the engine when he got into the car. As soon as he closed the passenger door she accelerated away, throwing him back into his seat. She braked with equal suddenness, almost flinging Lewis into the windscreen, did a lightning-fast three-point turn and sped away towards the car park exit.

'Left here,' said Lewis, quickly buckling on his safety belt as she stopped to scan the road for traffic. She seemed to hesitate, for the first time since he'd met her.

'Is it far?'

'No. Ten minutes.'

'Good.'

She put her foot to the floor and the white Renault shot off down the road at top speed.

'About two minutes if you drive like this,' said Lewis.

She laughed.

'Never could see the point of hanging around.'

'I noticed that.'

She gave him a sidelong glance as she changed gears.

'You think I'm too upfront?'

'No.'

'You wouldn't be the first. Do I keep straight on here?'

'Yes. Don't think I've met anyone called Grace before. What's your surname?'

'My, you are formal. It's Cornish. I know I haven't met anyone called Lewis before. That really does sound like a surname.'

'Well, it's really my middle name, but I've got used to it, and so's everyone else. Where are you from, Grace?'

'Why, do I sound like a yokel?'

'Not at all, but there's a bit of an accent. What is it? Yorkshire?'

'Say that again and I'll put a whippet down your trousers. It's Lincolnshire, if you must know. I wasn't even aware I had it any more.'

'Why, you been down south a long time?'

'A while. What's your real name then?'

'Sorry?'

'If it's not Lewis, what are you really called?'

'Lewis'll do fine, Grace. Take a right here.'

He was a bit late giving her the instruction. She spun the wheel hard and he was thrown against the passenger door. She didn't touch the brake but took the corner at full speed, unbothered by the squeals of protest from her tyres.

'Who taught you to drive then?' asked Lewis. 'Michael Schumacher?'

'No. The Surrey Police.'

'You're kidding.'

He had run through his repertoire of surprised looks by now. He could only gape across at her blankly.

'You telling me you're the fuzz?'

'Christ, Lewis, what time warp have you been in? The "fuzz", indeed . . .'

'Sorry, Grace, it's just that I can't bring myself to think of you as filth.'

'You trying to turn me on by talking dirty, Lewis?'

'Why do you keep saying my name like that?'

'Like what?'

'Like, it's in parenthesis, or something.'

'That's a long word for a bit of rough from the pub, Lewis.'

'There you go again. So I'm a bit of rough, am I?'

'You look it, but I admit you don't sound it. So what is it, if it so embarrasses you?'

'What's what?'

'Your name, Lewis. Must be something horribly posy and middle class. Quentin, perhaps? Or what about Tarquin?'

'You're not exactly Sharon or Tracey yourself, Grace. It's Michael, if you must know.'

'How disappointing!'

'Yeah, well. There were three other boys in my class at school called Mike, and I wanted to be different. Take the next left.'

This time he knew to hang on to the door handle. The G-force as they went round the corner was probably the right level for astronaut training, he reckoned. They were belting down the back roads now, shaking over potholes and scattered bumps. All he could do was pray they met nothing coming the other way.

'You do a lot of high-speed chases then?' he asked.

'Not any more. I left the force two years ago. I'm ex-fuzz, if that makes you feel any better.'

'I don't know. Maybe I'm disappointed.'

'You mean you'd like me to dress up in my uniform?'

'No, I don't –'

'You should never be too embarrassed to ask for what you like. I never am. Are we nearly there yet?'

'Nearly. So why did you leave?'

'The force? Oh, a lot of reasons. I joined because I thought it would be exciting, I didn't want a desk job. Which is exactly what it seemed to be most of the time.'

'It must have had its moments.'

'Oh, it did, once I got into plain clothes. But then it just got too much of a hassle. I had no problem with the criminals. Unfortunately most of my superiors seemed to consider it their duty to try and get into my knickers.'

'So what do you do now?'

'I work for myself, Lewis. Left or right?'

'Left, and then it's after the next bend. But if you don't slow down a bit, we'll probably overshoot it.'

They almost did overshoot, even with the warning. He got out and opened the gate. He indicated where she should park, then walked up to join her. The security lights came on automatically as he approached.

'This really is the middle of nowhere, isn't it?' she said as she got out of the car. She tossed her bag over her shoulder. 'I shan't bother to lock the car. Which way then?'

'Follow me.'

She came up as he set off towards the barn and slipped her arm through his. The simple, unaffected gesture surprised him. So far, in the whirlwind few minutes of their acquaintance, she had made all the running and left him feeling breathless in her wake. But they were on his patch now, it was time for him to assert control. As they approached the door he disengaged his arm and put it around her shoulder, gently pulling her in towards his body and giving her a proprietorial squeeze. When they stopped for him to fish out his keys, he let his hand slide deliberately down her arm and come to rest on her waist. His fingers slipped downwards to explore the swell of her hip as he took rather longer than he needed to find the right key. He unlocked the door of the barn, reached inside for the light switches and indicated for her to go in.

'After you,' he said, indicating the spiral staircase.

'Just as well I've got a good head for heights.'

She started to go up the stairs. He paused on the first step, watching her legs. She stopped halfway up and glanced back over her shoulder.

'Like what you see then?'

The expression on her face was perfectly neutral, but there was an edge in her voice that made him hesitate. It was unmistakeably the sound of a challenge. He couldn't work her out. He remembered the look she'd given him when they'd clapped eyes on each other for the first time in the pub. He knew she had the hots for him, so why did he get the sense that she was keeping him at a distance? She hadn't responded to him putting his arm around her outside. Perhaps playing hard to get turned her on. He decided that her coolness was beginning to irritate.

'Yeah, I'm coming.'

He followed her up the spiral staircase. By the time he reached the top she was standing in the middle of the room, hands on hips, surveying the four walls in turn.

'Well, well, quite the bachelor pad . . .'

She walked around the pool table, a ghost of a smile on her lips, giving a little nod of the head as she clocked the features of the room. The gallery bedroom prompted a raised eyebrow, the sheer glass wall of the Aquarium a little whistle. Idly she plucked the cue ball off the D and rolled it down towards the other end of the pool table. Lewis caught it before it hit the cushion.

'I've got a nice bottle of Chablis in the fridge,' he said.

'Trying to get me drunk, Lewis?'

The irritation surged through him. If she'd been looking his way, she'd have seen it flicker across his face, but she was wandering over to look at his exercise equipment. He decided to match her coolness.

'Do I have to?' he asked, as if the prospect bored him utterly.

She didn't answer. With one foot she rolled one of his dumbbells a few inches across the floor.

'I presume these aren't for decoration,' she said.

'I keep myself fit.'

'I can see that.'

Her back was to him, but he could see her giving him an appraising look in the long wall mirror. He folded his arms and leant back against the pool table.

'Like what you see then?' he said.

She turned around and met his stare full-on. He didn't allow himself to be distracted by the pretty smile and the dimpled cheeks. He measured the look of calculation in her eyes.

'What about that bottle of wine?' she said.

'I'll go down and get it. Maybe you'd like to put some music on. My CDs are over there.'

So it was a game then, he decided as he went downstairs. She wanted him, that much was obvious, but she wanted to spar first. She liked to be in control. Well, he'd have to see about that.

When he returned from the kitchen, a tray with the bottle and two glasses in his hand, Grace was at the pool table aiming one of the cues. She had pulled a random assortment of balls out of the pockets and was engaged in sending them back whence they had come, in no particular order. She had taken off her jacket and slung it over his exercise bicycle. Lewis carried the tray over to his office desk and poured the wine. She hadn't chosen any music. He walked over to his CD rack and selected a Phil Collins album.

'Trying to show your age?' said Grace, as he brought the wine over.

'I like Phil Collins,' he said, with a trace of pique, immediately cross with himself that he had allowed her to put him on the defensive. She chuckled as she potted a ball into a side pocket.

'It's all right, Lewis, I don't mean to criticize. Damn. Rotten shot.'

The ball she had been trying to pot almost jumped out of the mouth of the pocket before screwing back to rest on the edge of the D. The cue ball stopped in the middle of the table.

'Shall we sit down?' he said, indicating the sofa in the Aquarium with a nod of his head.

'In a minute. I'm enjoying myself.'

She bent over the table, her legs spread, her body pressed close to the baize. Her blouse lifted as she leant forward, revealing a strip of white flesh. Lewis came round behind her with the drinks, his eyes flicking between her bare back and the smooth curve of her bottom, stretched tight against the velvet material of her suit. He didn't notice her brown leather shoulder bag on the floor, and almost tripped over it.

'Sorry, I shouldn't have left it there,' she said, not glancing back, her concentration still on the shot into the top pocket.

Lewis had knocked the bag over, spilling some of its contents. He crouched down, put the wine glasses on the floor, and started to put her things back into the bag: a purse, a packet of tissues, chewing gum, a lipstick and a pair of handcuffs.

'I thought you said you were ex-fuzz,' he said.

He heard the smack of the cue ball striking home and saw the netting on the bottom pocket twitch and fill. Grace got up awkwardly from the table. For a moment, when she saw him holding the handcuffs, he could almost have sworn he saw her blush.

'Don't worry about it,' he said easily. 'I'm broad-minded.'

'I bet you are,' she said, trying to sound casual but not quite carrying it off. He grinned up at her from the floor, playfully twirling the links of the handcuffs between his fingers.

'They sometimes come in useful,' she said. 'You asked what I did now. I'm in the private security line.'

He must have looked dubious. It was her turn to look irritated.

'Something wrong with that?' she demanded.

'You mean like a private eye?' he said, giving her a glass of wine. 'Like in the films?'

She shrugged and took a sip of her wine.

'You're full of surprises, Grace. Cheers.'

He clinked his glass against hers. He pointed to the cue in her hand.

'Play a bit then?'

'A bit.'

'Unusual.'

'Are you being sexist?'

'Are you being oversensitive? Not many women are interested, that's all I meant.'

She looked like she was about to reply, but hesitated. She seemed nettled. He was amused, and he was enjoying letting her know it.

'Want a game then?' she said suddenly.

'If you like.'

'You think you're too grand, do you?'

'Did I say that?'

'You don't have to.'

She broke away and walked down to the other end of the table. She put down her wine, which she hadn't touched, on the floor. She started taking the red and yellow balls out of the pockets.

'What are we playing for?' he asked.

'Don't get overconfident, Lewis.'

'I won't. But you have to have a stake. To liven the game up. Make it worthwhile.'

'All right.'

She rolled the balls from her end of the table towards him. He bent down to pick up the triangle.

'You get to do what you want,' she said. 'That's the stake.'

'I'm sorry?'

'You do still want to fuck me, don't you?'

It wasn't easy remaining perfectly still, letting not the slightest trace of emotion register in his face. He heard himself speak, but the voice sounded strangled and unnaturally small, not his own at all.

'Yes. I still want to fuck you.'

She nodded briskly, as if indicating that some minor point in an academic argument had been settled. She picked up the chalk from the table and put both hands behind her back.

'That's settled then. You win, and you call the shots. I'll do anything you ask, anything at all. And if I win, then I'm the boss. OK? Which hand?'

She held out her two closed fists in front of her. He indicated her right hand. It was empty. She revealed the chalk in her left palm and began applying it to her cue tip.

'I'll break,' she announced.

He watched her bend down to take the shot. He imagined her, stripped naked over the pool table, squirming beneath him as he took his pleasure, and his time, that infuriating cool exterior cracked in the heat of passion, and all that teasing mocking aloofness discarded with her clothes.

The cue ball hit into the triangular pack, with a crack like a rifle shot.

6

The sex was rough and brutish. It was also over quickly. He held her down, her wrists pinioned above her head, the full weight of him crushing her against the mattress. She gasped for breath.

'You're hurting me!'

He ignored her and gripped her tighter. He wanted to hurt her, he was filled with incoherent anger. His features froze in an animal snarl as he reached a sudden, unsatisfying climax. He didn't look at her face as he released his grip and rolled off her.

'You bastard!' she whispered, a word she had never used to him before; the tone neither. 'What's got into you?'

He didn't reply. He sat on the edge of the bed, fishing his clothes up from the floor. The anger had been spent in that spasm of routine pleasure. The passion gone, he felt slightly ashamed.

'I thought you liked rough sex,' he said sullenly.

'It's him, isn't it?'

The sob in her voice was dramatic and contrived, but it made him look up. She was sitting against the headboard, her knees pulled up to her chin. Her eyes flicked briefly to the photograph of her husband by the bed.

'He was on about you last night, too. Said you'd been to the pub again with him. What a great guy you are. His new friend. Sick.'

'Julie, it's not –'

'It's sick, Lewis. What are you trying to prove? Does everyone have to love you, or what? I don't get it.'

'Me neither.'

He pulled on his pants and trousers. One of his socks had gone missing. He got down on to his knees and peered under the bed, holding the bedclothes up with his hand.

'What happened to your wrist?' asked Julie.

He found his sock and put it on. Self-consciously he fingered the red weal on his right wrist. His watch strap covered the corresponding mark on the other side.

'Nothing,' he said. 'Just a burn.'

'Funny-looking burn to me.'

'I said it's nothing. Forget it, OK!'

'All right, no need to shout.'

It was taking him forever to lace up his boots, his big heavy work boots with their rows of metal lace-hooks down each side. He tied quick rough knots and pulled his still-buttoned shirt on over his head as he stood up. He wanted to be anywhere but where he was now.

'Is that it then?' she said.

'Got to get back to work.'

'Oh, great. You've got to finish wallpapering his office, so you haven't even got time to be nice to his wife once you've finished screwing her.'

'Some of us have got to work for a living.'

'And what's that supposed to mean?'

It was her turn to shout now. Her eyes had a livid sparkle, to match her tone.

'You treat me like a prostitute,' she said bitterly.

He smiled coldly. He glanced at her huddled basque-clad figure. He noticed a ladder in her stockings.

'You dress like one,' he said.

He enjoyed her shocked silence. Her eyes brimmed with tears. For a few moments she was too hurt to speak.

'If you don't want to see me any more, Lewis, just say it. I know you have other women, but do I ever say anything? Don't think I'm not jealous. Sometimes when I'm sitting here, on my own or with . . . with him, and I think of you, out there and free as a bird, having a great time without me, oh I'm jealous enough then, I'll admit it. I lie awake sometimes with him snoring beside me, and I can't sleep because I'm thinking of you having sex with another woman. Is she prettier than me? Does she do things for you I don't? I know you have your pick, but I bite my tongue back, I don't ask. Everything I do is for you, to turn you on, to please you. I don't ask for much in return, do I? I know we've got no real future together, I know you're not interested. Sometimes you'll stay for a coffee and a chat after we've done it, but that's it. About ten minutes I get on a good day, and then it's time for you to make your excuses and get back to whatever job, or whatever woman, you've got lined up. How do I rate, Lewis? Do you keep notes?'

'I thought you –'

'Thought I was like you, you mean? No feelings, just cold. You've got a nice warm smile, I'll give you that, but the rest of you's cold. Great body, Lewis, shame about the rest.'

'If you're just going to insult me –'

'Oh, we couldn't have that, could we? The great love-god told off. My job's just to lie there and take it, right, and be grateful for what I get. I'm sorry, Lewis, I'm really sorry. I'm so so grateful, I really, really am, that you managed to find time to fit me into your busy schedule this morning, that you took all that extra effort to make me feel like a cheap tart.'

'Julie, it's no –'

'Don't touch me!'

She recoiled from his extended arm. She was hunched in a ball, as if she expected to be hit. She was fighting back tears.

'I don't know what's going on, Lewis, that's made you so angry. Hardly surprising, is it? You never tell me what you're feeling, what you're thinking, anything about you. I used to think you were a man of mystery, tall, dark and silent but smouldering with passion inside. But there isn't anything else, is there? What you see really is what you get, isn't it? I don't know what's bugging you, but would you stop taking it out on me, please?'

Now the tears came. He stood uncomfortably, glad at least that her accusing eyes were shielded behind her hands.

'Got to get back to work,' he said.

'Yeah, of course. You got what you came for.'

He bit back his angry answer, let it pass.

'I'll call you then.'

She didn't respond. He counted under his breath, gave it five, then walked out of the bedroom and down the stairs as fast as he could.

He was in Guildford in ten minutes, half of it on the tail of a Porsche whose driver must have been mortified by the blistering pace of the van sitting plumb in his rear mirror. He parked in the side road at the back of the estate agent's. McGovern's car was not in the space reserved.

'Is Peter not in?' he asked the only person in the office, a young man with fashionably cropped hair and a small gold earring.

'At the doctor's,' the young man responded laconically. 'Said he's not been feeling too good lately.'

Lewis had a vague sense of anticlimax. All the while he had been with Julie he had been suppressing a reckless urge towards confrontation. Quite what he needed to confront he didn't know, but it involved McGovern. He had found himself wondering what would have happened if McGovern had come home unexpectedly and caught them at it in the bedroom. Thinking about it had almost made him wish it would happen. The same thoughts had filled his head the night before, in the pub. He had decided he wasn't going to accept if McGovern asked him again, but before he could think of anything to say he had found himself nodding and following him over the road. He had told himself that he would have one, and then go, but in the event he had stayed for two hours and matched McGovern drink for drink. He shouldn't have driven home afterwards, but he had. Everything about the evening had been so mad he concluded that he must have a death wish. All the time, as the alcohol seeped into his veins and he listened to McGovern's endless spiel, he had felt an urge to bleat out the truth building volcanically inside him. At least it would have wiped the smug look off the other man's face.

'You need him for anything?' asked the young man with the earring. He was leaning back in his chair, his feet resting on a pile of leaflets. Lewis found his air of determined nonindustriousness irritating.

'It can wait,' he replied brusquely. 'No one else about back there, is there?'

'Nah, mate. Too bad, eh?'

The young man winked at him. His air of self-satisfaction had become so overwhelming that Lewis wanted to hit him.

'What's too bad?'

'Carol's not there, if that's what you meant.'

'What are you talking about?'

'Aw, come on,' said the young man with a smirk. 'I saw you staring at her arse yesterday. Don't worry, your secret's safe with me. We all do it. Boss doesn't let her out of his sight for long, you know. He's no fool.'

The estate agent gave a dirty chuckle. Lewis stared back coldly.

'Can't fault his taste, whatever else you might say,' the young man continued, either not taking on board Lewis's hostility, or just choosing to ignore it. 'Somehow I don't think it was her typing skills got her the job, eh? She's a bit simple in the head, if you ask me. Still, who cares? He's a dark horse, the boss. You wouldn't think he was no Romeo to look at, would you, but you should see his wife. Not too bright either from all accounts, but a cracker, mate, a cracker.'

The young man whistled softly. His grin had become wolfish. Lewis gave him the benefit of his hard-man glare before walking out.

The back room was a mess. Yesterday, Monday, had been his first day on the job and he'd spent it stripping the tatty remnants of the wallpaper and ripping out the old plasterboard partitions. Dust and muck were everywhere. He snatched up a broom and swept the worst of it away. He'd given himself until Saturday, but he didn't want to be around that long. He shouldn't even have been there in the first place, he knew that now. What was he playing at? he wanted to know. Seeing how far he could push it, he supposed, seeing how much he could get away with. It was that death wish again. But where had it come from? What was he trying to prove? Whatever it was he hadn't managed it. All he'd succeeded in doing was screwing things up with Julie, and that was just plain stupid. Julie was a cracker, as the man had said, and he was close to blowing it. It was stupid, stupid, stupid. He slapped the wall hard with the flat of his hand to emphasize the point. The gnawing charge of aggression that had got to him earlier was coming back. He'd been in a filthy mood all weekend, ever since he'd picked up that bitch in the Rose. It was worrying. He was losing his touch. Something to do with McGovern, and something to do with Grace. That bitch. He should have just told her to get stuffed, to hell with her silly games. He'd had her beaten, three balls up and no danger at all, and then he'd allowed his mind to wander, got himself too wrapped up in what he was going to do to her in the bedroom. A careless shot, that was all it had been, not even a real stinker, but somehow it had taken a flukey kiss and screwed into the black. He had just stood there, dumbly, with his mouth hanging open, watching the black bobble for an age in the mouth of the pocket before tipping in. She had been almost as surprised as he was, but she had recovered quicker. He couldn't get the image of her out of his head, her standing at the bottom of the table, smirking at him with one eyebrow raised while she dangled the handcuffs in front of his eyes.

He rubbed the still-red weal on his wrist, remembering his humiliation. She hadn't wanted pleasure from him, just his humiliation. She had left him handcuffed to the bed all night, the metal clips so tight against his wrists that he had hardly been able to sleep. In the morning she had been contrite, she must have known that she had gone too far, but he hadn't said anything, just as he had never complained that she was hurting him. At least he could derive a little satisfaction from that; she hadn't quite stripped him of all his dignity. But it should never have happened in the first place.

There were so many things he should have done, should do now, should stop doing in the future. And the first thing to do was get McGovern out of his hair. Ever since they'd met things had been going wrong. He wasn't the superstitious sort, but the thought kept flashing into his mind that McGovern was jinxing him. Well then, he'd better do something about it, hadn't he?

He carried his mobile phone outside, to get a better signal, and called Charlie. Charlie was at the Simmons place, tidying up loose ends, while Bill and a casual worker from the Job Centre were at the Larsens'. Lewis told Charlie to go and pick up the casual and bring him over to Guildford. The two of them could finish McGovern's office by Friday. Lewis would wrap up the Simmons job himself, then give Bill a hand. It wasn't what he'd promised McGovern, but if he didn't like it he could get himself another builder.

Lewis packed up his work bag and went out the back way. He allowed himself a passing moment of regret at the thought of Carol, but there were plenty more where she came from. It would have been worth cracking her just to see the look on the face of the geek with the earring. The geek could waste the rest of his life lounging in that office and leering at her body, but he wasn't going to get anywhere. Men like him, hands-off men who only dared think what they wanted, were beneath contempt. If you wanted to get anywhere, you had to take control.

Lewis revved up the van and drove off without a backward glance. The sensation of a burden having been lifted was overwhelming. McGovern had just gone straight back out of his life as easily as he had slipped in.

7

It was just coming up to eleven, and Lewis was preparing to go to bed, when he saw the headlamps of a car flash across the glass wall of the Aquarium. He paid the car no attention, assuming that it would continue on down the road, but as he started to climb the spiral staircase to the bathroom he distinctly heard the noise of the engine. He stopped at the top of the stairs and looked down through the huge glass window into the courtyard. The car was pulling up in front of the barn. As he watched, the headlamps went off and the engine cut out. A moment later he heard the faint sound of a slamming door.

People hardly ever visited him at home, and never this late, unannounced. He ran through the possible list of visitors in his head, and decided they were all unwelcome, but it was no use pretending he wasn't in, because the driver would have seen him through the window. Reluctantly he climbed back down the stairs.

By the time he had reached the ground floor he had decided that although there was just the faintest possibility that it was Charlie on a perfectly innocent errand, the most likely visitor was Julie. He had no idea what she could want, but having broken one golden rule about phoning him it felt somehow inevitable that she should break another and come banging on his door late at night. He had only ever let her come to the barn once, and that reluctantly, in response to months of wheedling. In her present mood, he suspected, anything he told her not to do would be treated as provocation. Through the glass at the top of the door he saw the security light come on. He took a moment to think what to say, then yanked open the door with an aggressive twist.

'I'm sorry to bother you,' said Peter McGovern softly, 'but I was wondering if I could have a word.'

'Of course,' said Lewis numbly, stepping aside to let him in.

Lewis was profoundly shocked, not so much at seeing McGovern, which was surprising enough, but at his subdued tone and look. His voice was so thin and indistinct that Lewis had barely heard him. And even allowing for the poor light it was obvious that his face, pale at any time, was utterly drained of colour. He shambled past with his shoulders slumped and his eyes down. When Lewis indicated the stairs he gave a little nod and started up them without a word.

Lewis had to grip the stair rail hard to steady himself. His legs were trembling. It was obvious to him what had happened, and what was coming. McGovern really had found out about him and Julie. If he'd been coming to make an angry scene Lewis could have coped easily, but this was going to be much worse. This was going to be wounded looks and tear-stained eyes. This would be talk of friendship spurned, betrayal, not 'How dare you!' but 'How could you?' Lewis could handle most things, but not guilt.

McGovern, at the top of the stairs, had drifted listlessly into the room and come to rest against the pool table. He was wearing a black woollen coat over his suit, buttoned to the chin in spite of the mild night. With the collar pulled up and his neck shrunk down into it he had the look of a furtive, if unconvincing, spy.

'Well, you did say you wanted to see the place,' said Lewis. He had put every effort into sounding casual, but he could hear the crack of tension in his own voice.

McGovern glanced mechanically to left and right. His pale, lifeless eyes seemed to take nothing in.

'Nice place,' he murmured.

His duty done, his attention returned to the pool table. He stared down at the green baize as if in a trance.

'Can I offer you a drink?'

McGovern took his time thinking about it. Eventually he nodded.

'Scotch?'

This time the nod was decisive.

'Why don't you take a seat?'

Lewis went downstairs to the kitchen. He knew how McGovern liked his Scotch by now, just a drop of water and no ice. McGovern scorned people who put ice in their Scotch. It made Lewis hesitate before he dropped a cube into his own glass, but that was how he liked it and he needed a stiff drink himself. He put the drinks on a tray, with the bottle and a jug of water. He was glad to have had an excuse to get out of the same room as McGovern. By the time he went back up his nerves were decidedly steadier.

He had indicated for McGovern to sit in the Aquarium, but instead he had headed for a canvas chair next to the filing cabinets in the office area. Lewis carried the tray over to the desk. He handed McGovern his drink and sat down behind the desk in his black leather swivel chair.

'So?' he said pleasantly, feeling like a bank manager interviewing a customer. 'What can I do for you?'

'I've been given three months to live,' said McGovern.

The smile which Lewis had so carefully put into place vanished. He wondered for a moment if he had heard correctly, but he knew that he had. McGovern had spoken quite distinctly. He carried on now, in the same vein, without emotion.

'Three months at the most. Probably less. I've had these pains in my chest for a while. I kept ignoring them, but I knew, somehow, that it was bad. When I did go to my doctor he said it was bronchitis. I tried to believe him, but it wasn't that sort of pain. It's funny how we always trust doctors. Bloody useless in my experience. I went to see a specialist today, to get the results of tests he did last week. That's why I wasn't in the office. I thought I just had a dose of flu I couldn't shake off. It's lung cancer.'

McGovern knocked back his Scotch in two swallows. Lewis began to reach for the bottle but McGovern waved him back.

'No, I've had enough. Been drinking all night, as you can probably imagine. I'm sorry to spring this on you, Lewis. I'm sorry, but I had to talk to somebody, and I didn't know who else to go to.'

McGovern had closed his eyes. The lines around them multiplied and creased as his chin began to tremble. He shook with dry sobs.

I'm sorry, he mouthed, no sound from his lips. I'm sorry.

Lewis, unable to think of anything to do or say, did and said nothing. Several minutes passed. By degrees McGovern began to get a grip on himself. When he started speaking again he sounded eerily calm.

'I can't say it's unexpected, but it's odd how you think it'll never happen to you. I've been smoking since I was fourteen, a twenty-a-day man all my adult life. My gran lived to be ninety-six, and she was a Players-untipped woman, almost to the end. Never did me any harm, last thing I heard her say. Been saying it myself ever since. I'm only forty-nine. I'm not even going to make fifty. Hardly past Gran's halfway mark. Did me some harm all right, didn't it? I've been staring at my fag packet half the evening, reading that stupid caption over and over again. Government Health Warning: TOBACCO SERIOUSLY DAMAGES HEALTH. Well there's a thing!'

McGovern gave a dry bitter laugh. Lewis heard the death rattle in his throat.

'No use crying over it though, is there? Even if I'd gone when the pains first started they probably wouldn't have been able to do much about it. Slowed it down a bit, maybe, got me another year, but that's all. It's one of the bastard ones, lung. Hardly ever cured. Hurts like hell too. It's spread, you see, got into the liver already, the spine. I've been complaining of a bad back for ages, keep having these massages, haven't done the slightest bit of good. Incredible you can be that far gone and not know it, but the doctor says it happens all the time. Worst thing is, now I know it's there I can feel it chewing me up. I woke up in the middle of last night with it. Excruciating. That's the bit I don't think I can take. Never been good at handling pain, I'm afraid. I'm no kind of hero, I have to admit. Great drugs these days, of course. They can dose me up till I'm a vegetable, but what's the point in that? You might just as well be dead. I'm sorry, Lewis. I'm sure you don't want to be hearing any of this, it's very selfish of me.'

Lewis found it almost harder to take in the candour in McGovern's gaze than the details of what he was saying. He had such a trusting, almost puppyish look.

'You're a good guy, Lewis,' said McGovern gently. 'I know I haven't known you long but you're a solid, straight guy. To tell you the truth I don't have many friends. It may seem a bit weird, and not the kind of compliment that'd do you any good, but I really couldn't think of anyone else to turn to. At times like this you've just got to talk, let it all out. Sorry it had to be you. Look, I've got a confession to make. I think I'd better have that refill you offered.'

McGovern leant forward and pushed his empty glass across the desk. Lewis filled it, concentrating all his effort into keeping his hand steady. He felt McGovern's gaze on him the whole time. He felt as if the man was weighing him up, deciding on an estimate.

'That's very kind of you, Lewis, thanks. I say there's no one else I could have turned to, and you might think that a little odd. But I haven't spoken to anyone else, anyone at all. I want you to promise that you won't mention it either. Will you do that?'

Again Lewis found it impossible to take that blaze of candour. He nodded, and pretended he needed another cube of ice in his own drink to give himself an excuse to look away.

'Filthy habit, Lewis, you really shouldn't, you know. I said I'd got a confession to make. It's not as dramatic as you think. When I say I've spoken to nobody, I mean nobody. I haven't said a word to Julie, and nor do I intend to. The fact of the matter is, we don't get on. I know I've spoken to you in glowing terms about her, I think I really talked her up. But we don't get on. Haven't for years, we shouldn't have got married in the first place. She's a smashing lass, I mean that, I've really got nothing against her, but unfortunately we've just got nothing in common. No shared interests, nothing. We don't even sleep together. You might think that's a bit crazy if you saw her again, because she really is gorgeous, but it's a mutual thing. There's just no spark between us. A dead marriage, common enough story, no sympathy required. I suppose we'd have got divorced in the end. No need for that now. But I couldn't bear it if she suddenly started getting all lovey-dovey with me for the wrong reasons. If there's one thing I can't stand, Lewis, it's hypocrisy. I'd prefer to give all the false sentiments a miss, if you don't mind. One day, very soon, it'll just be phut! and there I go. And that's the first I want her to know about it. I don't know if that sounds a bit cruel, but, to be honest, she's not exactly going to weep buckets when I do go. I've not got that much in the way of cash, but there's a decent amount of life assurance, and property, of course. She's going to be a wealthy woman. She'll be chuffed. Should be, anyway. I would be.'

McGovern laughed again. From somewhere he had dredged up a big smile, but the laugh was hollow.

'I guess you're thinking it might be hard to keep it from her, with me drugged up to the eyeballs and wasting away in front of her. At least I'm too far gone for chemo, so my hair won't all fall out. I think people would have noticed something then, don't you?'

Lewis did his best to respond to McGovern's big grin. The brave face he was putting on was unbearable.

'The thing is, though, I'm not intending to see it out to the end. I made that decision straightaway. I'm going to get some pills, something. When the pain gets too much, I'll just quietly see myself out. And that'll be sooner rather than later. I'm going to do this on my own terms, not let myself get dictated to by some bastard disease. I'm a fighter by nature, but there's no point arguing with the ref when you've been given the red card. Sorry, you don't like blokes talking about football, do you? I must remember that.'

McGovern reached for his glass, gave the whisky in the bottom a swirl, looked at it, and then replaced the glass untasted on the desk.

'I think I may have had enough. Alcohol usually makes me reach for the fags, it's a knee-jerk reaction. Not tonight. You don't smoke, do you, Lewis?'

Lewis shook his head.

'Sensible lad. You've a clean, healthy lifestyle. I envy you that. I'm not going to get self-pitying, though. If I start getting like that – you know, maudlin, sentimental – you have my full permission to give me a sharp nudge. Will you do that for me?'

Lewis nodded.

'Thanks, you've been a true pal. I'll be making a move. I'm sorry, I'm really sorry to have come round and inflicted this on you, but I was desperate. I know I can rely on you not to breathe a word to a soul, but I had to let it out, let out a bit of steam. I feel a lot better for it.'

McGovern got up, and slowly, purposefully, came round to Lewis's side of the desk. He laid a hand on Lewis's shoulder.

'Thanks. I really mean it.'

Lewis swallowed hard. The touch of the hand on his shoulder, the tangible physical weight of sincerity behind it, was hard to take. McGovern gave his shoulder a squeeze and turned to go.

'It's all right, I'll see myself out.'

'Don't be silly. I'll come down.'

They descended the stairs in silence. Lewis switched on the outside light from the hall and opened the door.

'See you then,' said McGovern, offering his hand. 'I won't be around tomorrow. I need a day or two on my own, just to sort my head out. But it'll be a comfort to me, in a funny sort of way, knowing you're in the office, taking care of things for me. Or does that sound daft already?'

Lewis shook his hand.

'Of course not,' he said. 'Are you sure you're all right to drive?'

'I know I'm over the limit, but I feel perfectly sober. What's the point worrying about it now anyway? So what if they take my licence? Not exactly a big deal any more, is it?'

'No. Look, if there's anything you'd like me to do, I mean *anything,* don't hesitate to ask.'

'I won't. Good night now.'

Lewis watched him drive away. When the car lights had

faded from view he remained rooted to the spot, staring into the darkness, until the cold got into his bones and sent him back inside. He went straight upstairs and rang Charlie. He told him not to come to Guildford in the morning after all. He said that he had decided to finish the estate office job on his own.

8

Lewis finished McGovern's office on Saturday morning. The boss hadn't been seen in the office all week and Lewis had had no contact with him. But he had spoken to his wife.

Julie had rung him again on his mobile, the morning after McGovern had been to see him.

'He's gone away for a few days,' she told him. 'Perhaps you'd like to come round. I think we should have a talk.'

He was on the A3, between Guildford and Petersfield, with one hand on the wheel and the phone tucked between head and shoulder. He pulled over into the slow lane, though as it was the morning rush hour the term was relative.

'Lewis, are you there?'

Her tone was cool, even clipped. It didn't sound like Julie at all, or at least not the pliant, simple creature he had first encountered fifteen months ago. That was twice now within a week that she had broken the rule and rung him.

'I'm sorry, I'm not getting you very clearly,' he said. 'I'll call you back.'

He put the phone down. He was feeling angry. So she wanted to talk, did she? And what did that signify? No good, was the short answer. Was she going to pull that classic woman's trick and start going on about commitment? Well, it was a bit late for that. Another possibility dawned on him, a thought as unwelcome as it was unexpected. She wasn't going to sit him down and tell him it was all over, was she? No, his women didn't do that to him, ever. He was the one who did the leaving. If that was her game she could forget it. He thought of her dying husband. He knew which of the two deserved his respect. So that was that then; no need for any stupid talks. It would have had to end sooner rather than later anyway. And fortunately he had his eye on a replacement.

It was nearly a quarter to nine when he pulled up in the drive of the big detached modern house on the edge of Petersfield. He had said that he would be there by eight-thirty. Ralph Carter came outside to meet him.

'I'm very sorry,' Lewis said as he got out of the van. 'Terrible traffic.'

'Don't worry about it,' said Ralph. 'Very good of you to come at such short notice. I've taken the morning off anyway, got to take the car in for a service later. Come in and have a coffee. Say hello to Laura before we go upstairs.'

Ralph wanted new windows and fittings in their bedroom and *en suite* bathroom. It was Laura's idea, Ralph told him as they went through to the back of the house. He couldn't see what was wrong with the windows they'd got, but she was very keen.

Laura Carter was sitting on a high stool at a breakfast bar in the kitchen. She was wearing a short nightie and a matching green silk dressing gown.

'My apologies for appearing deshabille, Lewis,' she said, offering her hand. 'It's a bit early for me.'

It might have been early for her, Lewis noted as he shook her hand, but it was obvious that she hadn't rolled out of bed five minutes ago. She was washed and fully made-up and her long auburn hair had been well brushed. Whatever had been in her mind when she'd dolled herself up it hadn't been a morning's housework. Lewis let his eyes drop to her bare legs, then move up, taking her in by inches until his eyes locked again with her own. He took his time and made no attempt to mask what he was doing. She raised an eyebrow as if to question the results of his appraisal.

'You know this kitchen better than we do, of course,' said Ralph cheerfully, pouring him coffee. 'Damned good job you made of it too. Didn't he, darling?'

'Oh yes,' agreed Laura, looking directly into Lewis's eye. 'He's always very good. He has an excellent reputation.'

Ralph chuckled as he brought over a mug of coffee.

'Seems like she's been speaking about you with her girlfriends,' said Ralph, giving Lewis a gentle nudge. 'You've created a bit of a stir with the ladies, my friend.'

'And which girlfriends would those be?' asked Lewis.

'Gill Seymour-Brown, for one,' said Laura. 'I recommended you to her, if you remember, after you were here.'

'Of course. I did her kitchen too, last year. Was she pleased?'

'Oh yes, very pleased. She said you're good. Not just good, but the best she's ever had. Quite a compliment, eh?'

'Yes, it is. I'm flattered. You mean you'd like the same service?'

'Exactly the same. In every particular. In fact, we insist on it. Don't we, darling?'

'What's that, darling?' said Ralph, who had been following the conversation only vaguely, with the smile of the happily ignorant plastered to his face. 'Oh yes, we want it all. The full monty.'

Ralph laughed heartily. Lewis laughed with him, and Laura joined in. Ralph seemed not to have noticed that the other two had silently excluded him. Three, as ever, made up a crowd, and a husband was nature's odd man out. Ralph was giving an Oscar-winning performance in the role.

Thoughts of Laura had kept him going the rest of the week. He hadn't made a move on her the year before because he'd needed Ralph's goodwill too badly. He still needed it, though his financial situation wasn't as bad as it had been. But he needed a new woman more. Laura was a class act, much more so than her friend Gill Seymour-Brown, whom he had only taken because she had offered herself so eagerly. Laura had the potential to be every bit as good a long-term prospect as Julie had been, just as sexy and a good deal brighter. He would have to be discreet, that was all. Fortunately Ralph's shrewdness was all reserved for money matters.

He hadn't returned Julie's call, not that day, the Wednesday, nor on Thursday, nor Friday. She had not called him again either, and with each passing hour the prospect of ever getting another call from her receded still further. So what? She'd be able to find herself other lovers soon enough, queues of them when word of the wealthy widow got about. It wasn't a situation that would have appealed to Lewis anyway, being the appendage of a rich woman, so he was doubly glad to be out of it. He thought about her, her shallowness, her unthinking self-absorption and lack of imagination, and was surprised that he'd stuck with her so long. And then he stopped thinking about her altogether.

Saturday morning was spent tying up loose ends in the Guildford office. Lewis wanted to get it all out of the way so he'd be able to give his full attention to Laura on the Monday. He finished the job off by noon. Before giving it a final check he popped across the road to buy a sandwich.

The little sandwich shop he had been using during the week was closed. He walked on down the road to a small supermarket, where he bought a stale-looking roll and a bottle of mineral water. As he finished putting his purchases into one of the flimsy plastic carrier bags heaped up by the cash register he caught a glimpse of a blonde head going past on the pavement outside. He looked up instinctively, a natural checker-out of passing talent, and the young woman glanced at that moment in his direction. Their eyes met and she stopped walking.

Why hello, said her lips through the glass. He managed the thinnest of smiles in response. Reluctantly he picked up his carrier bag and headed for the door. She was still standing exactly where she had stopped, waiting for him.

'I thought for a moment you'd forgotten me,' she said, smiling slyly.

'How could I? How are you doing, Grace?'

Grace Cornish shrugged. She was carrying a bagful of heavy shopping in each hand and she affected to look world-weary.

'Oh, struggling along, Lewis. Are you going this way?'

Lewis nodded.

'Good. Then we can walk together. What are you doing in Guildford?'

'Working.'

'Of course.'

'What are you doing?'

'I live here. You never rang. I'm offended.'

'You don't sound offended. Anyway, you're forgetting. I couldn't have rung because you didn't give me your number.'

'You didn't ask. Would you have rung if I had done?'

'No.'

She laughed, almost naturally. Though she was playing at being amused he sensed that she felt uncomfortable. That at least made two of them. They took the next dozen steps in silence.

'You don't seem very pleased to see me, Lewis,' she said with sudden gaiety. 'Was it that bad?'

'No.'

'I wasn't too rough with you, was I?'

He didn't answer. He kept staring straight ahead at the cracks in the pavement.

'Sorry, that was a bit heavy-handed.' She sounded contrite. 'This is as far as I go.'

They were outside a row of small shops, between a newsagents and an ironmongers. Grace transferred her shopping bags to the same hand while she fumbled in her coat for keys with the other.

'Is this where you live then?' Lewis asked. In front of them was a chipped blue door. An old brass plate advertised the services of an impressively qualified chiropodist. 'Is that a sideline then?'

'He's on the first floor. This is me.'

With her key she tapped a smaller brass plate next to the door buzzer. It read: Courtenay & Partner, Private Detectives.

'I'm Partner,' she said, not without pride.

'And you live above the shop?'

'At the moment.'

She unlocked the door. Lewis caught a glimpse of a narrow unlit hall, liberally carpeted with junk mail, and a staircase beyond.

'Nice to see you again,' said Grace. 'Where are you working?'

'I've just finished actually. It's an estate agents, down the road. Maybe I'll run into you sometime.'

'What estate agents?'

She sounded surprised. She had been on the point of going inside, but she stopped suddenly in the doorframe, awkwardly, holding back the blue door on its spring with her knee while she wrestled with her two big shopping bags.

'By the roundabout. McGovern's. You know it?'

'Yes. Yes, I do. Well, well . . . I actually rent this place through them. They do commercial lettings, too.'

'Small world, eh?'

'Seems that way. See you then, Lewis.'

He didn't answer. If there was one person he had no intention of ever seeing again, it was her.

He finished off the office, set the alarm as he'd been shown and drove home. He was planning to pick up his gear and spend the afternoon in the gym, but as he slowed down to enter his drive he saw that there was another car already parked in front of the barn. It was Peter McGovern's Mercedes.

McGovern was sitting in the front seat listening to the radio. Lewis stopped next to him. They lowered their windows and spoke.

'So you're back then?' said Lewis awkwardly.

'Yeah, I'm back. Had a couple of days away, get my act together. Not feeling too good, I have to admit, but I'm a bit clearer in the head. Hope you don't mind me bothering you like this.'

'Of course not.'

Lewis managed a sympathetic smile. In truth he was shocked by McGovern's haggard appearance. He didn't look as if he'd had much sleep. His skin was even sallower than usual, his hair unclean and greasy. His expensive suit was stained and creased.

'I've been thinking a lot, Lewis. I need some help. Are you doing anything this afternoon?'

'Nothing important.'

'Could you spare me a couple of hours? I'd like you to come with me down the road. It's not far, Haslemere way. Twenty minutes.'

'Sure. I finished the office, by the way. It's come up well.'

He gave McGovern details of what he'd done as he sat in the passenger seat of the Mercedes, admiring the way the noiseless engine effortlessly devoured the miles of country lanes. He wasn't a car buff himself, but he knew class when he saw it. If it hadn't been for the stale tobacco smell that clung to the interior, not helped by an ashtray jammed up with old cigarette butts, it could have been like something from a glossy magazine spread.

'I'm glad it all went well,' commented McGovern tonelessly when Lewis had finished telling him all about the paint finish in the back room. 'I've been making some enquiries about selling the business. It'll help if the head office looks smart.'

Lewis nodded, as if the point under discussion were purely commercial, not a matter of life and death. He wondered how long McGovern had got. Three months, he'd said, but the way he was looking he'd be lucky to stagger on for another three weeks. A phrase he'd often heard, lightly used with no real meaning, kept buzzing round his head. Like death warmed up. That was McGovern. Death warmed up.

They skirted round Haslemere and drove down familiar wooded lanes. The Larsens were on the right, a job that had dragged on because of Guildford and still needed finishing. A mile further on was a farmhouse where he had restored rotting timbers and rebuilt a Victorian fireplace. His own private landmarks littered this area, but he had never come across the house where McGovern pulled up at the end of a journey that had lasted a little longer than the twenty minutes advertised.

One of McGovern's estate agent signs, this one with the slogan 'Sold' blazoned in red across it, stood outside. The property was walled, and a long way back from the road, with no evidence of neighbours. There were nine acres, McGovern told him, two thirds of it wooded. After the build-up Lewis half expected to see something out of Brideshead emerge at the end of the long, winding drive, but the house when it appeared was disappointingly nondescript. It was quite big, but characterless, a solid fifties construction in red brick and grey slate, with an attempt at mock-Tudor in the doors and windows that hadn't quite come off. There were six bedrooms, McGovern told him, launching automatically into a professional spiel, three of them *en suite*, two other bathrooms, two reception, etc. It wasn't a place he would have cared to live in himself, he added drily, but both the previous occupant and the new owner had been greatly concerned with privacy, and there was certainly plenty of that. The new owner was abroad and wasn't planning to move in for another couple of months. He wanted some minor alternations made, and had left the work in McGovern's capable hands.

'And that's where you come in,' said McGovern as they got out of the car.

'That's very kind of you, Peter.'

'Not at all. It's not a big job. And besides, that's not the only reason I asked you here. Excuse me, I've got to get something out of the boot.'

What he got from the boot was a black leather hold-all. McGovern slung the bag over his shoulder and led the way round the side of the house, through a little kitchen garden. They came out on to an extensive patio and took a stone path that bisected a featureless oblong of lawn. At the back of the lawn was a long, low wooden building with a shallow felt roof. There was a door with a glass panel at one end, but no windows at all. McGovern produced a key, and they went inside. McGovern flicked some switches and two rows of powerful striplights came on.

There was just the one room, unfurnished apart from a couple of hard-backed chairs by the door. The dusty wooden floor was uncarpeted, and the walls and ceiling were covered in off-white polystyrene panels. A couple of yards in from the door was a wooden ledge, five feet high, standing square-on like a shop counter. The counter was divided up into makeshift cubicles by three more polystyrene panels, thinly visible in profile from the door.

'Know what this place is?' McGovern asked.

'Looks like some sort of firing range.'

'Spot on. Look, I'll show you.'

McGovern beckoned Lewis over to the wooden ledge. He positioned himself between two of the partitions and leant forward on both elbows, as if taking aim.

'My eyesight's not good enough for this,' he said. 'Couldn't even see the target from here.'

'Nor can I,' confessed Lewis.

'There isn't one in at the moment. Look.'

Underneath the ledge was a pulley fixed to a handwheel. McGovern turned the wheel and a metal target-holder, attached to what looked like a washing line, jerked its way towards them from the far wall.

'You stick your target in there, you see. Wheel it back, shoot, chalk up your scores. There used to be a cabinet with a collection of air rifles by the door. He was a gun nut, the last owner. Didn't just shoot air rifles either. He had .22s, a lot of handguns, you name it. A collector and an enthusiast. That's why he sold up. Because of the gun law changes he was forced to hand in the lot. Didn't get anything like the sort of compensation he should have got either, I heard all about it, he was pretty furious. He's gone to live on the continent, where they take a more relaxed attitude to these things. New owner wants this place turned into a playroom for his kids. Rip out all these soundproof panels, put in some windows and some lighting that doesn't look quite so industrial. Sound feasible to you?'

'No problem at all.'

'Good. Let's sit down for a minute. I'd like a chat.'

They sat in the two wooden chairs by the door. McGovern seemed tense, and Lewis, not exactly comfortable to begin with, felt his insides twisting in sympathy.

'I've got a few problems,' McGovern began, quietly, fixing Lewis with an earnest, anxious look. 'I seem to be going downhill very rapidly. Ever since I was diagnosed I've felt myself getting worse by the hour. I keep telling myself it's psychosomatic, but then I get that pain, Lewis, and I know I'm not imagining that. They're giving me morphine and they want me to do rad. therapy, but it doesn't help much. I know it's going to get worse, that's the horrible thing. And I can't take it. I'm not going to take it. I'm not. Sorry.'

McGovern's voice caught in his throat. He leant forward, his elbows on his knees, his head in his hands. He took a moment to recover himself, and continued.

'I've been trying to come to terms with my own reactions to all this. It's not easy, it's been a struggle to understand my own mind, to accept my own frailty. Most people, you see, fight to the last breath. You're told you've not got much time and your head drops, naturally. But then you recover and find the Dunkirk spirit within yourself. The doctors told me this. It becomes a conspiracy between doctor and patient. They tell you you've only got three months and then they work to eke out that little bit more. So then you survive for four months, five, six, and you've become a triumph for medical science. And the patient in all this is a willing accomplice, saying he'll fight on to the last drop and not let that bastard disease lick him. All that's left of him at the end is a useless husk but each breath makes him feel he's a part of the miracle. And each wave of pain has to be challenged and overcome. Why? For God's sake, why? I spoke to my specialist about suicide. In the abstract, of course. He told me that in thirty years of dealing with terminally ill patients he'd only ever known one who topped himself. Well, you've got to respect the will to live. It's a testimony to Darwin, I suppose. But the will to suffer is something I don't get. A tribute to masochism, I think. I can't begin to describe this pain in my spine, Lewis. I hope you never have to experience it yourself. It's like being eaten alive.'

His head sank into his hands for a moment. When he looked up he flashed Lewis a brave, wan smile. Lewis reached across and gave his hand a gentle squeeze.

'Thanks, Lewis. You've been very good to me. Better than I deserve. Maybe there's a way I can repay you, though. Listen: I've not led the best of lives, I have to admit it. Not that it's been disgraceful, it's just that . . . well, you know the score, we're all of us more sinners than saints. But at least I want to do the right thing now I know I'm on the way out. The right thing in my own way, that is. There aren't a lot of people who'd understand the way I'm thinking. That one in ten I told you about perhaps, though I suspect it'd be more like one in a thousand. I don't think I'm flattering you by including you in that number. Your strength of mind is evident. You've got what it takes to swim against the current, to play the game on your own terms. I didn't plan to go out this early. Of course not. I've got at least another twenty years in me, up here, I mean, in my head. Twenty years, maybe more, of wheeling and dealing and playing and winning the game. That's a lot of ingenuity going to waste, and something in me rebels against that, and not just the physical fact of death. Maybe it's sheer bloody-minded vanity, but I've got one last deal I want to pull off. It won't give me any satisfaction after the event, of course, because I'll be dead. But it'll enable me to face what I've got to face with something like equanimity.

'I told you that things haven't been great between my wife and me for a long time, but I want to leave her well-set-up. It's only fair, she's going to have a difficult enough time ahead of her. I've also got a couple of nephews up in Scotland, my brother's kids, I'm very fond of them, and they'll be carrying on my name. I've always said I'd leave them something, and it's a duty I take seriously. I never had any kids of my own, you see. Thought I never wanted them, but now this has come up I've been regretting it. I'd love to be able to pass on my business, my achievements, to another generation. I'd like to be remembered with affection. Don't leave it too late yourself, Lewis, a friendly word of advice. My nephews are only teenagers, too young to take over the business in any case. The problem's this, though. I'm not as well-off as I should be. The business would have been worth a packet in a couple of years, but meantime we're loaned up to the eyeballs. Big mortgage on the house too. There's a bit of liquid, but not enough. The money's in all the insurance policies. I didn't stint, Julie'll get the whole mortgage paid off, plus half a million cash. I've drawn up the will. She shares the money with the boys. Only one drawback though. If I take my own life the policies are invalid.'

McGovern paused. It was a suitably dramatic moment and he seemed to want it acknowledged. Lewis bit his lip and nodded.

'I see,' he murmured.

'It's a classic dilemma,' McGovern continued, seemingly satisfied at Lewis's contribution. 'I've got the guts to die, I know that. I had it all worked out. You should see the drugs I've got stockpiled at home, it's like a branch of Boots. Such an easy way to go, a pity. I've decided it's got to be a bullet now. Just as simple, but not nearly so clean.'

McGovern unzipped the black leather holdall he had brought in from the car. He pulled out a smaller case, about a foot long, also finished in black leather. He undid a catch and showed Lewis what was inside.

It was an automatic pistol. It rested in a red velvet interior, in a specially moulded niche, with other niches besides that held a magazine, a brush and flasks of oil and cleaning fluid. Lewis was reminded of the geometry set he had used at school. McGovern prised out the pistol.

'It's a Beretta, you know, a real James Bond type of gun. Quite a classic, apparently. You ever fired one of these?'

Lewis shook his head.

'Me neither. I tried, though, last night. A moment of weakness. I drank about half a bottle of good malt, got myself well mellowed. Then I picked up this gun and I put it to my head, and I squeezed the trigger. A gentle squeeze, just to see, to test myself. I was scared, oh yeah, even with all that good whisky firing me up, but I think I proved to myself that I could have gone all the way. I kept it there against my head till I couldn't take the weight of it any more. It's heavier than you'd think. You want to feel? It's all right, it's not loaded.'

McGovern passed over the gun. Lewis weighed it in his palm.

'You're looking a bit queasy, Lewis. If you'd prefer we can just stop here, forget this conversation ever took place. You don't have to get involved.'

'But . . . I don't even know what you want me to do.'

'Don't you?'

McGovern sounded faintly surprised. Lewis shrugged, and gave him a puzzled smile. McGovern didn't smile back. He was staring at him intently. His voice, when he next spoke, had a quality that made Lewis think of a hymn he had sung at school. It was a still small voice of calm.

'I want you to kill me.'

9

'I want you to kill me.

'I know there's something chilling about a bullet through the back of the head. It's like the secret police, or a gangland execution. But it's the quickest, surest way. Just put the tip of the barrel to the base of the skull, gently squeeze the trigger and that's that. I'll never know it's happened. And I know I won't feel a thing because I'm going to knock myself out first with pills. That's why I need you. You see, I was thinking at first that I might just shoot myself, but ransack the place a bit first, to try and make it look like a murder and not a suicide. But that's just stupid, there's no way to do it. What can you do with the gun? So I thought, I know, I'll get someone to take the gun away afterwards and dispose of it. But then I thought, they'll do forensic tests, and they'll work out the angles, and the velocity, and all that, and they'll prove that it must have been suicide. That's because I'd have to shoot myself in the side of the head, or through the mouth, and that would be suspicious. Then what if I didn't do it right, or lost my nerve? No, it has to be someone else's finger on the trigger. Someone I can trust. Someone above suspicion, with no motive to kill me, and someone with balls. Narrows it down, doesn't it? To a field of one.

'You don't have to say anything, Lewis. I can see you're shocked; I'd expect that. Just listen to what I have to say, then go away and think about it. Take your time and wait till the shock has worn off before giving me your answer. I've taken my time, plenty of it, to think it through these last few days. I'll give you chapter and verse.

'So the next thing I thought was that I'd hire a hitman. I

know that sounds ridiculous, this is the heart of the Home Counties, not the Bronx, for Christ's sake. But these people exist, you read about them in the papers. There was a case last week, a woman hiring a couple of guys to bump off her husband. Wealthy, respectable people, makes you wonder what the world's coming to. The problem is, you read about these cases because they've come to court. People just can't stop blagging, and nor can they stop flashing their wallets when they've got a big fresh wad of notes. These cases you read about, everyone involved seems a bit thick. You meet some guy down the pub, say here's a few grand, now do the business and keep your trap shut afterwards. As if! I know there must be real pros out there, but where would I find one? I'm an ordinary guy, it's not exactly my world. That's why people turn to the loudmouth in the pub, the one who sits at the bar telling everyone how tough he was in the army or the marines, how many people he killed in the Falklands, or the Falls Road. You don't want any of that macho crap. Someone has to keep telling you what a tough guy he is all the time, you know he's soft as shit.

'That's something I respect about you, Lewis. You are a tough guy. You don't labour the point, though. You don't have to. The first time I clapped eyes on you, I thought – now there's a guy who could handle trouble if it came his way. You've got the trick of inspiring confidence. That's why I took to you so quickly.

'It's pushing friendship a bit though, I'll admit. When you said you'd do me favours, I don't suppose you had this in mind. I didn't myself at the time, but the idea just suddenly got into my head a couple of days ago and it won't go away. I wouldn't ask you to do a thing like this for friendship's sake, though. I've got cash. Forty thousand pounds, it's yours. I'm not kidding. Here's ten, look, in the bag. It's all used notes, twenties. You can take it now, as an advance. Go on, feel it, it feels good. I've never seen this much cash myself, it's all plastic with me. Something satisfying about the feel of real money, isn't there? Take it, it might help you think things through clearly. It's like with the gun. Seeing it here, holding it, makes you realize it's for real. I'm going to fire it in a minute, see what it's like, and you have a go too. Illegal, of course, but what the hell? In for a penny, I say. No one'll even know we're here, that's the beauty of this place. I've got another one in the bag, by the way, a Webley, standard old service revolver, you can take your pick. The guns are quite untraceable, they've no criminal history. I've chiselled off the serial numbers. If you decide you can't go through with it, you can give me back the money. I'll understand.

'But I'm going to go on the assumption that you will say yes, all right? Now this is what happens, it's really very simple. I want this done soon, I'm not for hanging around. Survival's such a strong instinct, it's hard to explain to a healthy person why you'd want to die, but I've made my mind up, and this is the way I want to do it. Julie's going away next weekend. It's her dad's sixty-fifth birthday on the Saturday, she's taking the train up to Scotland Friday, won't be back till Monday afternoon. That's important, because our home help comes in on Monday morning, so Julie won't have to be the one who discovers the body. I'd like it done on the Friday night, that'll give you the whole weekend to cover your tracks. This is what you do.

'There's a lane down the side of the house, very quiet, gets about two cars a month. You can park there, no one'll see you. It's easy to get over the fence at the back of the garden, which is invisible from the main road. You know the kitchen of course, you rebuilt it. There's a little flower bed under the kitchen window at the back, with some big stones round the border. Use one of the stones to smash in the glass in the kitchen door, then lift the latch. The alarm'll be off, it's a piece of cake.

'I'll leave the lights on in the hall and the landing, so you'll be able to find your way upstairs. I'll be in the bedroom, which is at the end of the landing. The door will be open, and I'll leave the bedside lamp on. I'll make sure the curtains are shut. As I say, I'm going to knock myself out. I'll take some whisky and sleeping pills about nine o'clock. If you aim to get to me around midnight, that'll give plenty of time. I'll be on the bed, fully dressed. I suggest you put a pillow over my head before you shoot. That'll probably make it easier for you, and it'll also muffle the noise, but through the curtains and the double glazing I doubt if anything'll be heard outside anyway. I think you should shoot twice, to be on the safe side.

'The motive will appear to be robbery. I'll leave Julie's jewellery box out. There's nothing valuable, but I'll put the stuff ready in a carrier bag, so just take it away and dump it somewhere. It doesn't matter if it's found, it'll look like you dropped it in a panic. There's a safe in the bedroom. It's at the back of the clothes cupboard, pretty well hidden. I'll leave the cupboard open, and the panel at the back that disguises the safe. But the safe itself will be closed. That's where the valuable jewellery is, a ruby brooch, some gold, pearls. It'll look like you demanded the combination at gunpoint, I refused to give it, so you shot me. It might be good if you tied my hands behind my back. Use the dressing gown cord on the back of the door. I'll leave the rest of the money, thirty thousand, in a black bin bag by the bed. Now all you have to do is retrace your footsteps and you've got the weekend to dispose of the gun. You'll be wearing gloves of course, and we'll go through the whole plan in fine detail to make sure there's not the slightest chance of leaving any incriminating evidence behind. There isn't, by the way. I've been through all the angles, believe me, and you'll be in the clear. It'll look like a robbery that went wrong. Maybe they'll conclude that you found the safe, you tried to revive me, but I wouldn't come round because of the sleeping pills and you shot me out of frustration. If there are any loose ends like that they won't affect you. The police'll be looking for a professional burglar with a track record of violence. Should scare the neighbourhood shitless, a pity I won't be around to see it, could be amusing. Property prices in the locality might drop for a while, but I shan't be in a position to worry about that any more, will I?

'And that's about it, Lewis. They'll find the cancer when they do the autopsy, but that won't matter. It'll just look like the grim reaper got me a few months early. The insurance company'll have to pay up, and at the same time it'll put Julie in the clear. I mean, it's stupid to imagine Julie as a murder suspect if you know her, but that's the way the police think in domestic situations. But they'll have to eliminate her from their enquiries because it wouldn't make any sense for her to have me done away with if I was on the way out anyway. You see what I mean? I'm going to tell her about the cancer, by the way, just before she goes. The only thing you'd have to worry about is not giving yourself away, but I think you could handle it. You have to be discreet, above all not be seen splashing money about. You'll have to keep it under your mattress, unless you've got a dodgy offshore account somewhere. It's a fair amount of money, could be useful to you. The way I look at it, everyone benefits. I go out like a light, no fuss, and my family gets security. You get well paid and you can rest secure in the knowledge that you've done me the biggest favour possible. You have to satisfy your own conscience, of course, but as far as I can see there's no way this can be looked at as anything except voluntary euthanasia. That's no crime in my book. We're just aiming to be a little bit economical with the truth in order to get one over on a certain big bastard multinational insurance company. I don't know about you, but as far as I'm concerned that's not a crime either.

'Still, I'm not going to pressure you. As I said at the beginning, if you can't handle this, or if you don't want to know for any reason, just say the word and we'll forget this conversation ever happened. I'm just going to fire these guns now, even if only out of curiosity. If you want to join in I won't take that as a yes. Try the Webley. Here, it's heavy, isn't it? There's some ear pads in here, we'll need them. Why don't you think about it over the weekend, tell me Monday. There's plenty of time. Yes.

'All the time in the world . . .'

10

Time passed in a kind of haze, the minutes and hours rolling into days and nights, inexorably fulfilling the week. Later, thinking about it, Lewis could not pinpoint the exact moment at which he had made his decision, but he supposed he must always have known what it was going to be. On Monday morning he rang McGovern at the office.

'The proposal we discussed at the weekend,' he said in a businesslike voice. 'That would be acceptable.'

McGovern replied that he was pleased. He told Lewis what an excellent job he'd made of the office, and that there would be a cheque in the post. Lewis told him that he would return the office keys by the same method. McGovern asked Lewis to confirm that the financial situation was satisfactory. Lewis told him that it was quite satisfactory. McGovern said that they would speak again later in the week.

Lewis felt giddy with relief when he had put down the phone. In theory he could still back out, but while the prospect of what he was going to do appalled him, it also compelled him. He felt the compulsion like a physical grip. It was the first thing of which he was aware when he woke up, and it stayed with him through every minute of the day until it was time to lay his head once more on the pillow. And then, in his dreams, it got to work again. It was no longer possible to sleep through a whole night, he would wake up breathless and sweating in the dark, but his mind was so hyperactive that he didn't feel tired. It took him a little while to understand these feelings for what they were, but when he did he saw no sense in shying away from them. He was, quite simply, excited.

Competitiveness was an instinct. At school he had excelled in it, being good at games and powerful enough to scare his peers. He may not have shone academically, but the swots had all been terrified of him. He had never enjoyed that degree of respect since. He had revelled in that environment; he had been a lion. He kept thinking of McGovern's idiotic image, he couldn't get it out of his head: a flock of fat and woolly sheep baa-baaing their way in terror through the jungle, a lion crashing through the undergrowth after them. Other things McGovern had said had made an equally vivid impression. Lewis thought all the time about money.

He'd always told people that money wasn't a big issue with him. He needed enough to get by on, but he'd never wanted to be rich. Had he believed his own propaganda? Despising the rich had been an essential prop of his own self-esteem. Oh yes, he'd thought often enough, while he looked some client in the eye, and smiled his cold friendly smile, oh yes you've got it all, house job Porsche pool holiday villa, delete where not applicable, but you don't own me, and I can have your wife any time and any way I want, so still fancy yourself, do you? But the truth was more complicated. It was easy to say that he didn't want money, because he had never had the opportunity to acquire it. He worked hard, sometimes, but he'd never had the drive that motivated men had, that distillation of pure will applied with single-minded determination. But he should have had it, there were no excuses. He had consistently sold himself short. McGovern was right, and right again.

Forty thousand pounds, that was something to think about. The most Lewis had ever made in a year was thirty, much less after tax, even with all his fiddles. Not bad for a self-employed small builder with overheads and outgoings coming out of his ears, but not what it took to live comfortably in the Surrey/Sussex stockbroker belt. He was way out of his depth in this locality, even if the smart place he'd been able to build using his own sweat and skills meant that at least he didn't look out of place. With forty grand under his belt he wouldn't *be* out of place. Still, it was a pity that there wasn't more.

At least he had a downpayment, something to complement

the imagination. The ten thousand McGovern had given him was in twenties. He stacked them in piles of different sizes, and then, because there weren't quite enough to look substantial, he arranged them in fans, like cards spread from a deck, out on the pool table. Fifty notes made a thousand, five hundred notes in all. He fixed the look of them in his mind's eye and inwardly multiplied by four, but he couldn't grasp the image in his head. Two thousand notes, or forty thousand pounds, what did it matter how it looked? It was his, if he dared to take it.

He dared, he knew, but on the Monday he went out and spent some of the money, as if burning his boats. Work was slack, so he left Bill and Charlie to their own devices and took the train up to London for the day. He criss-crossed Regent and Oxford Street and bought a Paul Smith suit off the peg, a pair of Gucci loafers and some silk shirts. He peeled off the £20 notes as if he didn't have a care in the world, and left fat tips with cabbies and the Italian waiter who served him lunch. At the end of the day his wallet was the best part of a thousand pounds lighter. Spraying money around, he discovered, was akin to a pleasure of the flesh. He could get used to living like this.

He took the remaining money, wrapped it in the bin liner in which it had come and stashed it carefully under a floorboard in the bathroom. He had washed the spree mentality from his system, now he would think about more constructive ways of spending the rest. He decided that he might allow himself a short holiday, Greece or Spain perhaps, somewhere he could lie on a beach showing off his oiled torso to advantage and have the pick of the women. But after that the money would be used for acquiring more money. With a proper stake he could buy into something decent, move away from the donkey work into property development. It would require boldness, but that was exactly the quality he was in the process of proving that he had. He had been handed a life-changing opportunity on a plate. All he had to do was kill the man who had given it to him.

Kill a sick man, a miserable unhappy man in pain with nothing to live for. It didn't take much justifying. It was a weird situation, of course, but as McGovern himself had told him, he had to seize his opportunities, exploit accidents. McGovern was going to die anyway, and it wasn't going to be nice. In the same circumstances, Lewis decided, he too would kill himself. Thank God, he thought, for his own healthy lifestyle. The only thing that had ever frightened him was illness. Why did so many people with crippling terminal diseases fight on to the bitter end? McGovern had talked about the survival instinct, but perhaps that was a cover for cowardice. People were afraid of dying and would do anything to cling to life, no matter how awful it was. It was pathetic really. McGovern had the guts to say no to all that.

McGovern was an extraordinary man. Thinking about him, as Lewis did constantly, whether sitting in the Aquarium, or on the train to London, or walking in the woods around the barn, it was impossible not to admire him. He had made himself what he was in life, and he had constructed his own death with the same iron sense of purpose. The only guilt Lewis felt was when he recalled how seriously he had misjudged him. For over a year he had despised the man without even meeting him. And when they did meet, he had despised him even more. McGovern was physically unprepossessing, and weedy, and weak enough to let another man have his wife. But there was much more to him, as Lewis had discovered. He was sharp and clever, and had the knack of putting his finger spot on the button. He had made Lewis realize things about himself, about what he was and how he lived, that would never have occurred to him. All they'd had was a few boozy conversations, but McGovern had taken him straight into his confidence from the off, and his talk was all meat, no fat. He'd been a better friend than any Lewis had had since his schooldays. Lewis didn't despise him any more. Julie McGovern was another matter.

If he'd been really smart, he reckoned, he could have had it both ways. He could have kept in with Julie, then pounced to pick up the pieces after McGovern's death. Of course she was going to be shocked by his apparent murder, who wouldn't be? Even though she hated her husband she'd need someone to turn to, and who better than Lewis? She'd be coming in to a lot of money, much, much more than forty thousand, and she'd be open to advice on what to do with it. He could have helped himself, and she wouldn't have wanted much in return, except marriage.

The thought revolted him. Being tied to any woman would be bad enough, but Julie would have been unendurable. She'd only ever been good for one thing, and he was bored with that. How had someone of McGovern's intelligence put up with her for so long? It was ironic that he was colluding in his own violent death to leave the woman who'd betrayed him in clover. In other circumstances Lewis might have been the one to tell him that she wasn't worth it. In the event he almost told him anyway. Tuesday around midnight.

Lewis was in the Aquarium when he saw the lights of McGovern's car turning in to the barn. He went downstairs to let him in. McGovern was carrying his black leather holdall.

'Sorry to come round unannounced again,' McGovern said, as Lewis led him up the stairs, 'but I didn't like to phone, there shouldn't be any trace of contact between us. I'm sorry, please excuse me a second.'

Lewis heard the pain in his voice. McGovern had stopped halfway up the stairs and was leaning over the rail, breathing heavily. The noise was like the rasp of a woodfile.

'I'm sorry, Lewis, could you give me a hand?'

Lewis helped him up. He sat McGovern down where he had sat before, in front of the desk, and poured him a Scotch.

'Thanks, lad. I'm sorry to act like this, I'm not playing for the sympathy vote. The pain hasn't been so bad today, actually, but I don't much care for stairs any more. You keeping all right?'

'I'm fine, thanks.'

'Good. I just wanted to check that it was all on, and to look you in the face and say thank you. It's a brave thing you're doing, Lewis.'

'A brave thing *I'm* doing? The wrong way round, I think.'

'No, my part's easy. I don't want to live any more, it's as simple as that. I've tidied up the loose ends of my life, such as it is. Didn't take long, there's not that much to it really. I'm not frightened of death, never have been. It doesn't seem to me a logical thing to fear. You close your eyes and don't wake up, why be frightened of that? Pain's another matter, that's what's scary. I don't believe in an afterlife, but who knows, perhaps I'll wake up after all, pleasantly surprised. Nothing I can do about it either way though, is there? Either there is another life or there isn't, whatever you believe.'

McGovern chuckled and drank his Scotch. He declined a refill.

'Unlike me, I know, but funny as it sounds I'm feeling quite relaxed already. It's like a burden's been lifted from me. It hit me the other day, when I was looking through my diary, that I'm actually in a position of rare privilege. No man knows when the hour may strike. Well, I do. Date, time and place, I've got it all sorted. I was tempted to write it in, for my Friday diary. You know – "Die today". I didn't, of course, but it made me laugh. I feel strong, in control of my own destiny. And it'll be a relief. I wanted to be sure you hadn't changed your mind.'

'No.'

'Good. I'd understand if you did. You're quite happy with the arrangements, are you? I won't be coming round to see you again, no more nocturnal visits, I promise, so if you've got any questions, now would be the time. I think we've covered all the angles. You'll wear gloves, of course. I was thinking maybe it would be a good idea if you put something on your feet, wrapped a cloth, say, round your shoes, so as not to leave a footprint. What do you think?'

'Good idea.'

'Yup. We don't want to leave any clues of any kind. Have you got a balaclava? There'll be nobody around to see your face, but you don't want to drop any stray hairs. I'd burn your clothes afterwards, in case you leave any fibres.'

'I was going to.'

'Of course. I knew you'd think it through carefully. You've got to. It's as important to me as it is to you that you're completely in the clear, or the whole point of it's lost, but you know that. I've brought you this.'

He reached into the holdall and pulled out the black case which had reminded Lewis of his geometry set.

'You can have the Webley if you prefer, but you said you liked the feel of the Beretta best.'

'Yes.'

'You did well with it, I was impressed. You sure you'd never handled a gun before?'

'Only at the fairground. I didn't do so well with the Webley. Only hit the target with three out of six shots. You did better than that. I should be asking if you're the one who's sure he's never handled a gun before?'

'Beginner's luck. The Beretta was quieter, it's the right choice. It's ready and loaded, and there's a spare magazine. I gave it a good clean, but give it another wipe, for safety's sake. Have you got an alibi for Friday, just in case?'

'Do you think I need one?'

'I'm just being ultra-cautious. Why should you come under suspicion? There's nothing to suggest that our paths have crossed in anything except a professional capacity, is there? They might just as well suspect the milkman. They'll probably question the poor bugger anyway, for form's sake. Him and everyone I've ever known. Poor Julie. I don't know how she's going to cope with all this.'

It was then that Lewis felt tempted to say something. He began half-consciously to frame her name on his lips as an image of her materialized in his mind. He stared across at McGovern's drawn pale face and felt a surge of human sympathy. He wanted to say this: Look, I've a confession to make. Don't die worrying about Julie, regretting what has or hasn't happened between you. I've been having an affair with her ever since I did your kitchen, and I know her. I'm sorry to break it like this. She despises you, Peter, she won't miss you for a second when you're gone. She's faithless and shallow and stupid, and if you weren't about to die I'd tell you to divorce her. You'll probably hate me for telling you this, but I can't let you die worrying about someone quite worthless . . .

That was what he thought, and even as he thought it he knew he was never going to say it. Better to let the man die in ignorance. And anyway, if McGovern did suddenly see the light about his wife he might decide to hell with her, and just take an overdose as originally planned. Lewis didn't want that. He wanted the money. He wanted it very badly.

'There's just one thing,' he said suddenly.

McGovern had been about to speak, and the sharpness of Lewis's tone surprised him. It surprised Lewis as well. He hadn't meant to sound sharp. The thought had popped out spontaneously. McGovern looked at him with curiosity.

'It's like this,' Lewis went on. 'It's a lot of money you've offered me. Don't think I don't know that. Forty grand is not to be sneezed at, but, well, how shall I put this?'

'It's not enough?' said McGovern quickly. Lewis shrugged.

'What's enough? I could do it for nothing if you like, for friendship's sake. This isn't the kind of contract you can put a price on. But doing this is going to be a life-changing experience for me. I was thinking maybe I might move away, start up again from scratch. It could prove expensive. I don't want to be greedy, but –'

'It's not greedy. Only thing is, it's not easy getting cash together. I've got various accounts, a couple of building societies, banks. I've stripped them bare in the last few days, sold my shares, even raided the petty cash at work. There's a little bit over the forty already, as it happens. I could get a cash advance on my credit cards, knock up my overdraft facility at the bank and draw on that. I think I could get it up to fifty. Would that do?'

'That would do very nicely. I hope you don't think –'

'I don't think anything. Frankly, Lewis, you might just as well have it as anyone else. There'll be another forty in the bin liner on Friday, I promise. Julie'll have the insurance, and that's much, much more than you're getting. Now it's getting late and I don't want to keep you up any more. I just wanted to check everything was OK, and it seems to be. Thanks for the drink, again. I shan't bother to say don't trouble to see me out, because I know you will.'

'I will.'

'Let's go down then.'

Lewis walked McGovern out to his car. It was a cold but

clear night, the sky cloudless and starry. McGovern stopped with his key in the car door and glanced upwards.

'Quite beautiful, isn't it? Almost enough to make me want to go on. Almost. You do know I'm serious, don't you? You do trust me?'

'Trust you?'

'Yeah. I mean, you might think I'll bottle it at the last minute. That when the time comes I'll think I can't go through with it. Has that thought crossed your mind?'

'I know you're not a coward.'

'Good. It's important you know that, for your peace of mind. I won't call or see you again, Lewis. Make sure you do it right, OK?'

McGovern extended his hand. Lewis shook it firmly.

'I'll do it right, Pete.'

'Yeah. I know.'

McGovern got in his car, reversed and turned and headed for the road. Lewis went to open the gate for him. He watched him driving away until the red taillights had disappeared from view and the night had swallowed the sound of the engine.

He went back inside and sat in the Aquarium until after midnight, thinking about how he was going to spend the money.

11

It was coming up to eleven p.m. when Lewis drove past the front of the McGovern house on the Friday night. A landing light on the first floor was dimly visible, otherwise the house was dark. There didn't seem to be any lights on at the nearest neighbour's, the people a hundred yards down the road with whom, according to Julie, they had had only the most minimal contact in the course of ten years. The silence of the night was troubling. They had worn earplugs firing the guns in the shooting gallery, but the noise had still been tremendous. Even with the double glazing, the curtains and using a pillow for a silencer there would be some noise. Fortunately it was not the kind of area where there was much likelihood of encountering a dog-walker at an inconvenient hour.

Lewis turned into the little lane where he had always parked. He drove past the grassy verge where he usually left his car and continued round the first corner. It had been dry for days and the ground was firm, but he didn't want to risk leaving any fresh tyre marks. The lane was so tiny that it didn't even feature on his local road map, and in all the time he had been using it he had never met anything coming the other way. After another hundred yards he pulled off the road by a gate that led into a field. He had checked the spot out yesterday. The ground in front of the gate had been churned up by generations of tractor wheels, so the imprint of his own tyres wouldn't be noticeable.

He had taken a lot of care over things like that; he had been quite methodical. He knew that physically everything was taken care of, that he had covered all the angles. The gun, for instance, would be going into a lake on the road to Midhurst, heavily weighed down in a sack, while its case was earmarked for a dump at Petersfield, the velvet insides suitably ripped out to disguise the origin. But doubts nagged at him, as they were bound to. No one knew about his affair with Julie, but was there a danger of her blurting something out through shock? He didn't think so, but of course there was no way of knowing for sure. What if the police did sniff something out? OK, so he'd been sleeping with the man's wife, but why should that make him a murder suspect? He'd slept with lots of men's wives, that was no reason to kill them. He was just an ordinary builder, not a killer. This murder was going to look like a professional robbery gone wrong, as McGovern had said, nothing more, nothing less. They were bound to suspect Julie of hiring a hitman, of course. As McGovern had said, that was only to be expected in a domestic murder. But even the briefest of interrogations should be enough to convince the police of Julie's innocence. Her stupidity was a foolproof defence, just as his cleverness was his.

Sitting in the car, counting the minutes nervously, it was inevitable that these thoughts should go round and round in his head. The slow ticking seconds gnawed and nibbled at his doubts. He knew that he had the nerve to go through with it, but the waiting was emasculating. He tried to ration his glances at the watch, but was disappointed each time that the hands had advanced so little. He thought of Laura, to distract himself. He'd had to put back the Carter job, because of developments, but he'd be starting on Monday. He was willing to bet anything that she was a firecracker in bed, every bit as willing as Julie but not as passive. He liked his women submissive, but Laura positively wanted taming. That plump fool of a husband of hers, that pathetic bank manager, was a mouse to Laura's wildcat. No wonder she had wanted Lewis, and what a fool he had been to keep his distance for so long. He knew she wanted him and he wasn't going to hang around. He was going to have her first thing Monday, let out all the tension he was feeling tonight, slake his lust, and hers. He thought about what he was going to do, and enjoyed in slow delicious detail his private graphic images, frame by frame. When he next looked at his watch he was surprised to see that it was a quarter to midnight.

He got out of the car and checked himself. He was wearing an old pair of workboots, black jeans and a black vest. On top he wore a dark-green anorak with deep pockets. The gun was in the right pocket. Two pieces of sacking, string, a small chisel and a torch filled the left pocket. Black woollen gloves and a balaclava completed the outfit.

He set off up the lane in the direction of the house. Although there was some moonlight it was very dark under the trees and he had to use his torch. He kept it pointed at the ground and well-shielded with his other hand. When he reached his usual parking place, next to the fence, he took the pieces of sacking from his pocket and pulled them over his boots, securing them round his ankles with the string. When he was ready he took his bearings and climbed over the fence.

He didn't need the torch any more. He could see the black bulk of the house against the night sky, and in any case he knew the way. In the car he had wondered how many times he had made this journey, how many illicit liaisons it had presaged. At least seventy, he reckoned, maybe even more over the course of fifteen months. He'd had a lot of pleasure in that house, but he'd stuck around far too long. Julie had been good, of course, but Laura was going to be better. He thought about her body again, and felt his pulse quicken. All of his senses were at a pitch, but he could feel himself becoming aroused. It was the excitement, the danger. He had often wondered what he would have been like in wartime, whether he would have had the nerve for action. He had it all right, in spades, and the sense of his power thrilled him.

He stopped outside the kitchen door, took deep breaths for a minute and consciously willed himself calm. It was important to keep a clear head, to go methodically, by the book. He knelt down, felt for the flower bed and found a half-brick. With his other hand he felt for the glass in the kitchen door. When he had located the pane nearest the handle he smashed it in. There was little noise. He put the brick down, took out his chisel and knocked out the remaining shards of glass. Carefully he slipped his hand through the empty frame and located the handle. He turned the key and let himself in.

He felt his way round the kitchen table to the hall door and went through. The entrance and front door were on his left, the living room door on his right and the dining room ahead. Between them was the staircase. He could see well enough now by dint of a dim light shining up on the landing.

He climbed the stairs. None creaked. At the top he saw that the bathroom and spare bedroom doors were all closed. Only the master bedroom door was half open. He saw a reddish glow coming from inside; the bedside lamp, as promised.

He took out the Beretta. It was already loaded. He slipped off the safety catch. He went into the bedroom.

The shape of McGovern's body was visible on the bed. The sheet had been pulled up to the headboard, completely covering him. There was a half-empty bottle of Scotch on the bedside table and a box of sleeping pills. The jewellery, as promised, was also on the table in a plain blue carrier bag. Lewis checked behind the open cupboard door and saw the safe. He also checked the windows. They were all shut and the curtains drawn tight. He went to close the bedroom door.

The plastic refuse sack with the money was at the foot of the bed. He lifted it and was surprised at how heavy it felt. He gave it a shake and heard the satisfying rustle of paper inside. He resisted the urge to tip it out and count it. He had a job to do.

He walked round to the top of the bed. He could see the shape of McGovern's head under the sheet. He reached across him for a pillow, and eased it out from under the sheet. He put the pillow down on top of the head and pressed the tip into the middle. The end of the pillowcase was covered in blood.

He stared blankly at the blood, not understanding at first what it was. There was a lot of it, and it was fresh. He still didn't understand. He dropped the pillow and pulled back the top of the sheet.

Julie McGovern's empty eyes stared up at him. There was

a bullet hole in the middle of her forehead. Her blood and brains were all over the pillow.

A rushing, wailing sound was in his head. It was as if his ears were blocked, and the noise, like a tremendous waterfall, was trapped and magnified within his skull. He had lost all sense of feeling in his body, his brain was numbed and useless. He could only stare, without being able to move, or think, or react, at the bloody mess of the woman on the bed.

She was on her back, fully dressed but with her blouse torn, exposing a triangle of flesh that was covered in scratches and bruises. Her neck and throat were thick with red splotches. Her face, badly battered on one side and spattered with blood all over, looked like raw meat. The wide-open, sightless eyes, beneath the gaping red and open third eye drilled through her forehead, had the glassy sheen of a stuffed animal's. It didn't look like a human being at all.

He was on his knees by the bed. Though he had no control over his body, it was reacting of its own accord. Violent spasms racked his insides. He vomited over the sheet and carpet.

The waterfall was louder in his head. He was crawling across the floor, a baby who had forgotten how to walk, while a wall of white noise paralysed him. Another sound, more mechanical than the first, was infiltrating the insane mixing machine of his brain. Some distant remembrance from the real world began to penetrate. He recognized the sound of a siren.

They were coming to get him. A shock ran through him, starting his mind and body into action. Somehow he staggered to his feet.

They were coming to get him. The siren wasn't for anybody else, it was for him. The horror of the situation distilled into sudden clarity.

He brushed his own sick from his lips and chin and wiped his face on the sheet. The foul taste remained. He picked up the gun, which he must have dropped on the bed, stuffed it back into his pocket, and took a lunging step towards the door. In the same blink of an eye he saw the black bin liner on the floor, snatched it up and ripped it open. A shower of torn wastepaper fell to the floor.

He howled like a wounded animal.

He tumbled down the stairs, lost his balance altogether on the bottom step and went careering across the polished hall floor. The stupid pieces of sacking tied to his feet had no grip. He tried to pull off the string round his ankles, but his wool-covered fingers couldn't get at the knots. A flash of light made him glance up. In the glass above the front door he saw the reflection of headlamps. He picked himself up again and ran into the darkened kitchen. He could see the headlamps more clearly now, and the blue light on top of the police car that was coming slowly down the drive.

He bruised the same hip again on the kitchen table but kept on running. He crashed through the door and raced across the lawn, quite blind to where he was going. Somewhere over the grass the pieces of sacking fell away. He accelerated and felt the earth of flower beds under his feet. He had no idea where he was, he couldn't see a damned thing. Branches slashed his face, bushes pulled at his legs. His midriff ran into something solid and he fell, winded. There was a sound of splintering wood. He tumbled helplessly head over heels down a grassy bank, and came to rest, painfully, on a hard surface. He had fallen through the garden fence and was in the road. He pulled himself to his feet and staggered on down the lane.

Behind him he heard fresh sirens, the sound of an ambulance mingling with the police car's whoop.

12

Grace had lived above the shop for the best part of two years now. She had been hesitant when George Courtenay had invited her into the business, and the offer of the little flat, not forthcoming at first, had clearly been meant as a carrot. A wrinkled mouldy carrot some weeks after its sell-by date, as Grace was wont to say to George on his infrequent visits to the business he was still nominally meant to run. George would grin and show his broken teeth and tell her she should be so lucky. The bare-walled living room with its single tiny window up at head-height reminded them both of the holding cell where they had first been introduced, Grace sitting on top of a notoriously violent drunk and trying to keep his wrists pinioned behind his back as he heaved like a bucking bronco, while George, a cigarette dangling from the corner of his mouth, leant nonchalantly against the cell door murmuring, 'Good girl, good girl.' When she had remonstrated with him afterwards he had seemed surprised. He was a senior inspector and not used to being shouted at by a junior WPC. He had muttered something about having a dodgy heart and apologized.

The dodgy heart must have been at least half true because he took early retirement before the end of the year and set up his private agency in Guildford. He still kept in touch with his old pals, though, and when he heard that Grace was getting out he rang up immediately and offered her a job. She was surprised. She had put George down for a relatively affable but completely unreformable male chauvinist pig of the old school, an almost fully fledged misogynist. But he seemed very keen to have her, hence the offer of the flat.

'You're good and they're sorry to lose you,' George told her in the course of her formal interview, as they sat wedged between the lunchtime punters in a Guildford pub. 'Bob Challoner thinks you're the best he's got, and Bob knows his onions.'

George was famous for respecting people who knew their onions; his conversation was littered with expressions that marooned him firmly in the era of *Dixon of Dock Green*. The contrast with Bob Challoner couldn't have been starker. Bob was smart and streetwise and gratuitously foul-mouthed, a true modern copper with no time for anything, or anyone, not on the cutting edge. Everyone liked George, but almost no one liked Bob, not even his wife; especially not his wife. Bob used to complain about the fact that people didn't like him even as he was bawling them out for things they hadn't done or casually ruining their careers. And he really was a fully paid-up chauvinist, as good a reason on his own as the many Grace had actually given as her official reason for leaving the force. The real reason, that she had been ridiculously in love with the man, she had naturally kept to herself.

It had been a hopeless, stupid affair from the start, and both of them had known it. The point about Bob, as Grace had grasped immediately but almost everyone else seemed not to notice, was that he liked nothing better than an argument. His only principle in conversation was to disagree with the last person who had spoken, unless the speaker was a senior officer, in which case Bob said nothing. He may have been contrary, but he wasn't stupid. He had a knack of guessing what people least wanted to hear, and telling it to them straight. He was the best interrogator in the division, and the least forgiving colleague, feared more by his own subordinates than the criminal fraternity. Grace had dealt with him by paying him no attention, never rising to his bait and never allowing him to see for a moment that she was in the slightest bit intimidated or upset, although she was, frequently. She never responded to his lewd and sexist comments, but once, when they were in a car together, and his hand casually brushed her knee, she told him quietly but firmly that if he did that again she would report him. He had pulled the car over into a lay-by, turned off the engine and met her questioning look with a quiet but firm look of his own.

'What if I put my tongue down the back of your throat? Would you report me then?'

'No.'

A minute later and they were having wild uncomfortable sex in the back of the car. It was after dark, and they were off duty, but they were in an official vehicle no more than a stone's throw from a busy main road and it was the most stupid thing either of them had ever done. In the months that followed they did innumerable other stupid things, some of them bordering on the insane, such as the time they made love in a cell, he with his hand over her mouth the whole time to muffle her noisy cries, and the murmured conversation of the prisoners in the cell next door for background accompaniment. What they were doing would ruin both their careers when, not if, it came out, and they knew it. Grace was fast approaching a point of terminal disillusionment with her career, but she cared about his. She was the one who had to end it, because she knew that he wouldn't. And the only way to end it properly was to get out altogether and start a new life without a copper in sight.

So the last thing in the world she'd expected to do was go into business as a private detective. Private detection was a Mickey Mouse business for scumbags, that was the unofficial coppers' view and one she had always accepted unquestioningly. But when she thought about it, it seemed as good an option as any. She had no desire to go back into teaching, which was what she had originally trained for, and the vague notion that she might like to study computer programming was unlikely to be advanced in the absence of any suitable local courses. If she was prepared to wait until the new year, she was told, there could be places available, but in the meantime she had to earn a living. She had a goodish degree from Bristol University in French and Russian, but as George had not been the first to point out, that wasn't a lot of use in the practical world. His offer, and the flat that went with it, had assumed an attractiveness out of all proportion to their true merits.

To her surprise she found she rather enjoyed the work. She hadn't expected it to be glamorous, and nor was it, but at its worst it was no duller than routine police work, and at least she was her own boss. George was little more than a figurehead. He had a mysterious 'consultancy' with a retail chain that took up three days a week and more or less paid his salary. The rest of the time he was usually laid up with his heart condition, a debilitating ailment which required regular treatment in an assortment of pubs. Grace left him to it, because under the arrangement they quickly arrived at she more or less kept what she earned. There were numerous expenses to be paid, but the net amount in her bank balance at the end of each month compared reasonably with her police pay. The majority of the work was domestic, snooping on behalf of jealous wives or husbands. Sometimes it seemed to Grace as if the entire population of Surrey thought that its other half was having an affair. And quite often they were right. She had thought, and so had George, that women would feel more comfortable hiring her rather than a man, but in fact men made up the majority of her clients. George's theory, naturally, was that since they thought their wives were having affairs with other men they would try and retaliate by having an affair with Grace, but none of her clients had ever tried it on with her. A lot of her work ended up as evidence in the divorce courts, at which she felt the occasional passing twinge of guilt – how easily might the photographs and tapes of illicit couplings featured her and Bob Challoner? But she was a pro, and she did what she had to do with carefully studied neutrality. There was only one rule, said George, an avid collector of portentous truisms, and that was never to get involved. It was easy for him, she would answer, because he never did any work. Easy for her too, his shrewd twinkling eyes would seem to say, with a hide like a rhinoceros and sensitivity to match. It worried her sometimes that he thought she was so much tougher than she was, but at the level of their everyday badinage, and in the context of their work, she found it rather flattering.

If her professional life was more than satisfactory, her private life was less so. There had been no man worth a damn since her bruising finale with Bob, and, given the hours and the company she kept, the prospect of remedying the deficiency seemed dim. She was coming up to thirty, an uncomfortable age, and one by which, she couldn't help but think, she ought to have had at least one settled and meaningful long-term relationship. Some of her friends were now divorced and on their second marriages, but she had never even come remotely near to a first. She had been in love, but only with unsuitable men, like Bob Challoner. The suitable men, the ones who would have looked good in a morning suit and who might have been introduced to her parents without undue embarrassment, had all been drips. Her love life these days consisted of sporadic brief encounters, mostly one-night stands. She reckoned there was about as much chance of meeting a romantic handsome stranger in Guildford on a Friday night as there was of finding a Yeti.

It was still Friday night, just, when she unlocked the door to her little flat above the shop. The midnight pips sounded within moments of her turning on the radio and it was well and truly Saturday morning by the time she had finished brushing her teeth. She wasn't sorry to be getting into her notionally double bed on her own again, and she did wonder, not for the first time, why she had gone so tamely through the ritual of trying to pull a temporary accompaniment. The youths at the first wine bar Nikki had dragged her to had been spotty and hopeless, the kind who thought that sluicing their insides out with lager all night before inviting you to come for a curry ('we'll split the bill') was the way to impress a girl. The men in the second place had been worse, thirtysomethings with slick haircuts and well-greased chat-up lines who laboured under the misapprehension that they were interesting. In the third and last rendezvous of the night, a pub where the sweat dripping from the walls could have ended an African drought, four middle-aged salesman from Northampton, in Guildford to attend a conference on developing customer interface strategies, insisted on buying them champagne and regaling them with their life stories.

Nikki, predictably, took a shine to one of them, and had last been seen heading off with him in the direction of his hotel room. The collective charms of the others had made little impression on Grace. The least attractive, and most persistent, had followed her out to the Ladies on the pretext of trying to find the cigarette machine. When she emerged he tried to nuzzle her ear and wanted to know if she was wearing tights or stockings. She left him none the wiser, but quite prepared to wager that he was wearing Union Jack boxer shorts with a comical slogan.

With Nikki off her hands and conscience she had made her way home alone, failing as usual to find a cab and having to navigate on foot the depressing familiar streets. She was genuinely content to take a book rather than a man to bed, and she read for over an hour. It was coming up to a quarter past one when she turned out the light. She had not been asleep long when her door buzzer woke her.

She'd never been good at getting up in the mornings, and getting up in the middle of the night was out of the question. At first she just lay there and hoped it would go away, but on the third long, insistent buzz she realized that it wouldn't, and it occurred to her that it might be Nikki, perhaps in some sort of trouble. She clambered out of bed hastily and made her way next door into the office, where the intercom hung on the wall within reach of her desk.

'Hello. Who's that?'

For answer she received another protracted buzz, the horrible noise blasting out of the machine only inches from her ear and making her recoil in disgust.

'Nikki, is that you?'

No answer again; perhaps the damned thing had made one of its regular decisions to go on strike. She went next door to put her dressing gown on over the old rugby shirt she had been wearing in bed and to find her slippers. She went down the three flights of dingy wooden stairs to the ground floor and peeked out through the letterbox.

'Who's that?'

Something moved on the doorstep, but it was impossible to see who or what it was.

'I'm not opening the door unless you tell me who you are.'

The shape on the doorstep moved closer. By the dim streetlight she could just make out the whitish patch of a face as it bent down to her level to speak.

'It's me, Lewis. Please help me. It's an emergency.'

'Lewis? What the –'

She was too surprised to finish the sentence. Still in a daze she straightened up and released the catch. The door was flung back in her face and Lewis barged in, pushing her against the wall and slapping his hand over her mouth.

'Keep quiet and do what I tell you,' he hissed. 'I've got a gun.'

She could feel it, the cold metal tip of a barrel pressing into her temple. She concentrated on keeping still, and not panicking. So this is it, she thought, the line of unsuitable men finally ends with a rapist and murderer . . .

Lewis kicked the door shut with his feet. At that moment the automatic light in the hallway went off. In the darkness Grace was acutely aware of the smothering bulk of the man pinning her to the wall. He was rank with sweat and unpleasant odours, and his breathing was shallow and short. She could smell his fear.

'I'm sorry, I'm not going to harm you,' he said in her ear, his voice cracking. 'I'm in big trouble. Are you alone?'

It must have occurred to him she couldn't answer with his hand clamped over her lips. He snatched away his hand and she gulped in air.

'Am I alone? Christ, Lewis, it was only a one-night stand, don't you think you're overdoing the jealousy a bit?'

The bravado in her tone was all put on, but he wasn't to know that. He pulled the gun away from her head.

'I'm sorry. I'm not thinking straight. Can we go inside and talk?'

She told him to follow her. He wouldn't let her turn the lights on so it took an age to negotiate the three treacherous flights of stairs. She was glad that he couldn't see her shaking legs.

In her living room, once he was sure that the door and the

curtains were closed, he allowed her to switch on the small lamp in the corner. She was shocked by his appearance. His clothes were torn and filthy and there was a big cut and bruise over his eye.

'You've got to get that seen to,' she said, and made a move for the kitchen door. He levelled his gun at her.

'Where are you going?'

'To the bathroom. It's all right, Lewis, I'm on your side.'

She wasn't sure that she was, but her assurance seemed to satisfy him. She went through to the bathroom, but left the door open so as not to alarm him.

Bathroom was a considerable euphemism. It was a narrow corridor, with a fridge and a two-ring gas cooker at one end and a toilet cubicle at the other. Between them was a sink and a filing cabinet for the overflow of papers from next door. Where there had once been a store cupboard, next to the toilet, she had installed a plastic-walled shower compartment. The only way to traverse the room was to shuffle along sideways. She filled a bowl with water and took cotton wool and an iodine bottle from the shelves over the sink. She went back next door.

'You know that old line, this is going to hurt you more than it's going to hurt me? It's true, I'm afraid.'

The iodine made him bite his lip, but he didn't make a sound. When she had finished she went and sat down in the little armchair opposite the sofa, where he was sitting. She tucked her feet up under her legs and did her best to get comfortable.

'Suppose you tell me all about it.'

'I've been framed for a murder.'

It was a dramatic announcement, and he delivered it with a voice that was suitably quivering, accompanied by an expression of haunted desperation. When he had milked the moment for all it was worth, and he was positive he had her every last scrap of attention, he went on.

'I've been having an affair with this woman. We arranged to meet. When I got there tonight she was dead, shot through the head. The police turned up, almost caught me. Her husband set me up.'

Grace felt her insides go cold. The sound of her own voice, when she spoke, was tiny inside her head and far away.

'Who set you up, Lewis?'

'The husband. You know him, the estate agent. McGovern.'

'Yes. I see.'

She leant her head back against the chair and tried to control the mad rush of thoughts inside her head. Lewis, hunched forward with his elbows on his knees and fists clenched together, staring half at the floor and half at her, but without seeming to take her in, carried on.

'You've got to help me, Grace, I don't know what to do. I was going to London, to the station, but I'm not going to get far on my own, I need help. I'm innocent, I swear to you I'm innocent, but they're never going to believe me. All that blood, you should have seen it. I didn't know it was going to be so horrible, I'd never have . . . I'm sorry, I'm not being very . . . You're a detective, you know how to solve things. Will you help me, please?'

His head was in his hands now, his voice trailing away in his cupped palms. She was glad he had put the gun down; he was trembling violently all over.

'I don't know about you but I could do with a coffee,' she said gently. 'You sit there and I'll go and make it.'

The five minutes it took for the kettle to boil at least gave her time to think. She prepared a little speech in her head, and delivered it once she had put the tray down on the coffee table in front of the sofa and passed him the milk and the sugar bowl.

'I'll help you, Lewis, and I'll explain why in a minute. But first you've got to answer some questions, honestly. Where is the gun?'

He had forgotten. He patted his pockets, felt them empty, then found the pistol wedged down between the cushions on the sofa. He thought that she wanted it and tried to pass it over, but she shook her head.

'No, I don't want to touch it. Why have you got it, if you didn't kill her?'

He put the gun down swiftly next to him. She had noticed that he was wearing gloves.

'It's not the murder weapon,' he said. 'This is a Beretta, he did it with the Webley, I know. I've had time to think about it, I know exactly what he did, the bastard.'

'Where's the Webley?'

'I don't know, I don't know.'

'Why are there two guns, Lewis, and why have you got one of them?'

'I found it on the floor. You know, in the bedroom.'

'And you picked it up and brought it here? Where's the Webley?'

'I said I don't know.'

'Then how do you know it was the murder weapon?'

'I just know. Trust me.'

'Oh no, I bloody well won't, Mr Muscleman Builder.'

Her scornful laugh nonplussed him. He looked lost and helpless, this primitive hunk of a man with his chiselled film-star chin and flopping footballer hair. She decided that he had the look of that mythical schoolboy caught smoking behind the bicycle sheds.

'I will help you, Lewis, but only if you tell me the truth, the whole and exact truth, syllable by syllable, comma by comma. And if I find you've come up with even the littlest porky imaginable, I swear I'll have your bloody balls on toast for breakfast. Raw. All right?'

There didn't seem much option, so he told her the whole story, to every last syllable and comma. If he hesitated he had only to look into her unforgiving eyes and he was ready to continue. As the history of the last few weeks unravelled he became acutely conscious of his gullibility, and the picture he tried to paint of McGovern became more and more Machiavellian. He was sure that he knew exactly what had happened.

'I think he was there, in the house. I think he may even have waited until I came in before he killed her, so the body would still be warm. And then he called the police, so they'd catch me there and he'd be in the clear. There's no other explanation, is there? I mean, there's not some serial killer on the loose in Surrey who happened to get there five minutes before me. I'm just the fall guy, plain and simple. They almost got me too. They were coming up the drive as I was getting out the back. Ambulance, police cars, he really went to town when he dialled nine-nine-nine. A minute later and I'd be in a cell tonight. I got back to the car, I can't remember how. I didn't dare turn the headlamps on, I drove the other way, not the way I'd come, hit a ditch, went off the road and couldn't get out again. I ran off on foot, across a field, couldn't see a damned thing. I saw some car lights, hit a road and stuck out my thumb and got lucky. A van stopped, he was headed just the other side of Guildford, he dropped me by the A3. Then I thought of you. I know you've got no reason to help me, but you were here, I've got nowhere to go. I can pay you, I've got cash, McGovern's money, it's at the barn. What do you think I should do?'

'I'm afraid that's the easiest thing for me to say and the hardest for you to do. You should turn yourself in.'

'No –'

'They'll get you, Lewis, sooner rather than later, and you can't stay here, I'm afraid. Oh, don't worry, I'm not going to chuck you out tonight, but this is a working office, I've got a partner and a part-time secretary and, I'll be completely honest, even if I didn't have them to consider, I couldn't let you stay here. If it ever came out that I'd harboured a suspect then that'd be my professional career up the spout. I'm not a copper any more, it's true, but in here, deep down, I'm still on their side. If you give yourself up it'll look like you've got nothing to hide. Let them catch you and you won't have a chance in hell of persuading them you're innocent. I'll give you the name of a good solicitor, then you can –'

'No!'

It wasn't a word he shouted, it was an animal bark. His face was livid with tension, the veins on his neck and forehead bulged and throbbed. He was trembling almost as if he had a fever.

'You don't understand,' he said hoarsely. 'I can't. I couldn't take it in prison. Locked up, trapped. I'd go mad.'

'A lot of people think that, Lewis, but you're resilient, you'd adapt. And if you just walk in with a solicitor, who knows, you might even get bail, you don't even know if there's any real evidence against you. I mean, the police didn't see you there, did they? It's not as if they caught you with a smoking gun. The solicitor I use is called Terry Hoffman. He's very good.'

'You don't understand . . .'

He repeated the phrase wearily, sadly. He slumped back into the sofa and let out a sigh.

'You don't understand. How could you? You don't even know the man. I do. He threw out his bait, got me to bite and reeled me in. And by God did I fall for it. You should hear his spiel, the man's a master. I thought I knew exactly what I was doing before I met that man, I thought I was in control of my own life. Like hell. Julie warned me, I didn't listen. She said he was a clever, manipulating bastard. He twisted me round his finger, made me think he respected me, conned me into thinking I was his friend. He might just as well have had me on a string. That's exactly it, I was his puppet. I don't know what evidence they've got, but I know damned well that if it's McGovern who gave it to them then I'm finished. You just don't understand, because you don't know the man . . .'

Grace let him cry softly by himself for a minute, then she went next door to the bedroom to get him some tissues.

'I'll put the kettle on again,' she said, trying to make it sound consoling.

While she waited for the kettle to boil she went through the filing cabinet next to the sink. She found what she was looking for at the back, a thick orange folder. She balanced the folder on the tray next to the coffee things and carried them through to Lewis.

'I'm not quite sure how to put this, Lewis. You've had a few shocks tonight already, so perhaps one more won't make much difference. Here, you'd better have a look at this.'

She pushed the orange folder across the coffee table. He picked it up and began looking through, at first indifferently, and then with astonishment. He read the labels on the cassette tapes, and flicked with evident disbelief through the first of the thick wallets of photographs. He didn't need to see any more. A pile of the grainy photographs slipped through his fingers and scattered on his lap and over the sofa cushions. Grace smiled sympathetically. The wounded misery in his eyes was all but unbearable.

'I do understand, Lewis. I do know the man, you see. Listen, and let me tell you all about Peter McGovern . . .'

13

'You remember when I first saw you, Lewis? I thought I'd given myself away. I couldn't believe it when you walked into that pub, I just stared at you like an idiot, and you caught me doing it, I can still remember how I blushed. I've never seen a guy come over so chock-full of confidence as you. You really thought I was smitten, didn't you? I'm sorry, I don't want to bruise your ego unnecessarily, not after all you've been through, but the truth wasn't quite like that, as you've probably guessed from looking at these photographs. They're pretty graphic, some of them. Well, that's for two reasons, one because I've got a damned good telephoto lens, and two because you're not very discreet. I'd better give you the whole story, from the top.

'Peter McGovern walked into this office almost exactly a year ago. I checked it just now, it was November the tenth. He told me who he was and where he worked. If you lean out of the front window you can just see his office. He said he'd found our name in Yellow Pages and chosen us because we were so near. He only realized afterwards that he was our letting agent. It seemed like fate, he said. He was a pretty unattractive, twitchy sort of guy, I thought, it didn't come as a hell of a surprise when he told me he thought his wife was having an affair. He hired me to check her out and bring him proof one way or the other. He told me the name of his wife's lover. You. He had your address and phone number on an invoice. Apparently you'd done some work for him, although you'd never met. His suspicions had been aroused, he said, because there had been a marked change in his wife's personality over the previous months. She had become sullen and resentful, and he didn't know why. He said she'd gone off sex, but he had found a lot of expensive new lingerie in her drawer and a sex toy. He was very bitter. He said he'd come home from work unexpectedly one day and seen a man he didn't know walking across the back garden and climbing over the fence. When he went upstairs his wife was in the shower and the bed was unmade. He found a used condom in the bin by the bed. Another time he drove down the lane at the side of the house and saw your van parked. It was then that he made the connection, seeing your name on the side of the van. I told him the evidence sounded pretty damning already, I asked exactly what he wanted. He said he wanted cast-iron evidence that would be irrefutable in a divorce court.

'It wasn't difficult to obtain. He let me into the house and I put in phone taps and bugged the bedroom, although as I quickly found out you weren't the sort to limit yourself to conventional settings. The photographs are all numbered and dated and cross-referenced with the reports in the folders, by the way. The first incident was the Tuesday, the day after I started surveillance. I picked up your phone call – it's on the top cassette tape – inviting yourself round. I was a mile down the road, had plenty of time to get into position. You parked where McGovern had first spotted your van and I photographed you coming across the back lawn. These photographs here, in sequence. Here she is letting you in at the back door, here you are kissing, and here you are screwing her over the kitchen table. You seem fond of kitchen tables. Even fonder of screwing. Sorry, I shouldn't be flippant.

'I followed you round for a few days after that, to establish a pattern. That's what I said in the report anyway, but to be honest it was a bit of a smokescreen. It wasn't the most professional job I've ever done, I have to admit, but frankly I was intrigued. It isn't every week you get the chance to see a real genuine superstud at work, it's mostly pretty tame the stuff I get to work on. Not with you. As soon as I saw you I could see why Peter McGovern would be jealous. Not to mention Mr Seymour-Brown, but I don't think he knew anything about you. Don't worry, it wasn't in my brief to tell him. It was Wednesday morning I followed you to the Seymour-Brown house. I didn't know that was their name, of course. I found out from the milkman later. Incidentally, I thought that was always meant to be his perk, what you were doing. You'll be getting complaints from the milkmen's union. There aren't any photos, and it's not mentioned in the report because it's not strictly relevant, but you got round there about ten o'clock. No kitchen tables this time, but I saw you through the window – you went upstairs together and then she drew the curtains in the bedroom. Left the window open, though. Bit of a mistake. Very noisy, Mrs Seymour-Brown, though in fairness so are most of your women. I have to say, you are good at it, Lewis, you know all the right buttons to press. Mrs Seymour-Brown certainly looked pleased afterwards, and so did Mrs Garvey on the Friday. That's not officially in the report either, but it's in my notes. I don't know if you were being unduly prolific around that time, Lewis, but if you could bottle what you were on you might put Viagra out of business. Sorry, I'm doing the flippant bit again. Back to the main business, Julie McGovern.

'She was your number one, no doubt about that. I was following you for nearly three weeks, and you only serviced the other two once each. Mrs McGovern got four seeings-to, and they were always the steamiest. You made two casual pick-ups in that period too, both in pubs, though not the one where we met. I never found out their names; perhaps you didn't either. Those were the two I knew about anyway, perhaps there were more. By then I was following you about in my own time in the evenings, because I really was fascinated. I'd sussed the pattern very quickly, and I knew you were never going to see Mrs McGovern at night, so I didn't need to bother lumbering myself with the camera. Your married ladies were strictly daytime, and always at their place. Average age about forty, Julie the youngest. The evening pick-ups you always took back to your place, and the two I saw were about thirty, maybe younger. When you weren't on the prowl you stayed in on your own. I could see you through that big window in your barn, working out, watching TV, playing pool for hours. You went downstairs a few times, then I saw your workshop lights go on and could hear the sound of an electric saw or a drill or something. A pretty strange kind of life, if you don't mind me saying. No proper relationship, just sex. No men friends. You stopped off for drinks with your workmen a few times, but only in the early evening, briefly. No lads' nights out, no beer-drinking rituals, footy talk, no male bonding at all. Just women, and lots of sex. A kind of perfect lifestyle from a men's magazine, if you like, but I'd never come across it before. You'd have made an enthralling case study for a psychiatrist. Pity I was just a common-or-garden detective.

'My report must have made grim reading for McGovern. The evidence was overwhelming, and what must have really stuck in his throat was that Julie was having such a bloody good time. It's on the tapes, he insisted on playing them here when he came round, I got quite embarrassed. He sat exactly where you're sitting now, listening to the sounds of his wife thrashing around in ecstasy, looking through the photographs at the same time. I asked him if he was going to divorce her. He said he didn't know, which I thought was a bit odd having gone to all that trouble. For weeks, months after that I expected to hear from him, but not a whisper. The file was all made up, ready for presentation in court just in case. I'd given him the photographs and the original tapes, I'm not actually sure if he realized that I had copies. Sometimes clients insist that everything gets destroyed or handed over, but, as I say, he just disappeared abruptly. We got a cheque though, on the dot and in full a week or so later. You cost him a lot of money, £1,086.00 plus VAT, expenses included. It's all itemized, and that was without what I did in my own time. I saw your van out and about a few times after that. Scarcely surprising, we're both working this area. I was curious about you, tempted to check and see if you were still up to your old tricks. But I didn't. In the end I forgot about you. And then you walked into that pub.

'Nikki saw you first. Said Christ, will you look at that?

Said something along the lines of, I'd like to find out what he packs in his lunchbox. Birds can be as smutty as blokes when they want to be, Lewis, in case you didn't know. When I asked her to leave you to me she was well pissed off, but she owed me. I made up my mind on the spot I was going to sleep with you. I had to, I had to find out what it was like. You might not believe me, but I'm not normally that easy. Actually, I don't give a toss whether you believe me or not. It was a once-in-a-lifetime shot, normal rules suspended. Here you were, Mr Superstud himself, the kitchen-table king. Frankly I just had to see it in action for myself. I'd been completely amazed, to tell you the truth, sitting in my car those times listening to you go at it like a souped-up rabbit. It's never happened before, I'll tell you. It takes more than a few grunts and groans from a low-grade Swedish porn track to get me going. But you were different. You could shag for England, Lewis. I just fancied a one-off test drive, OK?

'You look shocked. I was quite shocked myself. I haven't behaved like that since I was a student, when it was two vodkas on a Friday night in the union bar and I was anybody's. No, I'm joking. It was three vodkas, minimum. Where was I? Yeah, your place or mine, that was the next line, wasn't it? Well, I knew the answer to that, didn't I? Daytime her place, nighttime yours, so off we went. Thought I'd better drive, though, so I could make a quick getaway afterwards. I wanted to see inside of that big glass fish tank for myself. But you weren't really happy, were you? You didn't like the fact that I was calling the shots. You're a bit of a control freak, Lewis, I knew that already. Not fair, I know, but I couldn't help teasing you. You thought you'd got it on a plate and I couldn't resist playing a game. It just went a bit further than I expected, that's all. I didn't mean to humiliate you, not seriously anyway. I could tell you weren't happy at being handcuffed to the bed, but you were a good sport and I should have been a bit . . . well, it wasn't fair and I really do feel guilty. In the circumstances it was hardly surprising that you weren't at your best. Didn't do me much good though, did it? I never did get the full amazing superstud service. I can hardly say I didn't know what I was missing. I'm sorry, I'm wandering from the point again. Are you getting the full picture?

'I'm a side issue. The important stuff is about him. I thought there was something devious about McGovern from the start. And I'm afraid I knew there was something gullible about you. Looks like he guessed that too. I believe you, Lewis. I think you're a schmuck, but I believe you. Anyway, you're a rotten liar, and that would be the dumbest story ever you've just told me, the kind only an idiot would make up. That could be a problem for you, but you've probably worked that out already. I know you don't like people telling you what to do, but you really haven't got any choice. In the morning I'll phone Terry Hoffman, he'll come here, you tell him everything and you go down to the station together. That's what an innocent man would do, and you are an innocent man. Well, mostly. The solicitor will be there the whole time, the interrogation will be recorded, they can't put the pressure on you or make you say anything you don't want to. Tell them everything, but leave me out of it, OK? I'll volunteer what I know about McGovern in my own time, and of course I'll testify in court. There is one piece of advice I would give you. I said just now you were mostly innocent. Conspiring to kill somebody with a view to defrauding an insurance company does rather blow that out of the window. If I was you I'd say you went to the house with the intention of telling McGovern that you couldn't go through with it. Impossible to prove or disprove, it'll be your word against his. Invent any excuse you like, but try to keep morality out of it. Policemen, as a rule, find that sort of thing suspicious.

'I'd try and get a few hours' sleep now. You'll need it. The arm of that sofa drops down, it's quite comfortable. I'll get you a blanket in a sec. I'll show you how the shower works. It's pretty primitive, I'm afraid, but at least the facilities are better than the nick. There's a clothes brush somewhere, I'll dig it out, you want to try and look your best when you turn yourself in. It's going to be tough for you, I won't try and pretend otherwise, but you're a tough guy, you can handle it. It's going to be a long hard slog ahead, but I won't give up on you, Lewis. I'll give you all the help I can, promise.

'Sleep now, if you can. You're going to need it . . .'

14

When Lewis came out of the shower Grace had gone and her bedroom door was closed. She had dropped the end of the sofa and laid out a blanket, as promised. He slumped on to it, a towel round his midriff, and stared blankly at the armchair where she had been sitting.

She had sat there, just there, and calmly shredded his life. She had lined up all his assumptions about himself, like ducks in a shooting gallery, and annihilated them one by one. He had been used at every turn, it seemed, and he had walked into every trap. Now she wanted him to walk into another, to give himself up to the police and cheerfully march into a cell. Here, Officer, allow me to turn the key myself . . . She wanted him to trust in justice; in Guildford of all places. She'd been in the police too long, her judgement was warped. If she thought he was going to put his trust in a bunch of plods with size-twelve feet and IQs to match then she was as deluded as he had been. As deluded as she had helped to make him.

Even through the shock of everything else that had happened to him he could still wince with embarrassment at the memory of the night they had spent together. She had toyed with him, humiliated him, then got off snickering to herself at her own private joke. And here he was, the big mug of the world, the original article, steeped to the neck in his own shit.

Disgust, and loathing, and fear consumed him. How easily they had all played on him. He had always taken such pride in his own cleverness, the way he had covered his tracks in his affairs, but it seemed that he had been an open book. He had been read, digested and spat out again.

He felt deep down within himself a physical knot of hatred, a twisting of the guts that made him ache. He closed his eyes and saw McGovern's spindly body dancing before him. He heard the grating mockery of his voice. How in God's name had he allowed himself to be suckered by McGovern's glorified salesman's patter? Julie had warned him, but he'd thought he'd known what he was doing. He remembered McGovern walking into the Coach. Three weeks ago, was that all? He had known right away that it was no coincidence, so why had he brushed aside his own instincts? Why had he let that weed, that pumpkin-head, destroy his life?

The tears he felt running down his cheeks were not from self-pity. His emotional turmoil was fuelled by rage and frustration. He held his fists up to his eyes and crushed his fingertips into his palms, imagining McGovern's throat in his grip. Yes, he would make him pay. To hell with the police, to hell with Grace. This was a score he had to settle himself.

He threw off the towel and put his clothes back on, trying to be as quiet as possible as his big boots came into contact once more with the bare floor. His clothes looked a bit of a mess, but with his face clean again and a plaster over his cut he would get by. He checked his watch. It wasn't yet five, still plenty of time before dawn.

He shuffled over as delicately as he could to the bedroom door, put his ear to the wood and listened. He heard nothing. He hoped she was asleep, but if she wasn't, too bad. She couldn't stop him. She had said she felt guilty. She had said she would help. But how? What could she do that he couldn't? What could she do that would harm McGovern? All she had suggested was that he turn himself in. Was she going to suggest the same to McGovern? He had a better idea.

The Beretta was on the coffee table next to the orange folder. He put it in his deep side pocket and felt immediately better at the reassuring weight against his hip. He wanted to see McGovern's face when he put the tip of the barrel to his head. Then they would both know how brave he was. Lewis knew the answer to that already. He imagined McGovern crumpling. He imagined the fear in his eyes, the whine in his voice. To shoot a helpless woman was one thing, to stare down the barrel yourself quite another matter. He would make McGovern confess, force the police to believe him. It wouldn't be as satisfying as pulling the trigger, but it would come close enough. He thought about poor Julie. Poor dumb Julie. Almost as dumb as himself.

He crept across the room and slipped out through the office to the top of the stairs. He negotiated the narrow steps in darkness, thinking how typical it would be if he slipped now and broke his leg. He didn't slip. He clicked the catch on the front door and headed off briskly up the hill towards the centre of town. He passed no one during his ten-minute walk. Guildford was fast asleep.

The little rows of terraced houses he came to all looked exactly the same. He couldn't for the life of him remember which one Bill lived in, but that didn't matter. The van was what he was after and he spotted it easily enough among the close-parked lines of modest saloons. He pulled out his bristling key-ring and selected the right keys by touch. He was glad that he hadn't thought of this before going to see Grace. Much better to know the worst, the truth.

The van started first time. The noise of the engine was startlingly loud, but no lace curtains were twitching as he pulled out and drove away. It wasn't exactly the perfect vehicle for a man on the run – conspicuously white and with his own name emblazoned on the side – but it was only a temporary measure. He would use it to get home, pick up some clothes, and, more importantly, the cash hidden in the bathroom. Then he'd come back to Guildford and dump the van at the station. He would go in and buy a ticket to Waterloo, and try and make sure the ticket clerk got a good look at his face. He would have to keep thinking ahead, never let himself forget for a moment that the police were after him. He wouldn't take the train, of course. He'd slip back out, get himself down to the A3. He shouldn't have any trouble hitching his way down to Petersfield, maybe further. He was aiming for the coast, Brighton probably, but he'd play it by ear. The first thing to do was change his appearance. His hair was getting long now, well over his collar and quite distinctive. He'd get himself a marine cut, then dye what was left blond. Not in Petersfield but further on, where there was no chance of bumping into someone he knew. Add dark glasses and he'd be unrecognizable. Grow a beard, perhaps. Find himself a little boarding house, then keep moving every couple of days or so. Spin a story about looking for work, but have as little contact as possible with people. Eat in his room, never mix with other guests. He'd work out the rules as he went. He would give it at least a week, wait for the heat to die down. Then he'd get some wheels, anything would do, pay cash, no questions asked. That would be the beauty of having McGovern's bundle. Use the man's own cash to get back at him. McGovern would probably lie low for a bit, go through the motions of being traumatized. Perhaps he'd move out of the house, but he'd be in the office, sometime. Lewis had never got round to returning the keys, they were still sitting in his desk at the barn. McGovern was always first into the office, he was so proud of that. Well, one day Lewis would be waiting for him. The man would freak out. Lewis would make him tell the truth, he'd buy one of those mini-cassette recorders and make McGovern spit out every word. And if he didn't, he'd spatter his brains all over the fucking wall.

He was driving much too fast and aggressively. He made himself take his foot off the floor. He hadn't seen a soul, let alone a policeman, but it would be foolish to draw attention to himself through a stupid traffic infringement. He'd already driven one vehicle off the road that night. He had to learn to relax. He had to learn to look like someone else. Soon there would be bulletins on the radio, announcements in the paper. There would be his picture and the tag, 'Wanted for questioning'. If he looked like a fugitive people would notice him.

He pulled off the road half a mile before his house. There was a bridle path, used all the time by a local pony club, rutted but wide enough to take the van. He bumped his way along it slowly until he was out of sight of the road, and turned off the engine.

The night had turned cloudy, there wasn't a single star visible and he couldn't see his fingers six inches in front of his nose. That was good. He fished the torch out of his pocket, shielded it with his palm and flicked the light at the ground as he picked his way between the trees. He climbed a stile, crossed the open field at the back of his house and swung his leg over the hip-high wire fence that marked the boundary of his property. He felt his way amongst the beeches and elms until he came to the garage. He crouched down against it and watched and listened. There was nothing to see, but there was nothing to hear either. The gate was somewhere up ahead of him. If the police had the place staked out already that's where they'd be. If there was a cop it'd be some half-awake sap on routine patrol, his car parked on the next bend. He'd never know a thing.

Lewis put the torch back in his pocket nonetheless, to be on the safe side. He could feel his way from here, he knew every inch of the place, inside and out. He slipped back to the trees and worked his way along to the side of the barn. It was good that the door wasn't visible from the gate, an extra line of insurance for the cautious creature he was becoming.

He let himself into the barn and climbed the spiral staircase to the top. He couldn't see anything, but somehow it felt OK. He was sure no clumsy policemen had been streaming through the place. He headed for the bathroom and tore up the floorboard under the sink. Oh yes, he thought as his fingers closed on the black plastic bag, oh yes . . . He felt both ecstatic and weak with relief. He slipped his hand inside and felt the reassuring bundles of money. He was still one good long step ahead of the law.

He put back the floorboard and went through to the bedroom. There was a soft canvas bag with shoulder straps up on top of his clothes cupboard. He pulled it down and stuffed the money in one end. Feeling blindly in his drawers he found a random assortment of clean underwear, a few shirts and a pair of jeans. There was just room for his trainers and a denim jacket. He zipped up the bag, slung it over his shoulder and crept back to the top of the stairs. Now all he had to get was the keys to McGovern's office from his desk and he was done.

Car headlamps were coming down the road. He stopped

in his tracks as he caught sight of the tiny pinpricks of light. No one in a passing car could see him from the road, but he would wait anyway until it had passed. He watched the lights come nearer through the glass wall of the Aquarium.

There was more than one car. The front pair of headlamps went into profile for a second as they hit a curve, and then at once a second pair took its place, and a third pair after that. Three cars together down a tiny country lane at five in the morning? No, that was impossible. They were coming to the barn.

He was running, falling down the spiral stairs in the thick darkness, like he was twisting into hell. He hit the floor in a giddy daze and only knew that he was going the wrong way when his thighs crashed into his workbench. The sudden pain would have half blinded him if he hadn't been blind already. He reslung the canvas bag and lurched towards the door.

He spilled out of the barn, hobbling and winded. The headlamps were playing on the garage, he could hear car doors opening and thumping closed. They were opening the gate and coming in. He heard voices.

He gritted his teeth and spurted for the trees. At least the spillage of light from the cars enabled him to pick out the denser clumps of shadows marking the tree trunks. Behind him he heard the car engines drawing closer. As he glanced back over his shoulder he caught his foot against something and fell forward in a bruising sprawl, his head fetching up painfully against one of the fence posts. He forced himself to his feet again, despite a sharp jabbing pain in his right knee, tossed the canvas bag over the fence and heaved himself over, using the post for leverage. He fell into the bank at the edge of the field and rolled over among the grass and nettles.

He pushed his face down into the dirt as a brace of headlamps swept the air above his head. When he looked up again he could see the three cars parked side by side in front of the barn. Only one of the cars was marked, and now the light on its roof was flashing. Shadowy figures of policemen were spilling out of the cars and spreading over the courtyard. One was coming towards the trees and the fence, the beam of a powerful torch preceding him.

Lewis snatched up the canvas bag and limped away. He couldn't run, he could feel the bruise on his knee spreading, making each step a torture. Soon it would be dawn and they wouldn't need torches. He quickened his pace and willed his brain to shut out the pain.

He was in the dense and comforting darkness at the boundary of the field, shielded by the thick hedge that ran alongside. He took his bearings from his trailing hand, and the irregular dancing lights behind his shoulder. They were making a lot of noise in his courtyard, he could hear them hammering on his door, but the voices were growing fainter. He had got out just in the nick of time.

He was almost there. He had reached the corner of the field, he knew because he had run smack into the right angle of the hedge, adding another line of bumps and scratches to the pitted landscape of his body. He found the stile and hauled himself over. It was a good thing the police were so far behind him, he thought, or they would surely have heard his rasping, rattling breaths.

He saw, dimly, the white shape of the van. It was good that he'd got spare clothes in the bag, his feet and ankles were covered in stinking muck. He chucked the bag down on the bonnet as he thrust his hand into his pocket for the keys.

A bright light exploded in his eyes. He reeled back, staggered. Someone was shining a torch into his face, someone standing only feet away on the other side of the van.

'It's him,' said a voice quiet with menace.

The keys, in his deep side pocket, slipped through his fingers. His palm closed on the pimpled grip of the Beretta.

'I've got a gun!' he squealed, his voice at the desperate pitch of a cornered animal's. He snatched out the pistol and tried to level it at the dancing light. Something hard struck his arm.

He had dropped the gun. What was happening? His right arm was numb and useless and there was someone behind him, grabbing him round the throat. He tried to twist away, and a fist slammed into his kidneys. He howled and almost burst with pain. His knees buckled and he fell to the ground.

There were two torches over him now, two men shining light into his face. He saw one of them swing a big heavy truncheon through the beam, and flinched. He threw his left hand up in front of his face. He felt his lungs and throat cry out, but no sound came through, only breath. He had never in his life felt fear like this.

'Don't hurt me!' he managed to whisper at the unseen faces hovering over him. 'Don't hurt me, please . . .'

15

They met in the wine bar where Grace had been chatted up by the champagne-drinking salesmen the Friday before. She was early and presumed she'd be first, but when she got there he was already sitting in one of the alcoves by the window. She put on her breeziest expression and hoped that he wouldn't notice her nervousness. His eyes, when at last he consented to look up from her figure and take in her face, were as studiously blank as ever.

'Not looking bad, Grace,' he said, deadpan.

'Same to you, Bob,' she lied.

Looking as bad as usual, she thought, especially since he wasn't drinking. He had told her over the phone that he was on leave, but he wouldn't let himself drink during the day any more. He looked a little fatter notwithstanding, a little more worn and a little balder than when she had last seen him, but just the same. The salesmen who had failed to get her into bed last week would have been offended to think that she could turn them down and still feel girly and weak-kneed in the presence of this nondescript, more than slightly seedy figure in a reject suit from Oxfam, the cigarette ash randomly distributed all the way down his tie. But she hadn't fallen for Bob Challoner for his looks.

'All right for some,' he murmured when she had asked the waitress for a glass of house white. He swirled around the ice cubes in the bottom of his glass and glared morosely at his orange juice. 'How's life then? Got a boyfriend?'

'No,' she said without hesitation. She had known that he would come directly to the point. The way to deal with Bob, as she knew better than anyone, was to take him head-on and not flinch.

'What do you do for sex?'

'Subtle as ever, Bob.'

'I know you. You're not cut out to be a nun, Grace.'

'I'm not going to bed with you, Bob.'

'Did I offer?'

'You don't have to. I know what you're thinking even before you do, and it's not going to get you into the church choir.'

'Not even once, for old times' sake?'

'How's your wife, Bob?'

'You do know how to hit below the belt.'

'Only part of your anatomy that's got any sensitivity.'

'She's all right, in a nagging unbearable sort of way. Why don't you come and live with me, Grace?'

'I hate crowds.'

'We could get a place. In Guildford, if you like.'

'You shameless romantic. You're a married man.'

'Will you stop reminding me?'

'Will you grow up and act responsible? You've got a wife, two kids and a career. Besides, we couldn't live together. You'd drive me round the bend.'

'Yeah, but we'd have great sex.'

'What about the rest of the time?'

'We could think about the next time we're going to have great sex.'

The waitress, returning with Grace's wine, was unable to pretend that she hadn't overheard the tail-end of their conversation. Not that Bob gave a damn anyway. He didn't modulate his voice for anyone.

'You said you wanted a favour, Grace,' he continued as the waitress scurried away at something quicker than her usual pace. 'It's obviously not a shag, so what are you after?'

'Inside information. I won't bullshit you, Bob. I need to know some things about the Julie McGovern case.'

'What you asking me for? That's Waverley, not Guildford. Anyway, as I told you on the phone, I'm on leave till I start my new job at the end of the month.'

'I know. But Jimmy Collins is running the show. You know Jimmy, I want you to talk to him, find out what he's thinking.'

'You know Jimmy too.'

'Yeah, but he just thinks I'm a thick bit of skirt with no nous.'

'Not far out there.'

'You know where you can stick your truncheon, Superintendent. Jimmy's scared shitless of you and he thinks you're some kind of genius, God knows why. I know you drink together, and I know Jimmy likes nothing better than a good blather.'

'Why are you interested?'

'I know the suspect. I think he's innocent.'

'Oh Christ no . . .' Bob pushed his drink away in disgust, though whether it was the nonalcoholic content or Grace's comment that had got to him was a moot point. He curled his lip at her scornfully as he fished a packet of cigarettes out of his pocket. 'You're out of the force five minutes and you start believing any old shit. So he's innocent, eh? Yeah, yeah. Innocent like every other bugger behind bars, all fitted up by the good old bent British copper. Still reading the *Guardian*, eh, Grace? I told you it'd rot your brains. He's as guilty as Jack the fucking Ripper, darling, and twice as nice.'

'What makes you so certain?'

'Oh come on! He's identified by the victim's husband, who's run away and dialled nine-nine-nine when the guy broke in. His fingerprints are all over the murder weapon. And when they try to arrest him he pulls another gun and threatens to shoot. Oh, and by the way, they found most of the money he'd blackmailed out of the guy in a bag he had on him. Open-and-shut case. Bugger should have his neck snapped at the end of a rope, not keep the taxpayers forking out for his useless keep the next twenty years.'

'I see,' said Grace thoughtfully. 'So you have been talking to Jimmy.'

He hesitated for a fraction of a moment before striking his match. Then he took a deep, deep drag of his cigarette, pursed his lips into a tight O and breathed his smoke very deliberately into her face.

'Still given up, have you?' he asked, with malice.

'I get all the nicotine I need through passive smoking, thanks, Bob.'

'You are smart, Grace, I have to give you that.'

'Big of you.'

'I was with Jimmy last night. He wouldn't stop talking about it, it's a hell of a big deal for him, this case. Did you see him on the telly, that local news programme? He was so proud, told me his mother was taping it for him. Good old Jimmy, if he handles this right then that'll be him set up, he'll retire an Assistant Chief at the very least. Couldn't happen to a nicer bloke.'

'Or a thicker one. What did he say?'

'What I said just now. Open-and-shut case. Man screws other man's wife, then gets jealous and shoots her.'

'Usually it's the wronged husband who does that, doesn't he? What was that about blackmail?'

'The builder – what's his name? – was creaming him.'

'His name's Lewis Young.'

'Yeah. Well, Young had been screwing the wife since whenever. McGovern was terrified that she was going to leave him for Young. He said he still loved his wife, he was desperate to keep her, and he went to Young, pleaded with him to leave them alone. Young's business was in financial difficulties, so he said, yeah, OK, but you've got to pay. McGovern even set up a job in his office, so he could pass some money through his books. But it was mostly cash, the bundle Young had on him when he was arrested. But Young didn't leave the wife alone, he continued to see her. And he was greedy. He wanted more money. McGovern said he didn't have it, Young got threatening. On Friday night he broke into the house. He made McGovern take him upstairs at gunpoint. There's a safe in the bedroom. But Mrs McGovern was there too. Young was shocked because he thought the wife was going to be in Scotland, but she hadn't been feeling very well and she'd cancelled her trip. McGovern says that when his wife realized what Young had come for she was livid. McGovern hadn't told her about paying Young the ten thou. She went crazy, lashed out at Young and started throwing things, accusing him of treating her like shit. Young was acting like a madman too, says McGovern. Young flipped, beat her up, then shot her through the head. McGovern ran away. Young fired at him, but missed. Forensic found two bullets, one in the doorframe, one in the wall on the landing. McGovern got out of the house, managed to get into his car and drive off. He rang the police from his mobile. Young ran and ditched the murder weapon, a Webley revolver, in a hedge. Jimmy's boys found it later, Young's fingerprints all over it. Sounds pretty innocent to me, Grace. What do you think?'

'What's Young's story?'

'It's a good 'un, brace yourself. Claims McGovern wanted to top himself because he was dying of cancer and hired Young to pull the trigger. We had a pretty good laugh, Jimmy and me, I have to admit. We've both heard some ripe ones in our time, but this is the peach. Jimmy's only worry is that Young's so off the wall the defence'll get in some smart-arsed psychiatrist to prove that he's doolally. Original story, you've got to give him that. But I don't think even these days the average jury's thick enough to buy it.'

'I presume McGovern's had a medical examination?'

'Hundred per cent healthy, even though he does smoke like a chimney and drink like a fish. Jimmy says the poor guy's a wreck. Weedy sort of a nerd, must have been scared shitless by that big hulk of a guy. What's your interest in him, by the way?'

'I know him.'

'Friend of yours?'

'Not exactly.'

'Screw him?'

'I don't go to bed with every man I meet, Bob.'

'Does that mean yes?'

'Bob, you're the one who needs to see the smart-arsed psychiatrist.'

'So you did screw him. Didn't know you were into psychos and weirdos.'

'I'm not and he isn't.'

'Was he good?'

'Stop it, Bob. I take it Jimmy didn't mention my name.'

'Why would he mention you?'

'Because a year ago McGovern paid me to snoop on Young and his wife and get enough evidence for a divorce.'

It was easy to tell when Bob Challoner was thinking, because thought wasn't his natural element. He was a creature of gut and instinct, a staunch believer in shooting first and asking questions afterwards. So when something rubbed across the grain, and forced him to press his grey matter into service, a resentful scowl would bloom sourly in his face and his permanently narrowed eyes would close up still further in suspicion and disgust. He produced a fresh cigarette and lit it from the stub of the old one.

'So what?' he said with a belligerent shrug.

She smiled to herself. She'd wormed her way just sufficiently under his guard to make him irritated. And that meant that something unwelcome was gnawing at his monolithic certainties.

'So what?' she repeated, quite relaxed now. 'Only this. I was wondering if Jimmy Collins had mentioned me. As I said.'

'And as *I* said, why would he?'

'Oh, it was just a little thought I'd had, about routine police procedure. Imagine the scene, Bob. Here's this guy, tells you his wife's been having an affair with another guy. So how does the husband know? The wife didn't tell him, and I don't suppose Mr Young was the first to broach the subject. You've done enough interrogations in your time, I don't have to paint the scene, do I? How long had your wife been having an affair with the suspect, Mr McGovern? Reasonable enough question, eh? Now how about a supplementary. When did you find out that she was having an affair, sir? Oh, about a year ago, says he. And how did you find out, sir? How indeed? That's how I was imagining it, Bob. Seem fair enough to you?'

'The poor guy was traumatized. How's he meant to answer every damn-fool trivial question?'

'Bob, McGovern is the only witness in a murder case. I don't want to sound pompous, but wasn't it you who told me that there is no such thing as a trivial question in a murder case? Doesn't it strike you that a private detective with a complete dossier, photos, tapes, the works, on the affair between the victim and the suspect is a significant witness? And doesn't it paint a slightly different picture of the relationship between the husband and the suspect than the official version? McGovern did not still love his wife, as he claims, I can tell you that for a certainty. He hated her. Perhaps that's why I haven't been mentioned.'

'What makes you sure you weren't?'

'Oh come on, Bob. You know damned well that if my name had come up Jimmy Collins would have split his sides pissing himself. And the first person he'd have called to share the joke with would have been you, his regular doubles partner in sexist banter and applied misogyny. I'd also have had a call from one of his minions by now, wouldn't I? Am I right, or am I right?'

'Whichever of the two, you're a cocky little bitch.'

'And I love you too, you miserable little prick.'

Bob's sneering lip curled into an expression that might almost have been a smile. He cocked his head a little to the side as he leant forward to flick the tip of his cigarette at the ashtray.

'Little?'

'Sorry. "Miserable prick" all right?'

'Better. So . . .'

He sucked the last remaining dregs of life out of his second cigarette and stubbed it out. He leant slowly towards her, put his elbows on the table, and rested his chin on his hands. He looked utterly bored, a sure sign that he wasn't.

'All right, I'll admit for the sake of argument that perhaps Jimmy's not the brightest. He never guessed about us, for one thing, and that was staring him in the face. Why don't you tell me everything you got . . .'

Grace didn't tell him everything, but she told him most of it. She told him about McGovern and how he'd come to her. She told him all about Lewis, how he operated, his vanity, his naivety. She explained how he had turned up on her doorstep the night of the murder, blurted out the same story which he'd given to Jimmy Collins, and how she had believed him, and still did. She had felt physically sick when she had woken up the next morning and found him gone, knowing full well that he wouldn't have a chance on the run. The circumstances of his capture, of course, had made a difficult position impossible. She'd read all the details in the paper, everything except the blackmail angle. She knew that on the evidence no jury could fail to convict.

'That's because it's cast-iron,' said Bob. 'Perhaps you're just another dumb bird who's fallen for the guy's bull-shit.'

'Well, I can see why you'd think that, Bob, but you'd be wrong. And I bet you anything you like that if you were handling this case you'd have twigged that there's something not right. I know what you'll tell me – go to Jimmy. But you know as well as I do he wouldn't get it. There are too many questions it just wouldn't occur to Jimmy to ask, so I'm going to ask them. And if you want to know the reason, it's because I'm here. It's true Lewis is a moron and he deserves no favours, but he's an innocent man, and some vague distant memory I've got of what it meant to be a copper makes me think that's important. You believe in what's important too, even though your insides would churn up in embarrassment if anyone dared accuse you of anything so woolly as idealism. I wouldn't dream of it. I'd just like you to help me, OK?'

'Better get yourself a cape, Grace, if you're going to start crusading. You're on a hiding to nothing.'

'I thought you'd think that.'

'What you going to prove? What can you do on your own, for Christ's sake?'

'Well, I won't be entirely on my own if you help.'

'Hang on, hang on. What was that you said earlier about my not screwing up my career? I'm starting my new job next month, remember, and I'm not blowing it for you, thank you very much.'

'Congratulations. What is this job?'

'I'm not supposed to talk about it. It's a new outfit, London-based, but not part of the Met. Report direct to the Home Office.'

'With you as boss?'

'No, I'm police liaison. Joint operation with M15, you see. It's the way things are going now with drugs.'

'I thought you said when you left the Met you never wanted anything to do with drugs again?'

'Yeah, well, this was too good to turn down, and I'm bored.'

'For something you're not supposed to talk about, you're doing a great job of being discreet.'

'I was under the impression I could trust you.'

'And I know I can trust you. So will you help, please? You just said you've got time on your hands. I'm not asking you to get involved physically, just listen out for me, right?'

'You mean be your grass. I don't get it, Grace. You're trying to tell me this guy McGovern's some kind of criminal mastermind, the sort who in the movies sits there stroking a white cat and smoking a fat cigar and cackling like an idiot to himself because he's just thought of another cunning plan to tear up the world. Until you burst in wearing your cape, that is. I never figured you for a fantasist, I must say, but let's just suppose for the sake of argument that you're right. So here's this guy, kills his own wife, sets up another bloke to take the rap, fills in all the background details so there's every bit of evidence in place and motives coming out of people's ears so thick that not even a clot like Jimmy Collins could fail to clock it . . . God, I don't believe I'm listening to this bullshit . . . so you're telling me all this, and still expecting me to believe that it hasn't occurred to McGovern that the police might like to talk to you? I mean, this is a pretty big story, the whole county's buzzing with it. Isn't it going to occur to him that you might perhaps contact the police yourself to tell them what you know?'

'Yeah, those are pretty much the questions I've been asking myself, Bob. And I don't know, maybe, just maybe, I *am* barking up the wrong tree. But I don't think so. I really do think McGovern is all those things you've just said, with or without the white cat. I think he's a pretty clever villain, and you know George Courtenay's first rule of clever villains.'

'They always forget the bleeding obvious. Yeah, yeah, I remember. How is the old bastard? Still got the dodgy ticker?'

'Nothing that four pints of Guinness can't put right.'

'Only four? Christ, he must be sick. So must I, to have sat here listening to this crap for half an hour . . .'

He was looking at his watch, but she knew that he wasn't registering the time. Wherever it was he was pretending he had to be, she knew damned well, wouldn't have precluded him setting aside a full few hours, just in case there was a chance of being invited back to her place.

'So you think I'm wasting my time?' she asked, as he reached across to the chair over which he had draped his coat. It was impossible to tell what he was thinking from his expression, of course. Nature had designed him for a professional poker player but by some mischance he had wound up as a detective. What Nature had really intended with regards to herself, Grace had yet to discover, but a part of her still hoped that it wouldn't require her to spend all of the rest of her life setting too much store by the wrong men.

Bob Challoner didn't answer her question. He seemed strangely preoccupied by the weather outside, as if the choice between putting on his coat or leaving it slung over his arm was the burning issue of the hour.

'Are you going to help me, Bob?'

As soon as she opened her mouth she wished she hadn't said it like that. She had sounded thin and plaintive. It was a tone to be reserved for appealing to someone's better side; and Detective Superintendent Challoner didn't have a better side.

'You know, Grace, when you rang me I got all excited for a minute,' he said. 'What's it been, a year and a half? I thought, maybe you'd been thinking about me, maybe even missing me. My fault, I know. Should know better than to harbour illusions at my age, shouldn't I?'

'Don't get self-pitying, Bob, it's not you.'

'Isn't it now?' For a second he showed her his teeth, his

shark's smile. 'Actually, I've got quite good at it over the last year. You asked if you were wasting your time. You know the answer to that. What are you going on? Impressions, judgements, feelings?'

'Call that instinct, Bob. It's got you quite a long way, hasn't it?'

'Not without any evidence to back it up.'

'That's what I'm aiming to find.'

'Good. Let me know when you've found it. I don't think it is going to rain after all, is it?'

The burning issue decided, he stood up and flipped his coat over his arm. He didn't stoop to kiss her cheek, that wasn't his style, and a handshake would have been ridiculous. So he just started to walk away.

'Will you ring me if you hear anything?' she called after him.

He paused for a moment to consider the question.

'If I feel like it.'

And that, she reflected as she watched him through the window crossing the street, never once glancing back, was about as committed as Bob Challoner was capable of getting. She finished the last of her wine and tried to imagine what she had not allowed herself to imagine at any time during the last year, what living with the man would actually have been like. And she decided that the passage of eighteen months had done very little to alter her opinion, and the truth was still that she couldn't think of anything more disastrous – or anything that she had ever wanted more.

16

When Grace said that she could see McGovern's office from her own front window it wasn't strictly true, but when she got back from the wine bar she did see the police car parked on the corner of the street and the clusters of pedestrians gathering and pointing fingers. The brutal murder of the estate agent's wife was the biggest thing to have happened in the area since the IRA bombing in the seventies. Early in the afternoon a television truck drew up and a crowd ballooned from nowhere in minutes, necks craning to catch a glimpse of the almost-famous local news reporter delivering the latest to the camera.

Grace got round in time to watch them packing up. The TV crew had been standing on the pavement in front of the estate agent's window. A bored policeman and a couple of print journalists were standing nearby. Grace knew one of them, the seasoned and suitably sleazy crime reporter for a local paper. He looked pleased to see her; no doubt he was glad of the distraction.

'Big story, eh?' she said pleasantly.

'Worse luck,' he muttered back.

He'd been there since nine o'clock, he told her. He'd spoken to McGovern's employees as they arrived to open up the office. He showed her his notes. 'It's too horrible for words,' one of them had told him. 'None of us can believe it,' said another.

'Could have stayed at home and made those up,' he told her sourly. At least he had some photos to go with the quotes. His photographer had just nipped round the corner to get some coffees. It would be just their luck, he reckoned, for Peter McGovern to turn up now.

'You're not really expecting him, are you?' she asked.

''Course not. Editor's bloody stupid idea. Can't say I've got a better one though. He hasn't been at his home since the murder. No one knows where he is.'

'Staying with friends?'

'Doesn't seem to have any. It's weird, I've never had so little to go on. Usually there's a whole rent-a-mob of friends and neighbours anxious to say their piece. I spoke to a woman who used to play tennis with the wife. Best I've been able to manage so far.'

Grace made sympathetic noises. She asked what the police were saying at their briefings, and he told her. In return she told him about Lewis's two employees. She didn't know anything about them, she said, other than that they were called Bill and Charlie and one of them lived in Guildford. He thanked her for the lead, but doubted that his editor would be interested. It was the innocent victim everyone wanted to know about, not the killer's workmates. The possibility that the suspect might be anything other than a hundred per cent guilty had clearly not entered his head, and nor, Grace reflected soberly to herself as she walked home, was it likely to enter anybody else's, prospective jurors included.

Back in the office she checked the answering machine, sorted through a late delivery of post and went through her diary for the week, crossing everything out. She had been scheduled to spend the next few days in London, on the trail of a sixteen-year-old girl who had gone missing. The girl had packed a bag and disappeared without leaving a note. After meeting the parents, Grace rather sympathized, but they were frantic, and more to the point they were loaded, and they wanted their little darling back desperately. Grace had got hold of a promising lead through talking to the girl's friends, but that would have to go on ice for a few days, grief-stricken parents notwithstanding. There was also a meeting scheduled with a woman who thought that her husband might be a secret transvestite. Grace rang to postpone the appointment. Then she rang Terry Hoffman.

Terry always dropped everything when Grace rang because he respected her so very much. That was what he said anyway. It probably explained why he found it so hard to concentrate on anything other than her neck or hemline whenever they met. She flirted mildly enough to keep his interest buoyed, but never sufficiently to give him any real encouragement. She knew that she was safe because although he had a reputation for toughness it didn't extend into his private life. His timidity, she suspected, was rooted in his fear of his wife, a frighteningly bright former barrister well known these days as one of the sharpest judges on the circuit. One glance at her across the breakfast table, Grace suspected, would have been enough to make any husband plead guilty and beg mitigating circumstances.

The only bright thing Lewis had done was to ask for Terry Hoffman at the police station. Terry had just come back from seeing him in Farnham, headquarters of Surrey's Waverley Division. Lewis had been charged and was still in the cells, waiting for a transfer.

'No, he's not looking too good,' Terry told her in answer to her question. 'I was going to ask them to put him on suicide watch, but apparently they've already done it.'

'I don't think he's the suicidal sort somehow. Still, better safe. Did he tell you anything?'

'Sort of. He's a bit fazed, I'm afraid, not with it. I asked him the questions you gave me. He perked up a bit when I mentioned your name. You have that effect on chaps, Grace, perhaps you've noticed. I did remind him, gently, that you didn't want your name dragged into it. I think he took that on board.'

Terry told her more or less what she wanted to know, some minor details to help fill in the picture Lewis had painted of his relationships with the McGoverns. Grace had made notes from memory of everything Lewis had told her on the night of the murder, but there were gaps, both of logic and fact. She had needed more information.

But what was she going to do with the information now she'd got it?

She looked at her two pages of densely packed notes. Despite her years of experience she was still affected with the filmic notion that if a mystery had a beginning then it must have an end, with a solution to neatly wrap up the untidy odds and ends. Detective work was about routine and procedure, not a matter of being struck by intuitive lightning. And yet that what was she waiting for, a bolt from the blue that would prove the unproveable.

Yes, there were holes in McGovern's story, but nothing that would cause more than a raised eyebrow in court. So what if she or anyone else were to testify that McGovern had hated his wife? In the circumstances it was hardly likely that the man would have volunteered the information himself. Under oath he could either admit that he had lied to save embarrassment, or try and pretend that everything had changed in the last year. McGovern was nothing if not a plausible liar. Lewis, with a story that sounded more like bad fiction every time she thought it through, wasn't going to have a chance. He was looking at life imprisonment, a twenty stretch at least, even the distant possibility of parole in his last years dependent on his admission to a crime he had not committed. Perhaps Bob Challoner was right. Getting involved was a waste of time. It wasn't too late to get out, of course, but there was that little nagging matter of truth and justice. She didn't have a clue how she was going to prove any of it, but in the meantime, while she was waiting for that lightning strike, she could at least go through the motions of methodology and routine. And she did have one advantage. McGovern was not going to have the slightest idea that she was after him.

She rang George Courtenay's number and told his message service that she would be mostly out of the office and on her mobile for the next few days. Then she changed into jeans and sensible boots and put on the old Barbour she always wore out of town. She filled one of the deep pockets with her purse and a thick bunch of keys she kept hidden in the back of the kitchen cupboard, for emergencies only. George called the outfit her country rambler's gear, and he could usually be relied upon to make the same quip about her going off in search of needles and haystacks. George's utter predictability, which she had once found only irritating, she now considered to be his greatest virtue. He was like a comfort food, a lodestar in an uncertain world. And the fact that he was never around made him the best of all partners.

She found her old white Renault more or less where she last remembered parking it and picked her way through the slow-moving traffic to the A3. She was at Lewis's barn in under half an hour. There was no sign of any police. She turned around, drove past slowly to make sure, then parked where Lewis had parked the night of the murder, down the bridle track. She crossed the field and climbed over the fence.

The central panel of the door to the barn bore the mark of a battering ram. The door had a shiny new lock, a replacement for the one smashed in during the forced entry. It was good to see her former colleagues behaving so conscientiously. She produced the thick bunch of keys from her pocket. They were George's prized possession, a set of comprehensive skeleton keys that would open ninety-nine per cent of all known locks. He had been given them by one of his oldest and most regular collars, an old-fashioned, which is to say nonviolent, petty larcenist and minor conman whose speciality was turning over hotel rooms. George, who had a soft side that is more common than policemen would like the public to know about, had visited the old crook in the hospice where he had been seeing out his final days, and the keys had been a parting gift. Not a lot of use to him where he was going, the once quick-fingered veteran with the clumsy arthritic fingers had admitted, unless there was one he had overlooked that could get him through the pearly gates. George loved to tell the story (or rather, he loved to tell any story). He reckoned the old boy could have conned his way past St Peter without the keys, under an assumed name.

A few moments of dextrous trial and error was all it took to effect an entry into the barn. Not for the first time Grace found herself reflecting on how much easier life was unshackled by regulation and that annoying impediment, legality. Whenever she engaged in a minor criminal act during the course of an investigation she found it hard not to enjoy the sense of guilty relish.

She went up the spiral staircase to the living area, and

found it exactly as she remembered. It would have been hard to tell with a casual glance that a whole squad of heavy-booted policemen had been rifling through the place only a few days before. The popular image of the police ransacking a suspect's place, ripping up floorboards and tearing the stuffing out of cushions, might look good in TV drama, but the mundane reality was that any damage had to be paid for. Whatever they had been looking for – another gun perhaps, or more money – the place had been politely pulled apart, then discreetly put back together again. The only signs of disturbance were a few quarter-open drawers in the filing cabinet and a carelessly ruffed-up rug beneath which someone had been sniffing for loose floorboards.

Grace started at the filing cabinet. In the top drawer she found a folder full of bank statements and she scanned through the most recent pages. Both Lewis's personal and business accounts were consistently and heavily overdrawn. It wasn't hard to see the appeal of McGovern's cash. There was nothing else of interest in the other drawers. She turned her attention to the desk.

She found Lewis's Filofax in the main drawer, and put it in one of her deep Barbour pockets for safe-keeping. The names and phone numbers of Charlie Thompson and Bill Cutler were scribbled on the first page and there might turn out to be other useful addresses tucked inside. In the left-hand drawer she found a heap of unpaid bills, more testimony to Lewis's shaky finances. The right-hand drawer contained fuses and lightbulbs and some bunches of keys. One bunch was tied to a brown cardboard tag, on which the numbers '26' had been scrawled in pencil. There were two chunky keys and a small one with a strip of sticky white paper wrapped round the head, on which was pencilled a single letter, 'A'. The keys joined the Filofax in her deep pocket.

That would do, she thought to herself. She flicked quickly through the rest of Lewis's collected paperwork but didn't spot anything of interest. Nor had the police, obviously. Fortunately, the keys hadn't meant anything to them.

Grace left the barn and retraced her footsteps across the field. Out of curiosity she drove back to Guildford via the

McGovern house. There was a police car parked ostentatiously across the front drive, but the ravenous media pack which it was meant to discourage was not in evidence. If they maintained that level of disinterest, thought Grace, they'd be giving the paparazzi a bad name.

Almost as bad a name as she'd be getting for herself if she carried on the way she was going now, she concluded a little later, a freshly made coffee on her desk, feet up on same desk, while she skimmed through the pages of Lewis's Filofax. Her own name of course, did not feature in the encyclopaedic lists of the owner's female acquaintances, an omission that was scarcely likely to have concerned him in the aftermath of their one dismal night together. He had hated her the next morning, she'd seen it in his eyes. She'd given him a much better motive for murder than ever poor Julie McGovern had, though she didn't suppose that it was the kind of character reference that would count for much in court. Poor Lewis, she thought, stuck behind bars and facing the prospect of life without his seraglio. It was cruel, like putting a lion in a cage. And who was she, to think that she could get him out? A would-be caped crusader, as Bob had sneered? No, just her own woman, with attitude. And she did have another good reason for doing what she was doing.

She had always disliked Peter McGovern.

17

He had turned up at the office without an appointment. He hadn't pressed the buzzer, someone on one of the other floors must have let him in. She was on the phone when he entered, knocking peremptorily on the frosted glass and not waiting to be asked in. He had spoken over her, while she was still in conversation.

'Is your boss about?'

She didn't like his voice, either because it was harsh and unfriendly, or because she'd already decided that she didn't like him. She had ignored him, and carried on talking, though it wasn't anything important. It was just Nikki, complaining about a man.

'Excuse me, I asked if your boss was about.'

The second time he spoke the tone was a little different, almost polite. He was no fool, as anyone who had dealings with him was quick to realize. Perhaps he had picked up something from her manner, self-confident and relaxed and very distinctly nonsecretarial. It might have been the way she leaned back and put her stockinged feet up on the desk, casually crossed at the ankles, a habit that hadn't always endeared her to senior police officers.

'And what makes you think that I'm not the boss?' she asked when she had got rid of Nikki and put down the phone. His eyes had narrowed. She could see him apprising, appraising, calculating. She stared back expressionlessly.

'It says George Courtenay on the door,' he said.

'It says George Courtenay & Partner,' she said.

'Then I stand corrected. Does the partner have a name?'

'She does. And does the prospective client, if that's what he is?'

He did, and he was. A transcript of their conversation would have probably given George a heart attack, but drumming up business would never, as far as Grace was concerned, justify anything approaching what he called good customer relations, and she called forelock-tugging. If anyone wanted her services, then bluntness came with the deal. They exchanged their names and she guessed at once who he was.

'That's right,' he said. 'Very astute of you, I am that McGovern, the estate agent.'

Well, at least you'll be able to pay the bill, she thought and almost said. She responded to his insincere and suddenly oh-so-friendly grin with a thin smile, still weighing him up. Would she buy a two-up two-down from this man? No, nor even a leaky caravan. She hadn't seen anything yet to contradict her first impression that he was a shifty-eyed slimeball. And she thought she was a pretty good judge of men, always excepting the ones she slept with.

'So, Mr McGovern, how can I help? You've misplaced your poodle, perhaps?'

He had been taken aback, but she had already decided that if he didn't like the way she spoke to him then he could lump it and take his business elsewhere, even though her casebook was far from full. He hadn't though. He had told her about how his wife was betraying him, and that was the word he used – betrayal. And she had been taken aback in her turn, by his vehemence and bitterness.

'I gave her everything. Nice home, as much money as she needed, never lacked for a thing. She was nobody before I came along. I made her somebody. She had a dead-end job in a hotel then. She's never had to do a stroke of work since, not even housework. Doesn't even know where the hoover's kept. She has a cleaner three times a week, a gardener. Nice home, nice car, all the expense accounts I can give her, swimming pool. I don't ask for much in return, but I do want respect. Not unreasonable, is it? So what does she do? She's not content with lounging about all day, reading her sloppy books and watching dumb stuff on the TV. Oh no, she has to start screwing another guy. It's not as if I was depriving her, giving her any reason, is it?'

The biggest reason of all, as far as Grace could see – acute boredom. That and the fact that she was married to a man who could only measure out his life in terms of commodity. He was no oil painting either, not that that would have mattered to most women had he possessed compensating qualities. If he did, they were not in evidence.

'It's humiliating,' he said angrily. 'She's changed. I didn't notice at first. I've been working so hard. Working to keep her in style. It's been going on for months, longer if it's the guy I think it is. A builder, for Christ's sake, would you believe it? Like one of those stupid old comedy films, a Jack the lad and a willing housewife. She's become cold and distant. Freezes up if I so much as lay a finger on her. I thought it was early menopause at first. Getting all she wants with him, I suppose. Big lug of a guy, all brawn, no brain. That's her problem, too, if you ask me, No brain.'

Then why had he married her? Grace wondered, not unnaturally. Because she was pretty and pliant, or at least she had been when he had brought her down from Scotland. Over the next few weeks she found it wasn't hard to come to conclusions. Julie McGovern was still a very attractive thirtysomething, and she must have been an astonishingly pretty twentysomething when she had succumbed to her husband's dubious charms. Her function was to be a trophy, and for ten years or so she had played the part admirably. But now, in time-honoured fashion, she had realized that there was a life out there somewhere and he had decided that it was time to trade her in for a newer model. It was a familiar story, even if the husband's bitterness was unusually acute.

'She's used me, but she's not going to take me for a ride any longer. I'm going to wash my hands of her. I want you to get the evidence in black and white. Let's see how she reacts when I tell her that cushy little life is over, that I've had enough and I'm kicking her out. I won't have her back even if she gets down on her knees and begs.'

She could have refused to take on the case, of course, but

she didn't. The business needed the money, and he didn't blink when she told him her fees. It would be twenty an hour, plus VAT and plus all expenses, although that didn't usually amount to more than a few gallons of petrol. She asked for a retainer of £200 upfront and he wrote her out a cheque. The other reason she didn't turn away his custom was because George had repeatedly dinned into her that theirs was a morally neutral business. It wasn't the same thing at all as having a badge and a warrant card. She might not sympathize with her clients, she almost certainly wouldn't like them, but that wasn't the point. This was a business without value judgements and if she found that hard to swallow then she should consider doing charity work for a living. She didn't find it so hard to swallow, and Christian Aid wasn't her style.

'I'm not going through this again. I've had it before, you see. At least my first wife had the decency to up sticks and jump before she was pushed. Just phht!' – with a snap of the fingers – 'now you see her, now you don't. Best way to do it. I was glad to be rid of her, if truth be told. Never heard from her again, thank God. Never will. No comebacks. But this is different. Julie may be dim, but she's grasping. She'll want to take me to the cleaners if I divorce her. That's why I want all the evidence I can get of her adultery. Photographs, tapes, whatever it is you do. As graphic as you can get. Don't worry about hurting my feelings. It's a bit late for that.'

He was a complex mixture of a man, Peter McGovern, and she observed him over the coming weeks with a degree of interest, suitably detached. It turned out that he did have charm of a kind, after all, but it wasn't natural, it was just a prop to be employed when the occasion demanded. He was energetic, and quick-witted, and knew his own mind. He had the gift of the gab and could hold an audience with his clever talk, even if his wit was too obviously cruel. In short, he had a few attractive qualities to make up for his unprepossessing appearance and his naturally unappealing manner. Grace didn't doubt that when the time came he would be able to acquire another female appendage to replace the one he was so anxious to discard. He was certainly interested in women.

Grace noticed him staring at her legs when he didn't think she was looking. Professional considerations apart, she felt not the slightest temptation to flirt.

His anger when she presented him with the concrete evidence of his wife's infidelity, the tapes and the photographs and the record of times and places, was impressively controlled. A little colour might have drained from his face, but he wasn't exactly ruddy-cheeked to begin with. Similarly, the narrowed suspicious cast of the eyes was nothing new. But the eerily even tone of his voice gave him away. Here was a man intent on wrestling his inner demons into submission while presenting a mask to the outside world. The contrast with his raw hurt during their first meeting could not have been more striking. He must have decided beforehand that there would be no ranting or raving. He wasn't quite able to feign indifference, but he did a pretty good job of suggesting that it wasn't that big a deal, after all. He was quite an actor. He had thanked her for all her hard work, as if it had been some secretarial assignment. She had handed him the dossier and he had put it into his briefcase.

'What do you think about this man, the builder?' he had asked her suddenly.

More than she was prepared to tell him, that was for sure. She said she knew little about him professionally other than that he seemed good at his job, and nothing about his personal life.

'I mean, do you think he's attractive, speaking as a woman? Good-looking, isn't he? From the photographs, anyway.'

She told him that he was good-looking in the flesh as well, if you liked that sort of thing.

'So you mean you can understand why she fell for him? Perhaps you sympathize. You'd have done the same in her place, maybe. Perhaps you think it's not her fault.'

She said that it wasn't up to her to apportion blame.

'But do you think I should forgive her?'

Not her place to say, she said.

'No, I can see that. I was just interested in your woman's angle again. You don't have to venture an opinion, but if you want to you can just shake your head or nod. This man, this builder, it's just sex he's after. He doesn't love her, does he?'

She hesitated, not wanting to take a step beyond professional necessity, but feeling uncomfortable under his intense stare. Reluctantly she shook her head. He seemed relieved.

'Good. That's not a situation I would relish, not . . . not now. Tell me. This man. Your report's very thorough, I commend your diligence, but . . .' He had taken the dossier back out of his briefcase and was flicking through it, apparently looking for something. He stopped suddenly and jabbed his finger at one of the pages. 'This credit check you ran is interesting. Obviously not his money my wife is after. Nor his brains from the look of it. One O level first time of sitting, three more at the retakes. Expelled from school too, hardly a model student. Academic ability doesn't mean anything, of course, but he's no rocket scientist, is he?'

She shook her head.

'I'm willing to bet my wife isn't the first employer he's seduced. Would you say I'm right?'

She nodded.

'Yes, so I don't have to worry about . . . I mean, they're not about to go and set up home together. Even so, it's not a nice situation, not nice at all. I bet he'd like to get his hands on her money. Correction, *my* money. He fancies himself from these photographs, I'd say. Type of man who can't walk past a window or a glass door without looking for his reflection in it, wouldn't you say?'

She nodded, impressed by his astuteness despite herself.

'And he never had the slightest idea he was being followed? You're sure? Good. Good. You've been very helpful. Thank you. I like to know what people are thinking. It helps me to keep ahead. Would you like me to write you a cheque now?'

She said that she hadn't yet made up the bill.

'Well, when you do I'll pay on the dot. You've done well, been very professional, very discreet. You know my office is only round the corner, of course, but I'd be grateful if you didn't just drop by with the bill, not that you would, I'm sure. Be sure to mark the envelope "Personal".'

They had shaken hands at the door.

'Thank you very much,' he said. 'I won't say it's a pleasure having done business with you, but it's pleasing to see you handle things so well. I expect I'll be in touch with you shortly, when I've decided how to proceed. This matter will, of course, remain strictly confidential.'

'Of course.'

'Where are you from, by the way?'

His sudden change of tack, and the dazzling if none too convincing friendliness of his smile, left her momentarily nonplussed.

'Er . . . how do you mean?'

'Your accent, Miss Cornish, it's very familiar. Let me guess. You're from Derbyshire originally, aren't you?'

'Well . . . no, actually. I'm Lincolnshire. Born and bred.'

'Really? I am surprised . . .'

And he seemed it. The smile disappeared as rapidly as it had arrived. He started to go out of the door, then stopped as an afterthought struck him.

'It's twenty-six by the way.'

'I'm sorry?'

'My office, for when you're addressing the letter,' he said over his shoulder, starting to go down the stairs. 'Number twenty-six.'

She banged the door shut firmly on him. She had never been happier to see the back of a paying customer.

18

It was three o'clock in the morning; starless, moonless, cold and drizzling; the kind of night when anyone sensible would be firmly tucked up in a warm bed. As she shivered and checked her watch by the light of a misty streetlamp, Grace rather regretted not being sensible. She put her gloved hands back into the pockets of her Barbour and walked on, passing Number 26, McGovern & Co, Estate Agents and Surveyors, Private and Commercial Lettings, etc. There was a pretty thatched cottage advertised in the middle of the window display, but the light was too dim for her to be able to read the price, although she suspected that that wouldn't be pretty at all. It was an expensive area not to be sensible in.

There was no one about, of course, it was just a routine reconnaissance, but going through the motions of surveillance helped calm her nerves. Look left, look right, and try not to look too guilty: it was just the highway code for the nefarious classes. She had already broken the law once today, but this was going to be much more serious than her discreet poke around Lewis's place. She went through her well-filled pockets once again, making yet another final mental checklist. She jangled the keys for reassurance.

She walked briskly round the corner, glanced over her shoulder and listened in stillness for a moment to confirm the emptiness of Guildford by night. Then she slipped discreetly down the alley that led to the back of Number 26.

She was being ultra-cautious and didn't want to use her torch, so it took her a while to locate the door. When her fingers brushed across the lock she held her breath involuntarily, not quite believing that the key would fit. It did. She turned it, twice, and crept inside.

The alarm cut in immediately. It was a harsh, persistent electronic pulse. Depending on its setting she would have between thirty and sixty seconds to disable it before the bell went off outside and, more importantly, in the police station. Now she had no choice but to use her torch.

She flicked it on and checked out the room rapidly but methodically. It was the office Lewis had done up, the walls were still bare and the furniture mostly bunched into one corner. There was nothing here. She opened a glass door and stepped into the main office. There was a desk and chair on her right, closed off by a freestanding partition. Between the partition and the wall she could see the glass of the front window. She aimed her torch at the walls, trying to ignore the frantic rhythm of the alarm, a sound like that of a heart monitor in a medical drama signalling an emergency. There was a metal cabinet to her left, just inside the main office, at head-height. She flipped it open and saw a tiny light above a panel, flashing in time to the electronic pulse. She put the small key, the one marked 'A' for 'Alarm', into the lock on the panel, and turned. How long would she have to get out, she wondered, if it didn't work? She needn't have worried. The noise, and the light, cut out at once.

She closed the panel door and leant back against the wall to get her breath. Now she was in there was no need to rush. She waited a minute until her heartbeat was stable again, then went back into the office at the rear.

She sat down at McGovern's desk. It was bare, apart from a telephone, a computer and a keyboard. There were three drawers. The one on the right was full of stationery, the one in the middle contained a desk diary. She held the torch over it and scanned through quickly. Anyone out in the alley could have seen the light, but now she was inside that was a million to one shot and not worth worrying about.

The diary was a record of appointments. The previous two weeks, up to the murder, were blank. Across the top of the first two pages, covering the first week, he had scrawled, in red ink, 'Away'. There were no future appointments, and just one entry, again in red ink, against December 12th. 'C – B'day'.

The drawer on the left was locked, but George's trusty skeleton set made light work of getting in. Inside were two boxes of floppy disks and four large manila folders. One folder contained petrol receipts, another bank and credit card statements. The third, marked 'For Filing', was filled with copies of recent faxes and letters. Most were from clients, but there was one fax from a hotel in Brighton, confirming a booking. It was marked 'For the attention of Mr Wilson'. She checked the cover sheet. It had definitely been sent to this office. There was another letter from an agent in Buxton concerning a cottage in the Peak District. McGovern, apparently, was the owner. The property was in serious disrepair and the agent was trying to explain that in the circumstances it wasn't surprising that there had been only one let all summer. Someone, it looked like McGovern from what she had seen of his handwriting, small and neat, had written the word 'Roughwood' across the top of the letter. The same word was on the front of the fourth manila folder, the thickest. She scanned through it. The dozens of letters inside all concerned the property in Derbyshire, which was called Roughwood Cottage. She flicked through to the bottom of the pile and saw that the earliest letter dated from eleven years earlier. It had been addressed to a Mr Wilson at a house in Godalming.

She glanced again at the hotel fax. It was dated two weeks ago, and confirmed that a double room had been booked from the 15th for two nights. 'We look forward to seeing you both on the 15th', it ended. She got out the folder with the credit card statements and cross-referenced them. A payment of £286.40 was recorded against the name of the hotel on August 16th. There were some other interesting payments on the same page, over £150 to Kookai, and £90 to La Sensa, the lingerie chain. She noticed for the first time the name of the account holder in the top-left corner of the paper. It was Peter Wilson. She flicked through the piles of statements. AmEx and Mastercard were in the name of McGovern and were sent to his private address. The Visa statements were sent to Mr Wilson at this office.

She got out the desk diary again. It was the small hours of Tuesday the 23rd today and Julie McGovern had been murdered on the night of Friday the 19th. Three days earlier her husband had been staying in a Brighton hotel, under a pseudonym, and he hadn't been alone. Who had been sharing the double room with him? Not his wife, that was for sure. It was getting intriguing.

Grace made certain everything went into the right folders and put them away again in the drawer before relocking it. She sat back in the high comfortable leather chair and tried to put two and two together. Acquiring an alias wasn't difficult in Britain. You didn't need official approval, you could just write to whomsoever it concerned and declare the name by which you henceforth wished to be known. It was one of the apparent benefits of living in a free society. Getting credit might present problems, but those were far from insuperable, and, in any case, it was very simple to make it official and change a name by deed poll. Tabloid papers were regularly full of individuals who had decided to rename themselves after their football teams, their favourite pop group, or even, in one case so bemusing she doubted she would ever forget it, after a car numberplate. But whatever McGovern's reason she didn't think that innocent eccentrciy lay behind it. Innocence and McGovern just didn't go very well together. Of course, a man could have very good reasons for operating two identities. Or else he could have something to hide.

She leant forward and turned on the computer. She wanted to see if there were any further clues on his hard disk, but when the machine had finished booting up she encountered her first obstacle. A box on the screen demanded that she type in a password. There were five asterisks in the box, five numbers or letters in a combination that would require a fair few monkeys equipped with keyboards to crack. She checked the diary for a clue. What about his birthday? It was usually something dead simple like that, but she had no idea of the date. The only 'B'day' marked was that of 'C' on December

12th, and that would be six numbers. She typed in his first name, Peter. The five asterisks remained unmoved. She toyed hopelessly with random combinations for a minute, then accepted defeat and turned off the computer. It was a pity, but she had other things to be getting on with.

She got up and came round to the front of the desk. The telephone lead ran into a socket in the corner. She laid the torch down next to it, removed the single plug and replaced it with the double plug in her pocket. A sharp-eyed observer could have noticed the difference, but it was hardly likely to occur to anyone to check. The plug contained a tiny transmitter, effective up to three or four hundred yards away, depending on conditions. The ledge of her office, about a hundred yards as the crow flew, would be comfortably within range. It would make a pleasant change from the hours she usually had to spend sitting in the car waiting for her receiver to click on.

The bug had been her main reason for coming, even though she realized it might be weeks before he came back into work, but the expedition had thrown up one unexpected bonus already and there might be more. She had a quick trawl through the filing cabinet in the corner but came up with nothing of interest. She went next door into the main office.

There was another computer on the nearest desk, the one screened off from the rest of the office by the partition. Grace turned it on and trusted there was still no one outside to notice the tinge of bluish light. She hit the same password problem again, though this time there were six asterisks. She rooted through the drawers, found a powder compact, a lipstick, and a box of Tampax. The secretary, she concluded, with Holmesian alacrity. There was also a desk diary, the same size and colour – red – as the one next door, and the same format, week to view. The secretary had written her name in the front, Carol Sanders, and her address, which was in a village near Petersfield. There was a six-figure number at the top of the page, but it wasn't the computer password. Idly Grace flicked through the diary, homing in on the day of the murder, Friday the 19th. On the previous page a black ink line had been drawn through the first two days. The word 'Away' was written across the line.

Grace wanted to smile, but she was too tense. So, the mystery of who McGovern had been in Brighton with was no mystery at all. It was oldest trick in the book, everyone's favourite number one suspect, the personal secretary. Of course it was possible that she was just synchronizing her absence with her boss's, but somehow it didn't seem likely. On a hunch Grace turned the page to December 12th, and there it was, in capital letters, with a bunch of exclamation marks trailing off to the edge of the paper: MY BIRTHDAY. Yes, of course, the B'day of C, C for Carol . . .

A birthday with six numbers; the 12th of the 12th. But how old would she have been? Grace had never even seen her, but she guessed young, because that was how he liked them, fresh and impressionable. Try twenty-five then, 12–12–74. She typed in the numbers on the keyboard, but nothing. Older or younger then? Try older. She typed in 12–12–73 and pressed *enter*. The password box disappeared and rows of icons filled the screen.

With a silent prayer to the God she had conspicuously neglected since her confirmation, she clicked on a folder marked 'current' and examined the most recent files: letters to clients, some the same as the hard copies she had found in McGovern's drawer, none interesting. She double-clicked on the *explorer* icon and began a trawl through the mass of document files. She was looking for anything relating to the house with the shooting gallery where, according to Lewis, McGovern had made his proposition. Somehow McGovern had got hold of two handguns. Obtaining firearms in Britain wasn't as difficult as popular opinion supposed, but Lewis's description of the carefully boxed Beretta made it unlikely that the gun had been bought under the table in some public bar. McGovern had told Lewis that the owner of the place was going abroad because of the new, post-Dunblane restrictions on gun ownership. Had he sold McGovern the Beretta and the Webley before going rather than surrender them for the measly amount of government compensation? Or had the guns been held illegally in the first place, leaving him with no choice but to dump them for nothing or sell them on? Either way he was unlikely to admit anything, but it might be possible to bring pressure to bear. If McGovern could be linked to the murder weapon it would obviously blow a hole in the police case. It had to be the most promising line of enquiry, not least because she couldn't think of any others.

It took her an hour to find what she was looking for. It was a three-month-old letter to a Mr Andrew Foreman, now living at an address in Brussels. It was brief, advising only that contracts would be exchanged shortly, but there was a PS: *Hope you're finding better sport these days. Good luck and good shooting!*

There was a reference number at the top of the letter. Grace noted it down on a convenient Post-It pad and cross-checked with a folder marked 'Prospectus' which contained hundreds of files identified by similar numbers. She located 'For/1173', double-clicked and found herself looking at a photograph of a large but plain-looking red-brick house. There were further pictures of the interior, and several paragraphs of text. Tacked on to the blurb about the number of bed and reception rooms was a reference to *Outbuildings,* including *a fully soundproofed shooting gallery, offering excellent opportunities for conversion.*

Grace wrote down the address on the Post-It pad. The new owners hadn't yet moved in, as she knew from Lewis. Before closing down the computer she copied two folders she hadn't had a chance to look at on to one of the floppy disks she had seen in McGovern's drawer. The disk was blank and he wasn't likely to miss it. And if she was ever going to be done for breaking-and-entering then they might as well chuck in larceny too. She checked her watch and saw that it was coming up to half past five. There would be stirrings in the street soon.

She tidied up, made sure all the drawers were properly closed and turned off the computer. Then she went to the panel on the wall and reset the alarm. She was out of the place within ten seconds and the electronic warning pulse had cut off almost before it had started. In the distance, she could already hear the cars of the first commuters.

She was home in two minutes without seeing a soul. She crawled into bed, exhausted but clenched up with nervous tension. By the time she fell asleep bright wintry sunlight was streaming through the blinds.

19

The steady rhythm of the train, the soothing whooshety-whoosh as the wheels ate up the miles of track, acted like a lullaby on Grace's poor tired brain. Had it not been for the constant ringing of mobile phones as the engine pulled out of Waterloo she would have dropped off immediately. As it was, she remained awake enough to register patches of Kentish countryside along with the braying voices of too many fellow passengers who thought that they were important. The tunnel, when at last it came, offered blessed aural relief. Grace rearranged herself into an almost comfortable position and managed to sleep most of the rest of the way to Brussels.

She had been up half the night two days running now. She had meant to sleep through the whole morning after breaking into McGovern's office, but with that perfect sense of timing for which local authorities are justly famed the council had decided that roadworks should commence directly beneath her bedroom window, starting promptly at eight. The pneumatic drills roused her without mercy after a pitiful few minutes of slumber. She tried to doze again, accepted after a brief struggle that it was hopeless, and roused herself. A pint or two of hot coffee went some way towards reviving her, and a generous handful of aspirin almost succeeded in banishing her headache. At ten o'clock, feeling semihuman at last, she had phoned Andrew Foreman in Belgium.

She told him that she was called Grace Evans, that she was a freelance journalist and she was writing an article on gun owners who had decided to emigrate rather than give up the sport they loved. Would he be prepared to talk to her? Oh yes, he would talk all right.

It took her a quarter of an hour to get rid of him, by which time he had done his best to furnish her with a condensed but encyclopaedic history of his thoroughly unengaging life. He was an accountant by training, originally from Nottingham. Now he wrote software. She had heard of Small Business Accounts 98, he supposed? She stalled, which was a mistake because it gave him the cue to explain to her in more detail than she cared to hear that it was one of the best-selling accountancy software packages in the UK.

She reminded him gently that it was his extracurricular activties which interested her more. His tone had darkened. The whole thing was iniquitous, he told her, an assault on civil liberties that had made Britain a laughing stock in the international community. The whole anti-gun legislation after Dunblane had been an idiotic knee-jerk reaction, hadn't it?

She hedged, but made sure the noises she made sounded sympathetic. She told him that much as she enjoyed talking to him over the phone she really would much prefer to conduct a face-to-face interview, and since Brussels was now only a few hours away by train she'd be happy to pop over any time at his convenience. Well, he had said, that could be tricky. He was going to a conference in Singapore on Saturday, moving on to Tokyo afterwards and Sydney after that, and was a bit tied up in the interim. He did have a small window the following day (his phrase), but he supposed the notice was a little short. Tomorrow, she had told him, would suit her just fine. She had rung and booked her Eurostar ticket she moment she'd been able to get him off the phone. Then she had driven out to Mr Foreman's former residence near Petersfield.

She had parked in a side lane, climbed over the fence and approached the unappealing red-brick house from the side. She knew the layout from the estate agent's blurb, and marched straight through to the back. There was the patio and lawn, as advertised, and the long low building, reminiscent of a Nissen hut, that housed the shooting gallery.

She was halfway across the grass, and reaching into her Barbour for the skeleton keys, when she noticed that the door was already open. She stopped walking, but before she could decide what to do a workman in blue overalls came out of the door.

'Hello there,' she said breezily.

The workman, a sallow youth with eyes as dull as the faded paint marks on his clothes, gazed at her without apparent interest.

'I'm from the Godalming office,' she said.

'OK,' mumbled the youth. 'Boss ain't here.'

She stared at him in her best policewoman's manner and he shifted his weight uneasily from one foot to the other. The trick was to stare and say nothing; use silence to make the other person feel guilty, even if he had nothing to feel guilty about.

'Getting more paint,' the youth volunteered after an awkward pause.

'What a pity . . .'

Grace permitted herself a sigh of relief; at least she hadn't lost her touch. But whoever the boss was he was unlikely to be as dull-witted as this gormless calf. His absence explained why no car or van was parked in the drive. Theoretically he could be back at any minute.

'How's it going then?' she asked pleasantly.

'Oh, all right.'

'Mind if I take a look?'

She didn't wait for his answer, which when it came amounted to no more than an indecipherable grunt, but strode on past him with a confident air. Confidence, or brass as Bob preferred to call it, was one of her fortes. She pulled the door right back on its hinges and thrust her head inside.

'Watch it,' said the boy listlessly. 'Wet paint.'

She could smell it. It was on the walls and the ceiling, both of which had been stripped of the soundproofing mentioned in the brochure. New windows had been put in and new floorboards had been laid. No hint of the room's former purpose remained.

'Well, that seems to be in order,' she had announced

grandly before marching off again. 'Excellent work, do keep it up. My compliments to your boss.'

And her compliments too to Peter McGovern, she might have added under her breath. He hadn't wasted any time. Knowing him he'd probably have had the alternative builders contracted and ready to go even before his wife's death. Obviously it had occurred to him that the police might just come and check out Lewis's story, even if only for form's sake. They might root around, they might even find a shell case, or a slug with an embarrassing forensic signature buried in the wall. No doubt McGovern had been careful to pick up all the pieces, but by stripping the place out he was giving himself extra protection. If she was to find the chink in his armour then she would just have to probe further afield – the other side of the Channel, for instance.

She was woken just as they were coming into Brussels by an announcement on the tannoy, repeated laboriously in three languages. She joined the queue on the platform and waved her passport at a man in a booth. It did not feel like coming into a foreign country. The station, the design of the shops, the style and the ambience all had that plastic universality of modern cities everywhere. The world was contracting into one huge advertising board for Coca-Cola and McDonald's. To eavesdrop on a conversation meant taking pot luck with any of at least half a dozen languages, but Waterloo had been a Babel too. A lot of her fellow passengers, she guessed, must have worked for the European Commission. She envied them their waiting limos as she stood in the queue for a taxi, trying to discourage an over-eager Fleming with good English and bad teeth who was offering to escort her round and show her a cool time. She told him firmly that she wasn't planning to stay in the centre of Brussels, cool times notwithstanding, but had to get out to Watermael.

'What do you want to go there for?' the man asked.

'It's where my fiancé lives,' she answered primly. He got around, her fiancé, whoever he was. Only a few weeks ago he had been enlisted to ward off the attentions of a man at a car park in Esher. Then he had been living in Kingston. He too was a citizen of the global village.

The taxi driver spoke little English and seemed uninterested in listening to her rusty French. She gave him Foreman's address on a piece of paper and he drove there at speed, through a pretty suburban landscape marred only by a profusion of potholes. After only ten minutes they had reached the outskirts of the city. They pulled up at a solid old walled town house with a prettily tiled red roof. Grace spoke into the entryphone besides the new-looking wrought-iron gates and recognized Andrew Foreman's voice. She paid off the taxi and walked through the gate into a cobbled courtyard.

Andrew Foreman was waiting at the door for her. He was tall and thin, fortysomething but with a sandyish, freckled look that made him seem boyish. He was dressed casually but expensively, in linen trousers and a cashmere pullover, though in an unfortunate choice of colours, beige and beige. His apparel merged seamlessly with his pale skin. His eyes, a muddy shade of brown, did little to dispel his general air of blandness.

He led her through to the kitchen, where a fresh pot of coffee was resting on the conspicuously gleaming Aga. The room was like something from a *Country Life* photo-shoot, all old oak furniture and sparkling clean tiled surfaces. She sat at the big old table while he poured the coffee.

'You didn't tell me who you were writing for, or I didn't ask,' he said pleasantly.

'I'm freelance. I'm hoping to sell this to the *Telegraph* or *The Times*.'

He seemed pleased. He didn't have the look of a *Guardian*-reading man. He brought over the coffee.

'We can go next door if you like.'

'Whatever you prefer, but I'm happy enough here.'

'Then we'll stay here.'

She took her mini-cassette recorder from her bag and placed it on the table.

'You don't mind, do you?'

'Be my guest. So, what do you want to know?'

She took a fresh notebook from her bag and laid it on her lap. She crossed her legs. She was wearing a navy-blue suit with a short skirt. She saw him looking at her legs as the skirt rode up her thigh. She let him look. She'd taken a lot of care to pretty herself up, and with the bags she'd had under her eyes at six o'clock that morning she'd needed to.

'Tell me,' she said earnestly, 'about your new life here.'

It turned out to be as dull as the life he had left behind, though he probably didn't see it that way. He hadn't been expecting to like Belgium, but he had been pleasantly surprised. The country was clean and well-regulated. Taxes were high, but of course his business was mostly offshore anyway. The infrastructure was excellent, and he particularly liked the roads, on which he was able to drive his Porsche at speeds he wouldn't have been able to get away with in England. He mentioned the Porsche several times during the course of the interview.

'And what about your new shooting club?'

It was home from home really, he said. He was one of a dozen new members from England. Most of the others still lived on the other side, popping over at weekends to pursue their sport (he corrected her smartly when she referred to it as a hobby). He was lucky, of course, in not being tied to any geographical location by his work. Lucky generally too, in not having ties of any kind. He was divorced, he said, no kids. He meant that he was available. She smiled sweetly. How could any girl react otherwise to the creator of SBA 98 and the owner of an electric-blue twin-turbo Porsche?

She recrossed her legs and showed him her other thigh. He apologized suddenly for being rude and asked if she wouldn't like something to eat. She had had nothing since breakfast and only put up token resistance to his suggestion that they share some cheese and pâté, and a rather good claret from his cellar. She took a much-needed break while he ferreted around for crockery and food, excusing herself with a request for the bathroom. She took the option of going upstairs because it presented more of an opportunity to satisfy her curiosity. A quick and furtive reconnaissance of the upstairs rooms confirmed a personality with an almost pathological need for neatness and order.

They continued the interview over lunch. He asked her about the journey, told her again how delighted he was that she had come this far to see him. It was a long way, wasn't it? She nodded. A long way to have to go back in one day. She was welcome, more than welcome, to stay the night, if she felt like it. There was plenty of room, as she had no doubt seen for herself. He lived all on his own.

She smiled even more sweetly than before. The box of sanitary towels in the bathroom cabinet must have been his then.

'Wouldn't your girlfriend object?' she asked innocently.

A touch of colour appeared in his pale face.

'I'm single,' he said, adding after a pause for thought: 'At the moment.'

She gave him a sympathetic look. She liked to see a man lie. Most men were hopeless at it, but there was a dangerous minority expert at deception. Fortunately Andrew Foreman did not belong to it, which made her job a great deal easier. A bead of sweat had appeared on his brow. He was expending a lot of effort in trying to look cool. No doubt he would be grateful for a change of subject.

'You know Peter McGovern, don't you?'

It took him a split second to register the name.

'You mean the estate agent?'

'Yes.'

'You know him too then?'

'Yes. In fact it was he who first mentioned your name to me. We were just having a general chat about guns, a subject in which I know he's interested, and your name cropped up.'

'Really?' He sounded surprised, as well he might have been. 'I don't know him very well. He sold my house.'

'I gathered. Peter told me about your shooting gallery. That was when I knew you must be serious about your sport.'

'I just used it for the air rifle,' he said quickly, and she knew that he was lying again.

'Terrible business about poor Peter, eh?'

'Yes . . .' He seemed distracted. 'I'm sorry, what do you mean?'

'Terrible business. About his wife. Or haven't you heard?'

He shrugged and opened his palms in a baffled gesture.

'I'm sorry. Heard what?'

'Julie McGovern was murdered last week. Shot dead in her home. Didn't you know?'

It was clear that he didn't. He stared at her.

'It's been in all the papers,' she said.

'I'm sorry, I . . . we don't see the English papers very often. Watch the BBC a bit, but . . . when did you say this happened?'

'Last Friday. She was shot through the forehead by a Webley revolver. No serial number of course, that had been filed off, but it was standard old army issue. There was another weapon found at the scene of the crime, a .22 Beretta, again no number but it had a very distinctive box, black leather calfskin, plush red velvet interior. The police are anxious to trace the original owner. Ring any bells?'

'No, I . . .' He seemed confused; again that baffled flapping gesture. 'What a terrible . . . I never met Mrs McGovern, but . . . who did you say did it?'

'Someone who'd been having an affair with her, apparently. I'm surprised the police haven't been in touch with you.'

'With me?'

This time he was too shocked even to make the gesture.

'Oh yes,' she continued glibly. 'Routine enquiry, of course, but they'll want to speak to all registered gun owners who've lived in the area recently. Those weapons, as I'm sure you appreciate, aren't Friday-night specials. They must have been in someone's collection for years. Have you ever owned a gun like that, a Beretta or a Webley?'

'No.'

She held his gaze. He didn't try to look away; he didn't even blink. His eyes were two empty muddy pools in a slack weak face. Either he'd learnt how to lie in the last ten seconds, or he was telling the truth.

'You seem to know a lot about this,' he said, a note of vague unease in his voice.

'Professional interest. Comes into my story, doesn't it? I mean the debate on gun ownership. Those guns came from a collector. Nothing like them has been reported stolen, so they must have been bought. So that could make whoever sold them an accessory to murder.'

'Now look . . .'

The unease had now spread all through his body. He was hunched forward, shoulders stooped and hands clasped together, his eyes wide with anxiety. He gave a little nervous cough.

'Look, I really don't want you to drag my name into this if that's the angle you're interested in. I'm sorry, but there's been a misunderstanding. I thought you wanted to talk about my sport and my moving abroad, not about . . . not about this.'

'It's a pretty big story back home right now, Andrew,' she said gently. 'I can't avoid it, but I do understand why you'd be uncomfortable at seeing your name in print.'

'Are you trying to stitch me up?' he demanded with a sudden burst of aggression.

If he was trying to impose himself it wasn't particularly convincing. An unfortunate high-pitched quaver in his voice rather undermined his attempted angry baritone. She didn't let on that she'd noticed. She put on her eyes-wide-open innocent look.

'Oh no, Andrew, I promise,' she said with aching sincerity. 'Look, I really do want to know about all the things we've discussed. The McGovern murder is just something that's in the news right now and has to be referred to, that's all, because people are bound to jump on the bandwagon and say that this just goes to prove why all guns have to be banned. We want to have a rational debate about it, but I know it's not easy when people get emotive. Now it's a pity, because I wanted to send a photographer out, get a shot of you with your collection in your new home, but if you'd prefer I could just quote you anonymously. You know, describe your circumstances but keep your identity out of it. How does that grab you?'

Pretty well, by the look of relief on his face. He allowed himself to relax a little back into his chair. His manner became sheepish.

'Look, I'm sorry, you probably think I'm making a fuss about nothing, but it's business. As you say, it's the emotive stuff that makes people overreact. After Dunblane, and Hungerford before that, telling people you shot was like admitting to leprosy. It dies down again, people forget, but when the papers are stoking it up – sorry, nothing personal – it doesn't do to get associated with it in the public perception.'

'You mean clients might think twice about putting in orders?'

'Well, yeah, stupid as it sounds, they might. I had a few comments last time. I can live without it, frankly.'

'I understand. I tell you what, I'm going to let you into a little secret. I'll respect your confidence, if you'll respect mine, OK?'

He nodded his head. She lowered her voice conspiratorially.

'I've got good contacts in the police. They reckon that the two guns might actually have belonged to Peter McGovern, that he kept them in the house and the murderer found them there. What do you think of that then?'

'Well I . . . I don't know.'

'Are you worried about getting him into trouble, Andrew? Because if you are, please don't. I swear this conversation is completely confidential and – wait a sec—' she flicked the off switch on her tape recorder – 'and now it's completely off the record.'

'No, no, it's not that. I wouldn't know how to get him into trouble, frankly, I don't know what he's supposed to have done. Look, perhaps I didn't explain clearly. Mr McGovern and I just had a very brief and entirely businesslike relationship. We only met a couple of times, we did talk a bit about shooting, and yes, he did seem to know something about guns, but he didn't say anything about having a collection, at least I don't think he did . . . hang on a sec, what was it he did say? I'm trying to remember . . .'

He gave the side of his head a little tap with his forefinger. Then he clicked his finger against his thumb.

'Yes, that's right, it was when I took him round to see the house. We were in my gallery at the back, and I asked him if he ever shot, and he said no, not for years. Bit of clay shooting, that was all, but he'd once been a member of a club when he lived up north. He gave it up, he said, when he got married again and came south.'

'From Scotland?'

'No, it was Derbyshire, I think. Not what I'd call north at all; he's been south too long. Yes, Derbyshire. We talked about the Peak District. I think he lived up Buxton way, either that or the club he belonged to was there. I really don't remember too well, it was just a casual conversation, but as I say, he was quite knowledgeable. Didn't say anything about owning guns, though.'

'Perhaps the police are barking up the wrong tree. It wouldn't be the first time.'

She laughed gaily, encouraging him to laugh along and dispel some of his tension. She picked up her tape recorder and put it back into her bag.

'Thank you so much, Andrew, I think I'd better be making a move.'

He didn't say anything more about her staying the night. He rang for a taxi to take her back to the station. While waiting for it to arrive they engaged in fitful, stilted conversation. She offered him further details of Julie McGovern's murder, but he didn't seem to want to know. He asked if she would let him see her piece before it was published. Since she had no intention of writing anything it was an easy promise to make. He did not try to disguise his relief when the taxi arrived.

'Don't hesitate to give me a call if you need to know anything else,' he said.

'Oh, I won't,' she said. 'You've been most helpful.'

More helpful than he could possibly have realized. He might have closed off what she'd thought was her most promising line of enquiry, but he'd given her something else to chew on. She thought about it on the train journey back from Brussels. When the mobile phones started ringing again she thought *oh, what the hell . . .* and took out her own. With more care for privacy than most she carried it down the corridor and only dialled out when she had locked herself into the first vacant lavatory.

It had rung about twenty times and she was about to give up when it was answered by a breathless but comfortingly familiar voice. He pretended to be annoyed that it was only her on the other end.

'I was in the garden,' he said. 'I wasn't going to answer it. It was your mother made me.'

She chuckled aloud, giving him further fuel to stoke up his irritation. It had always amused her that this big burly ex-rugby player, with a reputation for nervelessness and three police commendations for bravery to prove it, should wilt like one of his precious rose petals at the merest sharp glance from the five-foot-nothing stringbag (her own description) to whom he'd been married for thirty years. But he did, without fail.

'Good to see she's keeping you on your toes, Dad,' she said lightly, while she tried to get a fresh grip on a handrail as the train decelerated suddenly.

'Where the hell are you?' he asked.

'It's a long story but I'm on my mobile so I won't be long.'

'Watch out for them things, they give you brain tumours, I read it in the paper.'

'I was thinking more of the bill actually.'

'Glad to see you're still counting the pennies.'

'With you for a father how couldn't I? Look, Dad, I need to ask a favour . . .'

Despite his protestation on behalf of her health it proved difficult to shake him off. By the time he'd given her a rundown on the state of his arthritis, the state of the garden and, to a lesser extent, the terrible and declining state of the nation, her mother had come in and had demanded to be spoken to in a tone that could not be brooked. Grace tried to listen patiently while her mother filled her in on the latest developments in the lives of her brothers, cousins and the family pets, and did her best to ward off the quick barbed probing into her personal life. Between them, Grace and her father could boast forty years' experience of police interrogation procedures, but even combined they were no match for the diminutive Mrs Cornish.

Grace returned to her seat. Her conversation with her father had merely underlined how alone she was in all this. It was a bit much asking a retired pensioner to do her spadework, but who else did she have to turn to? She hadn't even bothered to mention what she was doing to George. Bob Challoner wasn't going to be the slightest bit of use. The only other person who had any idea which way she was thinking was Terry Hoffman, and she knew without any doubt that he thought Lewis was guilty and was only representing him as a favour to her. At least she had something to bite on now, another location. She remembered McGovern's surprise that her accent hadn't been Derbyshire. He obviously thought he knew the area well, and he had that cottage up there, the one his agent couldn't let. Her dad would do some rooting around for her and she could get Nikki, who was at a loose end and available for legwork, to run the standard checks on McGovern's business.

No, she wasn't completely alone, but it was still going to be up to her to get a result. What next then? She didn't have a clue. She remembered another of George's hoary old saws, delivered invariably with the ponderous gravitas of the born saloon-bar Solomon – when all else fails try the unexpected. What precisely wouldn't McGovern be expecting? She tried to think it all through logically, but the accumulated exhaustion of the last few days began to roll over her in waves. She was asleep long before the tunnel, despite the remorseless ringing of the mobile phones.

20

The girl was fussing over the tea things, laying out the cheap pyrex cups and saucers with a teaspoon each, though neither of them took sugar, and arranging the small assortment of biscuits she had taken from their cellophane wrapping on to one of the plates on the tray.

'Are you sure you don't want me to send down for some proper sandwiches?' she asked.

'No, thanks.'

He spoke curtly. He had already told her exactly what he did or didn't want and he wasn't the kind of man to change his mind, as she should know by now. It was a good thing she was going back to Guildford.

The kettle boiled and she filled the metal teapot to the brim, the little tags from the bags hanging limply down the side on their narrow threads. She brought over the tray and put it on the low table next to him. He was sitting in the only armchair. She sat opposite him, on the bed.

'Shall I be mother?' she said simply.

'Let it brew.'

She nodded. She usually did what she was told, she was a good girl really. It was impossible not to think of her as a girl, even though she was nearer thirty than twenty. She had a girlish way of talking, and a girlish way of thinking. She was uncomplicated and uncomplaining, and she thought he was the cleverest man ever. Maybe he had at last chosen right this time, even if her vacant twitterings did annoy him.

She was agitated. She kept feeling for the list he had given her, which was in her jacket pocket. And she kept looking at her watch.

'You'll have plenty of time,' he said. 'Pour the tea.'

He took the proffered cup and one of the biscuits. He spoke between munches.

'Don't worry if the press are there, they can't do anything. Don't talk back, if they speak to you. Remember, they're sending a policeman to be outside the house. If they start harassing you, go to the policeman.'

'What if they follow me away?'

'Well, you're not coming here, are you? You're just going back to your place. When they see I'm not there they'll lose interest. You're not frightened, are you?'

She shook her head, but he could see that she was. She was a timid creature, one who needed the world to be safe and predictable and easy. She was a sheep, like most of them out there, the natural prey of the cleverest man ever.

'Do I really have to go, big bear?'

No, she didn't. He said:

'Yes, Carol.'

She sipped at her tea unhappily. When she next looked at her watch he looked at his as well.

'I think you'd better be making a move, love.'

He fetched her coat for her from the peg behind the door.

'It'll be all right,' he said. 'You just have to get the suits and the shoes, nothing else. You don't have to go anywhere near the bedroom.'

It was the thought of being near where the murder had been committed that worried her, and he could understand. But the policeman was going to go into the house with her, be on hand while she went into the spare room at the back where he kept his overflow of clothes, the ones there had been no room for in the bedroom because of Julie's near monopoly of the cupboard space. She was to get the clothes on the list, nothing more, she'd be in and out in five minutes. He'd told her so enough times and he didn't propose telling her so again. The bedroom was still sealed anyway and the police would steer her well away. He pecked her on the cheek, patted her on the bottom and shooed her out of the door. Then he went back and finished his tea.

It was a relief to be alone. Although he'd booked separate

bedrooms for himself and the girl, for appearances' sake, she'd been hanging round him the whole time, in constant need of a level of reassurance which it was not in his nature to give. She actually felt guilt over Julie's death, ridiculously. It troubled her that she had been sleeping with him for the last six months, as if in some way her sin must be linked to the other. She had used that very word, sin. It was quite incongruous. She wasn't in the least religious, though she was consumed by superstition. She was an avid reader of horoscopes and couldn't leave home unless she was wearing her lucky brooch. If she hadn't been so devoted to him it would have been too tedious having her around.

He put down his empty cup and wandered over to the window, to check out the weather. They had been in Bournemouth for three days now, and it had rained on every one of them. It had been the police's idea that he should get away. With all the media attention, going back to the house was out of the question. The police had suggested that he stay with friends. In fact he had stayed with Carol, but the village where she lived was just too small, and it would have been only a matter of time before the reporters had tracked him down. It might have raised eyebrows if they'd found him living with her, however plausible and innocent-sounding his explanation. A hotel offered anonymity. He was registered as Mr Wilson.

He had been keeping himself to himself and he hadn't been spotted. He had watched the news bulletins and read all the papers with forensic scrupulousness. There hadn't been all that much about him, which was both satisfying and oddly aggravating. The coverage had all focused on Julie and the builder. He had given the media, through the police, some photographs of Julie, and they had somehow obtained good photographs of Lewis. They made a photogenic couple. The photograph he had given of himself was deliberately old and fuzzy, but they probably wouldn't have wanted anything better anyway. He knew, from experience. Far better, from the press's point of view, to concentrate on the obviously attractive pair, to squeeze every ounce of voyeurism from the twin horrors of sex and violence. The poor schmuck in the middle shouldn't be too surprised if he found himself squeezed out from such a juicy sandwich.

Nor was he. No, there had been no surprises. What he had expected had come to pass. Forward planning was not such a difficult art to master.

He lit a cigarette and enjoyed the long deep drag into his lungs. Nor was lying so difficult. It was just an extension of selling. Tell people what they wanted to hear. Convince any member of the herd that he wasn't exactly that and he'd be grazing out of your hand. You, sir, you're a man of taste, discernment, so this is just for you . . . The world was full of unexceptional people who wanted to be thought exceptional. But if it had to be thought, then it couldn't be real. The real world was the one you moulded with your own hands, not the one you dreamt behind your eyes. The dreamers were the buyers of scratch cards and lottery tickets. The realists bought stock in the company that sold them.

He was glad he'd chosen Bournemouth, the bad weather notwithstanding. He'd be moving away from Guildford shortly and this looked a promising area for a fresh start. Fresh starts were essential, he had learnt that long ago. It might take a while to sell the house, because of its notoriety, but he'd have no problem offloading the business, and for a handsome figure. He wouldn't choose the same line, though. Property development, that's what he would concentrate on, but he'd keep his eyes and ears open for other business opportunities. Why not? He was a wealthy man and could afford to dabble. He wondered how long the insurance company would take to pay up over Julie. Half a million pounds they owed him. When he'd taken out the policy a year ago he'd wondered about setting it even higher, but in the end he'd decided to rein himself in just this side of greed. He'd had half a million on each of them, so as not to draw attention. He hadn't ever mentioned it to her, of course. Why bother? He had never intended that she should collect.

So it was handsome profits all round. Instead of leaving himself in a position of vulnerability where she could take him to the cleaners at any time, demanding alimony and half his hard-earned capital, he was home free. Nor did he have to look at her stupid, grasping face any more, listen to her wheedling and whining, or worse, her reproachful silences. He didn't have to lie awake at night, hearing her deep, guiltless breathing, while he imagined how she had been writhing beneath her lover only hours before, calling out his name in her ecstasy, just like in the tape recordings he'd heard, not giving a thought to the poor fool who put the bread on her plate or paid for the sheets in which she sweated out her pleasure, unless to laugh him off, to blast him with her scorn and bile.

He took a last, very deep drag of his cigarette, wanting to calm himself down. It took nothing for the anger and bitterness to flare up inside him, but that was done, he didn't want to dwell on it any more. A fresh start, that was the agenda. He had to keep telling himself. But there were lessons to be absorbed. He'd keep a close watch on Carol. She would come and live with him, of course, but he wouldn't rush into marriage, not like he had done with Julie. Then he had been rebounding from Margaret, feeling insecure and in need of the uncomplicated adulation which Julie had seemed to offer so naturally. But Julie had been deceptive, more selfish than he had realized. He didn't think Carol was like that, but he would take his time, make sure first. Carol was weaker than Julie, more clueless and much more frightened of the world. Her bed was covered in teddy bears and soft toys. She'd always been a daddy's girl, but her daddy had died when she was little, and now she clung to him, her big bear. She had had boyfriends her own age, but she obviously hadn't cared for them. She wasn't much interested in sex, which suited him. He had his needs, of course, and she was suitably accommodating. But it was an overrated activity, and time-consuming. Julie had thought the same way once, until the builder came along.

He felt the anger flare again. He screwed up his eyes and closed his fingers hard around his lighter, literally getting a grip. There was no need for this, he told himself, no need any more. The revenge had been taken, and it had all worked out even better than anticipated, much better. What he had been expecting was that it would come down to cross-examining in court, the odds stacked heavily in his own favour, but still with that possibility of a glimmer of doubt in the jury's eyes – when push came to shove a matter of his word against the builder's. He would have had the scientific evidence on his side, of course, the man's fingerprints on the gun and his unquestionable presence at the scene of the crime, but he would have had to go into the witness box knowing that he had to perform. He would no doubt still be called as a witness, but not so much would ride on it now. Not only had the fool tried to run away, he'd pulled the other gun on the police and been caught with his bag stuffed with money. And to think that the thing that had most worried him had been the builder's shrewdness! Oh, the irony of it all . . . What a pair, Julie and Lewis; deserving victim, and deserving victim.

It was three o'clock. He turned on the radio to listen to the news out of habit, but there was nothing, of course. The media had already turned its attention to the case of a girl murdered in the West Country. The preliminary hearings were all done in his own case, the builder was remanded in custody and wouldn't be dusted down again for the cameras until the trial. That wouldn't be for at least six months, the nice Superintendent Collins had told him. So helpful, the police had been. He was on first-name terms with them all. Jimmy Collins was coming down to see him tonight, one of the reasons he had wanted to be rid of the girl, not that Jimmy would have noticed anything, or cared even if he had. Jimmy was so thrilled with the whole business it was clearly an effort for him to remember to sound sympathetic and respectful. Jimmy had said he should be down about five, five-thirty at the latest. Plenty of time, then, for him to take a walk. It seemed to have stopped raining at last. He'd better take advantage while he could.

He put on his raincoat anyway and took his umbrella. He went down in the lift and left his key at reception. The lobby was empty, in keeping with the general out-of-season air of both hotel and town. It was the kind of place where people seemed to mind their own business. He approved.

He walked down to the seafront, past the Pavilion Theatre and on to a stretch of green where an old woman was feeding the sea birds. It was beginning to get dark already and there weren't many other people about. He sat down on a bench and took out his cigarettes. The wind was gusty, it took him three attempts even with his spare hand cupped over his lighter to keep it alight. He enjoyed the feel of the wind on his face after so long cooped up in his hotel room. He smoked his cigarette slowly, pleasurably, down to the butt.

'Bracing, eh?' said a woman's voice close by.

He only half glanced at her, just enough to take in that she was youngish, blondish, tallish. He was annoyed. Why was she sitting down on his bench, when there were so many empty ones all around? He edged away from her instinctively.

'How have you been keeping then, Mr McGovern?'

He stopped in the act of putting his cigarette to his lips. He knew her now, from the voice alone. Lincolnshire, not Derbyshire, she'd put him right, of course. His mind went blank for a second, and then it started racing. Coincidence? Not likely. Then what? Nothing good, that was certain. Nothing good at all. He ground out the stub of his cigarette carefully with his heel, then took his time before turning his head in her direction, wanting to be sure that he had mastered his surprise, and the situation, first. He injected a tone of jauntiness into his voice.

'And what can I do for you, Miss Cornish?'

She returned his smile. Her own voice sounded unnaturally sweet.

'Well, you could always tell me why you murdered your wife . . .'

21

The wind was kicking up sharply now, muffling the noise of the sea birds wheeling overhead and making them sound more distant than they were. He noticed, with mild curiosity, a light flashing out to sea where the dim shape of a boat was making its slow way through a heavy sea. It seemed to be hanging still under the lip of the horizon, giving an impression of stateliness when in reality it was no doubt being buffeted from side to side. He had always been impressed by the brute force of the sea.

'That's not a very funny thing to say, you know,' he said mildly.

'Oh no,' she agreed. 'If I'd wanted laughs I'd have gone to the pier, not here.'

He kept his eyes on the boat. He had decided that he wasn't going to look at her, though he could sense her staring at him. He didn't like the cool confidence of her tone, though it had impressed him once, not long ago. Impressed him enough to hire her, despite his instinctive aversion to putting his trust in women. His hunch had been correct, and she had done her job well. She was probably only a little older than Carol, but there was nothing girlish about this one. He'd be very surprised if this one had a bedroom filled with teddy bears.

'Is there something you want from me?' he asked, resisting the temptation to reach for his cigarettes. Were he to light another straightaway, which he wanted to, it might just let on that he wasn't quite as relaxed as he was pretending to be. He brushed some ash from his coat, nonchalantly.

'Fifty thousand pounds,' she said.

Now he wanted a drink to go with the cigarette, to moisten the drying throat.

'Well, that makes a change from the wino who stopped me outside my hotel this morning. He only wanted the price of a cup of tea.'

'He didn't have what I've got.'

He twisted his neck suddenly and faced her. She didn't blink. He saw her blue hard eyes, as pale as the sea.

'I don't have the first idea what you're on about,' he said, putting anger into his voice. 'But I don't think it's in very good taste. I warn you that if you're going to harass me I shan't hesitate to call the police.'

'I'm sure you won't. It is what you did last week, after all. I know, because I was there.'

He needed the cigarette too much now. To his relief the lighter caught first time and the nicotine flooded his lungs in seconds. He recrossed his legs and leant back in the bench. His eyes sought out the boat on the horizon.

'Congratulations,' he said. 'You have a very vivid imagination.'

'That's true, but in this case I didn't need it. I saw Lewis Young go into your house the night your wife died. I saw him come running out a few minutes later. He looked terrified. Not surprising. She must have looked a sight, your wife. Bullet between the eyes, you'd have to hate her quite a lot to go that far. But you did, didn't you? Hate her, I mean. I remember the look in your eyes when you sat in my office. I wondered why you never went through with the divorce. Much cheaper this way. I reckon you must have saved yourself a fortune. Hard to put a figure on, but half the house and alimony over a lifetime would have come to millions. Can afford to push a little bit of it my way then, can't you?'

Clouds had obscured the wintry sun. It was getting too cold to be sitting out on a bench. He felt a drop of rain strike the tip of his nose.

'You've taken your time to think this little story up, haven't you?' he said.

'It's taken time to find you.'

'Well, I'm sorry it's been wasted. Very nice running into you again, Miss Cornish. You'll forgive me, but I have to be going now.'

'But if you go now, Mr McGovern, I'll have to talk to the police. And that would be a real waste. Why don't you at least finish your cigarette? You might as well enjoy it, seeing as you've made such a miraculous recovery from cancer.'

That hadn't been in the papers, he thought. The chill of the wind had got into his spine, he felt himself shiver.

'You must still have good friends in the police,' he said. 'I forgot, for a moment, but of course that's what you are, isn't it? You may have handed in your uniform but you've got that badge tattooed inside your skin. So you're trying to put the frighteners on me, are you? Think that by recycling that madman's story you're going to put the wind up me, screw some easy money out of me. Not just an ex-cop but a bent ex-cop. Commonest variety, I've always suspected. Well, the only thing that's going to get screwed round here, lassie, is you. You, screw yourself. Me, I'm going in now.'

'I've got photographs,' she said.

He had pushed himself to the front of the bench, ready to rise. He didn't move, except to pull his collar up to mask the wind.

'Good for you,' he said hollowly. 'I've always liked holiday snaps.'

'You wouldn't like these. I've got photographs of you with Lewis Young. He's been a nice little earner for me, that boy, your putting him away is cutting me off from a fair slice of my income. Let me tell you a story, to go with the holiday snaps. There's this man, you see, came into my office a month ago. A man rather like you, successful, hard-working, with a much younger and very pretty wife. Let's call him Mr Smith – why be original when nothing else is? Seems he wanted an extension built on his house. He hired the builder, said that he'd seemed topnotch. Polite, well-spoken, reliable. You can guess the rest, can't you? It's a more familiar story than you realize. You weren't the first man to be cuckolded by Lewis Young, not even the twenty-first. Such a lovely old-fashioned word, that, isn't it? Cuckolded. You're probably used to the sound of it by now. It's our builder's stock-in-trade. No extra charge and satisfaction guaranteed. You've got to hand it to him, he's a pro. Well, my Mr Smith wasn't a happy man. Much like you. He wanted me to get evidence to confirm his suspicions. It wasn't difficult. I knew our man's habits by now, it was a piece of cake. So you can imagine my surprise when I saw him hobnobbing with you.

'You don't get real, genuine copper-bottomed surprises like that too often in this line of work, I'll tell you. It's mostly the usual sordid, predictable stuff. So up went my antennae. It didn't take a genius to realize something was going on, but I couldn't work out what. So I started following you around in my own time, out of curiosity. What on earth were you doing, I wondered, going to Mr Foreman's old house that morning? Two boys playing with guns. Not just any old guns either. Thick as thieves you were, taking it in turns to blast away. The only window was the little one in the door, so the shots I got with my telephoto lens aren't great, but they're good enough. Put them together with my other evidence and a picture emerges. To give it its name in criminal law, a conspiracy. Lewis Young told the police what he says happened, and they didn't believe him. You told the police what you say happened and they did believe you. Now let me tell you what really happened.

'Lewis and your wife had fallen out. He'd stopped seeing her, I don't know since when, but I think your wife was pretty bitter about it, about him. You knew he didn't have any scruples, and you knew he needed money. So you paid him to kill your wife. Only that wasn't enough for you, you wanted your revenge on him as well. So you double-crossed him, turned him in and denied any involvement. He was caught with his pants down, tried to lie his way out of it, failed dismally. I don't know all the details, of course, but I know enough. About fifty thousand pounds' worth, I reckon. If you don't have it I'll just have to give them away for free. I'll chuck in all the stuff I collected last year about Julie and Lewis for good measure. Why not? Perhaps you think you've got it all. You haven't. I kept copies. Did you really think I'd say nothing? Maybe you're not as clever as you think. Seems like a waste, though. You're wrong if you imagine I've got any loyalties to the police. Why do you think I left? I wasn't going to take any more from those sexist, patronizing bastards. If I'd stayed in till it was time to collect my bus pass I'd never have got another promotion. Making the tea, that's all they thought I was any good for, besides the obvious, and I wasn't giving them that. You want their opinion of me, you ask your friend Jimmy Collins. He was the worst. Do you think I'd willingly give him this stuff, let him take all the credit for nailing you? He's a smug enough bastard already. Besides, he's happy with the way things are, he knows he's got the right man, he's not fussed. So why should I be? Why should I care if our friend the gigolo takes the whole rap? He's guilty, isn't he? There's nothing for me to gain from turning you in, spreading that guilt around. You wouldn't like prison, Mr McGovern. It'd pay you to keep out of it.'

He had sat back in the bench again as she spoke, crossing his arms and huddling his body against the stiffening wind. He spoke softly, into his chin, his head bowed.

'I don't see any photographs.'

'You'll see them when you bring the money. I want cash, of course, and I know it'll take you time to raise it. I'll give you a week. But in the meantime I want a downpayment. Five thousand sounds fair. You've still time to ring your bank this afternoon and transfer the funds. Cash the cheque tomorrow morning, come straight here. Ten o'clock, let's say.'

She stood up. He looked her in the eyes again, searching for signs of softness. He saw none. A fine drizzle had begun to fall.

'What if it's raining?' he said.

'Bring your umbrella.'

He watched her walking away, fast but somehow unhurried, so purposeful, so sure of herself. Was she trying to set him up? He thought through their conversation, trying to recall exactly what he had said. He'd been careful, he hadn't incriminated himself, he'd just listened. If she'd been wired then she wouldn't have got anything. What next then? He'd been caught flat-footed, but even the best-laid plans could go awry. The trick was to remain flexible. He knew that trick. He knew a lot of others too.

He sat in the gathering gloom, watching the flickering light on the distant boat, no longer feeling the cold. He had plenty of time before the policeman was due. He lit another cigarette.

22

The evening meal, advertised to begin at seven-forty-five sharp, had precisely as much appeal as could be expected in an English seaside hotel out of season. The only surprise was how quickly the dining room filled up. There were three couples, two elderly and wearing the grim pasty looks of weekenders determined as if by decree to enjoy the bracing sea air, and one, tucked with suitable discretion into a corner, much younger, who gave the impression of something altogether more illicit. Their constant touching, above and beneath the table, and heightened whispered conversation hinted at a kind of intimacy quite out of place amidst so much functional chintz. Some of the half-dozen unattached men, travelling-salesman types dotted singly about the room, stole occasional sidelong glances at them, perhaps out of envy, more likely out of curiosity. Some of them seemed quite interested in Grace too.

She sat, self-consciously at first, on her own. As the dining room had filled she had been gripped, briefly, by the fear that there might not be enough tables and she might be forced to share her square of faded floral tablecloth with a stranger. She buried her head in her newspaper, spread out in unwelcoming occupation of both the places set on the table, and waited for the danger to pass. Finally, when a full five minutes had elapsed since the arrival of the last stray traveller, and the soup was served, she permitted herself to breathe easy again. The diners proceeded to their task in a silence broken only by the scraping of spoons on china, and the occasional overheated whisper from the couple in the corner.

Soup was followed by something grey and overcooked that was unrecognizable from its description in the menu. The unappetizing nature of the food scarcely mattered. Grace was too tense to feel hunger. She scarcely even went through the motions of picking at her plate. The humourless overworked waitress removed it after a period of time without so much as a reproving glance. From its peeling faded portico to its topmost functional garret, this hotel was a take-it-or-leave-it establishment, with the latter the more popular option.

Grace declined a dessert and regretted ordering the watery coffee. It was a quarter past eight. Rarely had an evening stretched ahead with less invitation. In desperation she had consulted the television pages of her newspaper, but no joy was to be found there. The small portable set in her bedroom, one of the misleadingly long list of amenities to be found in the hotel brochure, would in likelihood remain unwatched tonight. What was there to do, in such a place, with so many blank hours to fill? There was a small and seedy bar next to the dining room, but even had it been more inviting she felt that it was to be avoided. She had enjoyed, up to a point, a single glass of white wine during the meal, but had too much self-knowledge to consider repairing to a barstool for the remaining licensed hours of the evening. The last thing she needed in the morning was to wake up with a hangover. She would need her wits about her if she was to have a chance of getting anything out of McGovern.

The thought of him filled her with dread. Until now she had worked in the shadows, but here she was out in the open. Surprise had been her biggest weapon, but McGovern hadn't crumbled. Had she expected him to? No, but he might have looked at the least a little nervous. She remembered his expressionless face, giving nothing away even as she had felt his eyes trying to strip her face. She hadn't blinked, but nor had he. A thought flashed into her head, a mental picture of herself lying in that little garret upstairs, turning restlessly into the small hours, too wound-up to sleep. Already she could sense a nagging tension foreclosing on her brain, that familiar presage of insomnia. It felt like a self-fulfilling prophecy.

She abandoned the watery coffee and her fellow diners and walked out into the lobby. She could hear the wind outside, and could see the glistening of raindrops on the glass in the front door. She went upstairs to fetch her coat and scarf.

Outside it was even windier than she had realized, though mercifully it was less wet. She walked briskly down towards the seafront, filling her lungs with the sharp air. It made her feel light-headed, and also a little hungry. Succumbing to a sudden chocolate craving she headed for the cafés and kiosks near the sea, but all were closed. There was no one in sight and the roads seemed equally deserted. Somehow she didn't think that this was a town bursting with twenty-four-hour shops. She walked on, though, because there was nothing to go back to, and a sense of motion helped keep the circling thoughts in her head at bay. And perhaps, too, there would be a chance of coming across a late-night garage. But the dark empty streets were a desert for impulse buyers.

She walked till her calves ached. At one point she had passed the facade of McGovern's hotel, faintly splendid and so far removed from the seaside shack where she was spending the night that it seemed like an idiocy of language for one word to embrace both locations. She had peered in through a brightly lit window and seen faces and figures, clearly enough to know that McGovern was not among them. There was a big party in the window, laughing and drinking and looking warm and at ease. Staring in from the wrong side of the glass made her feel like a starveling in a Victorian fable. She put her head down and walked back quickly to her hotel, determined to keep pathos at bay.

She was chilled through by the time she got back. It was just after ten o'clock. She hesitated, standing inside the lobby, her fingers playing with the room key on its bulky plastic tag in her pocket. Should she go up and watch something on TV? Whatever for? Because it would kill another half-hour. At least she could climb under the coverlet and warm herself up. Or she could stay downstairs and achieve the same effect by having a brandy. She wrestled with the two options, one completely unappealing, the other more than moderately attractive, for just as long as it took to convince herself that one really could mean just one, and that it might well help her sleep. Then she walked through to the bar.

She thought it was empty at first. It was only when she sat down on the nearest stool that she saw one of the window seats was occupied. One of the salesman types from the dining room was sitting on a wicker chair, a much-folded newspaper in one hand and a glass of whisky in the other. He smiled at her as she glanced across and she smiled back. He seemed quite presentable, in a salesmanish sort of way. He was thirtysomething, with a pleasant open face and nice eyes.

'You have to ring the bell,' he said.

She nodded. There was a little brass bell sitting just within reach on the counter. Feeling rather self-conscious, she stretched across and gave it a tinkle. Nothing happened.

'It's not exactly the Ritz, I'm afraid,' said the man. He was well-spoken, not posh but lacking the ubiquitous estuary twang she had grown used to in the south these days.

'I'd noticed.'

Grace rang again, more vigorously. After a protracted pause the waitress who had served them in the dining room, a thin middle-aged woman with hollow cheeks and a pinched mouth, appeared from the direction of the kitchen. She took up her position behind the bar counter and fixed Grace with an unwelcoming look.

'I'm on my own tonight,' she said, as if it were Grace's fault.

'I'd like a brandy, please,' said Grace.

The waitress picked reluctantly through the spirit bottles lined up on the shelf behind her until she found a litre of Martell. She measured it out in a metal thimble and relayed the bell-bottomed glass to Grace.

'That'll be two pounds twenty.'

'Can you put it on my bill?'

'Cash only.'

Grace produced a twenty-pound note. The woman's shoulders slumped.

'I'll have to get change,' she said grimly.

'Sorry,' said Grace, but the woman was trudging away

already and not listening. When she had disappeared from view the man in the window laughed softly.

'I've always wanted to stay in Fawlty Towers,' he said.

Grace started to laugh with him, but almost immediately saw the woman coming back across the lobby. She put her hand over her mouth and kept her eyes lowered. The woman put her change, all in coins, down on the counter, wordlessly. She started to go.

'Excuse me!' called out the man from the window.

She turned back with unconcealed annoyance. The man was out of his seat and coming up to the bar. He was holding an empty tumbler.

'Seeing as you're here, perhaps I could have a refill,' he said, putting down his glass. 'Scotch, please.'

The woman started at the glass for a few moments as if concerned that it might be a hand grenade. Then she refilled it.

'And another packet of peanuts, please.'

The man carefully added water from a jug on the bar while she raked in the heap of coins he had laid on the counter.

'You're ten pence short,' said the woman crossly.

The man patted his pocket for change. He seemed not to have any. Grace picked a ten-pence coin from the pile laid out in front of her and pushed it across the bar.

'Here. Be my guest.'

The woman scooped up Grace's silver along with the rest and retreated back towards the kitchen without another glance or word for either of them.

'Your good health,' said the man, raising his glass. Grace lifted her own glass to him and they both drank. He noticed her eyeing his peanuts. 'I expect you could do with something edible after dinner,' he said, pushing the packet along the bar towards her.

Grace returned his knowing smile.

'As you said, it's not the Ritz.'

'No. I don't think they'll be getting their second Michelin star this year.'

There was a pause, in which both of them looked at each

other, and then both smiled a little overbroadly to mask their awkwardness.

'I'm Alan, by the way.'

'Hi, Alan. I'm Grace.'

'Do you mind if I join you?'

She hesitated, and he blushed. He had seemed full of confidence coming over, something of which she was always wary, but now a kind of schoolboy shyness seemed to have gripped him.

'If you'd rather be left alone, I quite understand . . .' he mumbled, shifting his weight uneasily and developing an interest in the rim of his glass.

'No, it's not that,' she said quickly. 'I was just thinking that the chairs in the window looked more comfortable.'

'They're not.'

'Then you'd better pull up a stool.'

She watched him as he checked along the line of barstools, looking for the one with the least wobbly legs. He was about six foot, quite stocky in the body but with a narrow, almost boyish face. He had good cheekbones and the nice warm eyes which were the first thing she had noticed about him were big and hazel, the same colour as his hair. She remembered him from the dining room now. He had been wearing glasses then, sitting by himself on the other side of the room, reading a paper.

'You must be starving,' he said, offering her the packet of nuts again. 'You hardly ate a thing.'

So he had been watching her. Hardly surprising really, a lone woman, not unattractive if she said so herself, in a room full of lone men. She tried to recall the faces of the others, not that she had gone out of her way to notice. She remembered the paunchy man at the next table who had dandruff on his shoulders, and the thin, very bald one behind him who had slurped his soup like an anteater on liquids. She supposed that if she had to be stuck in the bar with any of them then this would do.

'Are you here on business or pleasure?' she asked.

'Strictly business. I'm not sure I'd come here for pleasure.'

'I can see that.'

'My secretary booked me in. I'll have to have a word. Yourself?'

'I came to see someone,' she answered without hesitation, and then, to change the subject: 'No secretary, I'm afraid, I've only myself to blame. I don't really know Bournemouth.'

'It's a good place to retire to.'

'I've heard.'

'My folks used to live round here but I think it was a bit too quiet even for them.'

'Where are they now?'

'Back where they came from, a little place in Surrey you won't have heard of called Shamley Green.'

'I know it well. Pretty quiet there too, I'd have thought. I live in Guildford.'

'You're kidding?'

'It's not something I usually joke about. Don't tell me you live there too.'

'No, I live in Kingston, but our office is in Guildford. Not that I'm there that often.'

'What sort of office?'

'A small one. I've never been a big-organization man.'

'And what do you do in it when you are there?'

'Computers, I'm afraid. I sell software. What about you?'

'Not accountancy packages by any chance?'

'Afraid not. Why, do you want one?'

'Not any more. Someone told me a lot about one recently. Enough to last for one lifetime.'

'Yeah, can be dull stuff. You didn't tell me what it is you do.'

'No.'

'Ah. Is it a secret?'

'No.' She hesitated a moment, then she said: 'I teach.'

'Really? That's what I did, once, long ago. Completely terrified me. Had to get out.'

'You mean you couldn't take spending your day in front of a bunch of sullen aggressive delinquents?'

'And that was just the staff room. You're a brave woman. You work in Guildford?'

'All around at the moment. I'm doing supply.'

'What's your subject?'

'Just at this minute I'd say it's alcohol deprivation.'

She looked down mournfully at her empty glass on the bar, wishing she hadn't wasted her time trying to be good and had asked for a large one.

'I'm not sure that I dare try ordering another,' he said, staring at the little brass bell on the counter.

'I was thinking the same. We might end up on the breakfast menu.'

'You'd have the right change at least, this time.'

'Not sure that I would after giving you that ten pence.'

'Damn. You mean for want of a nail?'

'Something like that.'

'I could risk it, though.'

'You're a brave man.'

He seized the bell and gave it a full, bold ring. Nothing happened. They exhanged glances of wry alarm and he rang it again, even louder. Still nothing happened.

'I think she's put her earplugs in,' said Grace.

'Perhaps I should go and knock on the kitchen door.'

'That'd be carrying bravery too far.'

'Perhaps you're right. Pity though.'

'Pity.'

They stared at their empty glasses. Alan cleared his throat.

'Look, it probably sounds a bit forward but . . . I've got a minibar in my room. You're welcome to come up for a nightcap, if you like.'

The suggestion took her by surprise. For a moment she couldn't think what to say. He coloured deeply.

'I mean, just a drink,' he said awkwardly.

She raised an eyebrow. It was always possible, she thought, that a man could be inviting a woman up to his hotel room for just a drink and mean exactly that; there had to be a first time for everything. She hadn't really been conscious of being chatted up, but she supposed that that was what had been going on. She supposed too that she must have been flirting at least a little in return. And why not? It was the best offer she'd had, or was likely to get, in this neck of the woods.

'I'd like that,' she said, swinging her bag up from the floor on to her shoulder and getting to her feet. He rose too. As he drew abreast of her she touched his sleeve lightly with a finger.

'Just a drink,' she said, looking him in the eye.

There was still so much colour in his cheeks that she couldn't tell if he blushed again. But he didn't look away. He held her gaze, and nodded gently.

'Then you'd better lead on,' she said, standing aside for him to go ahead.

She followed him into the lobby and up the stairs to his room on the first floor. The carpeting and wallpaper were rather finer than the faded specimens on her own third floor, while still falling some way short of the standards expected in a moderately respectable slum. She was more than a little surprised, therefore, when he unlocked the door to a room that was not only spacious and clean but also decorated with a modicum of good taste. The minibar was next to the large double bed.

'It's the bridal suite, apparently,' he explained, as he sorted through the array of miniatures inside the little compartment. 'I didn't know that, of course, my secretary just asked for the best room.'

'Well, I'm glad we're in yours and not mine is all I can say to that.'

'I take it you won't be recommending this establishment to your friends. Why don't you sit down? Another brandy?'

There was an armchair and a small sofa between the bed and the window. Alan's coat and briefcase were on the chair. She put her own coat on top of them and sat in the sofa. Alan came over with two plastic tumblers, one each of whisky and brandy, and sat beside her, self-consciously keeping his distance. They touched their plastic tumblers in salute and drank.

Grace leant her head back on a cushion and half closed her eyes, enjoying the warm feel of the liquor spreading through her. So much for just the one, she thought. She had to go easy, she made an effort to remind herself, and the reason why, with all its unpleasant associations, jolted her brain.

'Tell me again what it is you're doing in Bournemouth?' she asked quickly.

Just boring old business, he said. A local chain of fast-food outlets wanted to get into the twenty-first century and install a computer program to simplify the sales and invoicing. Of course it never worked out as simply as the clients wanted, in his experience, but he didn't suppose that she could possibly be interested in the boring details of his boring job. But she insisted that she was interested, and wanted to know more. It was obvious to her that he loved his work and didn't think that it was boring at all.

She wanted to hear him talk. She needed the sound of another voice, and his was warm, unthreatening. When she happened to glance at her watch she noticed to her gratification that the time was slipping by in his company. It was coming up to eleven when she noticed, just after he had poured her the contents of the second and last miniature brandy from his bar. She was beginning to notice other things too, about Alan. She liked the way he spoke. He was amusing and attentive and seemed at ease with her. She liked his looks too, and the way he moved, coming over to her with the drinks. At first glance she had put him down as a typical office-reared male, with the expanding bottom and beer-prone waist of the sedentary thirtysomething, but she could see now that he was lean under his loose-fitting suit and in good shape. He was charming and attractive and he was bringing her a full glass of brandy. What more could a girl want?

She was already feeling light-headed but she drank it down all the same, thinking of what she'd be doing now if she hadn't wandered into the bar downstairs. She pictured herself sitting on her own in her tatty room, joylessly sober, willing for the time to pass but dreading the moment of getting into bed and summoning sleep. She had never been an easy sleeper. She had too active an imagination and found it hard to shut off or compartmentalize her brain when under pressure. And she had never before in her life felt this much pressure.

Stop worrying it, she told herself, worrying it like a dog

with a bone, chasing your own tail, trying to scratch what you can't reach . . . the image, once started, rebounded in her head with a maddening impetus of its own. She would deal with it when the time arose, in the morning, as she had planned. She'd prepared the ground as best she could, now all she needed was the capacity to think on her feet, and she'd always had that. Too clever by half, Bob had always called her, whatever that meant, a typically absurd piece of Bob grumbling and sniping. McGovern now, there was someone the tag fitted. And there he was, buzzing round in her head again when for a minute or so she'd almost dared to think she had expelled him. That gingery head, that round soft face with its hard little eyes, clever eyes to mask the corruption in his mind . . . too clever by half.

'I'm sorry?' said Alan.

She had whispered the phrase aloud. She went stiff with embarrassment, aware now that Alan had been asking her something and she hadn't been listening.

'Sorry, miles away,' she said, shaking her head. 'What did you just say?'

'Nothing, I just . . . look, if you're tired why don't you go to bed? It's quite all right, I really don't mind.'

He sounded concerned. Perhaps she did look tired, even if she didn't feel it. She glanced at him to see if he was flagging. He didn't seem to be.

'I'm fine, really I am, and I'm enjoying talking to you. But I don't want to keep you up. Have you got an early start?'

'Ish, but I don't want to sleep yet. I'm enjoying talking to you too.'

'Then let's not stop.'

'All right, let's not. When are you going back home?'

'Tomorrow.'

'Busy week ahead?'

'Afraid so.'

'Where d'you go to unwind?'

'At home? Oh, different places. Wine bars, clubs, pubs; the usual.'

'Ever drink in the Bull?'

'By the river? Yeah, sometimes.'

'I usually end up there on a Friday after work, if I'm anywhere near the office.'

'Nice pub.'

'Yeah. Perhaps you'd like to have a drink with me there sometime.'

'Perhaps I would.'

'I mean, I don't want to pry, but . . .'

There was a slight awkwardness in his voice again, but it wasn't reflected in his manner. He was looking her square in the eye, without embarrassment.

'I mean, Grace, I know nothing about you and if there's someone else –'

'There isn't.'

The quickness of her own response surprised her. This time it was her turn to feel the colour rising in her cheeks.

'What about you?' she said.

'What about me?' he said.

'The same question. Silly.'

And she gave his hand a little pinch to emphasize his silliness.

'I'm unattached,' he said, and pinched her back, very gently, on the base of her thumb. He didn't take his hand away.

'I see,' she said. 'And is that why you go around inviting strange women up to your hotel room?'

'You're not that strange.'

'Ha ha. You think so?'

'Anyway, you accepted.'

'So I did. Just for a drink.'

'Just for a drink.'

'Drink's finished.'

'So it is.'

'Perhaps I'd better go then.'

'I'd rather you didn't.'

He squeezed her thumb again. After a moment he trailed the back of his finger across her wrist.

'That's very bold,' she said.

'Do you want me to stop?'

She didn't answer. Their eyes were still locked together.

His fingers ran all the way up her arm, slowly, over her shoulder and round to her neck. When she felt the gentle increase of pressure on her nape she lifted her head from the cushion, as he wanted. As she wanted. She came halfway to meet him and took his face in her hands as their lips parted to kiss.

It was awkward on the tiny sofa. They wrestled for position, arms and legs entwining and entangling, their hands all over each other, their lips glued together. Only when it became impossibly uncomfortable did she pull away, gasping for breath.

'I'm sorry,' he murmured, 'I don't want to rush you. I got a bit carried away, I don't –'

She pressed a finger to his lips and he shut up. He watched her with a quizzical expression as she slipped off the side of the sofa and repositioned herself, sitting astride him, her knees pressed in to his hips, her hands on his shoulders to steady herself. Somehow, mysteriously, all of the buttons on her shirt seemed to have become undone. She started to undo his in return.

'I don't want you to stop,' she said, taking his hand and pressing it to her bare stomach. She bent down and nuzzled his ear. 'I just think that big bed over there might be more comfortable. OK?'

'OK,' he breathed hoarsely, both hands now inside her shirt, stroking her. 'Look, I really wasn't expecting this, I'm afraid I haven't, you know, got anything.'

'I have.'

She broke away and reached for her bag on the floor. She took the packet of condoms from the inner pocket. There were two left and she gave him one. His innocent look of surprise made her smile.

'I suppose it's a bit late to worry about my reputation,' she said, 'but I don't want you to think I do this all the time, despite appearances to the contrary. I really don't, it's just . . .'

She hesitated. She was remembering where the third condom in the packet had got to. She thought of Lewis, of that night of cold and manipulative and joyless sex. She thought of Lewis in his cell and she thought of McGovern, waiting for her in the morning.

'What the hell,' she said quickly. 'It's a bit late to worry about what you think, even though –'

'Ssh!' he whispered urgently, taking his cue from her and stopping her mouth with the tips of his fingers. He frowned at her with mock-reproof. 'I don't think anything, OK? I don't usually do this kind of thing either but, I don't know, it just feels right. Doesn't it?'

She nodded. They started to kiss again but after a moment he drew back.

'I think you're right, you know,' he said.

'About what?'

'The bed. Would be more comfortable.'

'You think so?'

'Only one way to find out.'

They withdrew, by degrees, to the other side of the room. Although the distance was only a matter of a few yards it took them some time. Their path could be clearly discerned afterwards by the progression of discarded clothes on the floor, like clues in an amorous treasure trail.

23

She woke to see a sliver of grey morning light seeping into the room through a crack in the curtains. She had been deeply asleep and she came round slowly. The bed was deliciously warm and she snuggled down instinctively beneath the thick heavy duvet, wanting to delay the onset of consciousness. She put a hand behind her back and pushed it across the mattress. The other side of the bed was empty.

She turned around, suddenly awake and suddenly anxious. She sat up on an elbow and scanned the room. It was too dark, she could see nothing. She reached across for the lamp on the table by the other side of the bed and fumbled for the switch, shielding her eyes with her other hand from the glare.

His wallet and watch were on the table. His coat and briefcase were still on the armchair. She noticed that the door to the bathroom was closed. She heard the low whoosh of the shower.

She settled back into the pillows. Her own watch was on the floor somewhere on her side of the bed, together with her jewellery. Her clothes were where they had fallen on the floor. They had gone at each other last night like randy teenagers. She remembered his passion, and her own abandon, and smiled at the recollection. She remembered lying in his arms afterwards, her fingers entwined in his, murmuring to him in the warm darkness, the pauses growing longer between the questions and the replies, until, eventually, nothing. She had gone out in an instant and slept a deep uninterrupted sleep. She looked at his watch. It was twenty past seven.

The bathroom door opened and he came out, a towel round his midriff, his hair and upper body still wet. When he saw that the light was on and she was sitting up in bed he stopped tiptoeing into the room. He grinned at her.

'Thought you'd never come round,' he said.

'Your fault. You wore me out.'

He came over and sat on the bed. He bent his head to give her a peck on the lips, and she put her hands round his neck and didn't let go. He prised her fingers from him reluctantly.

'I've got to go, I'm afraid.'

'Not even time for a quickie?'

'Dammit, no. I've a breakfast meeting at eight.'

'You should have woken me.'

'God, I wish I had.'

He kissed her again, this time long and hard. When he let go she lay back on the pillows, smiling up at him. She stroked him lightly across the chest with the back of her nails.

'Nice body,' she murmured approvingly.

'And I thought it was my mind you were after.'

'Quite like that too. I hope the wall behind us is thicker than it looks. I think we might have kept the neighbours up.'

'You weren't that noisy.'

'No, but you were.'

He laughed. He ran his fingers through her hair and down to her cheek, stroking her. He took her face in both hands and kissed her, very tenderly. He pulled back, not letting go and looking suddenly serious.

'Can I see you again, please?' he said.

'If you like,' she said, giving the lie to her nonchalance with her smile.

'Where can I get hold of you?'

'I'll give you my mobile number. Got a pen?'

He reached for the wallet on the bedside table. Tucked inside it was a little silver pencil. She gave him her number and he scribbled it down on the back of a scrap of paper. He folded the paper carefully and put it back into the wallet.

'Shall I take your number too?' she said.

'Probably easier if I call you,' he said. 'I'm moving at the end of the month and they're giving me a new mobile too.'

'Oh,' she said.

'What does that mean?'

'It just means that. Oh.'

'You think I'm not going to call you?'

'Did I say that?'

'How it sounded to me.'

'Well, it did sound a bit like don't ring us, we'll ring you . . .'

'I'm sorry, that's not what I meant.'

'Really?'

'Really.'

He took a business card out of his wallet and put it down on the bedside table.

'I'm only in the office a few times a week but you can always leave a message for me there, right? But you won't have to, because I'll be ringing you first. Look, it's nearly half-seven. Sorry about this, but I've got to get my skates on.'

'Sure. Hey, Alan –'

He had started to get up. She pushed herself up from the pillows and put her arms round his neck.

'Sorry to doubt you,' she murmured, and kissed him lightly.

'So you should be. Do you really think I'd pass up on the chance of a repeat of last night?'

'You think I'm going to want to sleep with you again?'

'Damn. You mean I'm going to have to get you drunk first?'

'It worked last night.'

'Don't give away your secrets.'

'I'm trying to make it easier for you.'

'You mean you quite liked it really?'

'I mean I quite liked it really a lot.'

'Mm. I wish I had woken you.'

'Go on, you'll be late for your meeting.'

He rose reluctantly and picked up his clothes from the floor. He piled them in his arms, with some clean underwear from his suitcase on top, and headed back towards the bathroom door.

'Hey!' she called out to him as he was about to go in.

He turned back to her, wearing a faintly quizzical expression.

'About last night,' she said. 'I wasn't drunk.'

He grinned back at her.

'No, but I was.'

He had darted into the bathroom and closed the door long before the pillow she flung at him hit the spot where he had been standing. She heard him laughing on the other side, and then whistling over the sound of his electric razor. She lay back on the remaining pillows for a minute, one eye closed and the other on his watch, regretting the slow steady march of the hands. She had something of a busy day ahead herself. When the hands touched half past she threw back the covers and jumped out of bed.

She collected her clothes from the floor and dressed hurriedly, not bothering with all the buttons, and stuffing her scrunched-up tights into her pocket. She would wash and shower in her own room in a minute. She grabbed her coat and bag and laid them on the bed, ready to leave quickly. She sat down beside them and waited for Alan to reappear.

She looked at the card on the table and learnt that his surname was Russell. The card described him as a software consultant, whatever that meant. She saw the wallet sitting on the bedside table, next to his watch. A sudden mischievous thought popped into her head.

She opened his wallet and found the piece of paper on which he had written her telephone number. She unfolded it and found the silver pencil he had used. Underneath the number she wrote, in neat capitals: HOTEL VISITS A SPECIALITY. She refolded the paper and put it back, or at least tried to.

That pocket of the wallet was nearly full. There were a lot of other bits of paper already there. She pulled them out, a fistful of petrol receipts, to make room. She pulled out a photograph along with them.

It was a colour snapshot of Alan with a pretty young woman and a small child. Alan had his arm round the woman and her head was resting on his shoulder, the child between them. They were smiling happily at the camera. Grace turned the photograph over and read the inscription on the back: *For our darling husband and daddy, love Charley and Annie.*

Grace put the wallet and photograph down on the bed. She got up, slung her bag and coat over her arm, and walked to the door.

Alan came out of the bathroom, wearing his suit and tie, looking fresh and pleased with himself. She walked past him without a glance. He caught up with her as she reached the door and put his hand on her sleeve.

'Was it something I said?' he asked, trying to make it light but sounding concerned.

'Yes.'

She opened the door. He squeezed her arm tighter.

'Hey!'

She closed the door again and turned back to face him.

'Let go of my arm, please.'

He released her. She stared at him, at his open innocent face, at his warm, sincere eyes. He shrugged his shoulders.

'Whatever's the matter, Grace?'

'It's all right, Alan, you can stop pretending now.'

'What?'

He looked like a baffled puppy. But she no longer found his tousled boyishness endearing.

'You're pretty good at sounding genuine, you know,' she told him. 'One of the best. I've fallen for it before and I ought to know, but you fooled me. Only myself to blame, I suppose. If I'm going to go around acting like a trollop then I can't complain if I get used like one, can I?'

'Grace, what the –'

'Does Charley know what you get up to while you're away, Alan? You going to take a stick of rock back for little Annie, a memento of the seaside?'

His eyes froze with astonishment. Then he understood, and his surprise turned instantly to anger.

'How dare you look through my wallet?'

He was so furious that for a moment she thought he might hit her. Perhaps the same thought occurred to him. He turned away from her abruptly and stamped back into the room, putting distance between them.

'You think that's the issue here, do you?' she said bitterly, her own anger breaking through her mask of applied calm.

He was still walking away from her. He stopped at the bed and picked up the photograph. She saw him glance at it before putting it back into his wallet. He seemed to be making an effort to compose himself, and a reply.

'Trust, I think that's the issue,' he said, putting on his watch.

'Then we see things the same,' she answered evenly.

He went over to the armchair and put on his coat.

'I don't think so,' he said in a clipped strained voice.

He picked up his suitcase and briefcase and marched to the door. He walked past, as she had done to him a minute ago, without looking. He put his suitcase down and reached for the door handle.

'I see,' she said. 'You don't like the idea of me walking out on you so you have to be the one who walks out first.'

'If that's the way you want to look at it,' he said, and stopped. He was still angry, but not as much as before. She saw something else in his eyes, something like regret. He said: 'I did care about you, you know.'

'Yeah, yeah, I've heard that one before too.'

'Oh, for Christ's sake . . .'

He snatched up his suitcase again, plainly exasperated.

'Look, I don't even care whether you believe me any more, I really couldn't give a toss. But if you want to know, and even if you don't want to know, the truth is I haven't lied to you. I told you I was unattached, and I am. But I wasn't always. Charley and I were married for two years. It wasn't that happy, and the divorce was very messy, but I'm still quite sentimental about it, and we have got a lovely, lovely daughter who means everything in the world to me, and if you don't like me having a photo of them in my wallet then that's just too bad, you know what I mean, because I don't believe I ever asked you to go poking your fucking nose in there in the first place. And now, if you'll excuse me, I'm late for a meeting.'

He snatched up his bag and went out of the door. He probably didn't hear what Grace said, what with the speed of his exit and the slamming of the door behind him.

'Sorry,' was what Grace said.

Sorry. The most inadequate word in the language. She put her weight against the wall, closed her eyes and let out a long sigh. She wondered about running after him, trying the useless word on him again, this time so he could hear. And then trying to explain. Explain what? Her own general insecurities, or just the unnatural suspiciousness that was the legacy of the job she did? The real job, not the one she'd lied about . . . She felt sick and embarrassed and stupid. She heard herself laugh. Oh yes, she had to hand it to herself. Anyone want shooting in the foot? Then come for advice to crackshot Grace, the Annie Oakley of self-inflicted wounds. Dissatisfaction guaranteed.

She walked out of the bedroom and along the corridor. She stopped at the staircase. Was he still in the lobby paying his bill, or would he be in the car park at the back by now? In the car park, she reckoned, maybe even on the road. He'd probably pre-paid the bill, and, if he hadn't, what would she say to him? She trudged up the stairs to her room on the top floor.

A shower left her feeling unrefreshed. She went downstairs again and took a brief walk along the seafront, letting the wind batter some colour into her cheeks. When she got back the dining room of the hotel was thick with greasy frying smells but she braved them anyway, and even managed to get down some mouthfuls of scrambled egg to go with the statutory thimbleful of orange juice and the black coffee. Despite not having eaten properly the night before she didn't feel hungry. None of the other guests spoke except to ask quietly for more hot water. The waitress, a different one from last night but no less brusque, bustled clumsily but at speed, as if to suggest that the sooner they were all finished and out of her hair the better. It was a typical British seaside breakfast scene, down to the shocking wallpaper and the view of gathering raincloads through the window.

She took the newspaper she had ordered upstairs, tried to

read but couldn't concentrate. It was only half past eight. Why had she given McGovern till ten? She wanted it to be over with, to be out of this town, this hotel. Then, when she thought about it again, she didn't even want it to begin at all. What did she think she was doing? She faced herself in the mirror-fronted wardrobe and asked herself the question aloud. She wanted others to believe her. Who? Anyone who would listen: George, Terry, her father, Bob. Bob most of all, but perhaps there was someone else she needed to convince, herself. She did believe Lewis, didn't she? Of course she did, and she made herself say it to the mirror. But there was no evidence, so she had to manufacture it. It was possibly the most stupid thing she had ever done, but it was the only thing she could think of.

She had been through it in her head over and over again these past few days. Worrying it more, like that dog with a bone, wasn't going to help. It was time to stop thinking and just act.

She checked her tape recorder and put in new batteries. She was wearing jeans and a long black sweater. She clipped the recorder on to her belt and pulled her sweater down over her hips. The microphone was on a long lead, there was no danger of her tugging it out of the socket accidentally. She put on her Barbour and fed the microphone carefully through the narrow hole she had cut out on the inside, level with the lapel. A little spray of blue flowers she had bought yesterday was attached to the buttonhole. She worked the tiny microphone carefully through the hole and ensured that it was concealed. A strip of velcro kept the lapel pinned down, protection against the wind lifting the material to reveal the wire. She turned on the recorder and let the tape run for a minute, burbling away inconsequentially to herself about the view she could see from her window. She rewound and played back the tape. The tone was clear. So was the nervous strain in her voice. She looked at her watch, though she hardly dared. It was a quarter to nine. She took her folder of photographs out from her suitcase and checked that they were arranged in the proper order. They were old photos of Lewis she had taken a year ago with her telephoto lens. They weren't very clear, which was why she had never shown them to McGovern, but they might be enough to string him along for a while. She had to get him to say something incriminating before he realized there was nothing in them. It became a taller order every time she thought about it, so the solution wasn't to think about it. Ha bloody ha . . . she thought to herself. She unwrapped a stick of chewing gum and chewed furiously. She was desperate for a cigarette, as she had been yesterday. She had been envious of McGovern, sitting there casually blackening his lungs.

She put the gum packet back into her bag. She noticed her phone, sticking out from between her purse and Filofax. She turned it on, to check for messages. There were two. The first was from her father. He said that he'd been digging around in Buxton, as requested. He'd come across another retired policeman, Malcolm Thexton, also a keen horticulturist, well known in the Police Association for his roses. They'd had quite a chat, and he thought that she ought to have one too, because apparently he knew quite a bit about Mr McGovern. Her dad signed off with a cheery goodbye. She started to listen to the second message.

There was a knock on the door. She ignored it. She had the phone pressed close to her ear, the recording was faint, she was having trouble hearing. There was another knock.

'It's open,' she said distractedly, assuming it was the chambermaid.

'Good morning,' said Peter McGovern, standing in the doorframe.

He was wearing the same suit and coat he had been wearing yesterday. In one hand he held an umbrella, in the other a briefcase.

'Too grim to meet out there, I thought,' he said, with a nod towards the window. As if on cue a smattering of rain slapped at the pane. 'Mind if I come in?'

She nodded. She turned off her phone and put it down on the bed, next to the folder of photographs. He came into the centre of the room and looked around. A faint smile creased his lips as he saw the cracks in the wall and the threadbare carpet.

'I can see why you need the money,' he said.

He looked for somewhere to park himself. There was a hard-backed chair between the wardrobe and the bed. He dusted the seat with his palm ostentatiously. As he did so Grace sat down on the bed, slipping her hand under her coat and turning on her tape recorder through the material of her jumper. She cleared her throat to mask the tiny click, but no noise would have been audible above the sound of his fussing. McGovern sat down in the chair, laid his briefcase across his knees and gave it a pat.

'Here it is then. Five thousand pounds, like you said. In return for the photographs you were threatening to take to the police. It's in fifties, I hope that'll do you. You understand that I don't believe a word of your crackpot theory, but I want to be left alone. And if the only way I can achieve that is to give in to your blackmail threats, then so be it. I can't say I'm happy about it, but you've caught me at a vulnerable time.'

Oh, you're good, she thought to herself, so, so good . . . She had actually succeeded in throwing him off his stride last night, but he had made a quick recovery. And now he was returning the favour, giving himself the edge of surprise.

'How did you find me?' she asked.

'Not difficult. I've got a phone in my hotel room, and a phonebook to go with it. So they charge thirty quid a night for this, do they? Who said crime doesn't pay?'

'You should know.'

He didn't return her humourless smile. He clicked open the locks on his briefcase and flipped up the lid. He produced a thick brown envelope.

'Here's the money you're so keen to extort from me. Now, where are the photographs?'

There was no emotion in his voice. He spoke as if conducting a business transaction. No doubt he weighed up dispassionately the prospective profit and loss before embarking on any of his ventures, murder included.

'Why did you kill your wife, Mr McGovern?'

'Oh dear . . .'

There was a bit of feeling in his voice now, but it was

feigned. He was trying to look and sound pained and regretful, and at the same time rise above it all.

'I can't stop you airing your little crackpot theories, as I said, but I don't think it's very pleasant. You and I know who was responsible for killing my wife. I witnessed it, and it wasn't nice. I'm sure you've seen dead bodies, Miss Cornish, in your line of work, but when it's a loved one who's suffered a violent death it's a different matter, I can assure you. Let's have no more of these ghoulish questions, please. As you know very well, I'm an innocent man.'

'Then why are you trying to buy me off?'

'Oh come now . . .' There was a momentary snap of irritation, but that was all. He gave a little sigh and a shrug. 'Let's be clear what's going on here, shall we? You're blackmailing me for money in return for some photographs which, although I know they're perfectly innocent, could cause me further distress because of my delicate situation. Here, in my hand, is the five thousand you demanded as a downpayment when you accosted me yesterday. The ball is in your court. I suggest you show me your photographs and we can get this over with.'

The business tone was again in evidence. They might have been discussing a spot of conveyancing, or some such.

'I don't know what photographs you mean,' she said.

She spoke matter-of-factly. He hesitated, as if he thought that he hadn't heard correctly.

'You mean they're not here?' he asked, with a vague wave of his hand.

'I mean I don't know what you're talking about,' she said slowly and deliberately. 'Would you mind not doing that in here, please?'

He stopped in the act of taking his cigarettes out of his pocket. Grace nodded at the list of hotel regulations fixed to the back of the door, behind where he was sitting.

'You may think thirty quid's criminal, but I'm afraid it doesn't even give you the right to smoke in your own room any more.'

His hand fell back loosely to his side. He stared at her

intently, probing her, trying to work her out. She stared back, fascinated. She had never seen a look of such concentrated malevolence.

'What's your game?' he hissed at her.

'I don't know what you're talking about,' she repeated.

'Then what am I doing here?'

'Search me. I didn't invite you.'

'You arranged to meet me this morning.'

'I did?'

'You deny it? You deny accosting me on the front last night, demanding money?'

'The only thing I demanded was to know why you killed your wife, Mr McGovern, though of course I know. You did it to get revenge on her and her lover, Lewis Young. You did it because you're an avaricious man and it was cheaper than a divorce. You did it because –'

'You scheming little bitch!'

He stood up, giving himself a height advantage from which to glare down at her. Although he wasn't a big man he had a big voice, and his anger gave him physical presence. Grace found it impossible not to feel a little intimidated.

'If you're going to insult me then I shall have to ask you to leave,' she said.

'I wasn't aware that there were any nice words to describe a blackmailer, Miss Cornish,' he answered savagely.

'More than there are to describe a murderer.'

He stopped himself from making an instant rejoinder. She could see the rage boiling up within him, threatening to explode. He remembered himself just in time. He took some slow, deliberate breaths.

'I've no idea what you're playing at but it's sick,' he said. 'You know perfectly well what you said to me last night and I don't know how you've the gall to deny it. Why do you keep repeating your insane allegations? No one's listening to you, no one'll even give you the time of day –'

'Malcolm Thexton will, Mr McGovern,' she said quickly.

He stopped dead. For a fraction of a second he stood completely frozen, the expression on his face a mixture of shock and bewilderment. There was another ingredient present too, one she had not seen before. For the blink of an eye he registered fear.

Grace jumped eagerly to her feet. She hadn't known why she'd said Malcolm Thexton's name, it had just jumped out of her head and on to her tongue. But she'd landed a blow below the belt, that much was clear. McGovern couldn't take it. He turned on his heels suddenly and walked quickly to the door, his briefcase tucked awkwardly under one arm and the brown envelope filling his other hand. He fumbled awkwardly for the door handle.

'You harass me any more,' he called over his shoulder, blustering, 'and I'm calling the police.'

He jerked open the door.

'Give my regards to Jimmy Collins when you see him,' said Grace.

He turned back to her. He had regained some of his composure. He gave a hoarse chuckle.

'You think you're very smart, don't you?' he said.

She looked him squarely in the eye. She spoke softly:

'You've done it before, haven't you?'

He didn't answer. He didn't even blink. He went out and slammed the door.

Her knees buckled and she slumped back on to the bed. She was drenched in sweat, her limbs were trembling and the knot in her stomach felt like it was about to explode. For a moment she thought she was going to be violently sick, but the spasms subsided. Thank God, she thought. She didn't have time to waste emptying her insides.

There was a box of matches somewhere inside her bag. She had to empty the whole lot to find them. She tore the fuzzy photos of Lewis from the folder and held them to the flame, dropping them into the metal rubbish bin as they caught, trailing thick smoke. Fortunately it wasn't the kind of establishment to stretch to smoke detectors in its bedrooms.

She turned on her phone. She heard her father's voice again, and then the second message, the one she had been listening to when McGovern came in. She listened to Bob Challoner again, screaming abuse at her.

'You stupid bloody cow, what in Christ's name are you up to? I've just spoken to Jimmy, he's laughing his head off, he's set you up. Do you understand? He's going to do you for blackmail, send you down. When McGovern meets you he's going to be wired, with Jimmy outside. For Christ's sake, Grace, pick up the bloody phone . . .'

She didn't listen to the rest of it. She erased the message. Best to leave no trace of anything, just in case. She ejected the cassette from her mini-recorder, broke it open with her heel, and burnt the tape. She carried the smouldering bin over to the window, which she opened wide. She gulped in the cold air. Her head was swimming. What had McGovern told the police? Lies, of course, but he was so good at it, what did it matter? Her own lies now seemed puny by comparison. She thought of that old recurring line from her school reports. Must try harder . . .

There was a knock on the door, heavy and unsubtle. Grace turned in from the window. She took a moment to compose herself.

'Come in, Jimmy.'

24

She'd always known he was a thug, a big brutal policeman of the old school, the type who had thought nothing of knocking a suspect about in the days before taped interviews became the law. But she was still surprised when he hit her.

It was a slap with the back of his hand, a sudden venomous jab she didn't have time to flinch from. It caught her full in the face and sent her spinning to the floor. She lay on her side gasping for breath, a film of tears covering her eyes. She saw his short pitbull-legs pumping across the floor towards her, saw the toecap of his boot raised to kick her.

'Stop it!' she screamed.

His foot hovered in mid-air, then, after a second that seemed to stretch for minutes, he replaced it with an impetuous stamp on the wooden floorboards.

'You stupid fucking brainless stupid bitch,' said Bob Challoner.

He turned away from her and walked back sullenly to the chair in the corner of her office. That was where he'd been sitting half a minute ago when she'd come in. She'd hardly even had time to say hello. She had closed the door, taken one step into the room, and then he'd hit her like an express train.

Slowly she got to her feet. The right side of her face throbbed numbly. The inside of her mouth felt like it had been drilled out by a conference of sadistic dentists. Painfully she limped across the floor towards him, nursing her bruised cheek in her left palm. Bob looked up at her, something close to regret mingling with the rage that was dying in his eyes.

'I'm sorry, love,' he mumbled.

She drove her right fist with all her strength into the middle of his face. His nose squashed like a marshmallow as her knuckles hammered it in. His head snapped back and his chair tottered on its rear legs. He gawped at her with stunned, wide-open eyes.

'Don't you ever dare lay a finger on me again, you stupid fucking stupid pig,' she said. She turned away, still seething. 'Here, you'd better take one of these.'

She threw the box of Kleenex on the desk at him. He caught it and pulled out a tissue in time to stop the blood trickling out of his nose from spilling on to his shirt. Grace walked round to the other side of the desk and slumped into her comfortable padded chair.

'Who let you in anyway?' she demanded.

'Your friend Nikki.'

'Well, she shouldn't have.'

Nikki had been manning the fort while she'd been away. Her report on McGovern's business activities was lying in a folder on the desk, clearly marked.

'Where's she got to?' Grace demanded.

'Said she was going for lunch.'

Grace made a mental note to tick Nikki off for leaving a strange man alone in the office, though she didn't suppose that the big square thug in question had given her much option. She sat back in the chair, gently massaging her bruised face. The top of her cheek was very tender.

'Am I going to have a black eye?'

He shook his head, then tipped it back to stare at the ceiling, trying to stop the flow of blood. Grace laughed.

'What's funny?' he muttered.

'Us. It's like a casualty clearing station in here. Thanks for the warning, by the way.'

'What's this then? Gratitude?'

'Don't whine, Bob. It's not you. When did you speak to Jimmy?'

'He rang me first thing this morning. He was bloody excited. You'll never guess what, he kept saying, you'll never guess what. Funny thing, though, I did guess. Guessed that it was you involved, at any rate. 'Course I didn't know exactly what stunt you were trying to pull, but not even Alfred bleeding Einstein could have guessed anything that dumb.'

'I don't suppose Albert could have done any better either.'

'Oh, shut the fuck up, Grace. Shut the fuck up . . .'

He winced as he touched a finger to the bridge of his nose.

'I think you've broken it.'

'Let me know if I haven't. I'll come over and make sure.'

'Don't be vindictive.'

'All right. How about a coffee then?'

He nodded. She went through to put the kettle on, piling a mug on his behalf with instant granules and sugar. She knew he was going to moan because she didn't have any full-fat milk. Too bad, she thought, patting her swollen cheek with ice from the freezer. She didn't have that much sympathy to spare.

She took him his coffee. He was slumped in the chair, smoking and flicking ash on to the floor. She fetched him an ashtray and banged it down on the edge of the desk pointedly. She sat down again.

'I think you're right, you know,' he said.

'What do you mean?'

'We couldn't live together. Could have a future in tag wrestling though. What do you say?'

'Nothing without my lawyer present.'

'Jimmy give you a hard time then?'

'Not as hard as I'd given him. Thanks to you I'd ruined his day. No, more than that, probably ruined his year, his life. He really thought he'd got me. Putting the cuffs on me would have given him an orgasm.'

'Well, if you won't go to bed with him how else is he meant to get his kicks with you?'

'I was already going to bed with one thick, foul-mouthed copper. Remember?'

'What, and me as well? You put it around a bit, don't you?'

'Ha, ha. Jimmy was just mouth, the usual with him. Likes the sound of his own voice, especially at maximum volume.

Had a wet-behind-the-ears kid with him, I think he was just trying to save face. I let him have his rant, then I asked him politely if he wouldn't mind leaving.'

'What was he ranting about?'

'Oh, obstruction of justice, interference with a witness, hot air. I told him he'd arrested the wrong man for the murder of Julie McGovern. He didn't think that was very funny.'

'It isn't.'

'Don't you start.'

He hesitated. She could see the wheels of thought reluctantly turning. She'd thrown him off his stride by standing up to his bullying. As he didn't really posses a second weapon in his armoury it took him a few moments to gear himself up for an attempt at reason.

'Drop it, please, Grace. I had a long chat with Jimmy this morning, must have been while you were driving back from Bournemouth. He was well pissed off, as you can imagine, he needed to talk, let off steam. Seems like you handled the situation pretty well, by the way. It obviously didn't even occur to him that you'd been tipped off. He thought you must have spotted McGovern's wire.'

'I am truly grateful to you, Bob. I know what it'd be like if it ever came out that it was you that grassed.'

'Yeah, yeah. Anyway, he told me that you'd got this mad idea into your head that McGovern had paid Lewis Young to kill his wife. Not what you told me, but perhaps you've changed your mind. So we talked about the case. I was playing devil's advocate, just seeing if there was any mileage in your theory. There isn't.'

'Not in that particular version of it, I admit. I made all that up for McGovern's benefit, so he'd just think I was after money and easy to handle. What did McGovern tell Jimmy about me, by the way?'

'The truth. Everything you told me the other day. He told Jimmy he'd hired you to keep tabs on his wife. That was when he found out about her affair. He said he hadn't mentioned it before because he'd still been in shock, and was embarrassed. He said he didn't want people to know that he'd had his own wife followed. He was sorry he hadn't said anything, but he didn't think it was relevant anyway. Then he said you'd accosted him the night before on the seafront, threatening to show the police some photos of him with Lewis Young, proving it was some kind of conspiracy. McGovern said he hadn't seen the photos but he knew they were innocent. He said Young had been pestering him for building work, so he'd taken him to this house where a client had a shooting gallery that wanted converting. They'd mucked around a bit with this air pistol that was in there, and you were blackmailing him by saying that it was really the murder weapon they'd been trying out.'

'I see.'

She leaned back in her chair and put her feet up on the desk. She was cross with herself. She had underestimated McGovern, and for that there was no excuse. She knew better than anyone, even poor Lewis stewing away in his cell, just how devious McGovern was, and how clever. He had turned the tables on her without breaking stride and had had no difficulty in persuading the police of his version of events. Not that that would have been too difficult, of course, given Jimmy Collins's unshakeable convictions about both her and the crime that he was investigating. McGovern's angle on the photographs had been shrewd, or at least would have been had the photographs actually existed. Had McGovern guessed that she had been lying? If so, had he sussed that her whole line had been an act, that she was really after him, not money? Whatever his suspicions he couldn't be sure, and she had the added advantage that he thought she knew more about him than he wanted her to know. Having dropped the name with such effect into the conversation it was time to find out what Malcolm Thexton, Derbyshire CID retd., had to say for himself.

'Grace, what are you doing?'

She was getting up, putting her Barbour back on, checking her bag and pockets for keys and money. Her suitcase was still in the car, packed with enough clean clothes to see her through one more night at least away from home. With any luck she might even strike a more salubrious hotel than she had managed in Bournemouth. She went to check the answering machine.

'I've got to go and have a chat with someone,' she said, talking over a routine recorded message from George asking her if any bills had arrived. 'I'll probably be gone for a day or two. Now, will you get out of my office, please.'

There were no other messages. She reset the machine.

'Grace, for Christ's sake, drop it.'

He said it wearily, knowing it was a waste of time. She ignored him, as he had known she would. She stood by the door, holding it open and waiting for him to go. He rose with reluctance, still pressing his bloodstained tissue to his nose, although the bleeding seemed to have stopped.

'Better get that seen to,' she said.

'It'll be all right. Don't think it is broken, after all.'

'You don't mean to say you've been exaggerating, do you, Bob? Whatever next?'

He stopped on the threshold. With some wariness he took hold of her hand. When she didn't object he gave it a gentle squeeze.

'Just take care, please. Take care.'

She nodded. She locked up the office and followed him down the stairs. It was sensible advice. She was, after all, dealing with a murderer.

They went their separate ways at the front door. There was no parting intimacy, of course, not even a glance back over his shoulder as he slouched across the road, paying no attention to the angrily hooting car which had to brake sharply to avoid him. She watched him, though, with that private mixture of irritation and tenderness for which she'd always struggled to work out the right proportions.

She tried to put him out of her mind as she got back behind the wheel of her car and set out on the long drive to the Midlands. She had spoken to Malcolm Thexton's wife on the mobile outside Bournemouth. He was out for the rest of the day, but Mrs Thexton, pleasant-sounding and elderly, was sure that he'd be happy to see her in the evening. Malcolm had been expecting her call, she said. He was looking forward to meeting her.

She left Guildford on the A3 and headed north. By the time she reached the M25 she had pushed Bob Challoner out of her mind and was thinking about Peter McGovern instead. In some ways perhaps, though it was hardly fair to Bob, they were not dissimilar: cold, ruthless, selfish, egotistical. They had something else in common too.

They had both seriously underestimated her.

25

The Thextons' house was on the outskirts of Buxton, perched on the side of a steeply climbing road that led away into the heart of the Peak District. It was an old stone cottage, neatly kept and nestling in the middle of an even neater small garden. Although it was dark by the time Grace arrived, Malcolm Thexton was outside, raking over the drive by the light of a powerful porch lamp. She put her car into gear as a precaution against the slope and got out to meet him.

'Leaves,' he said mournfully, coming round as she got out of the car. 'Love autumn, hate leaves. You wouldn't credit how quickly they block up our drains. Sorry I'm not dressed for the occasion, but your dad didn't tell me you were such a looker.'

He opened his mouth wide in a big infectious grin. He was in his early sixties, Grace supposed, solidly built and hearty-looking, though when he moved there was a hint of arthritic stiffness. He took off his gardening gloves and offered her his hand.

'You'd better come inside or the missus'll get jealous.'

She followed him round to the side of the cottage. They went into the kitchen, where Mrs Thexton – Alice, as she at once invited Grace to call her – was peeling vegetables at the sink. Alice was as robust-looking as her husband, though she was a little older and greyer. They both had strong local accents.

'Ooh, get in out of that cold,' she said as they came in through the back door. 'It's perishing. And I thought I told you to put on your scarf.'

She jabbed an accusing finger at her husband. He muttered

something about not being able to find it. His wife was staring hard, with evident disapproval, at Grace's old Barbour.

'You'll catch your death in that,' she murmured threateningly. 'It's going to snow tonight, you know. Malcolm, you take her through, and mind you sit her by the fire, all right? Kettle's just boiled. I'll bring you some tea in a minute.'

Malcolm exchanged his wellingtons for slippers and led Grace through into a cosy low-ceilinged sitting room where a log fire was stuttering faintly in a low key. Malcolm indicated for Grace to take the sofa while he knelt by the grate and fed in more wood. As she waited for him to stoke up the fire she looked at the photographs on the wall. There were portraits of children and grandchildren, and a couple of group shots in which a younger Malcolm Thexton was standing in company with other men in ill-fitting suits who could only have been detectives. There was something about coppers and style that just didn't mix.

'That's the old crowd,' said Malcolm, noticing where she was looking. 'Dave Reynolds is in the middle, the one with the eyebrows. He handled the Wilson case.'

Grace could see what he meant by the eyebrows. They were like two thick bushes that had been overtreated with fertilizer. Had it not been for the intense staring eyes beneath he would have looked like the dotty professor in a film.

'Where is he now?' she asked.

'Drank himself to death three years ago. He never recovered from that case, you know. Was meant to be the brightest copper in the county, had a glittering future ahead of him. Never got another promotion, though, so took early retirement and spent his pension in a public bar in Manchester. Sad.'

Alice came in carrying a tray laden with cake and biscuits as well as cups and tea things. She put it down on a low table which was empty apart from a couple of photograph albums and a scrapbook.

'You come up all the way from London then, love?' asked Alice in a faintly disbelieving voice, as if London might have been somewhere on the moon.

'From Guildford actually. Not a bad journey, in fact. Four and a bit hours.'

'I went to Guildford once,' volunteered Malcolm brightly.

There was a pause while Alice digested this sudden revelation of her husband's reckless spirit. Evidently satisfied that it could have been only a mild aberration she turned her attention to the fire.

'You've got that going nicely then,' she said to her husband.

'I have that,' he answered, pleased. 'You can take your jacket off now, Grace.'

Grace did as she was bid. Alice put the offensively thin article over her arm.

'Where you staying tonight then, love?' she asked.

'I don't know yet,' Grace answered. 'A pub or a small hotel; perhaps you can suggest somewhere.'

'We won't hear of it,' said Alice grimly. 'Will we, Malcolm?'

'No,' he assented. 'We won't hear of it. Plenty of space upstairs.'

'Plenty,' confirmed Alice.

'Oh, but I couldn't –'

'Enough of that, young lady,' interrupted Alice in a tone that could brook no argument. 'I'll go and make the bed up. Tea'll be brewed now, Malcolm. I'll leave you two to have your chat.'

She went out and closed the door behind her. Malcolm poured the tea.

'So why are you suddenly interested in this man Peter Wilson?' he asked, handing her a cup and saucer. 'Your dad said he was calling himself something else now.'

'Peter McGovern. He changed his name by deed poll ten years ago. His wife was murdered. Coming up to two weeks ago now. Perhaps you read about it in the paper?'

She gave him the details. He seemed surprised.

'I think I did read something about this,' he said, 'but of course I didn't twig who it was. Did you say he was an estate agent? He wasn't in that line up here. Worked in land management or something, I think, up towards Derby. Same line of business, I suppose. I remember now, he trained as a surveyor. Pity Dave Reynolds is dead. He'd have been on to it like a shot. Here, you'd better look at these.'

He opened the scrapbook. On the inside page was a pile of yellowed newspaper cuttings. He explained while he opened them out on the table.

'This all happened twelve years ago. It was just a missing-persons case at first, but something about it made Dave Reynolds suspicious. Do you want to read this stuff on your own, quiet like, or should I talk you through it?'

'I think you'd better talk me through it.'

He took it from the top, methodically. Peter Wilson had lived with his wife Margaret at a farmhouse up in the Peaks, the other side of Ashburton. It was a remote and lonely place which he had inherited from a relative. He and Margaret were both Scots, living in Edinburgh at the time, and originally they had intended to sell the house. But by chance Peter had been offered this job in Derby and they decided to try living in it. Peter, being a self-contained sort of man, found that he rather liked it, but Margaret, who was by all accounts ebullient and outgoing, was lonely. It was a twenty-minute drive to the nearest shop and there were no neighbours to speak of. She got herself a part-time job as a receptionist at a dental practice in Buxton, but there was nothing to do in the evenings and she was still bored. Her husband was a bit of a workaholic and didn't have much energy left when he got in from his job. He was also away a lot. Margaret joined a local amateur operatic society. It was there she met Paul Bramall, a local man with a reputation as a bit of a rogue. Bramall had worked on oil rigs and as a seaman, but he was unemployed and drifting at the time. He had no interest in singing, but he was a handy carpenter and he'd been inveigled in to help with the set-building. Although he had a steady girlfriend he and Margaret began an affair. It lasted for a year, and then they both disappeared.

It was Peter Wilson who reported his wife as missing. He'd last seen her on a Friday morning. He said that when he came home that evening her car had gone and she'd taken a suitcase and some clothes. He admitted that they had been having some rows lately, and he had assumed that she had just gone off in a huff somewhere to stay with friends. But on the Monday she failed to turn up for work, and when he went into his bank to cash a cheque he discovered that over a thousand pounds, all the money in their joint account, had been withdrawn. The cashier remembered his wife cashing the cheque the previous Friday. Wilson rang the local police. They asked him routine questions about the state of his marriage and he told them about Paul Bramall. Wilson, who was by now highly agitated, told the police that on his return from the bank he had gone into the garage, which he hadn't used at all over the weekend because of the fine weather, and noticed a motorcycle standing in the corner. The motorcycle was Bramall's and enquiries revealed that he too had not been seen since the end of the previous week.

It was posted as a missing-persons enquiry, but Detective Inspector Dave Reynolds of the Regional Crime Squad saw Bramall's name and got involved. Later, when the investigation took a more serious turn, Detective Sergeant Malcolm Thexton came on board.

Dave Reynolds had arrested Bramall on a charge of passing stolen cheques two years previously. The case had been dropped for lack of evidence, but DI Reynolds had marked Bramall's card. Reynolds thought at first that Bramall must have persuaded Margaret Wilson to withdraw the money with the intention of conning her out of it. He expected her to resurface in a week or two without a penny and her tail between her legs. But he was a quick-witted copper, was Dave Reynolds, and as he began to look into things a little more deeply something stuck in his throat. Bramall, everyone said, had been really crazy about Margaret Wilson, it hadn't just been one-way traffic. Both Bramall and Margaret had told friends that she was going to leave her husband and that they intended to get married. They were quite open about it and had told several witnesses that they intended to stay in the area, possibly even live in the farmhouse. Peter Wilson admitted that his marriage had been rocky, but denied that Margaret had asked him for a divorce. When Reynolds went round to see him he noticed that there was building work going on in the back. Wilson said he was laying a patio.

Reynolds had a look on the way out and saw at once that it was a shoddy bit of work. Half of the patio had gone down already and the stones were all crooked and uneven. Just then a builder's merchant arrived with a delivery of sand. The driver told Reynolds that his cousin, a builder, had originally been employed by Margaret to lay the patio, but that Peter Wilson had rung first thing on the Saturday morning following her disappearance to cancel him, saying that he was now going to do the job himself. The driver had a look at the half-laid patio and agreed with Dave Reynolds that it was 'right cack-handed'. Wilson had seen them talking and had come out of the house. He had seemed nervous and agitated. Dave Reynolds had put a watch on the house.

Malcolm Thexton remembered the surveillance operation well. It was freezing out there in the hills and the long hours had been as uncomfortable as they had been tedious. It was the Friday a week after the murder and Malcolm had already done two shifts, watching with binoculars from a vantage point higher up along the road, when he saw Wilson dragging what appeared to be a heavy sack out of the back of the house and into the garden. It was first thing in the morning, and barely light, but it had seemed like the sack had been dumped in a hole on the site of the patio. Malcolm had seen Wilson working with a shovel for the next ten minutes. He had then driven off to work. Dave Reynolds, meanwhile, had been asking questions about Wilson and had come up with some interesting facts. Three months earlier Wilson had joined a local gun club. Most of the members shot rifles, but Wilson made it clear from the off that he was only interested in handguns. He had applied for a licence to keep a handgun, though the paperwork had not yet been processed. Nonetheless he had been seen shooting with a borrowed weapon and, according to one fellow member, he had been asking around how easy it was to obtain a gun illegally. Reynolds decided to pull him in for questioning and Malcolm Thexton had been the other officer present.

Reynolds told Malcolm he was convinced that Wilson had murdered his wife and Paul Bramall and had buried their bodies under the patio. Malcolm agreed that Wilson's behaviour was suspicious, though he wasn't at that stage as convinced as his boss. Margaret's car had been found abandoned in London and her credit card had been used to book a hotel in Bayswater for the weekend of the disappearance, though in the event no one had turned up. Reynolds was sure that Wilson, who claimed to have been in quietly all weekend, had made the booking and driven the car south, probably coming back by train. He said he was going to put the screws on Wilson and try and get him to crack before he applied for a search warrant.

Dave Reynolds was a hard man and a brutal interrogator. The first time Malcolm had worked with him he had been worried that he might lash out at the suspect, but in all the five years he'd observed him at close quarters he had never seen him lay a finger on anyone. The fact was he didn't need to. He had such an intimidating presence that the unstated but implicit threat of violence usually sufficed to do the trick. He had reduced bigger men than Peter Wilson to jelly.

Wilson cracked inside half an hour. Malcolm said he had never seen a man so petrified. Yes, he had blurted out, he had killed his wife and her lover. Yes, he had buried them under the patio. Yes, he had used a gun he had bought illegally from someone he met through the club, and yes, he had been the one who abandoned the car in London. Wilson was a sobbing wreck by the end of his ordeal. Dave Reynolds was cock-a-hoop. On the way out of the station to pick up his search warrant he told a local reporter he knew what had happened. It was over the front page of the paper the next day.

They dug up the patio that night under floodlights. They found two sacks. One contained junk, including an empty container of hydrochloric acid. Traces of acid were found round the bath in the house. The other sack contained bones. Wilson was arrested for the double murders. Dave Reynolds was the toast of the squad.

And then the results of the forensic tests came back. The bones in the sack had come from two dogs. Peter Wilson's lawyer issued a statement complaining that police brutality had forced a false confession from his innocent client. No trace of the missing pair was found either in the garden or in the house. The acid, said Wilson, had been in the house when they'd moved in and he'd only just got round to throwing it away. The bones were from two dogs that had belonged to the previous owner, Margaret's relative, and had been buried in the garden for years. He had found them as he was digging out the patio and had simply decided to rebury them in the sacks. He retracted his confesion and the case against him collapsed. So, more or less, did Dave Reynolds's career. Wilson went on to sue the police for wrongful arrest and won a substantial settlement.

'Poor Dave,' murmured Malcolm Thexton with genuine sadness. 'There's a photo here from the last time I saw him. It was a squad reunion, about three year ago.'

He pushed over one of the photograph albums that had been lying underneath the scrapbook. Near the back was a shot of more or less the same group of people featured on the wall. All looked much the same, if a little older, except for Dave Reynolds. He was hunched and thin and the life had gone out of his eyes. Even his eyebrows seemed to have shed their density.

'It was a bad time for us up here, there had been other allegations of police brutality in the press,' Malcolm explained. 'Dave was suspended. He was quietly reinstated a year later, but his career was finished. It was tragic, like. He had the best copper's brain of anyone I've worked with.'

Grace glanced again at the pathetic portrait of a broken man. There but for the grace of God goes Bob Challoner, she thought to herself.

'And what did this copper's brain tell him was really going on?' she asked.

'Oh, he was sure Wilson was guilty, one hundred per cent. He thought about nothing else for years, worried all the permutations of that case to death, until it turned the tables and helped do him in. The way Dave saw it, Wilson had planned the whole thing to turn out exactly as it did. He'd known that no one would buy the disappearance story and that he'd be number one suspect, so he'd taken care to cover up his tracks just enough to make it look as if he was hiding something. All that stufff with the patio had been deliberate. Dave was furious with himself, he felt like he'd been done by the equivalent of the three-card trick. Wilson had planted the acid and the bones deliberately so as to make us jump to conclusions and charge him. If Dave was right then he was the cleverest bloody villain in the whole country.'

'And what do you think?'

'Me? I don't know. Villains aren't usually that clever in my experience, but perhaps he was the exception. Who's to say with so much water passed under the bridge. We'll never know the truth now. Neither the wife nor the lover have ever turned up, of course, not a peep out of either of them for all these years. People do disappear into thin air from time to time, it's true, but why should these two have run away? She may have taken a grand out of their bank account, quite a lot in them days, but it was her husband who ended up with the gravy.'

Grace picked up one of the newspaper cuttings. There was a small fuzzy photograph of the scene of the suspected crime, under the headline 'Grisly dig on remote hillside'. The name of the place was in the text: Roughwood Farm.

'Perhaps that's why he's never sold it,' she murmured.

'Come again?'

'This place, Roughwood Farm. He calls it Roughwood Cottage now – just like him to change the name. He still owns it, rents it out as a holiday place.'

'Shouldn't imagine he's got many takers this time of year. Cheeky bugger though, if he's still making a profit out of it.'

'He isn't.'

She remembered the letter from the letting agent she had copied from McGovern's computer. Only one customer all summer, and for a cottage in the heart of one of Britain's most beautiful national parks. McGovern was wealthy, why didn't he do the place up? He was a shrewd businessman, it didn't make sense for him to let it go to waste. Unless he had a reason for leaving things exactly as they were.

'How far is Roughwood Farm from here?'

'Ooh, bit over an hour, if the traffic's not too bad. Do you want me to show you in the morning?'

'That's very kind, but there's no need, I've been quite enough trouble to you already.'

'Rubbish, you've been no trouble at all. It's good to have someone new to listen to my old stories. Alice got bored with them all years ago. That's a good smell coming from the kitchen, by the way. Hope you like traditional cottage pie.'

'Sounds wonderful.'

It was. And the bed to which Alice showed her some hours later, when she had tasted their hospitality to the full and sucked dry Malcolm's store of reminiscences, was delightfully warm and cosy. But she didn't sleep well. She lay awake for long hours, listening to the wind, and thinking about the kind of man who would be capable of killing not just one woman who had shared his life, but two.

26

She woke up after ten o'clock. She washed and dressed hurriedly, feeling guilty, and ran downstairs, her hastily packed bag in hand. Malcolm came in from the garden, where he said he had been working since eight, and put on the kettle for her. Alice, he explained, had gone into town to shop. When he had made the tea and offered her a choice of breakfast cereals he went back outside again. He told her she could stay as long as she liked. There was no hurry.

Why then did she feel that there was? She gulped down her food and coffee quickly. She hoped Alice would be back soon, but if not she'd just have to write or phone later. Her train of thought reminded her to turn on her mobile. There were no messages, but just as she was carrying her used breakfast things to the sink it rang.

'Sorry to be so late,' said Nikki, sounding embarrassed. 'Bit of a heavy session last night.'

Grace refrained from asking who with. She wasn't in the mood for chitchat.

'It's about that thing on the windowsill,' Nikki went on. 'You know, you told me to give you a buzz when it did anything.'

She took a moment to understand. Then she realized that Nikki was talking about the tape recorder she had set to intercept messages from McGovern's office line. There had been no calls at all, until now.

'What's it say?' she demanded eagerly.

'Be easiest if I played it back to you,' said Nikki. 'I've just rewound it ready, hang on a sec. I'll hold it to the phone. Hope you can hear clearly.'

It wasn't a great recording but McGovern's voice was instantly recognizable. He was talking to Carol.

'Something's come up,' he told her after a brusque preamble. 'Something the matter at the cottage, I've got to go up to Derbyshire for a few days.'

Her replay was tiny and indistinct, but Grace thought she was asking why the agent couldn't handle it.

'Something I've got to do myself,' he said, his voice strong with irritation. 'Unfortunately I've got a meeting I can't get out of tomorrow morning with the police. I'm back in Guildford now, at the office, they gave me a ride back from Bournemouth. Can you pick me up in an hour? Make sure there's a full tank of petrol. I'll be taking the car tomorrow, go up after lunch.'

There was a little more, mostly Carol enquiring after his wellbeing, but it was clear from McGovern's tone that he was in no mood to talk. The conversation ended suddenly with his reminder that she should be at the office in an hour.

'Is that all right then?' asked Nikki when the tape had clicked off. 'As I say, I saw the light on the machine winking at me when I came in. It must have recorded last night or first thing this morning.'

'Last night, I think,' said Grace. It was likely McGovern had come back from Bournemouth with Jimmy Collins. 'Thanks, Nikki. I probably won't be back today. Let me know on the mobile if anything else comes up, will you?'

Grace snatched up her coat and bag and went outside. Malcolm was kneeling on a little mat by one of his flower beds, attending to the stone border. There was a freezing wind, but Malcolm was seriously underdressed for the time of year. Hardy folk up here, Grace thought to herself as she shivered in her Barbour.

'Going back then?' he called out when he saw her coming. 'Alice'll be sorry to miss you.'

'And I'm sorry to miss her too. Thank you so much for your help and hospitality, Malcolm, I can't tell you how brilliant you've been, both of you.'

She tried to tell him, though, and he asserted with equal fervour that it had been nothing, nothing at all. She asked him the quickest way into town, saying she wanted to have a quick look around, seeing as she'd come all this way. Again he offered to guide her, and again she had to decline, firmly. He told her to have a look at the opera house and have a walk through the gardens.

She took his directions but stayed in the car. She wanted the Bakewell road. Under an hour, depending on traffic, he had told her. She was sure she could find the place, the descriptions in the newspaper cuttings had been quite precise and she had a map. Of course, it would have been quicker if she had allowed Malcolm to accompany her, but for what she was planning to do she needed to be on her own.

In the event it was harder to find than she had bargained for and it took her the best part of two hours. She managed to miss the last turn-off twice. There were no signs and the road surface was so rutted and cracked that she took it at first for a private track. After a mile or so the road improved and she came to a quarry that had been mentioned in the old reports and was marked on the map. She was high up now, in a bare bleak landscape. There had been a light snowfall the night before, as Alice had predicted. It was visible in the branches of the few and stunted trees. The sheep-cropped grasses of the hillsides glistened white with frost.

The road zigzagged, falling away sharply to the left where the hillside had been gouged out by generations of quarriers. On the right, where the slopes were gentler, a straggling line of pony trekkers was etched out against the skyline. It was the first sign of life Grace had encountered since turning off the main road. The riders were heading along a path that led in parallel with a long stretch of dry-stone wall into a shallow valley. There was a house in the valley.

Grace drove past slowly. The house was old and squat, built from the same grey stone as the low wall that enclosed its garden, the same as the wall on the neighbouring hill. The roof was covered with plain dark slates. It was a drab, cold and uninviting place. No wonder McGovern had difficulty renting it out to holidaymakers. And no wonder his first wife had been bored and lonely living there.

Grace drove on, following the road as it mounted the next

hill. It was single track now and halfway up there was a lay-by for passing cars. Grace parked and got out.

The cold wind cut her to the bone in moments. She zipped her jacket up to the chin, for all the good it would do. Fortunately she had a scarf in one of her pockets and gloves in the other. She put them on and walked briskly back down the hill. It was about four hundred yards back to the house.

By the time she got there she was wishing she'd just gone straight up and parked in the drive. She reproved herself for being unnecessarily cautious. It was only just after midday, McGovern couldn't possibly get here from Guildford before the evening, and it was hardly likely that anyone would have even noticed her car, let alone considered it suspicious. But old habits died hard. The pony trekkers were heading north into the next valley and were almost out of sight. Grace waited for them to disappear before she walked up the flat gravel drive. An old ceramic nameplate on the door, decorated with incongruously colourful pictures of flowers, proclaimed the name of the place as Roughwood Cottage, if she had been in any doubt.

A flagstoned path led round the side of the house. The path was narrow, squeezed in between the main wall of the building and a low flat-roofed double garage constructed from unattractive breeze blocks. There was a small window in the garage but it was boarded up. All of the windows in the house were equally opaque, drawn blinds and curtains hugging the frames from the inside. The place might have belonged to an especially misanthropic hermit.

At the back she found a small enclosed garden. A single sad thin fruit tree stood in the middle of the lawn, which took up half of the available space. The rest was covered with the patio.

She walked over the stones, relaid smoothly now, imagining the scene a dozen years ago, the place swarming with police, pickaxes and shovels digging out what they were all convinced was a burial chamber. There had been nothing, of course, but if McGovern really had killed his wife and her lover then what had he done with their bodies? Buried corpses had a nasty habit of resurfacing, even after this many years, and with modern DNA techniques identification was nowadays a likelihood. But as far as Malcolm Thexton knew there had been no discoveries of human remains that could have fitted the bill. Of course McGovern might have disposed of the bodies anywhere, but if, say, he had taken them in the boot of the car he drove down to London on the weekend of the disappearance, and dumped them somewhere on the way, then he had been taking a hell of a risk. Surely it would have been safer to dispose of them nearer to home, somewhere he could keep an eye on them? She tried to imagine herself in his shoes. He was a clever, resourceful man.

But he was cleverer now than he had been a dozen years ago. His disposal of his second wife had been even more cold-blooded than the first. The fall guy had been pumped and primed, the execution of the crime so faultless that the police didn't even begin to suspect the truth. Even so, he had made one mistake. He had forgotten her. She remembered the look of total surprise on his face when he had recognized her in Bournemouth. He had recovered quickly, but he wasn't used to being on the defensive and it showed. Had he made any other errors the first time around? If Dave Reynolds had been right then he had set the whole thing up with incredible nerve, actually putting his own head into the noose and inviting the police to draw it tight. He had known that suspicion would fall on him, so rather than try and sidestep it he had invited it. He was a psychologist of distinction, as his handling of Lewis demonstrated only too clearly. He had made himself the obvious suspect for the murder of Margaret, gambling that the police would be overhasty and spoil their own case. He had made an equally cool calculation in murdering Julie. If this first killing had been a dry run then he had no doubt learnt from his mistakes.

What were the mistakes?

Why was he driving up here? What did he need to do that couldn't be done by the agent? Had he grown careless and left something he hadn't meant to leave, never thinking that anyone would have a reason to pry into an old long-forgotten case again? Would she even recognize it for what it was if she stumbled across it? She reckoned she had a good four or five hours in which to find out.

She glanced around, for form's sake. Nothing stirred in the bleak deserted landscape. She walked across the stones to the double patio doors. Faded red floor-length curtains blocked her view of the interior. The lock was a Yale. She gave the doors a gentle push at the top and the bottom. There were no bolts, and one smart shove would have sufficed to split the cracked and slowly rotting wooden frame. There was no need for force, though, and nor did she need George Courtenay's keys. She rooted around in the bottom of her bag until she came up with a thin plastic ruler. It was stronger and more supple than a credit card. She slipped it into the gap between the two doors and tripped the latch. She stepped inside, closed the door and pulled the curtains shut again behind her.

It was very dark, and colder even than outside. She stood with her arms clasped, trying to rub some warmth into her shivering limbs, while her eyes adjusted to the gloom. It was a big room, too big, it seemed, to be in proportion with the low white-plastered ceiling. The plain blue-papered walls were almost bare, as was the floor. There was one door, half-open, through which she could just make out a staircase. There was no carpet, just a couple of threadbare rugs covering some of the floorboards. The furniture had been pushed to the sides and was covered with dustsheets, apart from one heavy wooden chair which was sitting in the middle of the room. She took a step towards it, drawn by its incongruity. There was something box-like on the floor next to it. She went closer. It was a brown leather briefcase.

The light went on suddenly. Grace threw up a hand to shield herself from the bright painful glare. Strange shapes danced before her startled eyes, one shape in particular advancing on her from the door.

'Good morning, Miss Cornish,' said Peter McGovern.

Although there was politeness in the words there was nothing pleasant in his tone, nothing pleasant in him at all, a wiry hard-edged unforgiving man, not hiding now behind the surface charm which was his prop of necessity. He had no need of it, now.

Not with a gun in his hand.

27

Grace Cornish was in the chair in the middle of the room. Her hands were tied behind her back, and her feet were tied to the legs of the chair. Her gag was a napkin, not tied too tightly, leaving her room enough to breathe through her nose, but secured in place with masking tape, wrapped twice around her face. More masking tape secured the cloths round her wrists and ankles. It was important to leave no marks on her body, not even a residue of the sticky tape, hence the careful double layering of the bonds. A towel taped around the top of her head acted as a blindfold.

Peter McGovern got up from the sofa in which he had been sitting and watching her, and walked twice around the chair, slowly, deliberately, his feet heavy on the bare floorboards. Her head moved to the sounds of his footfalls. It was the first sound she had heard in the half-hour since he had tied her up, though she could have had no idea of the time that had elapsed. A minute or an hour, what did it signify to her? She would sense nothing except her own fear. He imagined the intensity of it now, hearing him but not knowing what he was doing. She wouldn't know his intentions, though she would guess they were not benign. He had seen the terror in her eyes before he had covered them.

She had frozen when she had seen him with the gun. That had been the moment of danger, the one time when she might have tried to run for it or even attack him. She'd been in the police, no doubt she knew something of self-defence, and he didn't. Although he was stronger than he looked she might have been able to get away, but the gun had deterred her, the best irony of all. Yes, he had banked on it, of course; he had taken fully into account her knowledge of his willingness to pull the trigger, but still it had filled him with an intense feeling of satisfaction that was like a physical pleasure. A pity that he had not had time to savour it. He had been forced to move fast, to give her no time to think or to recover.

'Take off your coat,' he had ordered, taking a step towards her and pointing the gun at her face.

She had hesitated. Had it been shock or had she thought that he was going to interfere with her? The very idea had almost made him laugh.

'Take it off!'

He had snapped the order at her the second time. She was still too stunned to offer any resistance. He had advanced on her and she had taken a step back towards the chair, the coat slipping from her shoulders.

'Sit!'

And she had obeyed, like a good dog. He had gone behind her and put the tip of the barrel to the back of her head while he knelt and seized her arm. He had let her feel the hard cold metal. He had snapped on the handcuffs, one wrist at a time, then done the blindfold immediately to disorient her; then the legs and the gag. He had worked out the order beforehand and had all the materials ready in the briefcase. Lastly he had removed her gloves, taken off the cuffs lest the metal mark her skin, and retied her with the dishcloth and the tape. Then he had gone to sit in the dustsheet-covered armchair opposite and to watch.

To watch and enjoy. The terror she must have been experiencing was unimaginable. That didn't stop him from trying to imagine it.

He was almost sorry to break the spell by getting up to walk around her, but after half an hour he was stiff and cold, despite his heavy coat and gloves, and he needed to restore some circulation. When he had done his second lap of the chair he stopped behind her. He took off his glove and felt her face with the tips of his fingers.

She jumped at his touch. The heavy chair actually moved a fraction of an inch across the floor, he heard the squeak and scrape of the legs against the floorboards. The cry of her fear died muffled in the gag. All that came out was a tiny strangled noise.

He touched her face again. He felt her stiffen, but this time there was no sudden movement. Her cheek was frozen. He knelt and touched her bound hands. Her fingers were like ice already. That was good.

It was all good. She was dressed in jeans and a roll-neck black sweater. He felt the material between his fingers. Oh so thin; far too thin for a winter's day in a house with no heating, let alone what was in store for her later. He started to walk around the chair again. He counted the circuits under his breath. One, two . . . he walked faster; three, four . . . her head had ceased following his movements. It was a pity that the gag and blindfold obscured her features. He wanted to observe the effects of his silent torture. There would be plenty of time. It was only one o'clock. In another few hours it would be dark, and then there would be the long evening to get through. By the time midnight came, the appointed hour, she would be frozen both literally and psychologically. Then there would be no struggle.

He sat down again, his hand resting on the gun, which was on the arm of the sofa. She was no doubt expecting him to shoot her. After all, he had shot Julie, as she knew. Did she know that he had shot the others as well? No, she couldn't have known it for sure. But she had spoken with Thexton, and it was his boss who had almost broken him. He hadn't been frightened on many occasions in his life, but his interrogation by Dave Reynolds had been one of them. He didn't like to be reminded of it. It was another good reason to let her suffer. But he had so many good reasons.

It was strange being in this house again. He usually came up once or twice a year, but only after there had been paying guests, to check that nothing was amiss. There were not so many guests these days, and who could blame them? Because he wouldn't let in any decorators the place had gone to seed. But the last thing he wanted was workmen trampling in and out disturbing things. No one could understand why he kept the place on, but he had no choice. A new owner might not be so content to let it rot. It was useful for tax purposes anyway, provided he still went through the motions of letting it out.

Margaret had been standing about there, where the chair was, when he shot her. They had just had an argument about the money. That at any rate had been the pretext, though they both knew that it had really been about her lover. It had been his masterstroke, the money, or so he had thought at the time. These days his standards were so much higher. The money was in their joint bank account, but it had to be she who withdrew it, her signature on the cheque and her face fresh in the cashier's memory. He had agreed to pay the builder £200 in cash to lay the patio and repair the garden wall. The argument was about why he had insisted that she take all of the rest of the money out too, the full £1,000. He had told her that he had spotted a good second-hand car for sale locally. The plan was that they would drive over in the evening and if she liked it they could offer cash, get a better deal. She had been going on and on about needing a new car for years, and he had always told her that they couldn't afford it. No doubt she had interpreted his change of heart as a desperate ploy to keep her affections. He had been working hard for weeks to give her the impression that he was trying to win her back.

But on her return from the bank she had said that they shouldn't use it for a car. She had never had the chance to explain her reasoning, but his guess was that she wanted cash to set up home with her lover. As if he would ever have agreed to let her have the money, *his* money, for that. He had got cross with her and she had sulked, her usual tactic. She had turned her back on him and crossed her arms. He had walked across the room, taken the Beretta out of his pocket, slipped the safety catch, placed the barrel between her shoulder blades and pulled the trigger. He would always remember the look of surprise on her face. She had fallen backwards, almost knocking into him, and had lain for a moment looking up, shocked and bewildered. Then the blood had trickled out of her mouth, her body had twitched a couple of times and she had died. It had been very simple.

He had experienced revulsion when he had touched her,

but that had been because of who she was and what she had done to him, not because he was squeamish or anything like that. It was mere retribution, just and deserved. He had played the scene over too many times in his head for the reality to be shocking, though the surge of exhilaration he experienced had been stronger than anticipated. Her body had come to rest neatly where it was meant to, on the newspaper he had laid down earlier. They had almost had an argument over the newspaper too. He had said he didn't want workmen's boots bringing mud into the house, and she had said that if they wanted to come in it would be through the kitchen. He had said it so glibly; even in those days he could have lied for a living. He hadn't bothered to argue the point with her, because there weren't going to be any workmen. As it turned out there was only a smear of blood on the paper when he came to move her. The hole in her back had been drilled in precisely and there was no exit wound. A small-calibre low-velocity gun was as lethal as a Magnum or an Uzi if one only knew how to use it, and he did. He had acquired the Beretta from an old man, a sheep farmer called Wilkes he had met at the shooting club. Wilkes had bad eyesight and no longer shot, but he liked to take every opportunity of socializing with his old friends, because he was dying of lung cancer and didn't have long left. It was going to be a very painful death. The cancer was in his liver and his spine and it was agony. He had given lifts to Wilkes a couple of times. The old man was poor as well as ill and was worried about his wife coping after he had gone. It had seemed like he was doing him a good turn to offer him cash for his guns, the Beretta and the Webley. Wilkes had known that he didn't have a licence, so there was no danger of him letting on. Wilkes had taken the money, £150, and died a week later. The last time he had seen him he confessed that he would have used one of the guns to take his own life, had it not been for the life assurance policy. Wilkes had meant it. He had been impressed by the old man's resolution and lack of self-pity.

He had shot Paul Bramall with Wilkes's Beretta too. It had been just as easy. He had known that Bramall was coming round because he had overheard Margaret talking to him on the phone. He had heard her say that she was going to tell her husband that they were off to a meeting to discuss the casting of next season's musical at the society. It was obviously easier for him to come to her because his girlfriend was more suspicious than her husband. What a fool must that husband be! he had thought as he listened, his ear pressed to the keyhole.

He had greeted Bramall at the door just like that fool, jolly and unconcerned. Margaret was upstairs, he had told him, would he sit down and have a drink? Bramall had been at his ease, had sat just where he was now, on the sofa. My apologies for the dustsheets, he had said, laughing, talking about the builders as he brought his wife's lover his Scotch. So many apologies to make, and such little time! Where, he had wondered to himself, had she been planning to take her lover tonight, in the passenger seat of the car she was always complaining wasn't big or reliable enough for her? What did they usually do? Pull over in some lay-by and make awkward love in the back, or go to some cheap hotel? He would never find out now, not after giving him the drink and walking behind the sofa, saying he had to draw the curtains. Whoosh! the curtains had gone, and Bramall had never looked back. Bang! the gun had gone, one little bullet through the top of the skull and down into the brain, and he had never looked at anything again. And so, he had thought, looking down at the corpse, which of us is the fool now?

The killing had been easy. Disposing of the bodies had been the difficulty. He had thought about putting them into acid in the bath, but he had read too many cases of forensic scientists finding telltale remains in the drains. He had considered dismembering them, but that would have been messy and time-consuming. Many times, though, as the long night wore on, he had found himself wishing that he had cut them up, for the weight of the corpses nearly finished him. Margaret was comparatively easy, because she was so small, but Bramall, though not tall, was heavy, a good thirteen stone at least. He had wrapped both the bodies in blankets and dragged them out to the garage, where two trunks were waiting. He had driven all the way to Leeds to buy the trunks from a specialist luggage firm. They were old-fashioned and solidly built with metal corners, over five feet in length. He had lain them on their sides and jammed the bodies in, with difficulty. He had a two-wheeled trolley ready, but he hadn't been able to balance the trunks on it satisfactorily. He had had to drag them out, inch by inch, before standing them up and tipping them into the back of the car. The operation had required strength he had never known he had possessed. Although the car was an estate there was only room for one trunk at a time (the second one had come back from Leeds strapped to the roof rack) so he had been forced to make two trips. By the time he had finished, after two in the morning, he was so shattered he could barely move.

He had left the bodies at the abandoned quarry three miles down the road. The gate was padlocked and plastered with KEEP OUT and DANGER signs, but one of the sections of wire fence had been torn away in the distant past by scavengers and he drove straight through. There was nothing left to scavenge any more and there had been no visitors for years. There could be soon though, if the police were to launch a manhunt. The trunks were hidden under some old beams and strips of rusty corrugated metal and wouldn't have been hard to find.

But there had been no manhunt. There had been just the one well-publicized search, in the place he had directed them to look. The whole enterprise had been orchestrated with balance in mind. He had needed both to establish a suspicion of innocence should it ever get so far as a jury, and a more immediate suspicion of guilt. He had known that the police would sooner or later suspect foul play because they always did. He had worked his way through every book on true crime in the library and studied case histories. If a woman died or disappeared in mysterious circumstances then more often than not her husband or lover was involved. Sometimes it was the other way round and sometimes the combination of relatives was different, a stepfather and a stepdaughter perhaps. So it was natural for the police to search for a domestic solution to a domestic crime. It was a case of playing the odds. He had merely catalysed the process, and at the same time supplied them with enough rope to hang themselves.

He hadn't been able to go back for the bodies until nearly a week after his release from custody. It was a good thing the police had got off his back at last; the stench from the trunks filled his car for days. He had buried them in the place where no one would ever look again, in the hole in the back garden. The builders had come to relay the patio the next day, all paid for courtesy of the public purse. He had been going to throw in the two illegal pistols with the trunks, but he had decided that there was no point. If by some twist of fate the bodies ever did come to light the police weren't going to need a bullet match to ascertain his guilt. So he had kept the guns in a safety deposit box and they had come in very useful, all these years later. It was a pity he didn't still have them.

He sat back in the sofa of the chilly old living room and contemplated Grace Cornish. It would have given him as much satisfaction as Margaret and Julie combined to have put a bullet between her eyes. He had thought at first that she was just after money, but she was more dangerous than that. She had been after him. He picked up the pistol from the arm of the sofa and weighed it in his hands. Their confrontation in Bournemouth had put the wind up him. She had put him in hot water with the police. Collins hadn't said anything about Carol afterwards but he would have heard her innuendo all right, the seed of suspicion would have been planted. It hadn't occurred to the police to poke around in his private life, to dredge up his past. Why should it have done without her prompting? Fortunately the name Malcolm Thexton had meant nothing. Collins had asked him about it and he had shrugged, said he hadn't a clue what she was talking about. Still, she had caused him a lot of trouble, even if it had only been guesswork on her part. What had made her dangerous was not what she knew but what she might have found out.

He flicked off the safety catch on the pistol. It was a Smith & Wesson and it felt satisfyingly solid in his grip. He gave the trigger a little squeeze, watched the hammer begin to move.

It was a silly way to behave. Old Wilkes and his friends would have had him drummed out of the gun club if they'd seen him acting so carelessly. Only he wasn't.

The gun was a fake. A very good one, but a fake nonetheless. He had bought it a year ago from a replica shop in London, at about the time he had finally decided to kill Julie. It was a decision he had come to with the greatest reluctance, not because she didn't deserve it, but because of the risks it entailed. He had so much more to lose the second time around. He had actually given serious consideration to divorcing her, but after taking discreet soundings he had been appalled to learn the likely scale of any settlement. The injustice of it all had helped put his plans into focus. The replica gun had been in case anyone should have seen him by some mischance with either of the real weapons, when he would have claimed that the witness was mistaken and it was only a harmless fake. What a pity the woman would never know! He was almost tempted to take the blindfold off and show her. It might have been worth it for the look on her face. But he wasn't playing games.

Her jacket was lying on the floor where it had fallen, and her bag was next to it. He went over and got them, putting his feet down heavily again to let her know that he was there. He found an interesting set of keys in her coat pocket. That must have been how she'd got into his office to bug his phone. The security man who had come round yesterday had spotted the bug straight off. He had been surprised at not being allowed to remove it. But why disappoint a customer? It was so much easier to make a sale if you told people what they wanted to hear. So she had been through his drawers and found out about Roughwood Cottage. That had led her to Thexton. She had made her connections very quickly. Oh, she was dangerous all right. He had had to act immediately to eliminate her.

He had used the bugged phone for her benefit almost at once, then rung Carol again a minute later from his mobile to cancel his orders. He had hired a car and left for Derbyshire within the hour. He had been in the cottage for nearly twenty hours now, half freezing to death in the night as he waited in the darkness for her to come. That was another reason to let her suffer now.

He emptied her bag on to the sofa. The car keys were on a Renault fob. He had watched her park through a gap in the upstairs bedroom curtains. He would retrieve her car after dark; in the meantime he put the keys into his pocket. There was a diary, very unrevealing, two packets of tissues, a tube of mints, an unopened packet of aspirin and a lipstick. There was a pair of handcuffs, rather more solid and impressive-looking than his own, which had come from a sex shop in Soho. He looked in the side pockets and found an opened packet of Durex containing one condom. He wondered briefly where the other two had got to. Had she picked up a man at that seedy hotel in Bournemouth? So loose and free with their affections, these women; like Margaret; like Julie: these faithless whores. Her mobile phone was on and he was surprised to see a signal, albeit a weak one, because it was a bad area for reception. Fortunately the battery was low. It would be dead by tonight; in sympathy, perhaps, with its owner.

He looked at his watch. The hands had barely moved since the last time he'd looked. The whisky and chocolate with which he had sustained himself since yesterday were finished. But if he was hungry he was not tired, though he had not slept for thirty-six hours. His raw nervous energy would keep him going, and his patience. It was his ability to wait on events that had always given all his various schemes, in and out of business, such depth. He had read of a case last year where a man had taken out life insurance against his wife one week and murdered her the next. Rarely could a life sentence have been so richly deserved. He had forced himself to wait a year before cashing in Julie's policy. It hadn't been easy enduring her, but the delay had allowed his scheme to mature. Murder and a get-rich-quick mentality made for the wrong sort of bedfellows. And anyway, revenge, as they said, was a dish best tasted cold. He believed in the long-term view, the slow burn. Betrayal was the ultimate crime and it deserved condign punishment. The law was a disgrace. A man could slave all his working life and then his wife, a pampered stay-at-home, could turn around and demand half his house, his money. He had been generous to both his wives and each had responded with contempt, taking their brawny stupid lovers, feeding their own vanity from his wallet. All he was doing was reclaiming what was his own. Like going into the supermarket and asking for cashback with your chargecard. As Julie had done, often enough. How could she have had the nerve to charge her expenses to him while she was opening her legs to another man? That was women for you. Take the one sitting bound and helpless in the chair. She had promised confidentiality. She had betrayed him. Case made. Punishment approved.

He looked at his watch again, a reflex action; he had so much time to kill. It was a quarter past one. Why couldn't she have come last night, as he had anticipated? Then he could have had it all done and dusted. Now he'd have to start spinning some story to explain his absence from Guildford for so long. Not that he would need an alibi for this little excursion, that was the beauty of it. Miss Cornish was going to suffer a tragic accident.

He lit a cigarette. He was having to go easy, he had only half a packet left to get through the rest of the day. A pity the woman didn't smoke; he could have helped himself. They would find her diary and driving licence in the morning in her bag, it wouldn't take long to identify the body. The road near the quarry where she was going to end up was so little used that she might not be found until the afternoon, but sooner or later someone, probably a local farmer, would stumble across the scene. He imagined it to himself.

Here was the farmer driving his tractor, coming round the bend, that sharp dipping hairpin which in itself warranted a hazard sign. The little stone bridge came up so quickly, and was so narrow, that on the first occasion he'd used it himself, many years ago, he had clipped his wing mirror. At night it was potentially lethal, as the farmer would discover when he dismounted from his tractor. There would be her little white car, the front offside stoved in, glass from the headlamps everywhere, the result of a collision with the stone wall. Not a full head-on crash, more of a dodgems bump, but enough to put the car out of action. There would be a flat tyre too, just to emphasize the point; he had the hammer and nail ready along with all the other props in his briefcase. The driver's door was hanging open, and there was no one inside. No doubt the driver had wandered off, dazed and disoriented, to look for help. The weather forecast had promised more snow, so there might be footprints to lead the curious eye. Off down the road she had drifted. Along the way she had dropped her useless mobile phone, no doubt frustrated at not being able to get a signal. And then, in the pitch-darkness she had had her accident. The river bank was slippery and treacherous. She must have stumbled, poor girl. The water wasn't deep, but it was freezing and she was chilled to the bone already in her thin and unsuitable clothes. She hadn't had the strength to pull herself out. She had lost consciousness and just slipped in. A tragic accident? Of course; how could it be anything else when there wasn't a mark on her body and she had so obviously been all alone?

Naturally the police would ask some questions, but since there could be no suspicion of foul play they wouldn't be of the awkward variety. Perhaps Miss Cornish had told someone why she was coming up to Derbyshire, but he doubted it; everything she had done so far indicated that she was operating on her own. It would be obvious that she had been snooping around and poking her nose in, as usual, where it wasn't wanted, but there would be no reason to suppose that she had actually been into the cottage; and therefore no reason at all to suppose that he, or anyone else for that matter, might have had a hand in her death.

He finished his cigarette and got up to stretch his legs again. This time the hooded head hardly moved to follow him around. Had she given up already? Or was she one of those who would carry on clinging to hope when there was none? It was an interesting question. Julie had struggled to the end, but then again, she hadn't known what was coming. She had been due to catch a train after lunch from Guildford, the first leg of her trip to Scotland. He had gone up while she was packing. He had told her at breakfast that he was working from home that day and his presence had been annoying her all morning. The moment he came into the bedroom she had turned her back on him. Why did they always turn their backs on him? He had come up silently from behind, taking the piece of lead piping from one pocket and the handcuffs from the other. He had struck her once on the back of the head, not too hard but enough to stun her. She had fallen to her knees, groggy but not unconscious. He handcuffed her wrists behind her back, then pulled her up by her hair and threw her on to the bed, where he taped her ankles together and gagged her. Then he taped her hands and removed the cuffs, the same technique he had applied just now. By the time Julie recovered from the blow she was helpless, but that hadn't stopped her struggling. All afternoon and all evening she had struggled, twisting and turning on the bed, trying to chew off her gag. He had struck her many more times, shutting her up on each occasion for a few minutes only. She had been so filled with rage and fury, but she had never guessed her fate. At half past eleven, just after he had seen the headlamps of the builder's Range Rover go by, he had placed a pillow over her face and shot her through it. She had died without having had a clue what was going on. He had had plenty of time to untie her bonds, put two more bullets in the wall and get downstairs. He had taken off his gloves and carefully put the pistol into a handkerchief before transferring it to his pocket. On that day at Foreman's house he had ensured there was a smear of oil on the grip and trigger. Lewis had left at least one clear print above the safety catch which he had discovered afterwards with a magnifying glass and had taken pains to preserve. He had watched through the keyhole of the living room when Lewis came into the hall from the kitchen, ridiculously garbed like an amateur terrorist. He didn't wait for him to go up the stairs but went straight out into the garden and called the police on his mobile. He had seen Lewis come running out of the house five minutes later. The police car was coming already, he could hear a siren down the lane, which was impressive. He had only just had time to dispose of the Webley in the flower bed before the police car arrived. He had rather admired the unarmed officer who had gone up into the house and had discovered Julie's body. That had taken some nerve; as, indeed, had his own performance. His handling of Lewis had pleased him the most. He had gauged his weaknesses perfectly, his vanity, his bitter greed, his obsessiveness with the body beautiful. This was a man for whom death would be preferable to sickness and imperfection. He had also gauged his one abiding strength, and used that against him too. Lewis, the man with the shadow life, knew how to keep a secret. It was a secret he would have much time to ponder on, for the next twenty years or so.

He would have liked to interrogate the Cornish woman, to discover exactly how much Lewis had told her and how much she had found out for herself, but he could live without knowing. The only important thing now was to break her down, to deprive her senses and thus destroy her will before he destroyed her body. Tonight promised to be even colder than the night before. It would have been good to let her die of exposure, better than drowning and somehow neater. But the medical books he had consulted had been so vague. Sometimes people survived for days in freezing conditions. It depended on the toughness of the individual, and with this individual the proposition would have been too risky.

He took off his glove and felt in his pocket for the brown paper bag in which he had kept the chocolate. He fingered the discarded scrunched-up wrappers thoroughly, just in case he'd missed one. He hadn't. He was annoyed with himself for not having brought more food. It was her fault, not his. She should have been here last night. She had thrown his plans out of kilter, again. He sat down on the sofa, took the brown paper bag out of his pocket and emptied the wrappings into his briefcase. He smoothed out the bag, then squeezed it slowly into his palm, making a narrow funnel of the open end at the top of his grip.

He got up, quietly this time, not clumping his shoes down on the floorboards. He walked slowly towards the window, then along the wall, round towards the back of the chair. Her head hadn't moved. She just sat there listlessly, head sagging. He smiled.

He tiptoed towards her, right up to the back of the chair.

Still there was no reaction. He raised the neck of the paper bag to his mouth and breathed into it gently. The brown paper filled out into a balloon, making a crinkling but very gentle sound. She didn't hear it. He extended his arm until the blown-up bag was next to her ear. And then he burst it suddenly with the flat of his left hand.

The noise was like a gun going off. His own ears rang with it. The effect on the woman was dramatic.

Her head snapped back, her whole body jerked as if an electric shock had gone through it. The chair seemed to lift off the floor as her body jumped. She whimpered like a little animal.

Peter McGovern laughed out loud.

28

The cold was unimaginable, indescribable. There was ice in her blood, her bones. One thought kept her going.

She had no feeling left at all in her hands and feet, little sense of anything at all beyond her frozen crushing misery. It had got into her brain as well, slowing her furious fear-driven thoughts to a crawl. How long had this nightmare been going on? It felt like all her life.

She could see nothing. The blindfold covered her nose almost to the tip and came to below her cheekbones; there wasn't even the tiniest crack for any light to squeeze through. The gag was equally tight. She had tried to loosen it by working up and down with her jawbone but to no effect. The taste of the cloth on her tongue had almost made her choke; she had to keep her mouth closed tight. She could still breathe through her nose, but that was all she could do. He had absolute control over her. He could kill her whenever he chose.

She should have taken her chances when he'd first walked in. He would certainly have shot her, but it would have been better than this. Why hadn't he shot her already? There must be some reason he was keeping her alive, but it was only a stay of execution, not a reprieve. She was going to end up like Julie, like Margaret, like anyone who got in his way. Every time she heard his footstep she knew that it could be the last thing she ever heard. He wouldn't get away with it. He couldn't get away with it, not again. When they found her body they would know who had done it. Bob would know, Malcolm Thexton too. They would catch him. When she was dead.

Waves of self-pity rolled over her, swamping the all-consuming terror. She didn't want to die. God, she didn't want to die, to be another nameless statistic on the murder charts. She knew the processes, she had seen it all happen so many times, the dispassionate doctor slicing the corpse, her corpse, her name on the tag, little Grace, so loved once, so cherished, cut up on the slab, the sharp surgical smells co-mingling with the corrupt stink of putrid organs, decayed flesh. She had retched the first time she had witnessed an autopsy. Anyone would. The thing dissected was no longer human. By the time it was released for burial it was just a collection of spare parts.

Little Grace, boxed and dispatched with heartbreak and floods of tears. She imagined her parents' grief, her friends' uncomprehending shock; and her below in the cold black earth. What had she done to deserve that? She had done bad things sometimes, but she wasn't bad. She was little Grace, the apple of her daddy's eye. He used to bounce her on his knee whenever he came in from his shift, while she played with the buttons and the bright sparkling badge on his uniform and cap. Her brothers had been jealous, though he had loved them too. Her memories had a rosy glow. There had been so much love, so much warmth and goodness. They had always been such a close and happy family. When had she last told them she loved them? She remembered how hurt her parents had been when she'd gone through her difficult phase, shaving her hair and putting a ring through her nose and staying out late with her unsuitable friends, all engaged in their private pointless rebellions. She felt guilty. Other memories flashed at random across her mind, filling her with yearning and loss and helplessness. When had she last told them she loved them? Why couldn't she remember? Oh God no, please, let it stop . . .

She fought back the tears, succeeded somehow in reining in the terror. Get a grip, woman, for God's sake . . . she wasn't little Grace any more, that winsome dependent creature in ribbons and ponytails. She was a full-grown woman, independent and tough-minded. She couldn't give up. She wasn't dead yet, was she? No, and there had to be a reason why she wasn't. If she could just work it out it might give her a straw to clutch at, which was better than clinging to the sentimental flotsam swimming round her brain. She might be physically helpless but she could still think. If only it wasn't so cold . . .

Her thoughts kept drifting away. There was nothing to anchor them, no awareness of time, no sense of anything except the awful numbing cold. It was hard to focus in this silent sightless world. She would start to think it through, and then some unbidden image would dart into her consciousness and block everything out. Either that or she would succumb to the pack ice in her veins and sink into catatonic lethargy, only startling herself out of it when the full horror of her situation reared up again. And thus it went, in cycles of emptiness and despair, on and on for however long it had been; forever. It was as if she were drugged and hallucinating. It was the fear of death that kept her brain alive in sudden rushes. She fought to focus herself. One memory kept thrusting itself into the chaos in her head. She clung to it, that she might feed her will to live. It was the thought that kept her going.

It was his laughter, the memory of his dry sadistic cackle. She remembered his pleasure in her pain and fear. He had crept up on her and burst a bag next to her ear. For a second she had thought it was a gun, no doubt what he had meant her to think, but then she had heard him screwing up the paper and she had recognized the sound. It was a childish prank, but not done with the innocence of a child. He had done it because he enjoyed what he was doing. Just as when the time came he would enjoy the act of killing her. She forced herself to remember his face and pictured his thin colourless features splitting with mirth. Hatred fought with fear for tenancy of her consciousness. She kept thinking of his laughing face, willing her hatred to win.

She hadn't heard him for a long time. She had heard his footsteps a lot at the beginning, however many hours ago that had been, but he was quiet now. He was still there though, she could sense him. What was his game? Was he just prolonging his pleasure, tormenting her until he was sated? Or was he waiting for something? For what might a murderer wait?

For an accomplice? No, that wasn't his style: he was a loner who trusted no one. For darkness then? Yes, that was a better reason to wait. It meant nothing to her, for whom all was dark, but why else had he not shot her already? He had probably shot his first wife in this house, her lover too, perhaps in this very room. Their bodies had never been found. He would have taken them away, but not in daylight, even in as remote a spot as this. Maybe that was why he hadn't yet killed her. He had to get her to the burial ground, wherever that was. It would be easier to make her walk out of the house under her own steam, so much easier than having to drag the dead weight of her corpse, the blood smearing the back seat or the boot of his car. That would be just like him, clinical and efficient. He'd have it all worked out, like a railway timetable. Maybe you had to admire him in a way. No, no that was wrong. Admiration didn't begin to come into it. All that counted was hatred . . .

She had been losing it, slipping away into the void. She focused her thoughts on him again, sustaining herself with her loathing: that evil, manipulative bastard; that clever, ruthless sadistic murderer . . . such an ordinary man in other ways. Well-off and successful, yes, a role model for the material world, but with something dead or missing wherever it was inside a person that heart or soul or conscience – call it what you will – reside. Her time in the police had taught her that there were more people around who fitted that description than the rest of humanity would care to know about, but few, mercifully, made the transition from misfit to murderer. Something must have triggered the change; jealousy or greed, maybe, the usual suspects. Either that, or he had just been born with faulty wiring.

She concentrated on her body, willing herself to feel some sensation in her frozen extremities. Her well-bound hands and legs had long since passed from giving her pins and needles to mere numbness. Her limbs were just lumps of putty hanging from her torso. But she could make them move a little by rolling her shoulders and stretching her thighs from the hip. Her muscles protested, but they could still respond after a fashion. At least the bindings weren't cutting into her flesh. It was a small comfort. She hurt all over. The only other physical sensation of which she was aware was an unpleasant ache in her bladder. She wanted the bathroom. All she could do was grit her teeth and admit that it was probably the least of her troubles. She tried to flex the blood-starved muscles in her arms and legs again. If he was going to take her somewhere then he would have to untie her. Would she have strength enough to move? Her mind was slipping away again. She knew she couldn't take much more.

She was hearing things, voices and everyday noises, the tricks of her jumbled memory. There was a kind of humming in her head, a regular background beat to accompany the snatches of internal conversations and the chorus of unconnected sounds. She could see colours too, bright oranges and greens, more impossible tricks. Was she going mad? She could hear the revving of a car engine. It sounded close, almost as if it really were outside her head, almost real. The engine cut out. She heard a car door slam. It was real.

Suddenly there were no more sounds in her head. Even the background hum had stopped. She could feel her heart beating fast again, feel the blood pounding hard through her temples, reviving her sluggish brain. She was fully alert now, her ears straining to catch the slightest sound. There was a long silence. Then she heard a scraping noise and a click. A gust of freezing air blew across her face. Someone had come into the room. Someone had come to save her.

The patio door banged shut. Footsteps came towards her across the bare floorboards. A moment later she felt something tugging at her legs. With a shock she realized that her bonds had been loosed. It was true then. She was saved.

'Get up,' said McGovern.

29

He brought the car round on the dot of midnight. It was so dark he had to use the headlamps, but he turned them off again as soon as he was in the drive, coasting to a halt in front of the garage. The moon was out, bright and full, and the sky was dotted with stars, despite the forecast of snow clouds. It was so cold, though, that more snow was surely coming.

He got the car ready. It was an underpowered little thing with a tinny engine and a rattly exhaust. It was just as well he wasn't going far and had the big hired Audi sitting in the garage waiting to take him home. He cleared out the luggage space under the hatchback. There was a box with odd tools in it and a pair of old boots. He put them on the back seat, along with a stubby-handled broom with which he intended to brush over any of his footprints he might leave in the snow. He went back in and got the woman.

She didn't move when he told her to, so he yanked her up out of the chair by her hair. Her knees buckled and she fell to the floor. He'd had to cut her hands free to get her up, but she didn't even fling them out in front of her when she toppled over. She collapsed, like a rag doll. There hardly seemed any point in retying her wrists behind her back; he did so anyway. She lay gently shivering while he taped her arms.

He pulled her up again by her hair. She responded lethargically, took a few steps, stumbled and fell a second time. She seemed not to be fully conscious, which was exactly as he would have hoped but wasn't much help in the short term. He felt like kicking her to get her moving, but he didn't want to leave any bruises. He was pent-up, tired and tense after the long day's wait. He got her to the patio door and pushed her outside and along the passage between house and garage. The hatchback door of the car was open already. He tried to bundle her in.

She wouldn't fit. He had thought that he would be able to get her in on her side and fold her knees up into her chest. She would have been packed in like a sardine, but it hadn't occurred to him that she would be too big. But she was. Her legs hung out over the bumper and there was no way that he could close the door on her. He paused briefly to reconsider the situation and decided that he was being excessively cautious. The roads were certain to be completely deserted.

He went round to open the passenger door. The dim interior light came on, giving him enough to see by. He took the things off the back seat and rested them on the roof before returning for the woman. She was still half wedged in the back, her head crammed in to the side above the wheelarch indentation at an awkward angle. He pulled her by her legs, caught her as she fell out and laid her down temporarily on the ground. He examined the car more carefully. He'd never driven anything like it in his life, but he guessed that the back seat folded down in some way. He searched in vain for a catch, trying all the time to control the irritation that was mounting inside him. It was all taking much too long and it was exhausting him, just like all those years ago when he had disposed of Margaret and her lover. He paused to reconsider the situation. He was worried about the woman being seen, but again that was being overcautious. He was only going a couple of miles. He went round again to the front of the car.

The front seat catch was easy to find. He pushed the passenger seat forward and opened the door wide. The woman was lying on the ground exactly as he had left her, an inert lump. He raised her up by stages, first into a kneeling position, and then on to her feet by getting behind and lifting her up under the arms. He dragged her round to the front, her ankles trailing in the drive. She wasn't helping him much, but when he leant her against the car for a moment she tottered and swayed but managed to stay on her feet. He grabbed her by the collar and shoved her through the door on to the back seat. Her legs still stuck out. He went round to the other side and seized another fistful of her hair. It seemed to be the best way to get a reaction. He yanked her up from the roots and she slithered across the seat towards him half under her own steam.

He put the things on the roof into the boot, then went back inside the house for his briefcase and her coat and bag. He put the bag and case on the front passenger seat. He took the heavy fake pistol out of his coat pocket, placed it between the bag and the briefcase, and took off the coat. He laid both coats, his and the woman's, across the back seat, concealing her head and body, just in case. By the time he settled himself in behind the wheel and started the engine the windscreen had misted up again. He turned the heater up to full blast and was rewarded with a modest puff of lukewarm air. He wiped the glass in front of his eyes with the back of his glove and put the gears into reverse. He couldn't see a thing through the mirror. He wound down his window and stuck his head out. He reversed, very slowly, out of the drive. He checked his watch. He'd wasted a lot of time, it was almost half past midnight, and it was going to take him at least an hour to walk back once he had abandoned the car. At this rate he wouldn't be setting off for home until well after two. He put his foot down and drove as fast as he dared through the narrow lanes that led down to the quarry.

Mist concentrated around the headlamps, forcing him to slow down. It was just as well, for the sudden bend in the road, though so carefully anticipated, took him by surprise. He braked hard and felt the tyres slip on an icy patch. He slowed to a crawl as he approached the stone bridge. He'd travelled up in such a rush yesterday that he hadn't had time to come down and reconnoitre, but to his relief it was exactly as he remembered. He stopped in the middle of the bridge and turned off the engine. He took his torch from the briefcase and got out of the car.

The temperature had dropped even further. He reached back in for his coat. The woman was still lying exactly where he had put her in the back seat, her face covered by her jacket. He reached behind her, under the Barbour, and checked that the wrists were secure. He took off his glove and felt her bare back between her waistband and the bottom of her sweater. He felt cold enough himself, but her skin had the lifeless consistency of marble. He dug his fingers into her. She didn't react.

He buttoned up his coat and walked over to the parapet of the bridge. He pointed his torch down at the water. The light glistened off the black surface. The current was moving fast tonight, he could hear its steady rush above the rustling of the wind in the trees. He shone the torch at the banks. They seemed steep on both sides. He would have to take her away from the bridge, find a spot where there would be no danger of him falling in himself. Although she would be weak and confused she would still struggle once she realized what was going on. The trick would be to surprise her, which shouldn't be difficult. He'd find the spot, walk her down to the edge and trip her. Then make as if he was helping her up, but instead grab her head and force it into the water. With her mouth still gagged she wouldn't be able to breathe easily anyway and it shouldn't take long to drown her. He would remove the gag and bonds afterwards and tip her into the water. The only doubt was where exactly he was going to do it. He squinted into the darkness, trying to pick out the features of the river bank by the feeble light of the torch. All he could see clearly were a few white humps where the most recent snow had settled. It was no good, he would have to go down and have a look.

He heard the noise of a car. It was distant and muffled, but in the quiet of the night it carried easily. He held his breath and listened. It seemed to be drawing nearer. He jumped back into the Renault and restarted the engine.

He drove over the bridge. The road rose straight and steep. He hunched over the wheel, peering anxiously ahead through the headlamp beams. There was a wooden sign with writing he couldn't read. He stopped and flashed his torch at it, made out the words *Picnic Area*. That was new. There was a track leading away to the right. He revved the engine and drove up, the tinny little car straining all the way against the slope. He pulled on the handbrake, turned off the ignition and listened.

A minute passed. He heard nothing. The car had been on another road. Still, it had given him a fright. He had chided himself for being overcautious, but the truth was that it was impossible to take too many precautions. It was better, then, that he should leave the Renault where it was while he went to scout out the situation. It was annoying, another waste of precious time, but it couldn't be helped. He got out and checked his position. The car was only a dozen yards up from the road, but should any stray motorist happen to come by it would be quite invisible. He flicked the torch around. A few yards further up, the track curved around to a parking area. He could see dimly some picnic benches at the edges. He didn't think there was much danger of their getting any custom tonight.

He slammed shut the car door and walked back briskly down the hill.

The slamming door made the car shake. The humming noise hung in the air for long seconds. To Grace it sounded like the closing of a coffin lid.

He had gone. He had gone before, a few minutes ago, but had then come back almost immediately and driven off again a short distance. Was he still nearby? What was he doing? The questions buzzed around her head. She lay silently in her immolated world, listening for clues.

Where was this place? He hadn't driven far, no more than ten minutes, so they must still be near the house. She thought she had heard water when they stopped earlier, but she couldn't be sure. The only other thing she had heard was the familiar rattle of the engine. She knew nothing except that she was in the back of her own car, which was parked facing up a steep hill; she felt the force of gravity pressing her into the seat.

She tried to keep calm, above all to control her breathing. Her fear made her want to breathe faster, but she couldn't get the air in through her nostrils fast enough. She willed herself to breathe steadier, but it wasn't easy with the coat flung over her face. She needed oxygen desperately. She tried to push herself to the edge of the seat to free her head from the coat, but her legs and arms were still jelly. She sank back and found that she could hardly breathe at all. Despair overwhelmed her. She was helpless, she was going to die, there was nothing she could do. She was numb and frozen solid, like meat from the slaughterhouse. He was going to butcher her, like meat. A tiny spark of anger smouldered in her brain. Her consciousness fanned it and it grew. She thought of McGovern and her hatred intensified. She was trembling and shaking, but not from the cold. She jerked her head and a spasm ran through her whole body. She felt herself twitch like a landed fish. The coat slipped off her face with agonizing slowness.

She found herself staring up at a misty white light. She closed her eye, opened it again, and recognized the sheen of glass. She was puzzled, and then she realized she was looking at the reflection of the moon in the windscreen. She was looking . . .

She was looking. She could see. For a moment her mind was blank and uncomprehending, and then she understood. The cloth wound round the top of her head was loose. It still covered her left eye, but it had lifted on the other side. It must have loosened when he'd pulled her by the hair. He had pulled savagely enough. It had brought tears to the eye she could now see through again.

She pressed the side of her head down to the seat and rubbed as hard as she could against the upholstery. For the moment she had forgotten everything else, the cold, the terror, everything. She could see again. No matter that she was still bound and so weak she could hardly move, she had been freed from that which had made her weakest. She scraped her head up and down and from side to side in a bid to dislodge both the gag and the blindfold. He had tied the gag under her hair and it wouldn't shift, but the blindfold rode up and up until at last it was round her forehead like a bandana and both her eyes were uncovered.

She swung her knees up into her chest and guided her feet down to the floor. Her legs shook violently with the effort; they didn't seem to be a part of her. There was little feeling below the knee beyond a dull unpleasant tingling, but she managed to get both feet under the front passenger seat. She took a deep breath, summoned all her strength and levered herself up into a sitting position.

A silver of moonlight still fell across the windscreen. Her eyes adjusted slowly again to seeing, but the darkness helped; she couldn't have taken bright light. The thrill of being able to see anything at all again exhilarated her. She could make out the shapes of trees, a strip of white beyond where snow had piled up. She twisted her neck, but could see nothing out of the back window. For all she knew he might be standing there. Where had he gone? Why had he brought her here in her car? When was he coming back?

When was he going to kill her?

She propelled herself forward, against the slope, head first, trying to get herself into the front of the car. She managed to jerk and twist her body into the space between the two front seats, wriggling like a semiparalysed snake. She turned over, the top of her head pressing against the radio and the heater controls, the small of her back jammed painfully against the handbrake. She planted her feet against the rear seat and pushed. Her legs were shaking, but at least there was some circulation going again now, some sluggish blood to give her strength. Her arms and hands were another matter. Her wrists had been bound so tight for so long that there was no feeling at all in her fingers, precious little in her leaden arms. She pushed again with her legs, arched her back, and succeeded in getting herself up into a sitting position, her neck resting on the dashboard beside the wheel, the stick of the handbrake against her buttocks. She paused to get her breath back. Her heart was racing, she could even feel a trickle of sweat run down from her brow. She had forgotten about the cold, even though she could see the streams of breath rising from her nostrils in the bright silvery glare. The prospect of escape had galvanized her. All she had to do was get out of the car and run off into those trees and he would never find her.

She edged herself over towards the driver's seat painfully, inch by inch. Because she had no strength in her arms she had to swing her legs over the other seat, brace her feet against the passenger door, and push. It was awkward and inefficient and desperately uncomfortable, but there was no alternative. She got herself across the front seats, the back of her head up against the window, her feet planted against the other door. She felt for the door handle with her toes, and tried to get the tip of her shoe underneath. Her toecap was too thick. She sank back, trembling with exhaustion and fighting for breath. It wouldn't have worked anyway; only now did she see that the lock was pressed down. There seemed to be a lot of clutter under her legs. She lashed out in frustration and kicked something off the passenger seat on to the floor.

She heaved herself up into a sitting position, across the two seats. She pushed down with her shoulders against the driver's door to raise herself higher. The lock on this side was up. She could feel the armrest and the window handle pressing into her spine. She leant forward and trailed her bound hands up the side of the door. Her palms brushed against the door handle. She tried to grasp the metal grip with her fingers. Nothing happened. Her fingers wouldn't close. Her fingers were just hanging limply like a bunch of bananas.

She slumped against the seat. The moon had gone briefly behind a cloud but now it reappeared, splashing pale light across the front of the car. She saw that her bag was one of the things on the passenger seat with which her legs had been entangled. There was something lying next to it. It was his gun. She stared at it in disbelief. By God, but he must have been sure of himself if he hadn't taken the gun. He hadn't bothered to take the car keys either; she had heard them jangling in the ignition when she knocked her shoulder against the wheel. So he expected her to go without a fight, did he, to lie there meekly like trussed meat waiting for his knife? Well, she wasn't as helpless as all that.

She gritted her teeth and reached again for the door handle. She sweated and strained and willed every ounce of her strength into her fingertips. The dead nerves stirred. Just one more effort and she would be there. She tensed herself, leaning to the right against the wheel to compensate for the steep slope of the car. Her aching lifeless arm muscles stuttered fitfully. She pressed her shoulders back to get a better grip against the door, and then she slipped and her shoulder fell against the wheel.

The sharp raucous blare of the horn stung her ears. In the still night silence it was as loud as an explosion. She fell back against the seat, shocked and shaking violently. The horn had only sounded for a second but the noise vibrated endlessly in her ears. It would have been heard a mile away. He wasn't a mile away.

She clawed at the door handle. It was no good, her frozen fingers slipped from the metal every time. She lashed out pointlessly with her feet against the passenger door. The shock of the blow ran through her legs. At least it was good to know she had some strength back there. Whatever happened she wasn't going meekly; from now on she'd be kicking and struggling every inch of the way. Could she kick the glass out of the window? How would that help? There wasn't time anyway. He was coming back.

She heard him first, his footsteps crushing twigs against the hard earth. The hint of a human form seemed to take shape in the darkness outside, like a figure from a shadow play. The shadow moved from outside the rear window towards her. She jerked away from it instinctively, shifting her weight between the two front seats. She glanced back over her shoulder. The white blur of his face had materialized at the driver's window.

She rammed her head down suddenly, aiming at the back corner of the window where the slim cylindrical plastic lock was up. Her skull cracked painfully against the glass, but she hit the lock. She heard the little click as it went down. At the same instant the handle rattled uselessly outside.

She felt an electric surge of triumph. He was still pulling on the door handle, as if unwilling to believe that it wouldn't open. She couldn't see his features but she could imagine them contorted with fury. He didn't have the keys and he didn't even have his gun. What was he going to do now? She wasn't going to wait and see.

Her legs were scrunched up against the passenger door, her bottom resting uncomfortably between the two front seats.

She swung her legs over the passenger seat into the back and at the same moment heaved her body up and over to the driver's side. She flung her weight back into the middle of the driving wheel.

The horn burst out shrilly. It had never seemed a loud noise to her before, but now it sounded like a trumpet from Judgement Day. She jammed her feet against the rear seat and pushed, keeping her shoulder hard against the wheel. The single harsh discordant note reverberated through the night. Someone would hear it, somewhere; please God, someone would hear . . . She glanced at the white face in the window. It had gone.

The hatchback door flew open. The car trembled under his weight. She saw the white face now, looming over the back seat as he climbed in. His hands were on the upholstery, getting a grip so he could pull himself over the seat. She heard her own cry of despair die muffled in her gag as she slithered forward and took her weight off the horn. It hadn't occurred to her that the back might be unlocked. She lashed out blindly with her feet.

She kicked his hands. She heard him swear. He took another grip and tried to haul himself in. She connected solidly with his head and he swore louder. He grabbed her feet and pinned her ankles together. She had no strength left to resist. He was dragging her towards him, using her as a lever to pull himself into the car. She felt the handbrake gouging her back.

She slammed the heel of her hand into the tip of the handbrake. The button clicked in and the stick banged down. The car gave a lurch and began to roll down the hill.

He cried out in surprise. The sudden movement of the car had thrown him off balance. He was kneeling in the boot, still clinging to her legs as he tried to pull himself in. She bucked and heaved and flung him back. He lost his grip on her legs. Grace piled the sole of her shoe into his face.

The car had picked up speed and was racing down the hill. It bounced over stones and holes and rattled like an empty can. McGovern was grabbing desperately at the seat, but he couldn't get a grip and he was slipping back. Grace saw an onrushing streak of white, a bank of snow by the road below. The white blur hurtled towards them.

McGovern screamed.

The car crashed down on to the road with tremendous force and seemed to bounce up in the air. There was a hideous snapping sound and then McGovern's whole body jerked and thrashed and was flung against the roof. The car ploughed across the road and crashed into a tree.

The rear of the car imploded in a shower of broken glass and shearing metal.

30

Grace was in hospital for ten days. The doctors told her at first that she could expect to be in for anything up to a month and they were all astonished by the speed of her recovery. They were even more astonished by her luck.

She had been thrown into the back of the car when it hit the tree. The rear had caved in, but her body had come to rest, uncrushed, in the narrow space between the front seats and what remained of the back. She was bruised and battered all over and had a deep gash in the side of her head from a splinter of glass, but nothing had been broken. She had a cracked rib and a twisted neck, which necessitated wearing a brace for a fortnight, but although she was suffering from hypothermia she had sustained no serious physical damage. It would of course take time to gauge the extent of any psychological damage.

All this she learnt by degrees. She was barely conscious for her first few days in bed. The nurses were initially reluctant to tell her too much, fearful, perhaps, of her mental state. It was Malcolm Thexton who filled in the story.

The car had been found by a local man on his way to work the next morning. He had tried to summon help on his mobile but hadn't been able to get a signal. Nor had he been able to free Grace from the wreckage, but he had had the sense to cover her with a coat and blanket before driving off to summon help. He had also removed her gag. The Fire Brigade had cut her out an hour later.

Peter McGovern was already dead. His legs had been trapped and crushed between the car and the tree and he had bled to death. Malcolm had heard the story on the midday news and had called his old boss straightaway. The police were already at Roughwood Cottage. Over the next few days they took the house apart. They found nothing, but almost as an afterthought they dug up the patio again. This time they found the bodies of Margaret McGovern and Paul Bramall, although it was a while before they were formally identified. Forensics were able to match one of the twelve-year-old bullets discovered in the grave with the Beretta that had been found on the person of Lewis Young. The police officer in charge of the Julie McGovern investigation was at first reluctant to accede to the request for a ballistics test, but once Grace's statement was forwarded to him he had little choice. His reaction to seeing her name at the top of the paper was not recorded.

Lewis Young was released and murder charges were dropped. A decision was postponed on whether or not to charge him with a number of other offences, ranging from illegal possession of a firearm to attempting to pervert the course of justice. The threat of prosecution continued to hang over him for some time, but eventually the Crown quietly dropped the case. Bob Challoner had explained the reasoning succinctly. What was the point, he asked, in wading into a cesspool when you were up to your neck in it already?

In the fullness of time Grace received letters of commendation from two Chief Constables, her MP and a host of the great and the good. It was hinted that her name would be put forward for a public honour, but nothing more was ever heard on the subject. She was invited to tell her story on daytime television and offered the opportunity to sell it exclusively to a tabloid newspaper. When she said no she was offered double the amount. After much heart-searching she declined. She wanted the money, but she wanted to be left in peace more. Such attention as she did receive embarrassed her. A couple of times when she was out shopping in her usual supermarket back in Guildford she became aware of people pointing at her and whispering. Her photograph had been in the papers and there was no getting away from the fact that she had become a minor local celebrity. She gritted her teeth and bore it and accepted the upside, which was that it was good for business. New clients rushed to secure her services, to the unbridled joy of George Courtenay, who promptly jacked up the firm's hourly rate by twenty per cent. The workload kept Grace busy and helped take her mind off unpleasant things. For a long time after, her sleeping was erratic and she was troubled by bad dreams. She also seemed to have acquired, understandably, a fear of confined spaces. At her doctor's insistence she saw a psychiatrist, but she learnt nothing about herself she didn't know already and she stopped going as soon as she decently could. She had an innate distrust, inherited from her parents, of anything that could be construed as making a fuss. By the peculiar but hallowed definition of Cornish family usage, asking for help of any kind came into that category.

Lewis came to see her when she got back to Guildford. He turned up at the office, bearing flowers and champagne. She offered to open the champagne there and then, but he insisted that she keep it for a special occasion. He appeared to be embarrassed and didn't know what to say. He thanked her, of course, but he said nothing about his failure to do what she had told him. He left after only a few minutes, and made no attempt to disguise the fact that he was obviously pleased to be going. Later she read his account of his ordeal in a Sunday newspaper, and although he paid generous tribute to her detective skills it nonetheless struck her as being somewhat sparing with the facts. She didn't doubt that he had been well paid for the story, so she had no compunction in sending him a bill for services rendered that came to just under a thousand pounds with expenses, including a return Eurostar ticket to Brussels. It didn't seem a heavy price to pay for one's freedom, and he evidently thought the same way too. He sent her a cheque by return of post, attached to a compliment slip. There was no note. She did see him once more, some three months later.

It was a Friday night in Guildford. She had been out of town all afternoon and was stuck in roadworks and heavy traffic getting back. She didn't even have time to change. Despite her lateness she spent a good five minutes more in the car park, desperately trying to get her hair to behave in the tiny driving mirror. But it was hopelessly limp and refused to do anything other than sit like a dead animal perched on her head. She threw her comb crossly back into her bag and fished out lipstick and mascara. They didn't seem to do much good either. She stared back critically at the bag-heavy eyes and the drawn hollow cheeks and concluded that the effect was more drop-dead than drop-dead gorgeous. Nothing else she could do now, though, except give up and run away. She was tempted. She was nearly half an hour late already. Perhaps he had saved her the trouble and pushed off already. Perhaps it would be better if he had.

She left her tatty Barbour in the car. She was wearing a neat ivory sweater and her jeans at least were clean. She swung her bag over her shoulder. She hesitated outside the door. Was it just because she felt she wasn't looking her best that she was so nervous? Having come this far she should at least do her best not to let it show. She advanced into the wine bar with a display of confidence she certainly didn't feel.

He hadn't pushed off. He was sitting in a corner, with a bottle of white wine in an ice bucket and two glasses. He filled the second glass as she came over.

'I'm sorry I'm so late,' she said, rather breathlessly. 'I hope you didn't think I'd stood you up.'

He handed her the full glass of wine. He smiled.

'The thought did cross my mind, I have to admit,' he said. 'But it seemed a little unlikely given the trouble you'd gone to.'

'It would have been a bit silly, yes,' she said, taking the glass gratefully. 'Thanks for coming.'

'Not at all. It's nice to see you, Grace.'

'It's nice to see you too, Alan.'

They clinked their glasses and sat down. Alan was wearing a smart blue suit, sober shirt and plain tie. He looked a little formal, but relaxed. He had sounded cagey over the phone, which wasn't surprising really. But the smile seemed genuine.

'It would have been easier if you'd just picked up my card,' he said.

'It must have slipped my mind,' she said.

She'd told him how she'd rung round two dozen computer firms in the area asking for Alan Russell Esq, Software Consultant. It hadn't been difficult but he had still seemed surprised that she'd managed to track him down.

'No problem,' she'd told him on the phone. 'It's my job.'

He knew that by now. He'd seen the stuff about her in the papers. She had apologized for lying to him, and admitted that it was ironical that she'd been the one accusing him of duplicity when it was her stock-in-trade. She told him that she didn't usually go through men's wallets in her off-duty hours.

He said he believed her. He said that he'd found her note on the paper with her phone number and realized then why she'd been in his wallet. He thought it was a good joke on her part now, looking back, but at the time he'd been so angry that he'd just torn up the paper and thrown it out of his car window.

'Are you still angry?' she wanted to know.

'No,' he said, and he didn't hesitate.

'Then would you mind if I bought you a drink?'

And so they had arranged to meet, and here he was, only he'd arrived first so he was the one who'd bought the drink, a crisp and delicious Chablis. It was something she thought she could probably get through quite a lot of by the end of the evening, now that she was comfortably ensconsed and he had yet to give the slightest indication, even to her hypertuned and oversensitive private radar, that he was anything but pleased to see her.

He wanted to know all about her, now that he knew what she really did to earn a living. In the past some men had been rather frightened by her job, or perhaps rather the implication of her self-assurance and independence, while others had simply patronized her. Neither category had stuck around for long. It was another of her stocks-in-trade, the giving of short shrift.

But he just wanted to know, he wasn't alarmed or dismissive, only intrigued. She liked to keep her private and her public selves apart, but she felt she owed it to him so she told him what he wanted to know. The theory had always worked better than the practice anyway. Her personal life had always had this habit of disappearing suddenly from view, like the White Rabbit down his hole.

'Sounds a bit hairier than teaching,' he said, when she'd finished telling him about her time in hospital.

'Actually it's more dull routine than anything else. You don't come across murderers every day.'

'I'm pleased to hear it,' he said, and reached across to give her hand a gentle squeeze.

She squeezed his hand back. She left her fingers resting in his palm. They looked at each other for a while in silence.

'I'm glad you called,' he said.

'I'm glad you're glad. Took me a while to summon up the nerve.'

'I can understand that. I wish I'd called you first. I wanted to, when I read about you in the paper. After I'd got over my surprise, anyway.'

'Did you?'

'I thought about it. But I'd thrown away your number and I didn't know where to get hold of you.'

'Should have hired a private detective.'

'That's a thought. Yeah, it's a pretty lame excuse, I suppose. I could have used your method and just looked in the phone book. But I didn't think you'd want to hear from me again, to be honest. After all, we didn't part on the best of terms.'

'My fault. Shall we forget about that now?'

'Sounds like a pretty good idea.'

'I've got another one. Why don't I get another one of these?'

She pointed to the near-empty bottle of Chablis in the ice bucket. He hesitated.

'I probably shouldn't,' he said. 'I'm a way ahead of you and I've got to drive back tonight.'

'To Kingston?'

'Yeah.'

'It's not that far.'

'Hey, I thought you used to be a policewoman. You encouraging me to drink and drive?'

'You're right, that's completely failing in my duty. In fact,

I think you've probably had quite enough already. In fact, I categorically forbid you to drive anywhere tonight.'

'Do you now?'

'I do.'

'Sounds like I'm being arrested.'

'Mm, more a case of being taken into custody for your own good.'

'And where will you be taking me?'

'Not far. Walking distance.'

'I see. Will you have to handcuff me first?'

'Don't be cheeky.'

'Does this count as cheek?'

'What?'

'This.'

He leant across the table and kissed her firmly on the mouth.

'Oh yes,' she said, when they had had their fill of tasting each other. 'That'll get you time added on for bad behaviour. I'm going to get that wine.'

'Trying to get me drunk again?'

'Oh don't worry, I won't let you get *that* drunk. Maybe we should have some food, I'm starving. It's quite good here. I'll get a menu.'

She got up from the table, fishing her purse from her bag. She started to walk to the bar.

It was then that she saw Lewis Young.

He was standing at the bar, at exactly the point where she was headed, a small and pretty blonde tucked in beside him. Grace saw him slip his arm around her waist and recognized the style. He chanced to glance up and their eyes met.

He was in the middle of saying something to the girl. For a second he seemed to freeze. Grace smiled. He looked at her, and then, the difference was all but imperceptible, he looked through her. He had missed a beat, but he carried on whispering into the girl's ear as if nothing had happened. Casually he turned away. Grace felt as if she had just seen a ghost.

Grace walked back to the table. Alan greeted her with a quizzical look.

'I've had a better idea,' she said. 'I've got a bottle of wine at my place. We'll pick up a takeaway round the corner.'

He laughed. He held his wrists out meekly.

'Whatever you say, miss. I'll come quietly.'

He put his arm around her shoulder as they walked through the bar, and she slipped her hand round his waist and squeezed him tight. She leant her face across to his, and nuzzled his neck, and murmured in his ear about the delights of takeaway establishments in the vicinity and the odds of getting food poisoning in each and made him laugh.

The man at the bar with the pretty blonde heard them laughing. He didn't look around.